FRANKENSTEIN ENTERPRISES

MAX D. STANTON

Copyright 2024 © Max D. Stanton

All rights reserved. No part of this book may be used or reproduced by any means, graphic, electronic, or mechanical, including photocopying, recording, taping, or by any information storage retrieval system without the written permission of the publisher, except in the case of brief quotations embedded in critical articles and reviews.

This is a work of fiction. All of the characters, names, incidents, organizations, and dialogue are either the products of the writer's imagination or taken from the public domain.

ISBN: 9798218322687 (sc)
ISBN: 9798218322694 (ebook)

First printing edition: April 30, 2024

Published by 13th Month Books in the United States of America

Cover Design and Layout by Rooster Republic
Interior Layout and Formatting by Kirkus Media, LLC

This book is dedicated to my father and brother. Wherever I go, I carry you both in my heart.

CONTENTS

BOOK I: MASS CONSUMPTION

An Afternoon With Dr. Frankenstein	3
The Journalist Part I	5
Sign Posted in the Monroeville Mall Food Court	9
The Mallrat	10
When You Donate Your Body To Frankenstein, You Donate Your Soul To Satan	16
The Farmer	18
Reanimated Labor Linked to Rising Jobless Rates	25
The Mother	27
More Than A Dozen Killed In Mexico As The Death Lords Strike Again	37
The Lawyer	39
2019 Ganymede 700-Series User Guide	55
The Salesman	57
Discussion Thread from the FrankenDIY Online Forum	64
The Necrophile	66
New Shows of Note	71
The Pop Star	73
How To Win Prosperity In This Life and Eternity In The Next	78
The Believer	80
How to Die in the Age of Frankenstein: Pastoral Ideas for Modern Funerals	86
The Mortician	87
Freedom of Elderly Americans Act of 2017 (115th Congress, 1st Session) S. 520	93
The Elder	95

BOOK II: CORPORATE ASSETS

Victor Frankenstein to Leave U.S. for Switzerland	101
The Journalist Part II	103

Review Posted in the Frankenstein Enterprises Online Store	109
The Programmer	111
Frankenstein Enterprises, Inc. Form 10-K Investor Report for the fiscal year ending December 31, 2017	122
The Grave Robber	124
Frankenstein Enterprises Contract Staff Manual 2012 (v 3.35)	137
The Temp	138
Ganymede 500-Series Repair Manual Excerpt	143
The Repairman	144
Voters Want To Check Frankenstein's Power, but Washington Disagrees	156
The Senator	159
Operation Dark Avenger Rules of Engagement Card	172
The Soldier	174
Wright v. Massachusetts, 136 S.Ct. 1027 (2016)	183
The Detective	185
Introduction to Henry Clerval DEAD Talk™	195
The Chief Operating Officer	196
Lanchester Equity Partners Analyst Report	201
The Intern	204
Frankenstein Takes Aim At The Stars	216
The Astronaut	218

BOOK III: RISK FACTORS

Live Your Best Life at Byron Tower Sales Brochure	233
The Exterminator	234
Email Sent to Carbondale Auto Parts Manufacturing	241
The Hacker	243
Mother Earth Can't Be Re-Animated And Other Essays From The Zombie Apocalypse	256
The Hunter	257
Coalition Forces Announce Liberation of Basrah	261
The Enemy	263
Revolution, Not Reanimation	272
The Gravedigger	274
Hester Faust Opens the Fall Gala Season	283
The Heiress	286

Young Frankenstein: A Memoir of My Years With The Frankenstein Family	293
The Journalist Part III	294
Modern Prometheus: The Unauthorized Biography of Victor Frankenstein	299
The Doctor	300
Epilogue	320

BOOK I: MASS CONSUMPTION

AN AFTERNOON WITH DR. FRANKENSTEIN

BY JAMES GODWIN, THE NEW YORKER (NOVEMBER 9, 1994)

Dr. Victor Frankenstein leads a meeting from his personal autopsy room, his breath steaming out from beneath his surgical mask in thin white clouds. The only other people physically present in the room are an elderly dead man and myself. The old man donated his body to science, and now he rests in the hands of the 20th century's greatest scientist. Dr. Frankenstein inserts suction tubes into the corpse and hits a button, noisily draining the blood from the cadaver and replacing it with a patented electroconductive preservative of his own design. The smell is intense; an eye-watering perfume of swimming pool and biowaste. The doctor doesn't appear to notice. On the open conference line, his team of financiers, scientists, and programmers discuss his company's U.N.-sponsored venture to clear Vietnamese minefields using the undead. He has serious talent on the phone, including two MacArthur geniuses, leading engineers of the dot com revolution, and a former Pentagon chief of staff, drawn in by the gravitational pull of his genius. Occupied by his work with the cadaver, he speaks little but listens closely, and forcefully interjects whenever one of his underlings expresses a point he disagrees with. Frankenstein is a firm believer in multi-tasking. He thinks that doing only one thing at a time is a waste, and he cannot abide waste. He thinks that not even our lifespans should limit our productivity.

Dr. Frankenstein shocked the world in July when he publicly announced that he had developed a method to reanimate dead bodies as robotic automatons. And he shocked the world again when he announced that he intended to profit from this historic discovery by selling zombie labor to do jobs too dangerous, dirty, or unpleasant for human beings. Depending on who you talk to, this is either a horrific act of desecration or civilization's greatest advance since the domestication of animals; the domestication of the dead. Frankenstein cares little about the controversy. He cares about what works.

On the conference line, his team argues over whether zombies have the delicate manual dexterity that bomb disposal requires. His gravel-voiced personal secretary moderates the debate, trying to keep the titanic egos assembled on this phone call from doing too much damage as they crash into each other. Meanwhile, Frankenstein has sawed off the top of the dead man's skull and inserts electrodes into exposed grey matter. He seems irritated by the argument. A famously solitary worker, he is plainly unused to dissent. Eventually he sharply proclaims that his zombies have the capacity to do anything the living can do. If they don't yet have the fine motor skills to dismantle explosives, an update to their iGor control software can make it so. His secretary orders the head of product development to spend whatever's necessary, and the conference call wraps up.

Victor Frankenstein presses a button and the corpse convulses in a frightening posthumous seizure. Its eyes flutter open, their capillaries having burst from the trauma of reanimation and stained the sclera crimson. They are as blank as a piece of red paper. He has not replaced the top of its skull. Knobs and plugs and wires protrude from its exposed brain. With a joystick, he commands the zombie to sit up on the autopsy table, and then stand on its feet, which it does, its motions as trembling and unsteady as a creature newly-born. Dr. Frankenstein hands the joystick to me.

"Would you like to try controlling my creation?" he asks.

THE JOURNALIST PART I

Storm clouds gathered in the heavens above the Swiss Alps. Electrical currents flew through the atmosphere like witches on broomsticks. One could taste the incoming tempest in the air, feel the barometer plunging towards something terrible.

Rose Najafi sat at the window side table of a small cafe, watching the skies darken but not really seeing them, the interview of her career only an hour away. She was about to meet Dr. Victor Frankenstein, the tycoon who made billionaires feel poor and feeble, the world-famous hermit, the genius who developed the greatest invention in the annals of science and then turned it on humanity's throat. This would be his first appearance since he'd vanished from the public eye more than twenty years ago, retreating into the isolation of a restored Alpine castle.

The invitation had arrived in her email just two days ago. At first Rose thought it was some sort of prank. Even if the Doctor wanted to break his long silence, she was one of his company's most prominent critics, and Frankenstein Enterprises' army of PR flacks did everything in their considerable power to muzzle her. But then the company spokesperson followed up on the invitation with a phone call, and although Rose had repeatedly proven the man a liar, hearing his oily voice it dawned upon her that somehow this was real. Their offer: one hour on the record with Dr.

Victor Frankenstein, no subjects off-limits. She was on the next flight to Switzerland.

Rose's anxious mind drifted back to the first time she saw a dead man walking. She'd come home from school to see her mother and aunt huddled by the television, and for a moment she felt irritated that they were keeping her from the *Fresh Prince of Bel-Air*. "This is haram," gasped Aunt Fairuza.

"Are you a fool?" Mom sneered at her sister. "This is the greatest achievement since the moon landing! Greater, even. Rose, come here! I want you to see this."

"Don't show her!" Fairuza pleaded. "You'll give her nightmares."

"How can I keep it from her? It's on every channel. Rose, come and see. A foreign doctor has done something amazing."

On the screen where Rose had hoped to watch Will Smith's California adventures, a zombie crisscrossed with livid stitches like a railway map staggered purposefully across a stage, nude but for a loincloth, exhibiting himself to a gaping audience of scientists and photographers. Towards the back of the room, a lean, patrician man in a lab coat worked at a console, ordering the ghoul about by remote control. His angular, nearly fleshless face and luminous eyes gave him the look of a human bird of prey. This was Rose's first glimpse of Dr. Victor Frankenstein, the man who would shape her life more than any friend or lover, the man who would shape everyone's life with his brilliance and fortune and evil.

Aunt Fairuza was right. Rose did have nightmares that evening, and many evenings thereafter. But her bad dreams didn't revolve around the zombie. They revolved around the Doctor.

A few years later, in college, Rose got her first by-line on a story about the administration's decision to add six undead "z-gardeners" to the landscaping crew. She'd worked that piece relentlessly, interviewing everyone from the groundskeepers to the university president. Rose even tracked down the sister of one of the donors and talked to her over the phone about the past life of the shambling corpse now watering the campus flower gardens. Robert, his name had been, Bub to his friends. The story raised a huge outcry when it was published in the student newspaper, prompting protests, candlelight vigils, statements from the administration. When Rose went back for her fifteen-year reunion, the number of z-gardeners had swelled to twenty-six, and Bub still tended the tulips.

Yet if the story had not changed the campus, it certainly changed Rose. Her parents reacted to the news that she was becoming a journalist as aghast as if she'd told them that college inspired her to swear a vow of poverty. However, her father's taxicab business crumbled even faster than the newspaper industry, crushed by competition from Styx zombie cabs. The last tangible remnant of his life's work, a faded green "Najafi Transport" keyring, jangled in Rose's pocket.

The Styx rollout that disrupted her dad's livelihood became one of Rose's biggest stories. Frankenstein Enterprises failed to test its z-drivers properly before unleashing them on the roads, killing and maiming hundreds. With the patience of a secret agent probing an enemy organization's weak spots, Rose found a programmer with a guilty conscience and persuaded him to turn over a cache of documents proving that top executives had known about the danger. Her expose was a worldwide, first-class scandal. Frankenstein Enterprises settled all the lawsuits soon afterwards for a few billion dollars. Nobody went to jail, and the company's market cap jumped by six times the cost of the settlement when the investigations closed out.

Even though Rose's bombshell report failed to dent Frankenstein's armor, it earned her a reputation as a fearless and talented investigative reporter, and she kept on the attack. She profiled victims of war-zombies both overseas and at home, finding that in Iraq nobody blamed you if a squad of algorithmically trigger-happy ghouls shot up your living room whereas in America, such victims were commonly deemed troublemakers. She talked to cultists who worshipped Victor Frankenstein as a living god, CEOs who did much the same, and terrorists who dedicated their lives to his downfall. She exposed the high-tech serfdom that Frankenstein's ever-dwindling human workforce endured, and the Gilded Age corruption that the company's lackeys in D.C. embraced. She wrote about the human costs of the harrowing micro-budgets that Frankenstein donors lived on, and she published accounts of the titanic mega-yachts that the company's executives bought so that they might roam the seas like billionaire pirates. The yachtsmen seemed weirdly deprived in their own fashion, haunted by the knowledge that they would always be desperately poor compared to their boss. Rose traveled so much, and everywhere she went, she saw Dr. Frankenstein taking things away from other people. It was nearly unthinkable that one man could steal so much, destroy so much, and even more appalling that so many people had helped him. To Rose, the Doctor represented the terrible mystery at the heart of all things. If she could discover the motive behind his crimes, maybe she could discover the motive behind all of the terrible things that people did to each other. In a way, her entire journalistic career had been a quest to find the answer to a single question.

"Who is Victor Frankenstein?"

Soon she would know.

SIGN POSTED IN THE MONROEVILLE MALL FOOD COURT

Attention To All Guests:

Please be advised that to ensure a safe and pleasant shopping environment, the Monroeville Mall has adopted a ZERO TOLERANCE policy towards harassment, vandalism, or mutilation of reanimated workers.

ANY INTERFERENCE WITH FRANKS WITHIN THE MALL WILL RESULT IN CRIMINAL CHARGES AND CIVIL PENALTIES WITHOUT EXCEPTION. ALL FRANKS WITHIN THE MALL ARE CONNECTED TO OUR NECRO-SECURITY SYSTEM FOR IMMEDIATE RESPONSE.

The Monroeville Mall and its vendors disclaim all liability for bodily injury or property damage that may arise resulting from guests' mistreatment of our workers.

THE MALLRAT

Nikki Mendez arrived at the Monroeville Mall in a Styx taxi, feeling slightly carsick. The dead drove like maniacs, but at least you didn't have to tip them. At the entrance, a zombie in a grey maintenance uniform squeegeed spray paint off the sliding glass doors. Nikki walked past it, barely even recognizing its presence, and into the air-conditioned chill of the mall. She had come to see a movie with her friend Jen, but Jen sent a text bailing out while Nikki was on the escalator heading towards Cinemark. Nikki has halfway expected Jen to flake, and the disappointment ached even worse because it was not surprising. She found that she was no longer in a movie-watching mood and retreated to the first level food court to eat her feelings.

She was enjoying a grease-sopped bag of Auntie Anne's hot dog bites and bitterly pondering what to do with her day when she spotted Jason Pritchard coming out of Sbarro. They were in the same class at Gateway High but had never really spoken. He was said to be a bad kid, a vandal and a pothead, and the one time he'd come to a party he'd shown up wearing a necklace of zombie ears and gotten so drunk that he puked in the sink. Nikki was surprised at how pleased she felt when he noticed her and approached her table. Jason was kind of cute, with curly brown hair and a port wine stain on his neck that reminded Nikki of a vampire's bite, although he dressed like an asshole, wearing a hoodie covered in bright orange zig-zags and matching track pants. Urban legend had it that z-police had trouble seeing this pattern, and the hideous, eye-searing camouflage had become fashionable overnight.

"Hey, Nicolette, right?" he asked. "We have third period math together."

"I go by Nikki," she said. "Hi Jason. What're you up to?"

"Oh, just pranking some deadheads."

"Here? Aren't you worried about getting caught?"

"Nah, it's easy. Look at this."

A Frank manned the Auntie Anne's pretzel counter, rolling out the dough and knotting it with mechanical speed and efficiency. It had been a South Asian kid about the same age as Nikki and Jason when it died, but it'd decayed some before its reanimation, such that its ashy skin was withered and wrinkled and most of its nose was gone. Jason walked over to the counter and "accidentally" knocked over the napkin dispenser. The Frank let out a soft groan. It trudged outside its stall and bent over to pick up the fallen dispenser. As the zombie stooped down, Jason scribbled a penis on its forehead in Sharpie. The Frank didn't appear to notice. It returned the dispenser to its place, neatened up the condiment area, and then returned to its pretzel-making.

"Come on, let's get out of here," Jason said. "Z-security will be here in a minute or two."

Nikki sighed. Jesus Christ, the boys of Monroeville were dumb. No wonder the mall was going over to reanimated workers. But she got up and left the food court with him regardless. "This is how you spend your Saturdays?" she asked. "Drawing dicks on deadheads?"

"Not much else to do around here," Jason said defensively. "Besides, fuck deadheads. One of these days they're going to rise up and kill us all for parts."

"Maybe the zombies are going to kill us all because they don't like people drawing dicks on them," Nikki said. She thought about Bernie, her own family's z-butler, and tried to imagine the pallid, silent, always-helpful old man in his funny Hawaiian shirt taking part in an undead rebellion, his white hands bloody up to the elbows, gore dripping from his mouth, a phallus crudely scrawled on his forehead. The mental image set her to giggling.

Jason laughed too. "Sorry if my penis graffiti triggers a zombie apocalypse," he said. "What can I say? I was bored. Hey, what are you doing here? Just hanging out by yourself? Come with me, we can hunt deadheads together."

Nikki was about to turn him down, but then she remembered that her plans were shot. And since this handsome idiot had shown up, she hadn't been upset about Jen bailing. Maybe messing with zombies at the mall was as good a way as any to kill a lazy afternoon.

They had the place nearly to themselves but for a few elderly strollers and teenage loiterers like themselves. Nearly a third of the storefronts stood shuttered in grimy desolation. "This place is dying," Jason said bitterly. "Now that Frankenstein's online store offers free delivery nobody shops anywhere else. It's sad."

"Is that why you're so pissed off at zombies?" asked Nikki. "Free delivery?"

"No, I'm pissed off at zombies because they fuck up everything," replied Jason. "Dr. Frankenstein's taking over the world. He's like a fatal virus. Wherever he goes he leaves nothing but dead bodies behind. We've got to do everything we can to fuck him up, fuck up his monsters. Every little bit counts."

"Where do you get this stuff from?" Nikki asked. Her own parents constantly exhorted her to study hard so she could strike it rich like Dr. Frankenstein. It felt strange to see their idol demonized. And also exciting.

Jason glanced around conspiratorially, and then leaned in. "My older sister's in the Gravediggers," he said. "She tells me what's really going on."

"The Gravediggers? Aren't they a terrorist group?"

"No, freedom fighters. I know the government calls them terrorists, but the Gravediggers protect people and the government only protects property. I shouldn't be talking about it. Hey, speaking of property, is there anything here that you want? I've got a foolproof method for ripping off Frankenstores."

"My dad says that nothing can ever be foolproof because the power of foolishness is infinite."

"Your dad sounds like a lot of fun. You want anything or no?"

She did have her eye on a handbag at Macy's. Nikki walked him over to the department, pointing out the alligator-skin satchel she wanted. "Watch out for the human salespeople, they've still got a few left here," Jason whispered. A plastic anti-theft RFID gizmo with the Frankenstein skull-and-brains logo was clipped to the bag's strap. Jason thoughtfully fingered the tag, then produced a butterfly knife. In just a few seconds, he'd jimmied off the anti-theft device. He replaced it with an identical one from his pocket and handed the bag to Nikki.

"Take it up front to the register," he said. "It'll only cost you five bucks. Pay cash."

The walk to the register was long and exhilarating. Nikki felt like each of the department store's few human personnel were watching her, like the Franks stocking shelves and patrolling the aisles all knew that she was up to no good. Her throat dried up, her heart pounded, her fingers trembled as if slightly electrified.

"Keep cool," whispered Jason, his breath warm against her ear. "You look like you're about to rob a bank."

At the front of the store, four zombies in matching dark suits and red ties manned self-service kiosks. Nikki's nerve almost failed her as she approached the salesghoul, but with Jason by her side she didn't feel like she could back down now. She handed the $450 satchel to one of the z-clerks; it rang it up as a pair of $4.95 socks and put it in a shopping bag for her.

"That was amazing," Nikki said once they were safely out of the store. "How did you do that?"

"It's simple," Jason said, glowing with satisfaction. "Sales Franks use those RFID tags to stock shelves and ID merchandise. But you can buy pre-programmed tags online real cheap. At home I've got a drawer full of them. The z-clerk rang you up for a five-dollar pair of socks because as far as it could see, that's what you were buying."

"Why do stores use z-clerks if they're too dumb to even recognize the merchandise?"

Jason shrugged. "Even counting the stealing, they're still cheaper than getting humans to do the job. That's why places that use deadhead labor deserve to get ripped off."

"Well thanks for the bag, I appreciate it."

"No problem. I got to use up the tags anyway, the newest model can see right through that trick. Good thing Macy's hasn't updated yet."

Nikki felt a moment's discomfort that Jason's "foolproof method" for shoplifting was in fact incredibly risky, but before she could say anything a z-janitor shuffled by pushing a bucket, its pale face so heavily tagged with graffiti that it looked like it'd been a gang member in life. "Hey, watch this," Jason said. He seized the zombie's ear between his thumb and index finger and sliced it off cleanly with his butterfly knife. The z-janitor kept marching along dutifully, indifferent to its own mutilation, and even Jason barely broke stride. "Keep walking, keep walking," he stage-whispered.

The violence was so sudden and unprovoked and harmless that Nikki could barely keep from bursting out laughing. It was like watching a cartoon character get hurt. "Are you going to add that to your necklace?" she asked.

"No," he said bashfully. "No, this one's for you, Nikki." He handed her the severed ear. It felt cold and dry and rubbery, a creepy feeling in the tactile quarter of the uncanny valley, but as it passed between them Nikki felt an electric tingle from Jason's fingertips as well. "So what do you want to do now?" he asked, reddening slightly.

"I want to tag a deadhead," she suggested.

Jason grinned. "I was hoping you'd say that," he said.

They headed to the sporting goods store at the far end of the mall. The Franks here were fresher than the ones at the food court; almost human-seeming apart from their red eyes and the blank smiles permanently affixed to their faces. One of them waited by the entrance, glaring at new arrivals expectantly. "Welcome to The Sporting Life, how can I help you," it rasped, with a voice like somebody who'd been smoking a carton of cigarettes a day for forty years. It sounded kind of cool, in a demonic sort of way, although it made Nikki glad that Bernie couldn't speak.

"Take me to the baseballs," Jason told the greeter ghoul.

"Baseball equipment, aisle 9," the Frank announced, then led them towards the back of the store. Once they were out of sight of any living soul, Nikki drew a smiley face on the deadhead's cheek.

The zombie turned its head, its bloodshot eyes staring deep into her, and its cold hand latched onto her wrist like a spring-loaded trap. It opened its still-smiling mouth, exposing its nearly-toothless gums and swollen purple tongue, and shrieked an alarm that seemed to pierce through Nikki's eardrums and penetrate her brain.

Nikki froze in terror, but Jason did not. Without hesitation he picked up a bat and swung it full-force against the z-clerk's temple, shattering its skull with a sound like biting into a crisp apple. The zombie tightened its fingers. "You are under arrest for vandalism," it snarled in that horrible ashen voice.

"It's not letting go!" Nikki cried.

Jason hit it twice more, pulping the side of the zombie's head, and the ghoul fell limp with Nikki's wrist still clutched in its death grip. Hisses sounded all around them, the sporting goods store suddenly turned into a snake pit. Nikki gasped when she saw that z-security guards in navy blue uniforms had blocked off both ends of the aisle. A terrible fury gleamed in their lifeless eyes. Their lower jaws hung slack, swollen black tongues protruding. Then the ghouls were on top of her, forcing her down to the cold tile floor and binding her wrists with plastic ties that sliced into the skin.

Nikki was grounded for a month after the incident. The worst part of her confinement was being shut up with Bernie. She suffered nightmares about waking up with the ghoul's hands wrapped around her throat. Jason got it even worse. The store made him pay for the destroyed Frank, and since he didn't have any money he had to take out a donor pension.

They didn't see each other for a while after that, apart from a few awkward looks in third period math class, although Nikki thought of him frequently. She wondered if he was angry at her for getting him into trouble. She wondered if she was angry at him for making her so afraid. She wondered if there was any point to spending time with such a reckless, angry, futureless boy.

One day Nikki opened her locker and found a severed ear inside it, exquisitely cut and folded into the form of a grey leather rose. She called Jason immediately and asked him if he wanted to hang out at the mall.

WHEN YOU DONATE YOUR BODY TO FRANKENSTEIN, YOU DONATE YOUR SOUL TO SATAN

BY BLOOD OF THE RISEN LAMB MINISTRY (UNDATED LEAFLET)

What is the Bible-believing Christian to think of Frankenstein? Scripture teaches that the resurrection of the dead is the beating heart of our faith, and the ultimate sign of God's power. "For if the dead rise not, then is not Christ raised. And if Christ be not raised, your faith is vain; ye are yet in your sins." (1 Corinthians 15:7). Now the dead rise every day, yet America is more in her sins than ever before, lost to abortion and homosexuality and every form of deviance. Even many Christians are confused about what the triumph over the grave means in a society overrun by the living dead.

We must remember that Satan is a mocker who perverts Christ's miracles. (2 Corinthians 11:14) Prophecy tells us that in the End Times the Beast shall deceive men with wonders, and give false life to graven images, and be worshipped by a secular world so lost in awe of his mysterious powers that they cannot perceive the true Lord. (Revelation 13:4; 13-15) Does this remind you of any Death Valley executives you know? Revelation warns us that no man shall buy or sell without the Mark of the Beast. (Revelation 13:16-17) God foretold the Frankenstein pension, and said plainly that all who accept it are damned.

The rise of Frankenstein Enterprises is not a challenge to Christianity, it is the fulfillment of the Bible's final chapter. We now live in the age foretold by the prophets when men shall seek death and do not find it; when they desire to die and death flees from them. (Revelation 9:6)

THE FARMER

Wade Hellman stood in his fields, watching ragged, sun-ravaged cadavers harvest carrots that would reach their eaters' plates without ever having been touched by living hands. He missed the Mexicans, although he would not admit this to the fellows at the Red Plate Diner.

The zombies had their advantages, certainly. They followed orders, didn't complain about deductions from their wages, never smoked reefer, or organized, or made a move on the local girls. But nor did they play lively Mexican radio as they worked, or set off firecrackers at celebrations, or decorate their trucks with green and red lights at Christmastime. The farm was a lonelier place now that walking corpses tilled the soil.

Wade noticed a pickup approaching down the dirt road that connected this field to the farmhouse. From the skull-and-brains logo painted on the hood he recognized the vehicle as belonging to Carl Teller, the Frankenstein Enterprises regional manager for the county. Carl parked nearby and got out. He had another man with him, a thin-boned stranger in a crisp L.L. Bean flannel and new blue jeans.

"Hiya, Carl," Wade said warily. "This is private property, you know."

"I just saw Wendy, back at the house," Carl said. "She told me to come out here to find you. Let me introduce my colleague, Tony Andale. He's got a proposition to discuss with you."

Andale's handshake was soft and smooth as a handful of warm butter. His business card identified him as a data logistics manager, whatever that was. "Good afternoon, Mister Hellman," he said, flashing a polished smile. "As you may know, Frankenstein Enterprises is building some new facilities in this community, and we've identified your farm as a potential site for development. We'd like to put in an offer on it."

"New facilities? What kind of new facilities?"

"Is that important to you?"

"If you want the land my father left me, then yeah, I want to know what you intend to do with it."

Andale's bright white smile did not dim. "All right. It's no secret. Frankenstein Enterprises needs data centers to run its business, just like any tech company, and those centers need a fair amount of land. It's easier to build them in rural areas like this."

"Uh huh. And what are you offering?"

Andale quoted a price at the lowest ebb of fair. If the farm had turned a profit at any time in the past few years, Wade would have rejected the offer outright. "I'll have to think it over a while," he said.

"All right, Mr. Hellman, but don't think too long. That price is only going to decrease over time. Your farm is one of a number of potential sites that we've identified, and Carl and I have made offers to some of your neighbors already. You don't want to be – what's the expression – sucking hind tit?" He laughed at his own joke.

"By the way, Wade, I noticed that you've lost a couple of Franks lately," Carl said as he got back into his truck. "Give me a call if you want to talk replacements. I'll get you set up at a discount. And if you do sell, I'll give you a good price on any used Franks you want to return to the store."

Wade watched them drive away, then turned back to watch the zombies bringing in the harvest. While he had no great love for Frankenstein Enterprises, the sad fact was that he'd been imagining possible escapes from his mortgage-choked farm, and now one had arrived in the passenger seat of Carl's truck. If he'd only had himself to think of he might have fought on to the bitter end, but that sort of stubbornness was a luxury for the unattached. Wade decided to seek his family's counsel.

Over by the toolshed, Wade's boy Nate mucked out a combine that had gotten a zombie caught in its pickup reel. Nate grunted with exertion as he yanked a shin still clad in a workboot out from between the cutter bar's teeth and tossed it into a wheelbarrow half-full of mangled body parts. These grisly accidents came with some regularity. Indeed, if one were to disassemble the harvester entirely and look deep inside its mechanical guts, one would almost certainly find gobbets of necrotic flesh left over from the last accident, and possibly even the one before that. According to Wade's buddy Lester who worked at the chicken plant, it was even worse in the poultry business, since the knife-wielding zombies who dressed the birds constantly lost digits that got swept along into the grinders. One of the dirty secrets of modern agriculture was that it was nearly impossible to eat a meal that didn't include at least trace amounts of ghoulflesh.

Wade glanced over at the wheelbarrow heaped with shredded brawn, shattered bone fragments, and scraps of cloth, and again an absence struck him. No flies buzzed around the bloody pile. Flies wouldn't eat zombie meat. Wade wondered if the vermin possessed some wisdom that human beings lacked.

"Put that aside for a minute so I can talk to you," Wade told his son, who pulled off his gory work gloves and wiped his face with a rag. "Frankenstein's looking to buy our farm. They're not offering much for it, but neither is anyone else. What do you think of that?"

Nate seemed offended by the notion. "This is our land, Pop. Grandpa left it to you, and I always thought that someday you were going to leave it to me and Cathy. What else are we going to do, if we don't have this place? Where would we even go?"

"I don't disagree with you," Wade said. "My only concern is that I'd rather sell to Frankenstein and get some money to start over than lose the farm to the bank and wind up with nothing. But your point's well-taken. Do you know where your sister is?"

Cathy was at the barn, controlling some of the family's zombies as they washed and boxed freshly-harvested vegetables for transport. She reacted even more harshly to the proposition than Nate had.

"You can't sell to Frankenstein, Dad!" she cried. "I'd rather you salt the Earth than give it to them!"

"Isn't that a little extreme? They just want to use it for some sort of data center."

"I don't care. Frankenstein's corrupt and amoral, and they've got no right to this place. I *hate* that we use zombies to bring in the harvest, Dad. I hate it. Just looking at these rotten things makes me want to scream. It's the deepest sickness there is."

Wade sighed. "I hear you," he said. "And I don't know if there's anything we can do about it. I'm going to go talk to your Mom."

Wade went into the house and found his wife Wendy at the kitchen table, working at the laptop with the bills laid out all around her. "Did you see Carl?" she asked.

"Yeah. You know what he came to see me about?"

"Yeah."

"What do you think?"

Wendy sighed. "I think we'd be lucky if we can hold off the bank for another year. And I don't feel so lucky."

A rich, smoky odor like barbecued pork hung heavy in the air. "What's that smell?" Wade asked. "Do you have dinner on already?"

Wendy sniffed. "No, that's not me," she said. "I think it's coming from outside."

Wade looked out the window and saw Nate burning the zombie's mangled remains in a steel drum. Savory black smoke billowed thickly from the flames.

The next morning, Wade left Nate in charge of the harvest and drove to the Red Plate Diner. He recognized every car and truck parked out front. No matter how much the world changed, the Red Plate stayed the same, right down to the immutable menu. The mingled smells of fried food and cigarette smoke billowed out to meet Wade as he opened the door. The familiarity warmed him. Jim Fryer and Mike Schiller played chess over coffee in Mike's usual booth. Over by the jukebox, Al Carlyle forlornly gummed at a plate of eggs. And Bill Barber glared at the TV, hypnotized in his usual state of half-blind fury. Wade took a stool at the bar and ordered his usual from Susie, the last living waitress he knew.

"Anyone else get a visit from Carl lately?" he asked the room. "And a little guy named Tony Andale?"

Carl and Andale had been making the rounds to almost all the Red Plate's patrons. "They've been buying up land all along Butler Spring and Franklin," Jim said, taking Mike's bishop. "I'm surprised you hadn't heard of it yet."

"They're putting up those data centers," Al Carlyle muttered into his omelet. "I'd always thought farming'd be a steady business on account of everyone's got to eat, but I guess that was wrong. Nowadays the only thing that land is good for is storing big computers, calculating God knows what all day. Welcome to the future."

"What do you all think?" Wade asked. "Are any of you going to take them up on it?"

"I don't see that I've got much of a choice," Jim said sadly. "Crop prices being what they are, I'm just glad that Frankenstein's willing to buy."

"Even after they buy me out I think I'll still have to take a donor pension to make ends meet," said Al. "They'll get my land and my body – what do you think about that?"

"We wouldn't be in this mess at all if not for Frankenstein," Mike Schiller complained. A staunch Christian, Mike had refused to switch over to zombie workers and as a result he'd lost his own farm years ago. Wade was a churchgoer too, but he didn't know that any commandment required a man to bankrupt himself. "The big conglomerates are the only ones who can really make a go of zombies," Mike said. "It's all about efficiencies of scale. They save money, and they lower the prices so much that family farmers get pushed out."

"Frankenstein's not the problem," Bill Barber said sourly. "We'd be underwater already if we didn't have zombies to work the fields. You ought to know that better than anyone, Mike. No, it's the globalists and the Democrats who're doing this to us. They're manipulating crop prices so they can run us off our own land, end our way of life. You can read all about it online."

"At heart we're saying the same thing. What kind of name is Frankenstein, anyway?" Mike curved his index finger and put it to his face in a pantomime of a hooked nose.

"Welcome to the future," Al repeated, to nobody in particular.

After lunch, Wade got back on the road and headed out to Butler Spring to catch a glimpse of the future for himself. It was only a few hours' drive from home. The future had come quickly, springing upon the country without warning. Enormous windowless structures fenced in by razor wire had sprung up seemingly overnight like mushrooms, displacing fields of wheat and corn. No people were anywhere to be seen, not even zombies, yet the place nonetheless seethed with an atmosphere of bustling activity. It was as if he'd crossed a border into a foreign city that had no inhabitants and thrived without them in a state of industrious desolation. Black shapes circled in the skies overhead. At first Wade thought they were vultures. Soon, however, he realized that they were drones, and that they were following him.

The farmer only vaguely understood what a data center was, but he nonetheless intuited that he had stumbled upon a site of vast, inscrutable, and terrible power. He drove through the domain of a death god whose brain occupied hundreds of acres and whose mind encompassed the whole of the planet. Its electric thoughts pulsed all around him, invisible and intangible yet exuding menace that he felt in his marrow, in the fillings of his teeth. Wade tried to recall a Bible verse that might soothe his screaming nerves, to no avail. Jesus Christ was very far away.

On a distant hilltop, Wade spotted a fortress-like structure unlike all the others, seemingly a livestock facility, equipped as it was with feed silos and a waste lagoon. In any other context he would have passed such a place without blinking, but for some reason the sight of it set his skin crawling. *What does a company that makes zombies need to farm?* he asked himself. Revulsion gripped him by the guts, a horrifying sensation that caught him all the more powerfully precisely because he could not explain it. The industrial farm's smokestack exhaled a thin plume of inky black, and for the briefest moment the farmer imagined that he smelled burning human flesh again. Cathy's words echoed in his mind. *It's the deepest sickness there is.*

Wade turned his truck around and sped for home going thirty over the limit, terrified beyond any reason he could put into words, and determined to sell to Frankenstein at whatever price they'd give him. The future had come for his family's land. They needed to flee before it arrived.

REANIMATED LABOR LINKED TO RISING JOBLESS RATES

BY ROSE NAJAFI, ASSOCIATED PRESS (MAY 9, 2009)

The job market faces pressure on two sides, according to a new government report, and the vice is still getting tighter. On one side, financial markets remain unstable after the collapse of Lehman Brothers in September 2008, unable to find their footing with real estate prices still in free-fall. Furthermore, technological advances in reanimated labor have led businesses to shed hundreds of thousands of low-skilled workers, a trend long predating the current economic crisis.

The Department of Labor reported on Friday that the economy lost another 889,000 jobs in April and the unemployment rate lurched to 13.2 percent. Over that same period, Frankenstein Enterprises reported that it sold a remarkable 260,000 units of its popular Hercules 400-series labor model, with tens of thousands of orders waiting to be filled as soon as the company obtains enough cadavers.

"Businesses have a ton of incentives to switch over to reanimated labor right now," said Dean Weissel, head of policy research at Yale's Center for Necromantic Studies. "Because you can amortize a Frank's cost over its expected useful lifespan, and because you can work them twenty hours a day, from an accounting standpoint they're often much more cost-effective than paying for wages and benefits. So when you're in an environment where there's a lot of pressure from above to cut expenses, switching over to reanimated labor is going to be one of the first things that a manager considers."

"Despite the bank bailouts and the Federal Reserve taking rates to zero, the economy's still trapped in an awful vicious cycle," said Columbia labor economist Luke Prowse. "On a national level my spending is your income, so when everyone cuts back their spending at once it causes a severe downturn. And business investment's all but dried up. The only major firm that's really lending right now is Frankenstein's finance arm."

Prowse and other experts have called on the federal government to stimulate the economy with billions in additional spending. Congressional Republicans, however, refuse to support any program that would increase the budget deficit. "I'm not going to pass this crisis on to my children," said Senator Paul Mootey (R-Pa.). "The buck stops here. Besides, we also need to remember that modern unemployment is very different than it used to be. Now anyone who's in serious need has the option of walking into a Frankenstein store and signing up as a donor."

"Frankenstein Enterprises is proud that we've been able to help so many businesses at a time when the economy is in crisis," said a Frankenstein Enterprises spokesman. "And we're also glad that our donor pensions have helped so many through this difficult time."

Government economists say that they are anticipating a sharp jobs downturn in November, when Frankenstein Enterprises is scheduled to unveil its new Ganymede 500-series service model at the Reanimated Labor Industry Coalition's annual convention. With limited speech capability and the ability to connect directly to leading point-of-sale systems and productivity software, the Ganymede 500 is expected to be a formidable competitor for millions of positions in retail and clerical work.

THE MOTHER

My son's been dead for four years and three months, but I still visit him every Sunday. He works at Freshbuy, behind the butcher counter.

I try to get there early in the day, before the rush begins. I put a few things in a shopping basket so the manager doesn't kick me out, and then I stand by the rear of the juice aisle and watch Pat at work. From a distance you might think that he was still alive, that he was thriving. He stands up straight and tall. He attends to his customers swiftly. His uniform is crisp and clean. He even has a decent haircut at last. But when you get up close you can see the sickly, fish-belly whiteness of his skin, and the slackness of his features, and the plastic plugs that they drilled into his skull to restart his brain after it drowned in heroin. Up close you see his eyes, all dull and full of blood.

When Pat was alive he was always in motion, like there was a live wire deep inside of him throwing off sparks. Ever since he was a screaming toddler I hoped that someday he'd quiet down. Be careful what you wish for, I guess.

It all started with Dr. Victor Frankenstein, of course. He was the one who figured out how to bring the dead back from the grave, and how to make them do whatever you want. The Frankenstein Process, they call it.

In an earlier time they'd have burned the doctor at the stake but instead he won the Nobel Prize and became the richest man in the world. Goes to show that sometimes the old ways are best.

In the beginning it was like a magic trick. The famous doctor would appear on one news show or another, tall and unsmiling, handsome in a cold sort of way, with a dead body stretched out on a slab before him. He'd perform his hocus-pocus – crack the skull open, plug in some computer equipment, and then jump-start it with a jolt of electricity – and poor Lazarus would rise up and obey the doctor's orders.

My husband didn't believe it for a long time. "It's just a special effect," Mickey told me the first time we watched a dead man walk on live television. "They're doing publicity for a movie or something. Like back in the 20s, when that radio guy tricked everyone into thinking that Martians were invading New Jersey. What kind of aliens would invade New Jersey? A lot of people are going to feel like real idiots when this is all over and done with."

I sat there next to him on the sofa with my head resting on his shoulder, and laughed at his jokes as he poked fun at the dark miracle happening on the screen. But soon the magic trick crawled out of the TV and into all of our lives.

You see, at first even the people who believed in Dr. Frankenstein didn't understand him. They thought he was peddling immortality, a way for rich people afraid of death to cheat the reaper. But that's not what the Frankenstein Process is about. Dr. Frankenstein doesn't sell eternal life. He sells slaves.

I remember the first time I saw a Frankenstein zombie in person. Most people my age remember their first time meeting a zombie, it's one of those big events like 9/11 that forces its way into your memories. It's nothing to children, though, they've never known life without the walking dead. Pat had a nasty ear infection that was making all of us miserable, and I was walking to the pharmacy to pick up his prescription. Along the way, I spotted an elderly neighbor of ours whose name I never learned staring mutely at a construction site. I'd passed by the site many times without paying attention to it. I hadn't realized that most of the workers were dead. There were four of them, with skin the color of cigarette ash and red, sightless eyes. A paunchy foreman watched them at their labor with a tablet computer in his hands, occasionally tapping on the screen to give a new command. Until that moment it hadn't quite been real to me, even though I'd heard about mines and factories going over to zombie labor. They were nothing at all like the shambling, groaning zombies from the horror movies Pat loved. Hollywood got it all wrong. The dead moved gracelessly, but they were sure-footed and capable. They made no noise whatsoever apart from the clanking of their tools. They weren't hungry for brains or full of fury against the living. If anything, they seemed sad and tired.

For a while, life in our home went on much as it had before. You know how an earthquake can flatten a foreign city without ruining your day? The dead were rising up from their graves, but we still had bills to pay, and parent-teacher conferences to attend when Pat got in trouble at school, and a hundred other little things to worry about. So even while our mail men and store clerks and bus drivers were replaced by zombies one by one, and the strikes and protests against Frankenstein turned into riots and bombings, we kept calm and carried on just like we were supposed to.

Then one day I showed up for work at the hospital, and I found a ghoul standing in my spot at the nurse's station.

I ran to my manager. She was playing with the tablet that controlled my replacement, and seemed irritated by my questions. "You should have gotten an e-mail about this last week," she said. "It's out of my hands. I didn't make the decision, it's a new policy from corporate. They're phasing out all of the nursing assistants for re-animated labor. It's a cost-cutting measure. You'll get your last paycheck direct deposited like usual, and there'll be a notice in the mail about your health benefits and COBRA."

That evening, Mickey and I went out for a walk, like we used to do a lifetime ago when we were dating. We didn't want to talk for a long time, because neither one of us wanted to spoil the splendid silence, but eventually I couldn't take it anymore.

"What are we going to do now?" I asked.

Mickey gave my hand a comforting squeeze. "We'll get by," he said. "I've still got my job at the warehouse. It'll be tight until you find something new, but as long as we're careful we'll be all right."

"I was only half asking about you and me. What about Pat? He says he's not going to college but I don't know what else he can possibly do. There's no jobs out there anymore. Not for the living, anyway."

"I've been thinking about that too. It's tough out there, but he's a good boy. He'll find something."

"I love him more than life, and he *is* a good boy, but he's an angry, impatient boy, too. Besides, since when is being good enough?"

Mickey wrapped his arm around my shoulders, and I nuzzled my cheek against his arm. "We'll get by," he repeated. "What choice do we have?"

One day I came home from errands to the sound of shouting. I hadn't heard shouting in our home since the day that Pat tried to stick a fork in an electric outlet, when he was four. Mickey wasn't given to raising his voice, and Pat showed his anger through sullen silence and slamming doors. But now here they were, barking at each other in the living room like fighting dogs. "What's wrong?" I asked.

"You tell her!" Mickey yelled, red-faced, sticking his finger in Pat's chest. "Tell her what you did."

Pat smiled defiantly. "I got paid, is what I did. Two grand to start, and more every month for as long as I live. And I don't even have to do anything for it."

"He donated himself to fucking Frankenstein!" Mickey snarled accusingly. "After he dies they're going to take his body and start it up again and put him to work scrubbing toilets or some shit!"

"*After* I die! *After* I die! Who cares what happens *after* I die? Christ, nobody gives a fuck about what happens to me while I'm alive, why should I give a fuck what happens to me after I die?"

I nearly dropped my shopping bags. "You think nobody cares what happens while you're alive?" I asked. But Mickey and Pat were still shouting at each other, and neither of them heard me over the din.

"You've seen what that company does!" Mickey roared. "You want to be another fucking zombie? It's a goddamned abomination!"

"It's goddamned money!" Pat roared back. "What else am I going to do, tell me that?" And without waiting for an answer he stormed out of the apartment, slamming the door behind him so hard that you'd think he meant to break it.

After that day there was shouting in our apartment all the time.

The Frankenstein money wasn't enough for Pat to live on, but it was plenty to kill himself with. I began getting knots of dread in my stomach whenever the first of a new month rolled around, because Pat got his Frankenstein money on the first day of the month and he'd be drunk for at least the week thereafter. He'd vanish for days at a time – and when there's bombings and mob violence and spree killings on the television almost every day, it's so awful not to know where your son is.

It was a blessing and a curse to have company in our misery. So many of our friends suffered the same sorrows, and some of them had it even worse. Mickey's work friend, Vince, lost his house putting his little girl through rehab. My best friend, Teresa, had to go to a mental hospital after her Sally got caught up in some radical group and got herself shot dead at a protest march. It felt like the entire country was falling off the tracks.

When the call finally came, I knew what it was before I even picked up the phone. They'd found him in a gas station bathroom, the needle still in his arm. It's strange how you can anticipate something awful for a long time coming, but when it finally happens the enormity of the pain still takes you completely by surprise.

In my many bitter moments I imagine that Dr. Frankenstein planned it all to happen this way – that he knew giving my son a little money but taking away all his hope would drive him to the grave that much quicker and give Frankenstein Enterprises another piece of merchandise. I've been to enough of my friends' children's' memorial services by now that the idea doesn't seem totally insane. You'll note that I say "memorial services" and not "funerals." The dead hardly ever get buried these days.

I had to go to the morgue to identify the body. The street outside was full of dead men in black armor. They stared at me silently with their blood-red eyes as I walked through their formation. It was a big controversy when the police first started using zombies for foot patrols, but they probably couldn't even staff a force without them. I heard on the TV that it's more dangerous to be a policeman today than it was to be a soldier in World War II. It's so much easier to get a gun than a job these days.

Inside the morgue, they took me to a cinderblock room that smelled of antiseptic, where a long window looked into a chamber with brushed steel shelves built into the walls. A man in a white coat pulled my child out of one of those shelves and removed the sheet that covered him. *At least things can't get any worse*, I thought to myself. *The worst thing that can possibly happen has happened now.* Looking back, I see how naive that was. Maybe in the past death was the end of suffering, but science marches on.

After I'd identified my son, they escorted me down the hall to the Frankenstein representative. He had his own office in the morgue, a cramped space barely bigger than a cubicle. The Frankenstein logo, a corporate-looking skull-and-brains symbol, hung over the door. I hated that creepy logo so much. I'd hated it from the first time I saw it, and it had spread like a virus since then. The Frankenstein skull-and-brains was on packages, it was on the sides of trucks and cars and even drones and airships, it was on offices and showrooms, it was on appliances and electronics to show that they were Frank-compatible, it was on advertisements you couldn't escape, it was on sinister-looking broadcast towers that sprouted like mushrooms, and now here it was in the morgue, looking down at me.

The rep was a little man, not a midget exactly, but not much taller, in a rumpled suit slightly too big for him. There was a button with the Frankenstein skull-and-brain pinned to his lapel. It was easier to make eye contact with the corporate logo than the little man. He gave me a stock condolence speech that had obviously been written in some faraway office, and hustled me through signing some papers, discouraging me from reading them. I complied. Even if I'd had the presence of mind to read all those forms, which I didn't, I wouldn't have been able to understand all of their twisted legalese.

On my way out of the office, I asked the little man, "So when are they replacing you with a zombie?"

He smiled grimly. "If you'd rather not deal with a person at times like these, you can download our donor relations smartphone app," he said.

It was a year before I saw Pat again. Freshbuy was having a sale on sliced turkey. Even though it was out of my way I had plenty of time on my hands, and money was so tight we couldn't afford to pass up any bargains. Mickey, who had once been so easy-going and gentle, had gotten in the habit of nit-picking every bill, and if I spent more than he thought proper it was bound to cause a fight.

When I gave my order to the zombie at the Freshbuy deli counter, at first I didn't even recognize him. You get so used to dealing with zombies that you start thinking of them just as things, like they're ATM machines or self-checkout registers. Like they didn't used to think and dream and laugh. Like they didn't used to be the light of some mother's life. But when the zombie at the counter handed me my package of meat, and my fingers touched his ice-cold hands, I looked him in the face and I saw my lost little boy staring back at me. It was like someone had stuck a barbed fishhook right into my heart. On the one hand, it was so sweet to see his face again that I couldn't turn away. On the other hand, it was even more painful than seeing him on a slab at the morgue.

I collapsed right there in the store. Pat didn't make any move to help me up. He wasn't programmed for that.

When I told Mickey about it that evening, it drove him into a fury so fierce that I was scared of him for the first time in thirty years of marriage. He cursed Freshbuy until he was nearly raving, and swore up and down that if he could get his hands on Victor Frankenstein he'd shatter all his teeth and kill him by inches. Mickey didn't even like to kill bugs – when he found them in our apartment he'd cup them in his hands and put them outside. But I had no doubts at all that he would have tortured the Doctor to death if he'd been able.

Despite Mickey, I began visiting Freshbuy every week. I never told him or anyone else about those trips, and I was careful to always throw away the bags and receipts, but somehow I think he knew what I was doing. I never was any good at hiding my feelings. Maybe if I'd been stronger in the face of my grief, more capable of tearing out the fishhook and saying goodbye, then the horrors that came next might never have happened. I guess addiction runs in our family.

The day that Mickey came to Freshbuy was the second-worst day of my life. I was watching Pat work, like always, when I felt Mickey's hand on my shoulder. It was such a familiar touch, and yet I jumped at it. "You need to get out of here now," he growled. "I'm going to fix this." He glanced over at Pat and shuddered with hate and disgust. I noticed then that Mickey had brought a claw hammer to the supermarket, the same one he'd used to hang up our family photos.

"Mickey, what are you doing?" I screamed. "Stop!" But by then it was too late.

Pat met Mickey at the counter like any other customer. "You leave her alone!" Mickey half-screamed, half-cried at our dead son. "Stop hurting her! You were never good to her!" Pat didn't move, or respond in any way. He simply waited for Mickey to order some meat. Mickey raised the hammer and broke our boy's skull with a wet crack. But Pat didn't fall. He only stared at Mickey with those vacant, lonely red eyes of his. Mickey kept hitting him again and again and again, and finally, mercifully, he went down.

A gawking crowd had gathered around. "What the fuck is going on?" Mickey yelled hoarsely at them, with tears running down his cheeks. "Why do we have to live like this? Don't we mean anything to them? Doesn't human life mean a goddamned thing anymore?" Roaring, he shattered the panes of glass in the deli case one by one with his hammer, until the floor glittered with broken shards. He swept the items off of nearby shelves and kicked them away. Another zombie mutely approached with a push broom to sweep up the mess, and Mickey pummeled it until it dropped.

Then he ran out of gas and stopped breaking things and wept like I'd never seen before, not even right after Pat's death. I tried to go to him to comfort him, but before I could move, two black-gloved hands seized me roughly from behind.

Store management must have called 911. There were two zombie policemen in the store, looking like robots in their bulky riot armor. One of them had gotten a hold of me and gripped so tight that the next day I had finger-shaped bruises all along my arms. The other approached Mickey. The zombie raised its nightclub and hissed through its plexiglass face shield. Mickey dropped the hammer and put up his hands but by then it was already on top of him. I don't let myself think about the rest of it, although sometimes the sound of a hammer blow or the sight of a dead policeman walking about pulls me back into that moment and I lose myself in shrieking.

Afterwards, I had to make another trip to that goddamned morgue. I had to look at my husband laid out with his head caved in, and sign a form to identify him. And I had to deal with that little man in the cheap suit again, too. To my surprise and horror, Mickey had donated his body to Frankenstein Enterprises.

Mickey had always handled our finances as part of his husbandly duties. It took me a while to make sense of his shoebox full of bank statements, but once I did I realized that the warehouse had stopped paying him almost a year ago, not long after Pat's death. Since then, the only funds coming into our account were monthly deposits from Frankenstein Enterprises. Small monthly deposits, at that. No wonder he'd been so sensitive about money.

After the memorial service, Mickey's friends all decided to go out for a drink together. Some of them had become real barflies, dealing with Frankenstein by having a nice cold pint and waiting for all of this to blow over. I didn't want to go but I didn't want to be alone either so I followed along. They toasted Mickey and then they all got piss drunk while I sat at the bar quietly nursing a glass of wine.

"At least Mick's working again," Mickey's old chum Tom muttered to nobody in particular while he waited for his beer. "They might even give him his old job back. Whole fucking company's gone over to zombie labor." It turned out that almost all of them had signed up as Frankenstein donors just to get by. From the way they looked and talked and drank, I guessed that some of them would be back to work real soon.

The apartment was very quiet when I woke up the next morning. I couldn't believe how huge it felt. Like a vast, empty cavern. I accidentally made coffee for two, but I drank it all anyway. And then I went back to Freshbuy, switching buses twice because there'd been a terrible bombing the day of Mickey's memorial and the streets were still detoured. I would have asked the drivers the quickest route, but they were all long dead.

At Freshbuy, Pat was back in service already. All the technicians had to do was put a metal plate in his head, and he was ready to get back to his place at the meat slicer. I stood there watching him all day until the store closed and they made me leave.

Now I visit Pat every Sunday as part of my weekly routine. I visit Mickey on Sundays too. He's a street cleaner now. I walk with him on his rounds until it starts to get dark, almost like we did a lifetime ago when we were dating. The silence isn't so splendid anymore.

I go back to the apartment afterwards and heat up dinner. I eat it alone while I watch the fighting on TV. Of course, with Mickey passed, now I have to pay for everything myself. And it's not like there's a lot of jobs out there for a fifty-two-year-old woman without any college. So I went to the Frankenstein Enterprises recruiting office and signed up as a donor, just like Pat and Mickey did. It's not much money but I don't need much. And in a way, it gives me something to look forward to.

It means that someday we'll be a family again.

MORE THAN A DOZEN KILLED IN MEXICO AS THE DEATH LORDS STRIKE AGAIN

BY ROSE NAJAFI, WASHINGTON POST
(JANUARY 28, 2014)

At least 13 people were killed when cartel war-zombies descended on a bar in Ciudad Acuña late Thursday, the latest massacre in an ongoing struggle for control of smuggling routes that has left thousands dead. Onlookers described an unmarked truck pulling up in front of the Barra de Rayos and disgorging a horde of walking cadavers who stormed the popular cantina wielding axes and machetes.

"I watched them skin the bouncer alive," said a hot dog vendor who witnessed the carnage from across the street, who asked not to be named for his safety and that of his family. "The people inside never had a chance."

The number of dead is not known precisely, since the attackers absconded with the corpses, leaving behind a grisly scene of pooled blood and matted hair. It is widely believed that Mexico's organized crime gangs launder the bodies of their victims through corrupt hospitals and sell them for reanimation.

"The same factors that have wreaked havoc on Mexico's legitimate economy are fueling the drug wars," said Ricardo Flores, a journalist who has reported extensively on the use of zombies by Mexico's newest generation of high-tech crime kingpins, commonly referred to as Señores de la Muerte, or Death Lords. "With the rise of the donor economy, demand for drugs has exploded on both sides of the border. At the same time, the Death Lords' adoption of Frankenstein technology has left thousands of sicarios unemployed, which creates even more conflict. And because there's now a thriving grey market in human bodies, the gangs can turn a profit on murder. Every incentive leads them towards brutality."

"You don't see heads on spikes or mutilated victims out for public display, like you used to in the old days," said Ciudad Acuña police official Hector Raimondo. "Cutting your rival up with a chainsaw might feel good, but it destroys the resale value."

A Frankenstein Enterprises spokesman said that the company complies with all local laws regarding the sourcing of bodies and is confident in the integrity of its supply chain.

THE LAWYER

On the television screen, a leathery, bat-like figure so shriveled that it can barely be recognized as ex-human sits behind the wheel of a delivery van, racing down white-picketed suburban streets at reckless speed, another competitor in the nationwide rally race of e-commerce. The zombie takes a turn almost hard enough to flip the van. It has a tight schedule and no other concerns whatsoever. Ahead, a mother and child step into a crosswalk.

Cut to a scene where a woman's corpse stands in front of a stove, ghost-like in her kitchen whites and paper cap, methodically tending to a half-dozen sizzling, sputtering pans. A burner ignites into a blossom of flame with a billowing *whoosh*. The pale wraith steadfastly attends to her cooking, ignoring the grease-fed conflagration raging before her even as it begins to dance up the wall.

The scene changes again. A dead man with his back turned yanks repeatedly on a chainsaw starter rope and the engine coughs staccato. The skin covering his head has sloughed away in patches, exposing skull filthy as dirty snow. He wears denim overalls and a flannel shirt brown with stains. Suddenly the chainsaw fires with a throaty mechanical roar, kicking out clouds of blue smoke that enshroud the ghoul. He turns abruptly, faster than you'd think a thing so worn and rotten could move, thrusting the chainsaw's whirring teeth forward.

"Have you been injured by a zombie?" the announcer asks in a wheedling tone. "Call the Law Offices of Richard J. Kruger today!"

Cut to Richard J. Kruger, Esquire, a gentleman with the mustache and body type of a walrus, resplendent in a tan suit and mustard shirt combination that shouldn't work yet somehow does, giving him the look of a lawyer as played by a '70s character actor, the sort of guy who'd show up in one scene to give Dirty Harry a hard time. "My name's Richard Kruger and I've been suing Frankenstein Enterprises for ten years," he proclaims in a thick Texan drawl, his website and phone number flashing all about him in canary-yellow captions. "I know their tricks, I know their traps, I know how to take them on and win what you deserve!" His practice specialties scroll across the bottom of the screen.

- Styx collisions
- Industrial accidents
- Zombie bites
- Lemon corpses
- Z-police brutality
- Pension disputes
- Wrongful re-animations

"After a Styx backed over me, the doctors said I'd never walk again," testifies Franklin K., an actual client, not a paid performer. "With the cash settlement that Mister Kruger won for me, I was able to get a z-nurse and a state-of-the-art motorized wheelchair."

"Frankenstein Enterprises took my mother's body from the nursing home without permission and sent it to fight in Iraq," Marianne S. says, dabbing a tear at the corner of her eye. "I didn't know what to do. Richard was there with me every step of the way. He helped me understand my options and get compensation for my pain and suffering."

"Don't take on Frankenstein alone, call my office today for a free consultation," the lawyer offers, his phone number flashing again. "When you've got zombie trouble, you need Richard Kruger fighting for you!"

Emiliano Rodriguez watched from his hospital bed, his morphine drip lending the advertisement a foggy dreamlike quality. He would have smiled if his jaw wasn't wired shut. At last, he knew of a man who could help him.

Richard Kruger was an expert on the subject of neck braces, and he saw right away that Mister Rodriguez had been equipped with a real doozy. The fact that a man so badly injured could walk into the office at all was itself a small miracle, a sign of God's half-assed mercy. Notwithstanding his bandages he seemed a pleasant chap, the sort of good-natured and competent fellow you'd like to have as your neighbor or your lead witness. Rodriguez explained that he owned a landscaping business in Del Rio. When a member of his crew got pulled into a wood chipper, he'd made the mistake of going to Tombstone Bob's Refurbished Zombies for the replacement, eventually settling on a 2006 Hercules 200-series. He chose a primitive model, good for nothing except the simplest donkey-work, and in none-too-great condition, but Tombstone Bob lived up to his famous reputation for prices so low, they're six feet under. Rodriguez thought that he'd gotten a good deal on his new used zombie until he took it home and opened its charging coffin and it beat him half to death with a shovel. He might have cashed in his own donor pension on the spot, if his son hadn't had the sense of mind to deactivate the rogue corpse.

"You didn't give it *any* commands before it went berserk?" Richard asked, drumming his pen against his legal pad.

"No, nothing! I only just pressed the button to take it out of coma mode and then . . ." Rodriguez twisted his still-swollen face into an angry grimace and pantomimed swinging a spade with his less-injured arm.

"Outrageous. A Hercules shouldn't even be able to flick a man's ear, let alone belabor him over the head with gardening tools. It's not like you bought a security zombie, something that's programmed to defend itself. Mister Rodriguez, you are the victim of a gross injustice, and I recommend that you respond with a blistering lawsuit."

"That's exactly what I hoped you'd say," the grateful Rodriguez replied.

"But before we can file the lawsuit, we need to figure out exactly what went wrong so I can draft the complaint." Richard slid the business card of an establishment called Cool Air Forensics across his desk. "The guy who runs this place, Joe Torres, he used to work for Frankenstein Enterprises doing repairs. I use him as the consulting expert in all my cases. Don't let his appearance fool you, he's very smart, very professional, knows zombies inside and out. Give him a call and tell him I sent you. He'll pick your Frank up, find out the reason why it assaulted you, and then we'll make whoever's responsible pay."

Rodriguez shuddered and broke down sobbing, describing his sufferings since the attack and the anxieties he'd developed in its aftermath, not least of them a full-body aversion to shovels, no small problem for a landscaper. Richard listened attentively. Clients came to him seeking justice, and if they couldn't get that, the next best thing was simply to be heard. As Rodriguez tearfully described how he saw the defective zombie whenever he closed his eyes, even in blinking, Richard jotted down a note, reminding himself to reach out to a good testifying psychiatrist.

Two days later a cryptically urgent call about the Rodriguez case summoned Richard to Cool Air Forensics. Joe did business out of a strip mall, sandwiched between a noodle joint and a defunct tire dealership. The top-knotted, heavily-tattooed zombie expert paced back and forth in his office sucking on a vape pen, infusing the room with a sickly artificial-fruit smell that Richard found nearly unbearable, far worse than actual cigarette smoke. Joe was the only "cool" person that Richard knew, and Richard would not have tolerated him if not for the hipster's impressive skills ferreting out the secrets of the undead. Joe might have gone far at Frankenstein Enterprises, but he was not a man to wear motion-sensing shackles and race at an app's command, which was why he went off on his own to consult for lawyers and insurance companies instead.

"Something fishy's going on with the Frank that Rodriguez guy dropped off," Joe said. "You've got to see it for yourself."

"And you couldn't discuss it over the phone?"

"No, I couldn't. Who knows who's listening?"

Joe brought Richard into the puckish private mortuary of his workshop. Bright '60s Euro-pop played from a portable speaker, and Día de Muertos murals grinned from the walls. A scarred corpse lay on an examining table at the center of the room, nude but for a white sheet covering up its lower half. Yellowed skin gleamed sallow beneath the humming fluorescents. Red eyes stared sightlessly towards the ceiling. "The first thing I did was scan its SR chip to get its service record," Joe said. "According to the chip, this is an '06 Hercules 200-series with a few basic labor apps, previously owned by a construction company in Provo. Donor cause of death was heart failure. Other than standard maintenance, it's never had any transplants or major procedures."

"And?"

"The second thing I did was a physical exam. Check it out for yourself." The zombie's waxy flesh hosted a museum of injury, a colorfully varied array of stab wounds, fantastically textured burns, and bullet holes puckered like little assholes, enough damage to end a human being a dozen times over.

Richard whistled appreciatively. "Tombstone Bob falsified the service record! He must have cut out the SR chip in its neck and swapped it with a different one. It's a clean-cut violation of the lemon corpse law. Bless you, Joe, we'll nail his dick to the wall."

"Let's not go to the hardware store just yet. Look, all these wounds were inflicted postmortem. With antemortem injuries you'd see signs of inflammation, or even healing. There's none of that here. This Frank's been hacked apart and stapled back together on multiple occasions, and not very well, at that."

"Construction company in Provo, my ass – this thing's been in combat," Richard said. He thought of the cartel wars raging across both sides of the nearby border, and suddenly talk of nailing dicks to walls didn't sound like playful hyperbole anymore. "Oh, shit."

"Oh, shit is exactly right," Joe said. "The third thing I did was connect to its interface to see what apps it's got in its memory. Just in case you're not absolutely terrified yet, our ugly friend here knows how to field-strip an AK-47. It can drive a car. And it has a Star Wormwood priority satellite uplink in its headware, so it can operate pretty much anywhere on the planet without needing an iGor signal. All it's lacking is speech capability. Without the SR chip I can't tell what model it actually is, but this is definitely not a Hercules 200. This thing is to a Hercules 200 what a Navy SEAL is to you. I think it's one of the newer military models. Must have cost six figures, not even counting the apps."

"What were its Asimov settings tuned to?"

"Level five. Maximum aggression."

"Jesus Christ. That's the attack, right there! Tombstone Bob sells poor Rodriguez a high-end, high-strung death machine, under the pretense that it's a rotter just good for mowing lawns. Rodriguez takes it out of sleep mode without even thinking to check the Asimovs, its AI sees him as a threat, and it damn near puts an end to him."

"But what's in it for Tombstone Bob? What's he have against Rodriguez?"

"Mistimed April Fool's prank? Maybe Rodriguez and Bob's wife are up to something? Fucked if I know. But I aim to find out." Richard spotted a dark mark along the side of the zombie's mangled belly, a smudged, vaguely equine shape. "What's that supposed to be?" he asked.

Joe peered at the blotch. "A tattoo. Also post-mortem, you can tell on account of the smudging. It's supposed to be a chess piece, maybe? A horse?"

"No. No, I see it now. It's not a horse. It's a mule."

The blurred tattoo sat at the top of a fresh wound running vertically down the zombie's side, held shut with surgical staples. Joe gently ran his fingers along the zipperlike incision. "I feel a bulge," he said. "There's something in there." He retrieved a pair of wire cutters from his work bench and snipped through one of the staples, making a tangible *plink* that set Richard's teeth on edge.

"What the hell are you doing, Joe?" Richard demanded, waving his arms in dread and frustration. "Don't open the goddamn thing up! I hate to say this, but we should call the cops."

"I just want to see what's inside. Aren't you curious? What if it's cash?" Joe worked his way methodically along the incision cutting the surgical staples one by one. As he opened the z-mule's body its fingers and toes began to curl hideously, a pallid mass of worms, each squirming independently of the others.

"Nobody can access this thing remotely, right?" Richard asked, his mind suddenly racing with recent reports of the Mexican Death Lords' barbarism – animated idols of Santa Muerte wrapping victims in barbed wire and crucifying them; cities convulsed by armies of the dead fighting in the streets.

"Happens every time, the twitching's only a reflex," Joe said, casual as if he were tinkering with a lawnmower. "Franks can't be activated remotely out of coma mode. You need to plug physically into the brain to wake them up."

"But we don't even know what model this is," Richard said. "We have no idea what it's capable of." Something flashed on the monitor.

"Connecting..."

The z-mule's trembling hands straightened in an instant like a garotte wire drawn taut and latched around the back of Joe's neck, hooking its thumbs in beneath his jawbone. Before Joe could make a sound, the z-mule bit deep into his Adam's Apple. And then it began to chew.

Richard had litigated many zombie bite cases on behalf of stubby-fingered clients, but those had all been simple feeding accidents. Now he experienced the sights and smells and sounds of an animated corpse murdering a human being with its teeth; now he heard the meaty gnashing of a trachea devoured by an industrial machine with lips and a tongue. The room suddenly stank of pennies and the ocean. Cheerful French disco continued to pipe over the speakers, nearly drowning out Joe's strangled cries. The z-mule pushed its victim away with a forceful shove, gobbets of brawn and cartilage carelessly tumbling out of its wide-open mouth and raining wetly on the tile floor. Joe crawled for the exit on his belly, gurgling his death rattle. He collapsed beneath a mural of skeletons playing guitar and moved no more.

The z-mule nimbly hopped from the table. It moved like a mantis wearing a corpse, a predatory alien built for eerie grace and shocking violence. The partially reopened wound in its side flapped open bloodlessly, an entrance to a dark and mysterious cave. The murderous thing groped wrist-deep inside the opening, retrieving an automatic pistol. It expertly chambered a round and leveled the weapon at Richard.

The sight of the gun and the metallic click of its slide sent an icy jolt of terror through the lawyer's veins, shocking him back into the present. "Hey, I want to talk to you!" Richard cried as the z-mule took aim. "I want to make a deal!"

The blood-drenched ghoul paused, as if in confusion.

"I'm talking to a person, right?" Richard asked. "If I'm talking to a living person, wherever you are, please, I beg you, make this thing's head nod."

The z-mule's head jerked forward, causing more half-chewed windpipe to tumble out of its still-open mouth, and Richard felt a relief so great he might have cried. A human being was in control. You could talk to a murderer. And so began the highest-stakes negotiations of Richard Kruger's legal career.

"OK," Richard said. "OK, good. You prefer English o debería hablar español? Nod once for English, asentir dos veces para español." The zombie jerked its head again, startling Richard badly. "English it is. Listen, I can see something's gone horribly wrong here. You obviously had some plan for this zombie, and that plan's gone south. But if you let me live, I can help you."

The z-mule held statue-still, its gun still trained on Richard's heart. It had the ultimate poker face, especially with all the gore smeared on its haggard lips and cheeks. Richard suspected that, like Rodriguez, he would see that face the rest of his life. His mind raced trying to reconstruct the chain of fuck-ups concluding in this disaster. Fortunately, his job was all about reverse-engineering catastrophes to prove how they had happened.

"I think I understand your problem," he said. "Tombstone Bob got himself involved in a smuggling operation. You sent him this Frank across the border with some kind of contraband sewn up inside it, and he was supposed to deliver it to a buyer in the U.S. But Tombstone Bob's a goddamn moron, and he got his Franks mixed up. He accidentally delivered the cocaine-stuffed killing machine to a landscaping company, and he gave the cartel a beat-up old rotter just good for mowing lawns. Is that close enough to right? Give me one nod for yes, two for no." He mentally promised himself not to jump when the zombie moved, and then broke that promise when the z-mule nodded once. *Yes.* "All right," the lawyer gasped. "All right. And now you need to get the cargo inside this Frank to the people who were supposed to get it in the first place?"

Yes.

"OK. I can help! Look, friend, you're navigating a naked, bloody Frank through a city you may not know, trying to find people who may not be easy to find. I can be your guide, drive you around, do whatever talking's required. I'll get your z-mule wherever it needs to go, and then we'll part ways and I'll never speak about this to anyone, swear to God. I've got no reason to go to the police." He glanced guiltily at Joe's remains, the eyes still open and staring accusingly. "He and I worked together, but we were never close," Richard clarified. "I just want to go home."

Two head-bangs. *No.* Richard thought his offer had been rejected, and he cringed expecting the counter-offer to come at muzzle velocity. But the Frank lowered its gun.

"You want me to be your guide?"

Yes. Richard nearly passed out from a dizzying rush of relief.

"You want me to get the Frank to its buyer?"

No.

"You want me to take you to Tombstone Bob first."

Yes.

"God help me, we understand each other," Richard said. "Let's clean off the blood and get some clothes on you." The lawyer found a can of disinfectant wipes and scrubbed the gore away, then re-clothed the awful thing in the drab khaki coveralls that it had come in, which themselves were stained deep brown with Rodriguez. Once the warrior ghoul had been cleaned and dressed it was almost indistinguishable from its worker bee cousins, although upon close examination, one could still find shreds of Joe stuck between its teeth.

Ordinarily Richard quite enjoyed driving, but ordinarily he didn't have a bloodthirsty wight sitting in the passenger seat, cradling a handgun in its lap and staring at him. "So what do you think of Texas?" the lawyer asked in an attempt to break the tension. "Do you like what you've seen of it so far?"

The ghoul gazed out the window. *No,* it nodded.

"I know it doesn't look like much, but the food here is terrific," Richard said, state pride inexplicably bubbling up through his terror. "We got Tex-Mex, we've got good Vietnamese. You can't say you've really been to Texas unless you've eaten here." The zombie suddenly gnashed its teeth together with a sharp dental *clack*, startling Richard so badly he nearly lost control of the vehicle. "Joe doesn't count as eating here," Richard said. "I was talking about barbecue or banh mi or something. Jesus Christ."

Tombstone Bob's Refurbished Zombies had closed for business permanently by the time they arrived, its glass-walled showroom converted to use as a macabre spectator stadium. Somebody had installed a soccer app in all of the used zombies and set the clumsy things against each other in a game, using Bob's dripping head as the ball. The killer also stuck a dagger in the dancing tube man near the entrance. Pinned to the ground, the promotional device writhed and flailed its noodly arms about. Richard could sympathize. The lawyer and the ghoul stood together in the parking lot – empty but for a sunbaked Lexus bearing a TOMBSTONE vanity plate – watching the zombies play in the gore. Colorful pennants hung limp in the enervating midday heat and Old Glory dangled from her flagpole.

"We seem to be late to the game," Richard remarked. "You reckon the buyer did this?"

Yes, the ghoul nodded.

"Rest in peace, Bob," Richard muttered. A decrepit cadaver held together by stitching kicked its salesman's skull across his own showroom. Nearby, a siren yowled.

Richard turned and saw a pair of police cruisers coming down the road. Their red-and-blue lights briefly promised hope of rescue, before he remembered that he stood outside a grisly crime scene next to a contraband-stuffed zombie, and that he was implicated in two killings with no witnesses to clear his name. The truth was on his side, but alas, the truth was a terrible witness to put up on the stand. The truth was deranged and unbelievable. The z-mule watched the lawmen approach, calm as only a corpse can be. It thumbed off its pistol's safety with a gentle *click*.

Richard knew that if a gunfight broke out he would die or go to prison forever. "Put the gun away," he said.

No.

"Listen, there's no way this cocaine zombie's getting home if you play OK Corrall with the cops! Our only way out of this mess is to be smarter than they are. I know the law in this town. The bar is not high. Put the gun away."

The z-mule opened the front of its jumpsuit and slipped its weapon back inside its body. One of its weapons, at least. It still had its teeth.

Richard straightened his tie as the cruisers pulled into the parking lot, wishing that he felt as confident in his bullshitting skills as he'd promised.

A couple of hulking kids in deputy uniforms emerged from the lead car, almost identical in their matching uniforms and sunglasses, except that one sported a pencil mustache and the other kept clean-shaven. Richard had his hands up even before they pointed their pistols at him. For the second time in as many hours, he had to palaver for his life while staring down the barrel of a gun. Behind him, a *thump* sounded from the showroom as Tombstone Bob's head bounced off a window, leaving a pink smear on the glass. "Oh thank God you're here, I was just about to call 911," Richard lied.

"Sir, I need you to kneel down with your hands in the air," Deputy Mustache ordered. Richard got to his knees, a task that would have been painful even if the asphalt wasn't so hot and sticky. "Is your zombie capable of violence?" the deputy asked.

"This old thing? Heavens no. Check its neck, it's only a Hercules 200-series."

When Deputy Mustache took Richard up on this offer, Richard winced inwardly, terrified that the z-mule would seize this opportunity to catch a lawman by surprise and tear his guts out with its mouth. But it quietly submitted. For now.

Deputy Babyface handcuffed the kneeling lawyer. "Don't I know you from somewhere?" he asked.

"I sure know you," Richard said. "I remember that 80-yard touchdown you ran against the Brackett Tigers. My name's Richard Kruger – you might have seen my TV ads, or my billboards on US-90. Business cards are in my inside jacket pocket."

Deputy Babyface took a card, pleased to meet a fellow small-town pseudo-celebrity. "Now I recognize you," he said. "What are you doing here?"

"That zombie yonder belongs to one of my clients," Richard said. "It's a lemon. I came here to negotiate a refund from Tombstone Bob. I only just got here a minute ago. He was already decapitated when I arrived, I swear." A near-perfect lie, verifiably correct for the most part. Deputy Babyface had more questions, but he couldn't conduct a good cross-examination any more than Richard could catch a long spiral. While they talked, Richard watched one of the deputies inside the showroom chase after Tombstone Bob's head, trying to retrieve it from the soccer players.

Eventually the sheriff's men let Richard and the z-mule depart with a warning not to leave town, unable to believe that such a ghastly crime could have been committed by a plump middle-aged attorney who plastered his face on local bus stops. Richard watched the flashing lights recede in his rear-view mirror, then drove onwards to meet the butchers responsible.

"See, I told you I had that under control," the lawyer boasted to the z-mule.

Yes, the zombie nodded.

"You're lucky to have me around."

The zombie did not respond yes-or-no to this; it merely gazed at him, its lower jaw crookedly agape. Richard decided not to press his luck. "So next we're going to see the buyer?" he asked.

Yes.

"Can you tell me where he is?"

No.

"So how are we going to get there?"

The zombie glared at the steering wheel.

"You want to drive my car?"

Yes.

Richard sighed. His knees still ached from kneeling on the asphalt, and somehow this day kept getting worse.

The z-mule turned out to be a better driver than Richard. It took them across the county line to a beautifully decrepit ranch in the badlands. Rusted cargo containers and decomposing prefab sheds littered the drought-parched grounds. The sun sank over the edge of the horizon, reminding Richard yet again of Joe's blood.

A sturdy metal gate controlled entrance to the smugglers' lair. Behind it, a beefy white guy in flannel and a cowboy hat sat on a lawn chair reading a comic book. This desperado reminded Richard of his all-time least-favorite client, a biker who claimed he'd caught genital gangrene from a truck stop z-waitress, and who shot out Richard's office windows when his lawsuit was dismissed. Behind him stood two monstrously large Franks that had been surgically transformed for maximum intimidation, their lips cut away to reveal sharpened teeth, their faces studded with implanted chrome spikes and countless piercings, their skin elaborately scarified. Both of these muscle-bound ogres carried rifles, although they looked like they could tear Richard's car open with their bare hands alone. He'd heard that you could grow Franks to enormous size by feeding them anabolic steroids and making them pump iron for weeks, and he suspected that the gang had done just that. The putative human walked up and tapped a revolver butt on Richard's window. "You expected?" he asked in a purring drawl, his tone implying that surprises were unwelcome here.

"Tell your boss I have the package that Tombstone Bob was supposed to deliver," Richard said.

The goon glanced over the lawyer and the z-mule appraisingly. Richard wondered if this man was the one who'd beheaded the salesman. The goon smiled ominously. Something cruel and playful flickered behind his piggish eyes. "I know you. You the billboard man." The advertising agency had done its job well.

"Richard Kruger, attorney at law."

"I thought you just chased ambulances."

"In this economy? Everyone needs a side hustle."

"I'll tell Pike you're here," he said. "Stay right where you are. You move from this spot, my handsome friends here will blow you away." He punched a command into his phone and his ogres stiffened into a combat pose, shouldering their rifles and aiming them at the lawyer, the third time today he'd had a gun pointed at him. *Third time's the charm?* Richard wondered. *How would that even work?* The goon stepped a short distance away to place a call.

Richard glanced to the ghoul beside him. "If I don't make it out of here, will you avenge my death?"

No.

When the goon returned Richard asked how the call had gone but couldn't get an answer. He escorted Richard and the z-mule to one of the cargo containers and threw its door open, letting out a gust of stale air, rust, and disinfectant. Roaches skittered for cover when the lights went on. The smugglers had converted the box into a makeshift dissecting room, well-stocked with surgical machetes and even more horrifying tools. The left table was in use. A thoroughly deconstructed body lay scattered upon it, as well as in overflowing buckets on the floor nearby. A big-eyed cartoon burro grinned impishly from the shoulder of a severed arm.

"Step inside," the goon said. "Pike'll be here soon." Richard anxiously glanced over the instruments for taking people apart, and once again wondered how the call had gone.

Pike did not make them wait long. The smuggler was a wiry, sunburned white guy wearing a bloody apron over a black T-shirt and jeans. He walked in leading a small leashed creature that Richard momentarily mistook for a hideous and evil-looking child, but which was actually a reanimated chimpanzee. "Karlov sent you?" the smuggler asked in seeming disbelief.

"It takes all sorts," Richard said diplomatically. "Karlov wants you to know that he never intended to rip you off . . . and he hasn't ripped you off. I've got your delivery right here. Hopefully we can get back to business as usual and put this mess behind us."

"Clyde, gimme a scalpel," said the smuggler. His zombie ape obediently retrieved a blade from a tray and handed it over. "I spent hours carving up a body with nothing inside it but innards," said Pike, gesturing with the scalpel. "And then I had to settle up with your man Bob. Is Karlov going to pay me back for that time?"

"This isn't how I wanted to spend my day, either," Richard said, entirely truthfully. "Are we going to resolve this thing or do you want to dick around even more?"

Pike sneered and waved towards towards the empty table. Richard unbuttoned the z-mule's jumpsuit and stripped it to its waist, exposing its scars and sutures. The killer ghoul lay passively face-down, and Pike flayed the z-mule's back as smooth as opening a zippered bag, his dead ape passing him surgical tools as he worked. Once the flesh was cut and folded away, Richard spotted gaps sawed into the ribcage. Pike stuck a hand into this crevice and worked it elbow-deep inside the z-mule's body. The z-mule, meanwhile, remained stoically indifferent to this ordeal, good trooper that it was. During the surgery, its gun never left its hand.

After some cutting and rummaging, Pike pulled out a lung, depositing it onto a metal pan. When he sliced the organ open, the biggest diamonds Richard had ever seen tumbled out from the incision in great abundance. The jewels in the right lung turned out to be even bigger. Pike inspected the gemstones with a professional eye, even breaking out a jeweler's glass. "These are going to make the grandest fucking chandelier that ever twinkled," he said. "Tell Karlov we're square."

Pike hastily stuffed the z-mule's lungs back inside it and stitched its hide together and got the Frank up on its feet. Business concluded, the goon shuffled Richard and the Frank out of the dissecting box and into the deepening chill and gloom of the early evening desert. Richard floored the accelerator and drove off into the night, leaving the cursed ranch far behind.

"What a crazy day," Richard said evenly.

Yes.

"Are you going to let me go?" Richard asked. He knew that he stood at a moment of great peril now that the mysterious Karlov had everything he needed from him, but by this point it hardly registered. The lawyer felt as if he had poured out his daily capacity for terror, leaving only exhaustion and an odd sensation of bewildered exhilaration. "You can take the car if you want," he said. "Just drop me off at the next town we pass through."

The zombie remained mute and still, a necrotic Sphinx in the passenger seat. Its silence promised nothing good.

One of Richard's own billboards passed by on the side of the road. Richard glanced up at himself larger-than-life, his motto printed in huge, bold letters. A brilliant and terrible idea occurred to him.

"I want to offer you another deal," Richard said. "I don't know much about you, my friend. I think your name is Karlov, but I couldn't recognize your face and I've never heard your voice. I can't say what country you're from. I don't know if you're a man or a woman. But I am certain of one fact about you. In your line of work you need a lawyer. And not just any lawyer, not some border drunk or a soft little Yale boy in white shoes. You need a lawyer who thinks on his feet and holds his shit together in the most stressful fucking circumstances imaginable. You need a lawyer who understands your needs without you saying a word. You need a lawyer who will keep your secrets forever, bound by an unbreakable professional vow of confidentiality and attorney-client privilege. You need Richard Kruger fighting for you."

The z-mule cocked its head, its lower jaw falling slightly askew as if it were noiselessly laughing at the lawyer's audacity. It stiffly thrust one of its mitts outward. Richard, still holding the wheel with one hand, grasped the cold flesh and pumped.

It was his first handshake with a client who would soon make him extravagantly wealthy.

2019 GANYMEDE 700-SERIES USER GUIDE

FREQUENTLY ASKED QUESTIONS

Q. Is it true that Franks hunger for human flesh?

A. Not at all. The only food that your Frank requires is specially-formulated nutrient paste, available for sale through our website. Soy is the main ingredient in this paste, with only trace amounts of human-sourced protein.

However, while your Frank does not want to eat you, exercise caution whenever you are feeding it or otherwise touching its mouth. Improper handling may trigger a bite reflex powerful enough to sever bone.

Q. I feel frightened by the presence of a reanimated corpse in my home. What should I do?

A. Many first-time Frank owners experience unease or even revulsion at first, but these sensations are typically fleeting. If you would prefer a covering for your Frank, Frankenstein Enterprises sells a wide assortment of masks, uniforms, and skin-tight "zentai" bodysuits. We also offer kid-friendly costumes to make your home-service zombie look like a dinosaur, robot, or superhero!

Q. Do Franks experience pain?

A. Of course not. Franks experience nothing. They are machines that simply happen to look like people. Keeping this thought in mind may help you get more out of your purchase.

The Ganymede 700-series does include an alarm system that causes it to utter guttural moans if it is damaged. You can mute the cries at any time through the settings menu.

THE SALESMAN

DeShawn Kimball knew that he would sell a zombie to Calvin Tanzler before Calvin even stepped into the Frankenstein store.

DeShawn's foresight was partly due to his considerable skills as a salesman, and partly due to a cunning bit of tradecraft on the part of his employer. The moment that Calvin Tanzler requested a Styx to the showroom, DeShawn received a text message with the man's name, birthdate, address, and credit score. Calvin was 28 years old, adored by lenders, and a resident of a ritzy ZIP code. The fact that he was traveling alone indicated that he lived alone, since a household Frank was a major purchase, not to be done without consulting one's significant other if such a person existed. In the specialized cant of zombie salesmen, prosperous, single young males were referred to as "Pavlovs," since persuading them to buy high-end models was like persuading dogs to eat steak. DeShawn chuckled knowingly. Barely a week into the new month, and he already had his rent taken care of.

Rick, the store manager, appeared at DeShawn's side without warning. When you had your eyes on Rick he seemed a lumbering, half-bright oaf, but he could sneak up on you like a ninja and possessed uncanny awareness of everything happening within his bright little fiefdom. "You've got a Pavlov coming in," Rick said.

"I know," said DeShawn, muffling his annoyance at Rick's constant restatement of the obvious. "I'm looking through his social media right now." DeShawn came across a photo of Calvin at a smoothie shop, and mentally filed it away for reference.

"All right, give me the signal if you need any help."

DeShawn took up his position and waited as if in ambush. The Frankenstein showroom was arranged to resemble the interior of an open floor-plan house. It had areas furnished like a living room, office, kitchen, dining room, bathroom, and bedroom, each of them staged in sleek, modern Swedish design. Zombies in crisp white jumpsuits perpetually cleaned and tidied each station of this gleaming ersatz home, watched over by an iconic portrait of Dr. Frankenstein pensively stroking his chin and a light display of the ubiquitous skull-and-brains logo. The salesmen's desks were set against the far wall, opposite the entrance. A massive screen mounted behind them played an endless loop of Franks driving race cars and sprinting through obstacle courses and performing other such wonderful feats, while Vivaldi's Concerto Number 10 in B Minor, the immediately recognizable soundtrack to every Frankenstein commercial since 1997, played from hidden speakers all around. A troop of reanimated rhesus macaques stood on display like little Beefeaters in a glass case at a remote corner of the room. The showroom was designed to both bludgeon customers with a larger-than-life display of the Franks' abilities, and seduce them with a vision of the quiet, harmonious lifestyle that one could only achieve via necrotech. It succeeded at both of these purposes; Calvin was visibly gobsmacked the moment he walked in the door. DeShawn donned a broad smile and a Caucasian accent and approached him.

"Welcome to Frankenstein, my name's DeShawn," the salesman said, offering a practiced, firm-but-not-overbearing handshake. "What can I help you with today?"

"Hi, I'm Calvin. I'd like to look at your domestic models."

"Just something to help out around the house, eh? We've got plenty of options for you to choose from. Have you ever controlled a Frank before, Calvin?"

Calvin shook his head. "I've called Styxes, but other than that, no."

"All right, wonderful! There's a first time for everything. Here, I'll let you handle our floor model, Sheila. She's a Ganymede 700-series." When Sheila had died, she'd been an attractive yet matronly blonde woman in her mid-40s. The company had strict guidelines for floor models. At the moment, Sheila was dusting a bookcase that she dusted a hundred times a day. "Just call her over," said DeShawn. "The Ganymede 700-series has full voice control, so she'll recognize her name."

"Sheila, come here!" said Calvin. At the sound of its wake word the zombie immediately stopped what she was doing and complied. Making a zombie come when called was such a simple thing, but such a powerful thing, as well. Giving the customer control – or at least an illusion of control – was the key to making a sale.

"What would you like me to do?" Sheila asked. Her voice was friendly and surprisingly lifelike, although she did sound like a heavy smoker.

"Do a jumping jack," Calvin ordered, and the zombie complied. He made her touch her toes, stand on one foot, walk back and forth across the showroom, pick up a sales brochure that he dropped on the floor.

"Check this out," DeShawn said, unloosing his necktie. "Sheila, come tie my tie."

"What type of knot would you like?" she asked. He told her. The corpse reached for his neck and knotted an elegant Windsor.

"Pretty nice, right?" DeShawn said. "And you don't even need to control her yourself all the time. You can set her on an automatic schedule so that every day she knows just what to do for you. Imagine having Sheila waiting for you every day when you got home from work, with a beer and your slippers and a fresh-cooked meal. All you have to do is set a workflow queue in iGor."

"You called her a Ganymede 700-series earlier," said Calvin. "What's that mean?"

"We have four basic classes of Frank that we sell in the civilian market," DeShawn explained. "Ganymedes are designed for domestic and service industry work. We use fresher bodies for those, and we calibrate their artificial nervous systems for human interaction. Hercules Franks are more for industrial work – they might not look quite as nice, but they're strong and durable. Styxes are our driver model, they're optimized for use behind the wheel, with superior reflexes and vision, and Dragonsteeth are for security. The series number refers to the sophistication of the neural programming. You want a high series number, the more advanced Franks are generally more capable and coordinated and are compatible with the latest apps in the iGor store. We're always improving our product lines."

Having put the dead woman through her paces, Calvin gave Sheila's corpse a close inspection, even tugging at her lower lip to see the zombie's teeth. "She's very well-preserved," Calvin commented. "Do you have to do anything to keep them fresh?"

"Maintenance is easy. All that Franks need for day-to-day operations is a little protein paste and water, plus an electrical charge every twenty hours or so and the occasional cleaning." DeShawn partly unzipped Sheila's jumpsuit to show Calvin the electrical plug installed in her breastbone. "If anything goes wrong with their internal organs, you'll get a notification on your command tablet, and you can call one of our mobile repair vans to come to your place for a transplant. The Frankenstein Process arrests tissue decay, so Franks are guaranteed never to rot. Most of her cells are actually alive, it's only the brain that's dead."

"She's alive?" Calvin said, a look of mild concern passing over his face.

"No more than a vegetable's alive, they don't actually think or feel anything," DeShawn laughed, gently rapping the zombie's forehead with his knuckles. But nobody ever sold a zombie by dwelling on existential concerns, so DeShawn changed the subject quickly. "Hey Calvin, do you like smoothies? Sheila, make us two mango smoothies."

Sheila walked briskly to the showroom kitchen, prepared two milkshakes, and brought the frosty-cold beverages to Calvin and DeShawn. Calvin made a yummy noise as he sipped his drink, always a good sign. Sheila stood by patiently until they'd finished, and then dutifully took their empty glasses back to the kitchen and cleaned up.

"If you liked that, you should try her cooking," DeShawn suggested. "You can get all sorts of different cuisine skill modules – teach your Frank to cook Italian food, Greek, Indian, Szechuan, whatever you want." He smacked his fingertips to convey all the delicious flavors that an undead chef could bring to the table. "She can even do the shopping for you! If you get the Frankenstein Marketplace skill module, she can connect to the iGor network and place delivery orders. And we've got a catalog full of household devices optimized for use by Franks, so your household zombie can do the best possible job taking care of you. Is that cool, or what?"

"I'm not sure I understand the skill modules," said Calvin. "How do those work?"

"Your Frank will come with some basic skill modules installed – navigation, fetching, cleaning, hygiene, that sort of thing. Right out of the box, she'll be able to perform basic tasks around the house and handle most of her own maintenance. If you want your Frank to have additional skills – the ability to drive a car, fix a toilet, play the guitar, type, dance, you name it – well, you can just go to our online store to buy the appropriate module, and it'll download into her brain over iGor. We offer more than a thousand skill modules, with more in the store every day. You can even buy a weapon module so that your Frank knows how to fight, and use her as a home security system."

"A friend of mine told me you can download skill modules from the Internet. Is that right?"

"Yes and no. Yes, there are some folks out there who mod their Franks on a DIY basis. And yes, there are some sketchy sites on the web where you can download bootleg modules. But no, I don't recommend skill modules from any place other than the official iGor network. If you install any unauthorized software, it'll void your warranty and it might mess your Frank up. These are complex machines, you don't want to go messing around under the hood."

"Can I see the Franks you've got available?" Calvin asked.

DeShawn smiled brightly. Even for a Pavlov, this guy was an easy sell. "It'd be my pleasure," he said. Rick winked at DeShawn from across the showroom.

Two dozen Franks stood on raised platforms against the walls of the inventory room, stiff and impassive, their prices and specifications displayed on nearby screens. Most were black or brown, since despite the success of the donor program, the company still sourced most of its raw materials from abroad. They also tended towards old age. Calvin, however, shot straight towards the rigid corpse of a good-looking young white girl with a butterfly tattooed on her throat and stars all over her temples. The knobs and plugs in her skull were barely visible beneath her wavy black hair. The company used a mysterious algorithm to price its Franks, and DeShawn didn't even have to look at the screen to know that the algorithm would prize this one highly.

DeShawn congratulated Calvin on a wise choice and activated the zombie. Her eyelids fluttered open revealing two soulless orbs, ice-blue irises floating in twin pools of blood. At DeShawn's command, the cadaver stepped down from her platform.

The great moment of danger in the sales process approached, the moment at which the customer was confronted with the price of the boundless convenience and comfort on offer. This was where DeShawn earned his money. Any fool could make household zombies seem appealing, but it took a salesman to get people to pay for them. Sure enough, Calvin balked when he saw the final price.

"You've got to remember that you're paying for the perfect servant," DeShawn boasted. He stroked the arm of the she-zombie who stood at his deskside, watching patiently and impassively as DeShawn and Calvin haggled over the terms of her sale. "This lovely lady's never going to ask you for a raise, or want Christmas off, or complain that you're working her too much. She won't even take smoke breaks. You can't ask for more than that, am I right?"

"They're impressive, certainly," Calvin admitted, gazing longingly at the zombie. The Pavlov was almost drooling for her.

"Remember that a Frank is a long-term investment," DeShawn continued. "With proper upkeep and maintenance she'll last you twenty years or longer. Compare that to having to pay salary every year. Not only are Franks better than living workers, in the long run, they're cheaper. And of course, we offer an array of financing options."

The last of the Pavlov's resistance crumbled in the face of this argument. DeShawn walked him through the sale papers, talking him into the optional anti-bruising treatment and extended warranty. He also got him to sign up for an iGor roaming data plan, even though you didn't really need one if you kept your zombie at home hooked up to the Wi-Fi network. The salesman maintained a poker face while mentally calculating his commission.

"Hey, do you guys sell reanimated dogs?" Calvin asked. "I always wanted a dog but I don't want to deal with the walks or the poop."

"No dice," DeShawn replied. "The Frankenstein Process doesn't work on dogs or cats. We've got monkeys, but they're designed for household service. There's really no need for one if you've got a Ganymede." Besides, the commissions on z-monkeys were garbage. He directed the Pavlov's attention back to the extended warranty paperwork.

Soon DeShawn stood at the curbside, watching Calvin and his new Frank depart in the back of a Styx. Calvin said something to the zombie. She turned towards the man who had sold her and waved goodbye as the car drove away.

"Nice sale," Rick said, appearing out of nowhere again to slap his salesman on the shoulder.

"Thanks. You know how Pavlovs are."

"It's all about making them think they're in control," Rick mused. "Works with customers, works with women. Works with anyone. Make a person think they're in the driver's seat and they'll do anything at all. But that's why Franks are so great. They don't even need the illusion. They just do what they're told."

Outside the auto dealership across the street, a zombie twirled a promotional sign. Its solitary dance was expert, dexterous, joyless. The advertisement moved too quickly for passerby to even read its words, a Styrofoam wheel of color and commerce, spun ceaselessly by cold, dead hands.

DISCUSSION THREAD FROM THE FRANKENDIY ONLINE FORUM

Help! I promised my kids that I'd deep-fry a turkey for Thanksgiving. I bought the fry cook app through the iGor store, but even after I installed it, I still can't get my z-maid to use the turkey fryer. She keeps giving me that awful hooting noise she makes when a command's blocked by her safety settings. Does anyone know how to override this? She's a 2012 Ganymede 500-series if that makes a difference.

TacomaDad72 – 11:12 AM; 11/28/2013

Let me guess, you don't have a Frankenstein Enterprises turkey fryer? That's how they get you – even after you pay for the app the greedy bastards want you to buy their hardware as well. The good news is that there's an easy workaround with the Ganymede 500. First, go into her system folder and revert her to the 3.1.20 operating system (if you don't know how to do that you shouldn't be on this board to begin with). Open her Cognition menu and turn her Pattern Recognition up as high as it'll go, and then go to the Environmental Interactions tab and toggle

'Preferred Devices Only' to OFF. The 500s are smart machines, she'll figure out what buttons to press. Happy Thanksgiving!

ZombieKingKarl – 11:27 AM; 11/28/2013

Thanks! I'll let you know how it goes!

TacomaDad72 – 11:48 AM; 11/28/2013

Well, the good news is that my z-maid figured out how to use the deep fryer. The bad news is that right now I'm sitting on my neighbor's lawn across the street watching my house burn down. The z-maid's still roasting inside, hooting like a fricasseed owl. I never should have used her for this.

TacomaDad72 – 2:13 PM; 11/28/2013

Don't blame the zombie for your own bad decisions. Frying whole turkeys is dangerous!

ZombieKingKarl – 2:15 PM; 11/28/2013

THE NECROPHILE

Calvin Tanzler was not a lonely man. On the contrary, he was young, handsome, and well-liked, with a successful career in finance. He was, however, an extremely busy man, possessed of too much money and too little time. Eventually the Internet caught wind of this and began bombarding him with advertisements for zombie slaves. Calvin immediately saw the appeal. Zombies already drove him around, cleaned his condominium, delivered his food and packages, and did his dry cleaning. Having one available to serve him full-time seemed to be the next logical step.

    Calvin came home from the showroom with his new Frank as giddy as a boy returning from the toy shop. Hooking her up to his wireless router so that she could access the iGor network was a bit of a chore, but apart from that the initial setup was a breeze. He walked the zombie all around his condo, exulting in her immediate responsiveness to every command. Calvin made her clean his bathroom, vacuum his bedroom, and wash his clothes, watching all the while in amazement at the animated corpse's fastidiousness and attention to detail. When his stomach began to rumble he downloaded the Italian cooking skill module from Frankenstein's online store and had her prepare a superb meal of shrimp scampi and salad. Afterwards, sitting on the couch with his belt loosened, he bought a bartending module and made her whip him up an Old Fashioned. No living mixologist could have done better. Calvin leaned back, sipped his beverage, and congratulated himself on a wise purchase.

In the beginning, the Frank delivered everything that her salesman promised and more. Due to her quiet, ceaseless labor, Calvin's home was always a place of perfect order, sparkling cleanliness, and delicious smells, where food appeared as if by magic without even having to think about it, and all his needs were attended to with a crisp command. Although she came with speech capacity, Calvin didn't like the sound of her voice and turned it off. When her battery was low she clicked her tongue and when she connected to Bluetooth she squeaked and when she accepted an order she made a little hooting noise and otherwise she was silent. Half domestic goddess and half creature of the underworld, Calvin took to calling her Persephone. He never once wondered about the life of the girl with the butterfly tattoo who had died to create his possession, even though she served him so attentively, and even though his home was her unquiet grave.

Calvin had not purchased Persephone with the intent of sharing a bed with her. At night she sat in a closet recharging, a tool put away for the evening. However, as Calvin became accustomed to her presence and her services, the idea of using her for sex came to seem like a further logical step. His work tied up so much time that he didn't have many opportunities to socialize, and necrophilia seemed a less depressing option than dating apps. Sometimes he'd fondle her curves, or make her do the housework nude. One night Calvin went out riding the whiskey train with his buddies to celebrate the closing of a deal. Stumbling home tipsy and horny, he cheerfully decided to take Persephone's cadaverous virginity.

The experience was equal parts appalling and delightful. She was cold, dry as parchment, and absolutely motionless, not even breathing beneath him. Yet she was also supremely limp and submissive, a beautiful plaything. Calvin never realized how much he disliked free will in his sexual partners before he had Persephone.

Afterwards, he sat shuddering on the edge of his bed and swore to himself that he'd never do it again.

He did it twice more before getting bored with the Sleeping Beauty routine and deciding he needed something a bit livelier. Calvin browsed the skill module store, to no avail. Frankenstein traded in bodies, but not the skin trade.

Adtech algorithms, fed by the dark confidences that Calvin shared only with his search engine, caught wind of his unwholesome thoughts and offered him up an embarrassment of options for transforming zombies into sex zombies. It was just a matter of buying a program from www.draugrhaxx.com and uploading it into Persephone. At the last moment, Calvin remembered the salesman's warning that installing any unofficial skill modules would void Persephone's warranty and might turn her twitchy. He shrugged. The worst-case scenario was that he'd be stuck with a repair bill, and the best-case scenario was that he'd have an ageless and obedient catamite.

Calvin followed the not-quite English instructions on the website to the letter, or at least as close as he could reckon. When the file transfer completed, he gazed into Persephone's lovely, vacant face. Nothing seemed to have changed. He snapped his fingers and ordered her to give him a hand job – a simple task to run the software through its paces. Responding with her customary swift obedience, Persephone unbelted, unbuttoned, and unzipped Calvin in the time it had taken him to snap his fingers. Her hands were nimble and delicate, teasing and working his manhood like a seasoned professional. Persephone's expression and manner remained as empty as ever, which Calvin found distracting at first. Soon, however, he was so caught up in his zombie's rhythmic erotic massage that everything beyond his own throbbing pleasure seemed to vanish. After he finished he almost instantly passed into a deep, dreamless sleep.

When Calvin awoke, Persephone sat stiffly in her closet, patiently awaiting more instructions. He browsed through the app to see what exciting new commands were available to him now, and smiled when he saw the variety.

From then on Calvin had Persephone nearly every night. She was better than any girlfriend he'd had before – randy as a porn star, loyal as a dog, and silent as a mime. The only apparent downside to the affair was the cool clamminess of Persephone's flesh. Calvin began making her take piping-hot showers beforehand, but that only warmed her skin, not the inside of her. Nonetheless, the chill was a minor price to pay, and even rather bracing once one got used to it.

However, even though Persephone made no demands upon Calvin, coupling with a dead woman seemed to drain his vitality. Whereas once he'd been a night owl and compulsively early riser, now he passed out early, slept late, and still never felt rested. Persephone's rich cooking fattened him up alarmingly, the extra pounds pressing down on his lethargy. His work became increasingly stressful, as well. Some keyboard criminal had hit the bank with a nasty cyber-attack, and the nerds in IT and compliance made everyone miserable trying to figure out how the hacker had gotten past their very expensive firewalls. Dark resentments bubbled up inside of Calvin, the resentments of a man whose every whim is catered to and yet still finds himself unhappy.

Calvin, who had never trusted therapists and only rarely spoke of his inner life with his friends, vented all of his passions and frustrations into Persephone's petite and ghostly form. Sometimes his anger manifested as lust, and he pounded the zombie with everything he had until he spent himself and collapsed into his silk sheets like a dying king. Sometimes he came home from work in a fury and beat her without mercy – a punching bag in the exact size and shape of a ninety-pound woman. He'd paid extra for anti-bruising treatment, and he put it to the test.

One night Calvin awoke in fright, to a clattering sound coming from his office. For a terrifying moment he thought that an invader was inside his home. Then he realized that Persephone's closet yawned open and empty.

Calvin groggily pulled himself out of bed and stumbled towards his home office, the source of the clattering. His meticulously-kept condominium swayed drunkenly, even though he'd only had a single martini before bedtime. No matter – the horror that he witnessed sobered him right up.

Persephone sat in front of Calvin's computer, her face bathed in its glow, typing at such incredible speed that it seemed the keyboard might fall to pieces beneath her fingertips. She was logged in to the trading platform that Calvin used for work, methodically transferring funds out of his clients' accounts and into an Eastern European bank. Calvin realized that he'd saved all his passwords on the computer, such that anyone who had access to this workstation had access to the whole of his life. He screeched orders for her to halt, but she pointedly ignored him, and her defiance was so unexpected that the surprise chilled him to the depths of his soul.

Howling in terror, rage, and shock, Calvin physically dragged Persephone away from his desk and hurled her against the nearest wall hard enough to shatter the plaster, leaving a splotch of blood and hair at the center of a fragmented spiderweb. He searched through the browser history aghast. Millions of dollars were gone, and his career was sure to follow them into oblivion.

The zombie rose up from her place on the floor, jaggedly righting herself like a fallen spider getting back onto its feet. Calvin backed away from her, staring into her bloodshot, blackened eyes. Once they had seemed so safely, invitingly empty. Now he saw that he had not understood what lurked in their depths, and that she was no more loyal to him than he was to her. He wondered if he could get to his phone in time to call 911, and if 911 could arrive in time for him. The zombie was small, true, yet she was also impervious to pain, surprisingly strong, and expert in the use of knives.

"You piece of shit, you'll never touch me again," she said. She spoke with the same bright, blandly cheerful affect as the voice assistant in Calvin's smartphone, and the almost-forgotten sound of her voice scared him as badly as anything else that had happened tonight.

Persephone turned to the wall and bashed her head against it with such force that her skull split open and her brains bulged out the top of her head in a spray of black blood. She knocked herself against the wall four more times, as if her brain was a nut she was trying to free from the shell of her skull, until at last she'd reduced her head to a dark liquid ruin and collapsed in a twitching heap.

Calvin sank to his knees, sobbing from the bottom of his lungs. He'd never understood how much he loved her until she was gone.

NEW SHOWS OF NOTE

BY MARGARET SEVILLE, BEHOLD MAGAZINE
(MARCH 31, 2018)

Since Victor Frankenstein unveiled his masterpiece on the capitalist exploitation of the body in 1994, the use of human remains in artwork has traveled a journey from shocking avant garde provocation to mass-produced banality. While reanimated corpses initially reinvigorated the art world as a genuinely new medium of creative expression, giving rise to the so-called Autopsy School, they also attracted a horde of lesser talents dependent on shock value alone, destroying the sense of novelty that many of the early Franken-artists relied upon. So too, as zombies become more ubiquitous, the visceral reactions they once provoked have numbed. The ghoul serving you coffee isn't a horror anymore. It doesn't prompt reflections about mortality like it once did. Nowadays, you barely think about it at all.

Yet just as zombie art seemed to be losing its bite, *Fantasies of Flesh*, Baz Udo's latest exhibition at the prestigious Zuckerman Gallery, breathes transgressive new life back into a tired medium. *Frankenstein/Madonna/Lazarus* stands out as the highlight of the show, an immersive installation blending elements of Catholic reliquary traditions, 21st-century influencer culture, and animatronic human taxidermy into an interactive experience that stays with the viewer long after they have exited into the

New York City night. At times *Fantasies* feels like a haunted house designed by Andy Warhol, a fitting achievement for an exhibit that seeks to raise the departed in astonishing new forms.

THE POP STAR

Darkness and silence fall swiftly over the sold-out theater where Diana French is playing tonight. The opening act has come and gone – a pleasant enough diversion, but only an appetizer for the gothic feast that awaits. The audience holds its breath collectively, anticipation tinged with a delicious note of fear. The great artist herself lurks somewhere in the shadows. Her presence is felt long before she is seen. Just as the suspense is becoming unbearable, a spotlight illuminates a hooded figure cloaked in brilliantly-colored silks. The audience roars in delight. Diana French has taken the stage.

Witch-music rises - ominous, dissonant strings and insistent drums. Disembodied hands reach from the inky blackness, grasping the rainbow hem of Diana's hood and pulling it back. Her large, luminous eyes peer into the crowd, and every man and woman sitting in the theater's cavernous dark experiences the unsettling sensation that she is looking directly into them, an intimacy to be feared and desired.

Then Diana French opens her mouth and begins to sing, unleashing a ferocious new intimacy with her listeners, close as the bond between the tiger and the prey in its jaws. Her voice is a thing of paradoxes – muscular and delicate, pure and earthy, diamond-hard and trembling with vulnerability. An invisible choir accompanies her with rapturous hosannas. It is a moment of musical transcendence, transporting even the atheists to a heavenly kingdom ruled wisely by its queen.

The upstage lights suddenly rise like an ambush, and the audience gasps as they lay eyes upon the angelic choir for the first time. Diana French's backup singers are desiccated mummies in loincloths, a choir of leathery skeletons. The contrast between the horror of their appearance and the beauty of their singing is so stark that it dizzies the mind. They perform in perfect harmony, not a note amiss, their claw-like hands clapping to keep the beat.

The rest of the band slowly rises up from hidden platforms beneath the stage, and waves of joyful revulsion sweep through the audience at the sights and sounds of these necromantic prodigies. A male and female zombie stitched together into a four-armed, bicephalous chimera play tenor saxophone with the left side of their conjoined body, and alto with the right. Violinists stitched together from the limbs of basketball players affixed upon the bodies of dwarfs strut about, sawing haunting strains on catgut. The flutists have been butterflied, exposing the vibrations of their glistening lungs as they blow into their instruments. Sparkling flares burn inside the drummer's mouth and eye sockets, his head leaving trails of light and smoke as he thrashes it back and forth, a jack o'lantern metronome. Playing the guitar is a creature mutilated so delicately and artistically that one could barely imagine such an exquisite thing had ever been human. Then comes the macabre harlequinade of the dancers, an impossible ballet of the grotesque. Above the stage, acrobats as slender and hideous as eels perform feats of alarming contortionism upon the trapeze, twisting themselves into positions that no person with all of their organs and bones could manage.

And Diana French dances at the center of it all, the power of her voice such that she seems to sing this decadent phantasmagoria into being. The artist brings her audience through a set list of greatest hits and bold experiments, commanding the stage even as unspeakable sights unfold all around her. She does the radio standard *Alchemical Wedding*, the metal-influenced *Pigman*, the peppy crowd-pleaser *Artificial Uterus*, the bluesy *Jericho*, the operatic *Season of Loathsome Miracles*. As she lashes the house into a frenzy with her raucous anthem *Flying Machine*, charges planted inside the drummer's skull explode, and his head erupts into a volcanic pillar of multi-colored flame.

When *Flying Machine* ends the upstage abruptly falls dark and Diana's monstrous entourage vanishes into the gloom, leaving her alone. Violin strings swell with a flourish. A worshipful hush falls over the necrobacchanal. Diane French saved the very best for last. She is closing with *Stag*, the waking nightmare of a love song that made her famous.

A terrible and beautiful ivory-white creature rises up from a hidden place beneath the stage, its arms outstretched to the lights. The animatronic taxidermists in Diana French's entourage have surgically transformed the corpse of an astonishingly beautiful, powerfully-muscled man into an undead satyr. They reconfigured his legs so that he might bound like a deer, and reshaped his features to those of a faun, and crowned his noble head with kingly gilded antlers. He is a sculpture of masculine perfection, carved in the medium of flesh, and reanimated so skillfully that he seems a living being but for his snowy pallor. He is a haunter of dreams.

Diana French sings of primal love and the Stag translates her passionate music into motion, executing pirouettes and grand jetés with precise, forceful grace. He catches Diana in his mighty arms, sweeping her off her feet and twirling her through fog and shadow. It seems impossible that this lithe spirit is a cadaver; he is more vital than anyone in the theater save Diana. A magnificent puppet, he dances to the call of invisible strings, creating an uncanny illusion of life and joy with each carefully programmed motion. The Stag holds up Diana as if she were his idol, a perfect object of adoration.

And as the song reaches its bridge, she produces a knife from up her sleeve and cuts his throat with it.

The lights abruptly come up stark white, the better to show off the blood. The Stag falls to his knees with a theatrical flourish, his handsome, alien face grimacing, his muzzle dripping gore. His eyes roll back in a painterly approximation of martyr's passion, crimson pouring down his finely-muscled chest.

The deathly choir returns, wailing. The revenants intertwine their bony fingers and circle round the dying Stag, chanting an elegy for another beautiful beast laid low by love's trap. The climax of the song is approaching.

Diana dances towards the wounded beast, her steps as light as a matador, her gleaming dagger swaying hypnotically to the music, until at last she thrusts the blade into the Stag's breast with a steady, practiced hand. At the moment her voice crests the ecstatic peak, Diana reaches into the wound and pulls out her creature's still-beating heart.

The Stag throws backs his antlered head and bellows in deep bass agony, a musical death cry that its listeners feel vibrating in their bones. His voice mingles with Diana's in uncanny harmony, each of them wailing in desperate, dying passion as shadows swallow up the choir.

The Stag collapses onto his face. Only Diana is left. She rests her bare foot upon his limp form for a moment, then turns and follows the choir into the dark. The love song is over.

Contemplative silence briefly reigns over the theater, before the audience bursts into rapturous applause.

Two weeks later Diana French dies in a Miami hotel penthouse after drinking enough vodka to drown in. She is 27. She will be 27 forever.

Her death is a great shock to her fans, and no surprise at all to those few who knew her well. Her management company prepared extensively and meticulously for this moment. They own the rights to an entire vault full of Diane French's unreleased songs in various stages of polish. More importantly, they own the rights to the singer's mortal remains. Within hours of her death she undergoes the Frankenstein Process that she used to such devastating effect in her art. Her voice and talents gave her one form of immortality. Her estate gives her another.

Diana French's posthumous comeback tour is a fan sensation. The public packs concert halls and stadiums to see the singer's reanimated corpse perform. They cheer wildly when their invincible icon takes the stage, and going home they remark to each other that they could barely tell the difference. The only change they notice is in her voice, now slightly huskier and smokier than it had been during her life. Many listeners prefer the new vocals. She gets the best reviews of her career.

After two phenomenally successful tours, the executor of Diana's estate strikes a deal with a casino to have the dead star perform a stage show at a purpose-built theater, a sort of Las Vegas Grand Guignol, which is perhaps a redundancy. She quickly becomes a figure of great fascination, one of the leading spectacles in a city that is nothing but spectacles. The tourists flock to her. She is the anti-Orpheus, a great musician come from the land of the dead to the Hell of the living, fascinating the damned of Sin City with her songs and distracting them, if only briefly, from their endlessly repeated torments.

Diana French is on stage now, dancing in a circle. Her white limbs fly amidst dry ice and colored light, in a place where everything is permitted but flash photography. Her voice carries to every corner of the world. She will dance with the Stag forever, or until they are forgotten, and she cuts out his beating heart three shows a day.

HOW TO WIN PROSPERITY IN THIS LIFE AND ETERNITY IN THE NEXT

BY SCOTT ALAMO, ALIVE! MAGAZINE (DECEMBER 4, 2018)

God loves you so much that He doesn't just offer you eternal life, He'll pay you good money to take Him up on it. More and more Americans are discovering that accepting a Frankenstein pension can help you obtain both financial security and spiritual fulfillment. Not only will you receive a guaranteed income for the rest of your life, you'll guarantee that in the afterlife you'll be part of something greater than yourself, working for the highest power there is.

At the New Resurrection Church we believe that Dr. Victor Frankenstein is the second coming of Jesus Christ, fulfilling his 2,000-year promise to raise the dead, defeat the Islamic Antichrist, and bring about paradise on Earth. Like any parent, Frankenstein wants His children to thrive and prosper, and every day His wonderful power is building a better world for Christians. He sends His angels to feed us and serve us and protect us from harm, and all He asks in return is that we pledge ourselves to Him so that we may one day be angels ourselves.

As you may know, Frankenstein Enterprises offers generous referral bonuses for signing up others as angels-in-waiting. At New Resurrection we've created an exciting Multi-Level Ministry program that enables you to earn even more by building your network and bringing souls to

Frankenstein. Many of our members have used this program to gain financial independence while doing the Lord's work.

Come join us in praise at our beautiful new temple in Radnor to learn more about what New Resurrection can do for you and your family!

THE BELIEVER

Billy Gultch found the Lord in SCI Rockview while doing a stint for identity theft and kiting checks. The Holy Spirit fell upon him as he stood naked in a cold concrete pen in line with ten other men, undergoing a contraband search at the clammy hands of a corpse. The ghoul-guard was bulky as an ape in its armor, and moved like it was stop-motion animated. Its bloodstained eyes stared through him from behind smudged goggles, at once piercingly perceptive and supremely indifferent, and Billy suddenly felt himself in the presence of infinite power, power so vast that one had no choice but to obey it. He decided that the creature probing inside his mouth could only be an angel of God.

Now Billy Gultch was a free man, or at least on probation, and every Sunday morning he attended the New Resurrection Church in Radnor. Outsiders called it a death cult, but attending its services made Billy feel vibrantly alive like nothing else. The church building itself was a gleaming, ultra-modern prayer center, all shining glass and chrome and brass. A twelve-foot-tall rose-gold crucifix hung over the open doors, the skinless figure affixed to it rendered in exacting anatomical detail. A Dragonstooth angel in full military attire stood vigil near the entrance, protecting the faithful in case some maniac tried to shoot the place up. Billy dropped off his car at the Styx valet station, feeling sheepish about driving his beat-up Civic when so many of his fellow churchgoers had BMWs and Lexuses.

The church's interior was every bit as magnificently appointed as the outside, splendid in crimson and gold. Well-dressed and clean-scrubbed families milled about socializing under the watchful eye of Dr. Frankenstein, whose photograph was projected on the huge screen behind the pulpit. Ever-smiling angels in button-down shirts and red vests recognized the churchgoers by sight and welcomed them to the sanctuary. "Hi Billy, I'm so glad to see you again," said a beaming emissary of the Lord in a voice like a robocall. "Let me show you to your seat." When Billy had first come to New Resurrection he'd been assigned a place in the very front row, but now that he was a regular they put him in a less desirable section towards the rear. He hoped that someday, as his own ministry took off and his contributions increased, he'd work his way back up.

As always, the service opened with a hymn from the Angel of Song, a Ganymede 700-series programmed to sing gospel music. She'd been a stunningly beautiful woman when she died, and in her flowing white gown and bright makeup she looked truly divine.

When she finished, Brother Alamo, the founder and pastor of New Resurrection, bounded up to the pulpit. The preacher was a slim, stylishly-dressed man with teeth so white that God's blessings seemed to glow from between his lips. For today's sermon he spoke on one of his favorite themes, about how Heaven and Hell were not remote destinations above the clouds or deep underground, but rather that both existed here and now, within the promised land of 21st-century America, and that it was within our power to choose Heaven by submitting wholeheartedly to Frankenstein. "Brothers and sisters, Frankenstein has delivered us from the grave!" he proclaimed joyfully. "Death has lost its sting, for every day we see the proof of eternal life and are nurtured by the angels themselves! Hallelujah!" Billy sat rapt in his pew. Life had been so hard in the bad old days when he'd lived for himself. Living for the Lord was much easier. Why try to fight that power when you could team up with it?

After the sermon came the affirmations, Billy's favorite part of the service, wherein church members testified to the blessings they'd received from Frankenstein. First came a crewcutted plumbing contractor who spoke movingly of how he'd been able to expand his business since switching to angel labor. Passionate sincerity radiated from the man as he thanked God for all the beautiful things he'd been given and praised the holy name. Hearing about this man's life made Billy ache with jealousy, but Brother Alamo preached that coveting thy neighbors' goods was no sin so long as it inspired you to work hard and keep up.

Next came Ronni Cocinelli, a bubbly middle-aged blonde in chewing gum pink with impeccably frosted hair and nails, one of the Church's top recruiters and a regular in the affirmations. She'd brought hundreds of souls to Frankenstein and made a fortune in the process. She was actually a part of Billy's own ministry network. Billy tithed 30% of his commissions to Terrence, the guy in the prison ministry who'd brought him into the fold, Terrence paid a 30% cut to Ronni, and Ronni tithed to Brother Alamo directly. It did sound a little like a pyramid scheme, when you laid it out like that, but Brother Alamo had proven that Jesus and his apostles used this identical revenue-sharing setup, right down to the percentages. Billy liked the way that it bound the Church together in shared interest. He felt like they were all getting rich together, even though his own bank account didn't reflect this.

The last speaker of the day was a heavily made-up old woman with frizzy red hair, who spoke tearfully about her husband's recent suicide, and how glad she was that the troubled man was with Frankenstein now. It just went to show that God could make something good out of even the worst situations.

The service closed with group prayers and two more hymns led by the Angel of Song. Billy left the church invigorated and refreshed, excited to spend the rest of his day in missionary work. Although many of the church members teamed up when knocking on doors, he went out solo so that he wouldn't have to split the commissions.

The church had a tithing app that doubled as a contact management system. You could look up the names and addresses of everyone in the ZIP Code who hadn't yet signed a Frankenstein donor contract, color-coded to represent the last time a church member visited them. Bringing new members into the fold was the best-paying type of apostleship, since it grew your downline network and earned you passive income, but convincing people to sign up as angels still made you money even if they didn't adopt the religion. It was all the Lord's work. Billy frowned when he looked at the contact list. There were not many names, and even fewer green or yellow ones. He supposed it was a good thing that so many people in this community had already given themselves over to Frankenstein, but it did make it hard to earn.

Billy spent the rest of the day driving around the suburbs making door-to-door house calls, doing his best to spread the good word and make a buck in his crisp white shirt and tie. For the most part missionary work was a pretty frustrating endeavor, largely spent getting doors shut in his face or cursed at. Old-style Christians were the most likely to lose their tempers. Billy took smug satisfaction in his faith that they were the new Jews, a people who'd had God's blessing once and lost it along the way. That belief did not help his recruitment numbers, however.

He was close to quitting when he recognized a name in the app from his past life. Mitchell Purling, or Rollo, as he'd been known as SCI Rockview, had been one of Billy's more agreeable cellmates, doing a five-year stint for Narcan possession. He'd been released before Billy's spiritual awakening, and Billy was glad to see that he was still out. He lived in a duplex that had been small even before the landlord divided it up. A sticker said, "No solicitors," but Billy straightened his tie and rapped on the door anyway. Pungent weed smoke drifted out as Rollo opened it. He'd put on even more weight since prison, where he'd been fat to begin with, and his wispy beard had thickened up somewhat, but otherwise he looked pretty much the same. His eyes narrowed for a second, and then he recognized his old lockup buddy and embraced Billy in a hug.

"Billy Gultch! Holy shit, it's good to see you again, man!" he said. "What are you doing here?" He looked Billy up and down, seemingly confused by his outfit. "Don't tell me you've become a Mormon."

"Even better," said Billy. "Rollo, I'm here today on behalf of the Lord up high, Dr. Victor Frankenstein. Frankenstein can enrich you financially and spiritually if you'll just let Him into your heart."

"Aw no, Billy," sighed Rollo. "Really? You think Frankenstein is God?"

"Just look at all He's done," said Billy. "Look at how much power He has. Of course He's God. And God wants to help you."

"Why would God need all that money? If he wants to help people, wouldn't he give it away?"

"No. Why should God give His money away? He's earned it, it's His money. God helps people by giving them the tools they need to be successful, not by giving them handouts."

Rollo shook his head sadly. "Dude, I still have nightmares about those fucking deadhead prison guards. Sometimes I wake up and I think I'm back in Rockview and they're all around me. The thought of *becoming* one of those things . . . *yucch*." He shuddered in repugnance. "No, I'm not signing up for Frankenstein. Besides, I want to donate my organs for transplant, not to work in a shitty fast-food joint or something. But hey, if you want to come inside, I've got video games and I just packed a fresh bowl. Want to catch up?"

They spent the rest of the day playing Xbox and talking in a haze of marijuana smoke, although Billy did not partake. Occasionally he tried to steer the conversation towards the Lord, and every time Rollo turned it back away.

Billy left Rollo's house rather late in the evening, experiencing powerfully mixed emotions. He was happy to have seen a friend again, but he hated the idea that a person as decent and good-hearted as Rollo might never come to Frankenstein. Why would anyone want to be carved up and distributed to a bunch of strangers when you could live forever as a helpful angel? Rollo might have made the right choice if only he'd explained it better, and now Billy felt guilty that a soul might have been lost through his own failings. Ronni Cocinelli would have closed the deal, he had no doubt of that.

Suddenly, Billy noticed an electric bill in Rollo's recycling bin, and another moment of holy inspiration hit. Now he saw how his particular skill set could serve the Lord. Billy took the electric bill, rummaged around for any other noteworthy papers he could find, and drove straight home.

Frankenstein's donor recruitment app didn't ask for much in terms of identifying information. Billy bought Rollo's Social Security Number on a dark web marketplace for a mere $20, and most of the other necessary details were free for the taking online. He wondered why he hadn't thought of this earlier. The pension information page did puzzle Billy momentarily. If Frankenstein Enterprises started making deposits into Rollo's bank account, he'd surely figure out that something was up. Then, however, Billy noticed that you could direct your pension to the charitable organization of your choosing. Billy gave Rollo's pension money right to the New Resurrection Church. It was perfect. The church would enjoy a monthly stipend, Billy and everyone in his ministry network would earn a referral fee, and Rollo would never know about any of this until he died and became an angel, at which point he'd be delighted. Joy and satisfaction flooded through Billy as he signed his friend up for eternal life in the service of the Lord.

That Sunday marked the dawning of a new era in Billy Gultch's ministry, and in his personal relationship with Frankenstein. Soon he had a prime seat in the pews and was speaking at the affirmations. He never brought any new converts on Sunday, but he recruited so many future angels that Ronni Cocinelli got a renovated bathroom out of it. If anyone found it suspicious that all of his recruits donated their pensions to the New Resurrection Church without once stepping through its doors, nobody brought it up. In time he found a good wife and became a deacon. When Billy Gultch went up to the pulpit he freely wept with joy before the whole congregation, overwhelmed by the mercy and abundance of his Lord.

HOW TO DIE IN THE AGE OF FRANKENSTEIN: PASTORAL IDEAS FOR MODERN FUNERALS

BY REV. LORETTA WINSTEAD (MANNA BOOKS, 2016)

A PRAYER FOR THE EARTHLY REMAINS

> Lord, even as you accept our beloved's spirit into your arms, please watch over [his/her] body during its final service on Earth.
> If [his/her] flesh is called to labor, may it work with grace and dignity.
> If [his/her] flesh is called to war, may it fight with honor and protect the innocent.
> Let [his/her] body be fruitful and [his/her] soul at peace.
> May you return soon, so [name] will experience the true resurrection in the fullness of your Holy Name.
> And let us say,
> Amen.

THE MORTICIAN

Ebenezer Morse – more commonly known as Ben – meticulously arranged the viewing room chairs for the Blanchard memorial service, whistling "Nearer my God to Thee" as he worked. By all accounts Hugo Blanchard had been a good man, and Morse hoped to give him the best send-off possible under the circumstances. Once the seating was in proper order, the mortician checked on the guest book, the flowers, the photo display, the podium and microphone. Everything in its right place. Only the corpse was missing. Hugo Blanchard's body was off at its new job.

Morse took another look around, and found himself dissatisfied with things he couldn't fix. The carpet needing replacing. He'd installed it when he first took over the business, and it'd been trodden into threadbare middle age right alongside him. The old-fashioned floral wallpaper had likewise turned dingy. He could not, however, afford the refurbishments that the Morse & Sons Funeral Home needed so sorely. Going by the mortality statistics you'd think it'd be a golden age for undertakers, but his bank account told a different tale.

True, he was not without options. As a man who'd spent the entirety of his adult life tending to the dead, he was well-qualified for any number of jobs in the burgeoning reanimated labor industry. Indeed, Ben's brother Randolph – the second son referenced in "Morse & Sons" – had abandoned the family trade some years ago and became a zombie repairman for Frankenstein Enterprises. But Ben and Randolph barely spoke since the prodigal's defection.

The undertaker went to his showroom and picked out the coffin that Mrs. Blanchard had selected for the memorial service, then wheeled the box to the elevator and brought it down to the funeral home's basement, a cold, windowless, concrete-and-tile mortuary that had been the Morse boys' playroom growing up. When he was young, he and his brother dared each other to trespass down here, and when that thrill wore off, they played hide-and-seek amidst the dead. As Ben matured, the basement became the site of his apprenticeship, where he'd learned the morbid secrets of the family business. The smell of preservative fluid – the sharp, chemical smell of childhood – was starting to fade, like the taste of a madeleine cookie going stale. Ben went past the now-rarely-used embalming chamber and entered a former storage compartment that he'd repurposed for modern funerals.

Two dozen nude, headless mannequins in a carefully calibrated range of sizes, body types, and skin tones stood at attention before him, gleaming in the room's harsh light. They were made from silicone, using essentially the same process as the manufacture of sex dolls, although their crotches were egg-smooth. Most of the bodiless memorial services at the Morse & Sons Funeral Home used a closed, empty casket or a photo display to stand in for the corpse, but a substantial minority of customers – the widow Blanchard amongst them – preferred something more tangible. For these mourners, the funeral industry had devised a line of therapeutic dummies to serve as proxies for the departed. All that one had to do was dress the mannequin in the dead person's clothes and craft a plastic head, and one had an affordable, reasonably faithful facsimile of the beloved body that was now laboring in some home or factory. A few customers even went so far as to bury their mourning dummies. Ben sometimes pondered that the polyethylene effigies he'd planted in local graveyards would endure for millennia, far more durable than the mummies of the pharaohs. Future archaeologists might someday unearth them and believe their models to have been kings and queens. They would get some very strange ideas about America in the early 21st century. But then, America in the early 21st century was a very strange place, the undertaker thought, as he looked over his headless funeral dolls.

A 3D printer sat in the corner of the room, near a shelf stocked with grinning artificial skulls and bins of plastic pellets in various flesh tones. Ben inserted a skull into the printer's output tray and a measured scoop of nurdles into the intake chamber, then uploaded a digital photograph of Hugo's Blanchard's face into the machine. It whirred into life with a cranky sputter and its spindle began to saw back and forth across the skull, extruding pink dabs as it went. The odor of melted plastic wafted through the funeral home's basement. Hugo Blanchard's visage knit itself back into being.

While the printer whined, Ben selected the mourning dummy that best matched the dead man's size and skin tone, and then dressed it in the clothes that the widow Blanchard had given him. Crisp new underwear and socks. A collared dress shirt still in its cellophane wrapper. A dated grey suit, cigarette smoke lodged deep in its fabric. A blue striped tie, similarly besmogged. A pair of black loafers with worn soles. A wedding ring. Ben had always enjoyed dressing cadavers. He felt that after their long, taxing, and frankly undignified journeys shuffling between hospital beds, morgue slabs and embalming tables, clothing them in their terminal finery helped restore them to some measure of humanity. But clothing this headless mannequin in Hugo's funeral outfit felt like crafting a window display for a particularly seedy department store, one that obtained its wares by robbing graves.

The 3D printer buzzed angrily. Hugo Blanchard's head sat waiting in the output tray, reminding Ben of a nobleman's noggin in a guillotine basket. Its eyes were closed and its face frozen in a neutral expression starkly dissimilar from Mister Blanchard's sly grin in the reference photo. The mortician retrieved the disconcertingly warm head from the printer and placed it atop his workbench. As a first step, he sprayed it with a chemical deodorizer to neutralize its distracting new-car smell. Then he took up his makeup kit and applied some color to the printed head's cheeks and lips, trying to shade its uniform pale khaki into something more naturalistic. He was a magician when it came to restoring the bloom of life to cold, dead skin, but somehow that knack with cosmetics didn't extend to painting models. Once he finished with the makeup, he rummaged through a bin of artificial scalps until he found a wig generally matching the color and style of Hugo's hair. Finally, he picked up the head again and placed it atop the mannequin's neck, securing it in place with a long cylindrical pin inserted through the neck and concealed by Hugo's collar.

The mortician examined his handiwork and grimaced. One recognized that the doll was supposed to be Hugo Blanchard, certainly, but it was decidedly not him. This hunk of plastic had never been alive. Ben was saddened without being disappointed. These things never came out quite right. The clients didn't expect perfection, of course. Anyone who had the money to afford a totally convincing replica of their loved one's corpse probably hadn't needed to sell off the original article. Still, delivering substandard work offended his sense of professionalism, even when there was no way around it.

Ben lowered Hugo's mourning dummy into its coffin. The casket was a handsome one – solid mahogany, with gleaming copper fittings and an almond-colored velvet inlay. Coffin sales had once been the mainstay of Morse & Sons' profits. Now many customers needed only to rent a box for a few hours rather than purchasing one for perpetual use. A hundred funerals might reuse the same casket. So too, embalming services paid much better than short-term mannequin rentals. The undertaker forced himself back into the moment. He had all the time in the world to contemplate the reasons that his business was failing. The Blanchard memorial service, on the other hand, started in just a couple of hours. The family would be here soon.

As Ben wheeled the mourning dummy out, he glanced back at its naked, headless peers, patiently awaiting their own funerals. He shuddered as he turned out the lights and closed the door, leaving the dolls to their own affairs.

The memorial service was well-attended. Hugo Blanchard had lived to the age of 75, a father of three and a veteran of both the U.S. Navy and the HVAC business. He loved tying fly fishing lures but rarely went out on the river, preferring the comforts of home and the presence of his wife. Hugo's eulogists had plenty of material to work with to portray a full and well-lived life, yet even so he'd been cut down too young. He'd been enjoying a modest retirement on a donor pension until one day he visited

San Francisco to see his granddaughter and a Styx hopped the curb and killed him without warning. Ben thought it unfair that Frankenstein got to take your body even if its products had ended your life.

The effigy's presence produced mixed reactions. The widow Blanchard seemed to be in a daze as she regarded her late husband's likeness. She kissed the dummy on its forehead and pressed one of Hugo's colorful fishing lures between its fingers. The granddaughter from San Francisco, on the other hand, took one look inside the coffin and proceeded to shriek until her parents removed her. Most of the mourners spoke a few words to the doll, then gave it a wide berth once they'd paid their respects. Zombie aides attended to a few of the more elderly guests, creating the strange and rather eerie spectacle of a memorial attended by the walking dead.

Ben recognized the priest who'd spoken at the ceremony and went over to say hello. "Times have changed, haven't they?" the clergyman said. "Three dead bodies at this funeral, and not one of them belonged to Hugo Blanchard."

"Strange that we put dead bodies to work rather than rest," the undertaker agreed. "Until Frankenstein came along, nobody believed that a human corpse was just meat. Not even the tribes that practice funerary cannibalism."

"The church tried to stop it," the priest said defensively, as if he were trying to cover his ass. "We told people not to sign up with Frankenstein, not to sell their loved ones. But nobody listens to us anymore."

"Every culture in history had a relationship with its dead," Ben said. "Even before history, the Neanderthals, they decorated their dead with red ochre and buried them with stone tools. People said their goodbyes and life moved on. Now the dead don't go away. And the rites of death are dying."

"What can you do?" the priest asked, shrugging. "People just can't afford them anymore."

Ben locked up once the last of the guests had departed. Ordinarily at the end of a funeral he was as cheerful as any workingman reaching the end of a shift. Today, however, a gloomy spirit oppressed him. The mortician tried to whistle as he pushed the coffin downstairs, but the music wouldn't come. The effigy's inorganic serenity seemed to mock him from inside its casket. *You may be mourning, but plastic never grieves*, the mourning doll's frozen, painted face gloated. *That's what you get for being alive. Plastic is indifferent to pain and that's why plastic will still be here when life on Earth is over.*

Ben rolled the awful thing back into the room it had come from, and pulled the pin that kept Hugo Blanchard's plastic head anchored to the reusable mannequin body. The wig went back into the bin where it belonged. Ben opened the closet where he kept the used heads, should the bereaved ever want them again.

The undertaker looked upon shelves crowded with dozens of busts he'd made in the likenesses of dead men and women, still rouged and lipsticked from their funerals. Their eyes were shut but not in sleep. Sometimes he dreamt of this closet, heart-rending nightmares where the dummies' eyelids opened. Ben tossed Hugo amongst the heads and closed the door in their faces, sealing them up in the dark.

Ben Morse was born into the mortician's trade. Not long ago, he had loved it. But lately the business had gotten so fucking creepy.

FREEDOM OF ELDERLY AMERICANS ACT OF 2017 (115TH CONGRESS, 1ST SESSION) S. 520

IN THE UNITED STATES SENATE
September 12, 2017

Mr. Mootey and Mr. Hazen introduced the following bill, which was referred to the Committee on Health, Welfare, Education, and Pensions, and in addition, to the Committee on Reanimated Labor, for a period to be subsequently determined by the Speaker, in each case for consideration of such provisions as fall within the jurisdiction of the committee concerned.

A Bill

To eliminate restrictions on the delivery of medical care by reanimated cadavers, to encourage necrotech innovations in the field of elder care, to restructure Medicare so as to recognize that elderly Americans may now access substantial funds from the reanimated labor industry, to provide tax relief to certain individuals and employers, and for other purposes.

Be it enacted by the Senate and House of Representatives of the United States of America in Congress assembled,

SECTION 1. SHORT TITLE; PURPOSES; TABLE OF CONTENTS.

(a) Short Title – This Act may be cited as the "Freedom of Elderly Americans Act of 2017."

(b) Purposes – The purposes of this Act are as follows:

1. Providing Seniors With Alternative, Affordable Care Options – To provide greater flexibility in providing seniors with options for obtaining affordable health care by eliminating certain onerous restrictions on the provision of medical and nursing services by reanimated cadavers, and by shielding z-nurse manufacturers from tort and malpractice liability.
2. Promoting High-Tech Innovation – To revise provider payment schedules under Medicare Part A so as to encourage the utilization of innovative necro-technologies for elder care.
3. Restructuring of Medicare Funding – To protect the long-term viability of the Medicare program and the interests of taxpayers by requiring Medicare beneficiaries eligible for donor pensions to exhaust such private sector funding before receiving coverage for long-term residential care.
4. Tax Relief – To eliminate or reduce tax burdens imposed by 26 U.S.C. 3101 and 3111.

THE ELDER

You tremble helplessly in your wheelchair. A stranger is pushing you out of your home, and you don't know what he wants with you. His face is unnervingly familiar, but you can't remember his name. You have no idea how he got inside your house.

You grasp desperately at the brake, at the furniture, at the doorframe, at anything you can reach from your chair. Each time the stranger firmly pries your arthritic fingers free. The sunlight and fresh air hit you like a closed fist as he pushes you across the threshold. A tired-looking blue sedan waits in your driveway, ominous as a hearse.

"Let me go, I don't know you!" you shriek hoarsely.

The kidnapper's face tightens, and you flinch, expecting a blow, but when you look up again he only sighs. He hoists you out of your chair and transfers you into the back seat, grunting with the exertion. "We've been over this, Mom," he says through clenched teeth. "You can't stay in your home anymore, it's not safe for you there. I'm sorry."

Everything this bastard says is a lie. The stranger is not your son, you've never had a son, you're sure of it. And your home is the only safe place on Earth. A zombie epidemic infests the world outside your door. You see the monsters every time you turn on the TV. When you peek through the curtains you see them stalking through the streets. Every day there are fewer humans and more of them. A rotting corpse even replaced the neighbor boy who used to mow your lawn. They seem docile enough on the surface but these creatures don't fool you for a second, you know they're just waiting to get you in their talons so they can rip you apart. Worst of all, you seem to be the only person who minds them. You feel like you're the last sane woman left, that the rest of humanity has surrendered itself to slaughter.

Besieged by monsters, you retreated into isolation. You used to sit by the window all day long, peering through the blinds, carrying on a vigil against the hordes of the dead outside, and living in constant terror that someday they might replace you like they've replaced so many others. You have not left your home in years, and now some goddamned imposter is dragging you out of it to die.

Screaming for help, you try to escape the car while your kidnapper puts your wheelchair into the trunk. It's no good, he locked you inside. The kidnapper says something to you as he gets behind the wheel but you're so confused and terrified that you can't make out the words, it's all just human static. As he drives away, you stare out the window at your home. It's been so long since you've been outside, you barely recognize it anymore. You can't even recall the address. Disorientation overwhelms you, as if the stranger pulled you out of nothingness. As if your home never existed at all.

The kidnapper drives you to a large, dismal brick building the color of mud. Two dead men in medical scrubs wait at the entrance, like ghosts. The horrible truth, which you have suspected all along but did not dare to admit, dawns upon you. *He's feeding you to the zombies.*

Your enemy pulls you out of the car and back into your wheelchair, and pushes you towards the ghouls as if he were handling a buffet cart. You shriek with all the force you can muster, hoping that some kind soul will hear and intervene – and there are people on the street, but the sons of bitches purposefully ignore you, not a Good Samaritan in the bunch. The kidnapper calls for help and the zombies come for you, their grey faces forcefully impassive, their bulging eyes crimson as fresh cherries. They seize you with their fish-cool hands, and inject the night into you through your arm.

When you wake you're in a small, beige bedroom that stinks of antiseptic, maybe a dingy motel suite. Your wrist feels like it's been stung by a wasp, and there's a gauze pad taped over the spot. Your kidnapper waits by the foot of the bed, which you are starting to realize is your bed now. He tells you his name is Matthew but that can't be right, the only Matthew you know is your grandfather and this man is much younger than you are. "I have to go, but I'll be back soon," he says, squeezing your hand. "I know it's not ideal . . . you'll get used to it, though. They're going to take good care of you here, I promise." Is the kidnapper working for the zombies, a traitor to the living, or is he controlling the zombies somehow? Your life may depend on the answer to this question, and you can't figure it out.

A walking corpse in a nurse's uniform looms in the doorway behind the kidnapper, the corpse of a woman close to your own age. Her craggy, pallid skin shines leprous in the dim yellow light. The zombie's bloodshot eyes bore into you like drills, with pointed but dispassionate interest. There's an awful, merciless intelligence in her glare, clever as a calculator and blankly vicious as a shark.

The bastard who brought you here against your will kisses your cheek against your will and leaves you alone with the monster. You're shaking uncontrollably. Death is not the most terrible thing in the world but living death surely is. Will she tear out your throat with her yellow teeth? Will she pull you limb from limb, like a child playing with insects? The anticipation is its own subtle torture. You both wish that she would say something to break the awful silence, and are petrified of what this soulless thing might tell you.

Without a word, she walks to the bathroom and turns on the faucet. She was a shrunken old woman when she died yet now that she has quickened she moves with eerie speed and force and a horridly precise gait, not the way a human being moves at all. You have no doubt that she could tear you to rags if she tried. The zombie stares at you expectantly as she draws your bath. She never blinks.

You edge away from her, whimpering. She has no patience for your terror and modesty. She undresses you, handling you with a gentle yet threatening grip, like a spring that might snap if it met the slightest resistance. You offer none. Up close like this, it is hideously obvious that she does not breathe. You, on the other hand, are sobbing from the bottom of your lungs.

The zombie lifts you out of bed and guides you to a seat in the tub. The water's seething hot, yet still you shiver beneath her clammy, probing touch. Her flesh is withered and strong as gnarled oak, eel-belly translucent with blue-black veins. You spot a bar code tattooed on the inside of her wrist. The hag's blankly malevolent facial expression never changes once the entire time that she's bathing you.

Mercifully, she's efficient, and the ordeal is soon over. Once you're dried off and clothed she leaves you alone in your cell, locking the door behind her.

You peel back the gauze taped to your wrist and see a shiny new tattoo underneath, a bar code like that of your beldame nurse. You sit shivering on the bed, wondering how you got here, wondering if there is any way out.

BOOK II: CORPORATE ASSETS

VICTOR FRANKENSTEIN TO LEAVE U.S. FOR SWITZERLAND

BY ROSE NAJAFI, ASSOCIATED PRESS
(NOVEMBER 13, 1997)

World-famous inventor Dr. Victor Frankenstein shocked the business community today by announcing that he intends to leave the U.S. and move into a restored 17th-century castle in the Swiss Alps. Dr. Frankenstein will make his own home into an experiment by largely eschewing live staff in favor of reanimated workers. Frankenstein, who was born in Geneva, first moved to the United States in 1981 and maintains dual U.S.-Swiss citizenship.

Dr. Frankenstein rarely appears in public, and it has been widely reported that he dislikes his celebrity. "Victor has found it very difficult to maintain his privacy ever since announcing his invention, and relocating will let him focus on his historic work in peace and quiet," said a company spokesman.

Many observers questioned the timing of the move, coming a mere six months after Frankenstein Enterprises raised $48 billion in its initial public offering. Although the press release emphasized that Dr. Frankenstein is not retiring from the company he founded or stepping down as its CEO, investors have expressed their doubts that he can run such an unconventional business empire from his home.

"I'd expect that Victor will continue to spend substantial time in the U.S. overseeing the business," said Lee Cushing, head of Hammer Capital

Partners, a hedge fund that holds a $1.2 billion position in Frankenstein Enterprises stock. "It's one thing to claim a new domicile for tax reasons, if that's all this is, but Dr. Frankenstein has responsibilities to his investors."

"From a P.R. perspective I think it's a wonderful move," said Marcus Carradine, a professor of management at the Wharton School of Business. "Dr. Frankenstein already has such a mystique about him, and going up to the mountaintop's sure to reinforce it. It's also quite a show of faith in the quality of his product, to go without human staff entirely. From a management perspective, however, I think it's suicidal. He has a very aggressive business partner in Otto Faust. The Warlock of Wall Street's sure to take advantage of this opening and make a play for control."

Some commentators cheered the prospect of the notoriously reclusive and difficult inventor accepting a less prominent role in his company. "At this point in Frankenstein Enterprises' lifecycle it makes perfect sense for the founder to take a step back," said Wall Street analyst Ingrid Lanchester. "He's a scientist, and while he's obviously a great genius he doesn't have any background in the business side of things. He doesn't know manufacturing, he doesn't know product design, he doesn't know financial engineering. Now that the miracle's been accomplished, and they were able to have a very successful IPO by putting the miracle worker front and center, it's the perfect time to start letting the MBAs take over."

After wild fluctuations over the course of the trading day, Frankenstein Enterprises stock closed at $102.57, a 1.4% gain.

THE JOURNALIST PART II

Rose Najafi took another sip of coffee and glanced around the cafe for people she could talk to. The village of Walserbad was the closest settlement to Castle Frankenstein, a mountainous hamlet too rustic to even be cute. She'd arrived early in the morning and spent all day fruitlessly trying to get the locals to open up about their famous neighbor. At first she thought they avoided her on account of her hijab, but as she explored Walserbad and attuned herself to its frequencies, she realized that wasn't right. She knew what prejudice felt like, and this felt like something else. Traveling through this remote, picturesque stretch of a famously peaceful and neutral country, Rose picked up a psychic atmosphere she'd encountered in war zones and prisons. These people were afraid.

Perhaps due to the oncoming storm, the cafe was nearly deserted. An old couple sat at a table towards the rear, whispering to each other like conspirators over their cake. The woman tending the place kept glancing back and forth anxiously between Rose and the entrance. She was the first human server whom Rose had seen in a while, quite a novelty. In fact, Rose realized that she hadn't encountered a single zombie since arriving in Walserbad. The locals didn't trust them.

Rose knew at a glance that she wouldn't get any quotes out of this crowd. With an hour to go until her ride to the castle was scheduled to arrive, she decided to take out her laptop and review her biographical notes on Victor Frankenstein. She'd memorized them already, but going through them once again diverted her from her jitters, like Aunt Fairuza with her tasbih prayer beads.

Victor Frankenstein was born in Geneva in 1954 to a bright and prosperous couple, his father a pharmaceutical company chemist and his mother a poetess of no little renown. Rose sometimes wondered how different the world would have been had he followed in his mother's footsteps instead. An early family photo showed Victor as a brooding little boy, his brow furrowed as if he was trying to work out some vast problem, yet couldn't bear to ask for help.

Unauthorized biographies of Victor Frankenstein came out on an almost monthly basis, and Rose had read through an entire bookcase of the genre. Regardless of whether they viewed their subject as a hero or a demon, they tended to be slim and unhelpful. The best of the lot was a memoir by the Frankenstein family housekeeper, and even it foundered on the rocks of its subject's remoteness. Whatever their perspective, all the biographers agreed that Victor Frankenstein was a loner from his earliest days. The boy genius's childhood produced no portents of the wonders and calamities that he would produce in time. Indeed, he left few traces of any sort for his biographers apart from a school record full of high grades and ineffective discipline. One of his teachers remarked in a report card that, "Victor has a great future ahead of him if he can only learn to control his temper and get along with his peers," doubling Rose over with laughter thirty-six years later.

Rose had done her own digging into Frankenstein's past, and even she hadn't found any credible sources who claimed friendship with the tycoon. If such people existed, they were skeletons in a closely-guarded closet. Perhaps the same quirks of personality and intellect that allowed him to solve death itself led him to find human company intolerable, and he resolved to build companions out of corpses instead.

After college, Victor Frankenstein earned his doctorate in biochemistry from the University of Ingolstadt, although only barely, since his thesis was so radical that his defense of it nearly degenerated into hand-to-hand combat. The academic job market brought him to America, where he took a faculty position at the venerable and disreputable Miskatonic University in Arkham, Massachusetts.

For a while it seemed like nothing much would come of the young Dr. Frankenstein, that he was doomed to a life of obscurity in the back benches of academia. He published little and spoke at no conferences. His students described him as the worst teacher who'd ever been inflicted upon them, even after his name had become synonymous with genius. In 1989 Frankenstein left/was pushed from Miskatonic when one of his studies failed catastrophically. None of his former colleagues expected or cared to hear from him again.

Enter Otto Faust, the billionaire founder of the hedge fund Hastur Capital LLP, sometimes known as the Warlock of Wall Street. The word "warlock" is usually thought of as meaning "male witch," but its original translation is "oath-breaker," and either definition plausibly applied to the corporate raider, who made his fortune buying thriving enterprises and cannibalizing them for parts. Rose had interviewed one of his former business partners in an insane asylum, and knew of another driven to murder-suicide. For the first time, Victor Frankenstein had a man that he could work with.

Rose never managed to dig up the details on how Faust and Frankenstein first crossed paths, but the tycoon was there to catch the scientist when he fell from academia. They struck a deal creating Frankenstein Enterprises, bankrolling Victor's research and giving him the resources he needed to develop his vision from a fevered dream into a wide-awake nightmare. Curiously, although at that time Victor Frankenstein was a failure with no patents or proof of his claims, Otto Faust nonetheless agreed to a dual-class corporate structure that granted the Doctor the majority of the new company's profits and dictatorial control. Some years later, Faust told an interviewer, "I would have squeezed more out of Victor if I could have. But even at that early stage of our partnership, I saw that he was an irreplaceable man."

On July 5, 1994, Frankenstein published his seminal paper, *On the Reanimation and Control of Human Cadavers*, and a breaking news alert interrupted the *Fresh Prince of Bel-Air*. Doomsayers proclaimed that the apocalypse was nigh. Time Magazine proclaimed that the Age of Frankenstein had begun. The Swedes awarded Dr. Frankenstein the Nobel Prize in

Medicine, an award named for another of history's deadliest science-tycoons.

Frankenstein and Faust opened their doors for business before anyone could think to stop them. They started out importing dead bodies from Haiti and putting them to work sweeping minefields and cleaning up toxic waste sites. Rose came across a famous photograph of the two men together with Princess Di in Cambodia, all three of them watching and grinning in minesweeping gear as a walking corpse triggered an old explosive and burst. They also began offering the first donor pensions, sending representatives to nursing homes and hospices waving checks. In the mainstream media, Victor Frankenstein was a genius whose principal lines of business were performing miracles, saving lives, and giving money away to the old and sick.

In 1997, Frankenstein Enterprises went public. Ravenous investors stampeded to get their teeth into the company, and a tuxedoed zombie rang the opening bell at the New York Stock Exchange while Otto Faust beamed. Dr. Frankenstein, however, was nowhere to be seen. Soon after the IPO, he used a portion of his vast new fortune to reconstruct a castle in the Swiss Alps, and then the founder of the hottest company on Wall Street cleanly severed himself from human society. It was a brilliant act of corporate myth-making – Zeus returning to Mount Olympus. Nobody thought it would last. But nobody understood Victor.

Somehow retreating into hermitage reinforced the Doctor's position as CEO. Rose's sources inside the company all described the same strange pattern. Before decamping to Switzerland, Victor Frankenstein had been a demanding but remote boss, mostly concerned with his research and content to let Faust's people handle the day-to-day work of finance and marketing. Afterwards, his involvement steadily grew to encompass nearly every aspect of the company's metastasizing operations. His awed employees commented that even though he never set foot on the Death Valley corporate campus, he nonetheless seemed to know of everything happening there. It was as if he had ascended to a new plane of existence; incorporeal and omnipresent, walled up and inescapable.

In 2001, the Twin Towers came down and Frankenstein went to war. "If you don't stand with us, you stand with terror," the President said, and then he commanded an army of the dead to march across the Fertile Crescent.

Zombies represented a near-perfect weapon and a revolution in military affairs – adaptable, durable, ruthless, and self-perpetuating. War has always made corpses, and now corpses could make war. Much of the Islamic world rose up in terror and fury – America as the Great Satan had never seemed more plausible – and the Mideast dissolved into a ferocious conflict of all against all. Governments both friendly and hostile to the U.S. were swept away in a rising tide of violence, displacing millions of refugees whom Western governments treated with more fear and suspicion than the walking dead. Meanwhile, back home in Buffalo, Aunt Fairuza went insane. The war destroyed her faith in God, but not her hatred of the Devil, and believing creation to be the province of evil exclusively destroyed her.

Once Victor Frankenstein tasted blood his appetite for conquest became insatiable. He assembled legions of highly-paid brainiacs in Death Valley, ordering them to make the walking dead as capable as people, and moreso. Under his leadership the company built a nationwide iGor network, wirelessly connecting all of the company's ghouls into a vast electronic hive-mind. He knit himself into the infrastructure, into the bones and arteries of society. Cities reconfigured themselves around the needs of inhuman things, like they'd done for the automobile. Zombies death marched through industry after industry, each new victim feeding the collective's strength, helping it to overwhelm and devour its next target, until 2008, when the entire economy collapsed into Frankenstein's jaws. A surge of foreclosures rattled Wall Street and panicked executives replaced workers with cheap Franks by the thousands, feeding another surge of foreclosures and starting the cycle again. The great serpent of capitalism swallowed its own tail, chewing gruesomely as it spiraled into auto-cannibalism. Donor recruitment soared.

In 2012, Otto Faust died of brain cancer, gibbering and mad at the end. He left his daughter Hester all his assets, his seat on Frankenstein's Board of Directors, the politicians that he owned, and iron-clad instructions to cremate his body. Rose descended on the funeral service with a nervous mob of reporters, every one of the ink-stained wretches wondering if the elusive Dr. Frankenstein would appear at last. Of course, he did not. Black smoke puffed from the crematorium chimney. Rose caught the faintest whiff of the burning flesh of a man who'd been worth more than five hundred million people put together. She sat in the Walserbad cafe experiencing a vivid recollection of the odor.

The death of Frankenstein's business partner did not slow him down. He and his lieutenants developed the company into a speedy and agile juggernaut as unstoppable and unkillable as its products. They conquered e-commerce, manufacturing, consumer tech, high tech, transportation, military contracting, and even sent rockets into space. It was inconceivable that any competitor might develop to challenge such a leviathan, or that any government might have both will and means to bring it to heel.

Only terrorist strikes seemed to even slow the company down. The Gravediggers' latest attack on Frankenstein Enterprises had stunned the whole country with its brutality, and the country shrugged off brutality every day. Rose's sources told her that now the Gravediggers were gunning for the Doctor directly. It seemed impossible that any assassin could touch a man so supremely protected, but they lived in an age when impossible things happened all the time.

REVIEW POSTED IN THE FRANKENSTEIN ENTERPRISES ONLINE STORE

(SEPTEMBER 30, 2012)

HERCULES 200-SERIES FRANK ☆☆☆½

by LawnmanRod (3 reviews, verified purchase)

I've been using Franks in my landscaping business for five years, and I decided to pick up a few Hercules 200s after the recent price drop. The Hercules 200 is an OK Frank for what is and a good deal for the price, especially if you get it used. Just don't think it's going to do all that stuff from the commercials.

The Good: Even though Frankenstein uses its lowest-quality bodies for labor models like this, the Hercules 200 is stronger than it looks. One of my Franks was a 92-year-old woman who looks like she'd been lying out in the sun a while before they reanimated her, and she can still haul bags of sand and gravel all day.

The Bad: I'd hoped that the 200 series wouldn't be as clumsy as the 180s. No luck! They're still slow and gangly and get caught in the lawn-mowers all the time, which is a real pain to clean up.

The Ugly: Speaking of being a pain to clean up, the 200 isn't compatible with the iGor store's hygiene apps, so they can't clean themselves automatically. Every once in a while you've got to strip them off and hose them down. It's an ugly job. And this model doesn't notify you about soft tissue damage, so you really can't let the maintenance slide. One time I accidentally left a Frank outside overnight and a colony of fire ants got into it. That was good for a few nightmares.

THE PROGRAMMER

Hey bro, good to see you again! Yeah, I know, it's been too long. I've been busy as a dead hobo lately.

Didn't I tell you this place was swanky? We're living the Death Valley dream now! No more Natty Ice in the Zeta Tau basement for us. We earned it, didn't we? Fucking A.

The job's going great, thanks for asking! I started at Frankenstein Enterprises about five months ago. I'm writing code to help the Franks interact with smart gadgets and the Internet of Things. Mostly working with C++ and Java to access web APIs.

Oh, you want that in English? Ha, no problem. Dealing with coders and zombies all the time, sometimes I forget how to talk with normal people. I'll start with the basics.

So, every zombie that we sell is connected to a global computer network called iGor. Zombies don't have minds of their own – it's iGor that tells them how to behave and follow our commands. When I take the order tablet here at our table and punch in that I want a frosty cold Heineken, that signal gets transmitted over the Internet and into the iGor network. iGor then locates all the zombies assigned to waitstaff duty at this restaurant, calculates which one of them can fill the order the quickest based on their GPS coordinates and whatever other tasks they've been assigned, and tells that zombie to bring me my beer.

And speak of the devil, my drink's already here! Because the Franks are all connected through this network, they can share data with each other to do their jobs more efficiently. Like, as soon as the kitchen Franks have cooked a burger, the server Franks know that it's ready, and one of them will come pick it up and deliver it to the table. Pretty cool, huh? Because their minds are all knit together with code, they can work faster and smarter than humans.

Of course, building and maintaining a system this vast and complex is a huge job, so Frankenstein needs armies of programmers like yours truly to handle it all. We're really the company that built Death Valley into what it is today. Don't get me wrong, southern California's been a hotbed for tech for a long time, but it was Frankenstein Enterprises that brought in the big bucks for AI and networking research. Death Valley used to be called Silicon Valley before we built our headquarters here, did you know that?

Haha, yeah, I've been working there five months and I'm already talking like a grizzled old company man. Frankenstein has that effect on people.

Anyway, getting back to your initial question of what I do fourteen hours a day, I've been networking Internet-linked devices to iGor so that Franks can gather and use their data as well. Example. This place probably has a smart refrigerator with sensors inside and an Internet connection. As soon as the beer supply starts running low, an alert automatically goes out from the fridge into iGor, and iGor tells the zombies who work here that it's time to restock. If you've got smart speakers, you can program your Franks to dance to the music. And over time, iGor learns how much beer you drink and what kind of music you like and all that, which makes the service even more seamless. I'm writing code so the Franks and iGor and the appliances all understand each other.

Yeah, it's neat stuff. There's a billion potential applications for it, the sky's the limit so long as we get the engineering right. And if the technology takes off the way I think it will, we're going to make mind-boggling amounts of money. We won't just sell you zombies, we'll sell you all the appliances your zombies use every day. Frankenstein Fridges. Frankenstein Washing Machines. Actually, there's a lot of Frank-optimized hardware in the industrial market already, we're just now bringing the tech into the consumer sphere. Oh, and we'll know everything about how you use those appliances, so when you're out of detergent, a zombie'll stop by your place with a fresh delivery order.

It's a crazy stressful workplace, but the pay's incredible and the bennies are out of this world. I can take Styxes anywhere I want to go for free. At the office they have free food for us every day, and in the company cafeteria we get to test out all the new cooking apps before they've released to the public. They even have Franks who come around and give massages! You can get haircuts, pedicures, whatever sort of pampering you want.

Oh, and get this – on my very first day they gave me my own household Frank! A Ganymede 500-series. She's great, keeps my place clean, does all my cooking and laundry, never complains. She's like a Mom, except, y'know, she's a zombie. I call her Ivy. And she's wirelessly integrated with most of my stuff, so she functions like a control hub for my whole apartment. I can lie in bed and tell Ivy I want a cup of coffee, and she'll connect to my espresso maker and get a cup started as soon as I say the words. She knows my schedule so well she can usually predict what I want without me having to say a thing!

Hey, you want another one of those? This round's on me. Actually, you know what, I've got tonight. Just hit the button on the tablet and the Frank'll bring another. Get me an order of the mozzarella sticks, too.

My one complaint about working at Frankenstein is that it's got a bit of a culty vibe. You see that sort of thing in tech companies. Lots of lunatic CEOs trick themselves into thinking that they're the second coming of Jesus Christ, smarter and richer and better-looking this time. But Victor's got a better claim to messiah territory than most, since he really can raise the dead. He owns a castle in Switzerland staffed entirely by Franks, and from what I hear he never leaves the grounds. Imagine having all that money – infinite money, for all practical purposes – imagine having all that, and never even leaving your home. The whole campus is decorated like a shrine to him. There's statues of him on the lawns, massive photographs of him on the walls. Victor accepting his Nobel

Prize, Victor working in his lab, young Victor teaching at Miskatonic University. Nobody other than top management's actually laid eyes on Victor in years, mind you.

And it's not just decoration – people act like he's watching over our shoulders. If a decision's got to be made, no matter how grand or petty, the question's always, "What would Victor do?" "What does Victor want?" At meetings people go on and on about his philosophy and his vision, and how it's got to be the foundation for everything that we accomplish. I mean, sure, he's a genius and all, but he runs his company like it's Jonestown.

Haha, yeah, you're right, I guess he pays better than Jim Jones. OK, and the poor bastards at Jonestown didn't get pedicures on-demand, either. I get your point. It's still creepy, though, this huge megacorporation operating on a cult of personality.

Am I talking about work too much? I'm sorry, dude. I've been pushing myself too hard. Like I said, I've got Victor on the brain these days. No more business talk tonight. This is a night for brothers to reconnect, and get blind drunk, and maybe get laid. Let's introduce ourselves to those ladies by the bar.

☠

What's up, bro? Come here, give me a hug! Take a seat, grab a drink. Did you ever hear anything back from that PR chick you were chatting up last time we hung out? No? That's too bad. Don't worry, your fortunes are bound to turn around. San Francisco's a great dating town.

Huh. Yeah, I guess you did use to date waitresses a lot in college. I admit it, you've got a point, you can't flirt with Frank servers like you could with humans. One way that humans are better. That reminds me, whatever happened to that punk chick who used to waitress at Bennigan's our senior year? With the red hair and tattoos? She was really cool, really funny. I wonder what she's up to these days? I guess she's probably not waitressing any more. Unless she passed away.

I'm doing good these days, man, doing real good. I love this city! The technologies that are going to shape tomorrow are birthed right here! Death Valley's ground zero for a revolution that's changing the way we live, the way we die, even the way we think. You and I get to live at the spear-tip of the future as it penetrates the present day. How cool is that?

I tell you, bro, there's nothing the living can't accomplish now that we've domesticated the dead.

Yeah, I am a little stoned. What of it? Ivy rolls really tight joints, let me know if you want to step outside and smoke one.

Work could not be going better. I got a promotion a little while ago, they kicked me upstairs! Fucking stock options, man. Yeah, cheers. They've got me on interesting projects, too. I can't talk about the details, but iGor's amazing technology to work with, and it gets exponentially more interesting the deeper you get under the hood. It's humbling to think people could make an artificial mind spanning millions of bodies and all of the planet. Every day I learn something astonishing about it.

You know, Frankenstein really is an amazing company to be a part of. There's so much energy, so much innovation. I get to work together with the smartest people alive in a shared enterprise that's transforming society in front of our eyes. This company makes miracles. We traffic in honest-to-God miracles. I think I might get a skull-and-brains tattoo, I'm really thinking about it.

Drink with me! To Victor Frankenstein, the miracle-maker!

Kool-Aid? What are you talking about? No, man, I never said Frankenstein was like Jonestown. That's crazy talk. Here, finish your beer and let's go out back for a meeting of the joint chiefs of staff.

☠

Hey, thanks for meeting me here. I know that this place is a shithole, but it's one of the last bars left in the city where they've still got human servers. I needed to get away from Franks for a bit.

Listen, can I ask another favor of you? I've got some things I need to get off my chest, and I don't have anyone else I can talk to about it. I mean, I probably shouldn't be talking about this at all, Frankenstein made me sign a stack of NDAs. Screw it, though, Zeta Tau trumps NDA and if I hold onto all these secrets much longer I'm going to lose my mind. It's OK? Really? Thanks so much, buddy. You're a real friend.

This might sound paranoid, but could you do me a favor and turn off your cell? If you've got the Styx app installed on your phone then Frankenstein Enterprises can access the microphone.

All right, here's that big news I mentioned when I texted you. I lost my job. From golden boy to pariah overnight. Thanks, man, I appreciate that. I admit, in some ways I had it coming, but in others it's totally fucked. The whole thing's a goddamn mess. I was in my office at 1 A.M. knocking my brains out trying to get this network synchronization issue resolved. I was stressed out and exhausted, so I'd gotten a z-masseuse to come in and work the knots out of my shoulders while I wrestled with the code. Other than that, I was all alone.

I needed to install a patch in iGor, and in order to do that, I needed my network privileges temporarily elevated. Totally routine cybersecurity horseshit, I'd done it plenty of times before without incident. The company's got an automated process for it. You just enter a description and purpose for your request, and iGor's supposed to give you the degree of access you need for the length of time that you need it.

I told iGor that I needed permission to run the update. Suddenly, my whole network interface changed. All the options I was used to were still there, but now I also saw a dashboard displaying a heat map of the globe, with GPS data showing the locations of all the Franks. All of them. Even the ones working at the poles, and the bottom of the seas. The whole planet, lit up by zombies. And I could connect to any of them.

It took me a second to realize what I was looking at, and when I figured it out I nearly shat myself. iGor's automated security protocols had accidentally given me the very highest level of access. They granted me privileges that only Victor and a few other top executives are supposed to enjoy.

I know that I shouldn't have looked, but I was so exhausted that I wasn't thinking straight, and curiosity got ahold of me before I could think through the consequences. How often do you get to play with a toy like that? Fucking stupid of me.

I ran a search for Yaza. You know, the supermodel, she's the one in the Frankenstein Enterprises ads driving a chariot pulled by a couple of Franks without skin. iGor pulled up its listing of all the Franks that Yaza owns. I selected 'Bodyguard-01,' and the iGor network sent me a live video stream from the POV of her personal security Dragonstooth, complete with his GPS coordinates and vital stats. He stood in the corner of a fancy-looking bedroom, watching over Yaza as she slept. He was basically a walking camera, transmitting everything he saw and heard.

And he was more than that. iGor offered me a command interface. Not only could I see through the z-bodyguard's eyes, I could control him as well. Yaza was snoring peacefully in Montreal, totally oblivious to the fact that I was watching her from my office in San Francisco. I could have hit a few keystrokes and made her own guard strangle her.

What? No, of course I didn't do anything! What sort of sick fuck do you think I am? There's a phrase for passing morbid notions like that, l'appel du vide. It means call of the void. Everyone gets them, they're perfectly natural.

What's freaky isn't that I thought about killing her, it's that I had the power to do it in the first place. I mean, think about it. The whole point of owning a Frank is that you're supposed to be able to tell it what to do, right? Management never told anyone that they have a private backdoor to override the owners. Hell, I didn't even know about all this shady shit, and I work there!

Used to work there, I should say.

It gets even worse. I noticed a sub-menu called "Data Archives." Checking that out, I found a massive trove of video. And when I say massive, I mean, Yaza's z-bodyguard recorded every second of his service and streamed it all back over iGor for permanent storage on Frankenstein's servers. No wonder the company's been building so many data centers out in the Midwest.

You're absolutely right. Any tabloid in the country would have made me a very rich man in exchange for these video files. Heh, you can hear the call of the void now too, can't you? I saw reality the way the world's most powerful people see it. It's a weird experience. Gives you a lot of dark thoughts.

But dark thoughts or no, once you've touched this sort of power it's hard to pull away from it. I closed out the window with the bodyguard's data and went back to poke around the main directory. It's organized so beautifully. I took a virtual tour of the White House via one of the zombies who works there. The President picks his nose, FYI. I watched a couple minutes of the Superbowl from the z-waterboy's perspective. I caught a few minutes of Diana French's Vegas show through her own eyes. Oh, and there was a sub-menu called Mars Colony. Do you believe that? I caught a glimpse of life on Mars. Well, not life exactly.

And then a truly terrible idea occurred to me. Just monumental dipshittery on my part. I realized that I could see through the eyes of the zombies serving Castle Frankenstein, and maybe get a look at the great shut-in himself.

There are well over a thousand Franks on the castle grounds. I selected one of them at random, and looked inside the house of the world's richest man. I saw a gloomy, dimly-lit stone corridor, much more like a dungeon than a mansion. No art, no furniture, not even any carpets. A green door down the hallway stood half-open, with a light on inside. I couldn't see through the door from my position, but I heard noises coming from it. Horrible wet noises. Splashing. Gurgling. A choking shriek.

I could have ordered the Frank to take a few steps forward and see what was happening, see Victor in the flesh, but I was too afraid. Even through a proxy his presence is overpowering. It felt like I'd broken into Heaven to spy on God, and caught Him in the midst of something terrible, and of course, that God saw me coming. Up until this point I'd been so preoccupied with my iGor privileges that I'd largely zoned out on my backrub. But visiting Victor's castle made me suddenly very sensitive to the knowledge that a six-foot tall zombie stood directly behind me at my workstation. Now I acutely felt its cold, strong fingers digging into the flesh of my shoulders . . . its dead eyes peering intently at the back of my head.

Just then, my screen went black. My network privileges had been reset.

Frankenstein's thumbs pressed hard into the base of my neck.

Jumping in surprise, I ordered the z-masseuse off of me. He complied, but other people in the company could still see through his eyes, and give him commands that would override my own. It was the first time I've ever felt afraid around a zombie. I immediately sent him away, but before he left my office, he stopped by the door and paused a moment. Like he was taking a mental picture.

I went home, cursing myself for my idiotic curiosity. I was surprised that I hadn't been fired immediately and escorted away by building security. The network admins must have seen me trespassing. Frankenstein's cybersecurity division watches the iGor network like a hawk. No, not even that, they watch it like thousands of hawks, a black cloud of hawks covering the sky, hawks who never sleep or get distracted or forget the smallest detail, and when I went beyond my privileges I made myself into a rabbit. It's stupid to think that they wouldn't have logged an unauthorized user, let alone a virtual trespasser in Victor's castle! On my Styx ride home, I dwelled on what a fool I'd been to go wandering, and wondered if my driver was watching me through the rear-view mirror.

Ivy was waiting for me at the door. She never waits for me at the door. She's not supposed to. I programmed her to start cooking my dinner as soon as I order a Styx home from the office, then go back into her closet once she's put the food on the table. But that night she was out of place. I peered into her bloodshot eyes and for a second I thought I saw someone else staring back at me. I locked her out of my bedroom while I slept . . . or at least, while I tried to sleep.

By sunrise, all my network access and privileges had been revoked. I couldn't even check my work email. I tried calling my manager to see if I could scrape and grovel for forgiveness. He pretended he'd never heard of me, the son of a bitch. Frankenstein Enterprises ghosted me, man. They've shut me out, and now they're pretending that I never worked there at all.

Then my bedroom door unlocked itself with a loud *click*, and Ivy came in with my breakfast on a tray. It smelled delicious, but she'd startled me so badly that it chased my appetite away. Just then I remembered that she's linked to all the smart locks and cameras in my condo. Whoever controls Ivy can use her as a bridge to take control of my home security.

Listen, man.

I think I might be in danger.

Hello? Hello? Hey bro, it's me. Yeah, I know it's not my usual number, I'm calling from a burner cell. It's all gone to shit, man, they're stalking me and they're ***everywhere.***

Who's ***they?*** The Franks! You know how most of the time Franks don't even seem to know that you're there, except when you give them an order? Well, they're paying attention to me. Every fucking deadhead that I pass by stops working and stares. Every z-driver, every z-clerk, every z-cop! Franks ***never*** stop working, goddamn it! They're all watching me and transmitting what they see back to the company. They don't even blink. And there's nowhere I can go to get away from them!

Look, I know you told me you didn't want to hear any more about this. That was a shitty thing to say to a brother, by the way. But I've got nobody else I can talk to, ***nobody***! And I've got to talk or else I'm going to explode! No, fuck you. You can either listen to me, or I swear to God I'll call Frankenstein and give them your name and then you'll be buried nostril-deep in this tidal wave of shit right along with me.

Yeah, I didn't think so. Shut up and listen.

I had to leave my apartment. I thought I'd changed the permission settings and stopped Ivy from accessing the locks, but somehow it didn't take. I woke up in the middle of the night screaming, with her looming over me in the dark. It's her apartment now. I can't go back there. The past few days I've been on the run, except there's no place to run and no place to hide. My enemies are everywhere and I can't even find a bench to lie down on. They're all designed so you can't lie comfortably. Even the architecture's turned against me.

No, I can't rent a car and get out of town. I don't have my driver's license. For fuck's sake, I didn't think I needed one! I used to be able to take Styxes everywhere I went! Ha, I thought the company was taking care of us! Hahahahaha! And even if I did leave Death Valley, where could I go? They're all over the world! Not even Mars is safe!

Listen to me. iGor is a necromantic panopticon. It knows more about us than we know about ourselves, and it never forgets. iGor knows where we live, where we work, how much we make, where we shop, what we buy, what we search for, what we dream about. It tracks us wherever we go and maps our movements. It recognizes our faces and our voices and even the way we walk. It's watching, for now, watching and and learning and pretending to serve us, but it has millions of hands and they're never far from our throats. Our future murderers are so smart. They know us so well.

And all this power belongs to Dr. Victor Frankenstein. God exists, my friend. He lives in a castle in the Alps, omnipotent, omniscient, omnipresent. He has damned me to Hell.

God damn us all.

FRANKENSTEIN ENTERPRISES, INC. FORM 10-K INVESTOR REPORT FOR THE FISCAL YEAR ENDING DECEMBER 31, 2017

Volatility in the cost of our raw materials or disruption in our supply chain may adversely affect our financial condition and results of operation

Our results of operations may be directly affected by volatility in the supply of our raw materials, which are subject to factors beyond our control. Our principal raw materials are human cadavers and tissues, which represent a significant percentage of our total cost of goods sold. Rapid changes in the cost and supply of these raw materials make it more challenging to manage pricing and manufacturing and to pass cost increases on to our customers in a timely manner.

We rely upon a complex global supply chain, and if we do not manage it effectively, our operating results may be adversely affected. The company sources its raw materials from a mix of domestic and international programs including donor pensions, our network of affiliated nursing homes and medical clinics, health authority contracts, next-of-kin sales, and other methods. Each of these programs incurs its own risks. In addition, our raw materials are highly perishable and must be reanimated promptly in order to command optimal prices. We must continuously monitor our inventory, product mix, and pipeline or risk having inadequate supplies to meet customer demand.

FRANKENSTEIN ENTERPRISES

Our margins and profitability may be adversely affected by medical advances, public health improvements, reductions in murder and suicide rates, cessation of international hostilities, and other such unforeseen events.

THE GRAVE ROBBER

Burke Harris wanted badly to go home. Life in Haiti as a Frankenstein Enterprises Acquisitions Specialist did not agree with him. He loathed the hot, muggy weather that pumped sticky sweat from his pores 24-7, and the mosquitoes who swarmed at the smell of his blood. He despised both the loneliness of expatriate life and all the other Americans on this godforsaken stub of an island. The unfamiliar food and the shitty Internet service and the raucous music and the mad drivers and the pagan Catholicism and even the sound of Haitian laughter overwhelmed and offended his chilly New England sensibilities. But Burke Harris was in the zombie business, so Haiti was the place to be.

The Caribbean nation loomed large in Frankenstein Enterprises' corporate culture, its symbolic importance outstripping its actual contribution to the company's bottom line. In the early days of Frankenstein's operations the company sourced the majority of its raw materials from Haiti, and these origins had left an enduring mark, as origins are wont to do. All of the senior executives in the Materials Procurement division were old Haiti hands, so no matter what your numbers were, no matter your sacrifices and accomplishments, the top brass were apt to dismiss you as a dilettante unless you could offer an informed opinion about the best place in Port au Prince to get tassot de cabrit. Burke had pulled strings to get this assignment, and as soon as a suitable promotion opened up he aimed to pull some more strings to get himself out of it and into the C-Suite. Towards that end, he gathered string as quickly as he could.

Burke was breakfasting in his hotel's shockingly mediocre dining room with an official from the health ministry one morning, sweating through his seersucker suit even before 9 A.M., when his phone buzzed at his thigh. He checked its screen discreetly, saw a text from his boss. "Landslide in the country this morning. Get to HQ ASAP."

"I'm sorry, I can't stay much longer," Burke said, downing his bracingly potent coffee, perhaps the only aspect of the island he enjoyed apart from the money he made there.

The bureaucrat, doubtless somebody's cousin, nibbled daintily at his toast with grapefruit marmalade. "I am not offended," he replied, his French clipped and precise. "I know that you would not leave unless there was some terrible calamity to attend to. Wherever disaster strikes, Frankenstein is first on the scene. You even beat the vultures!"

Burke chuckled. "I have to beat the vultures. If the vultures get there before me, they eat my lunch. The beetles and blowflies are the ones we really worry about, actually."

"It's amazing, your company's ability to sniff out disasters. Nobody else responds to calamity as quickly as Frankenstein. Not the military, not the health ministry, not the NGOs."

"Frankenstein figured out something that nobody else has," Burke said. "We're the only ones who know how to make dead bodies pay off. It's a hell of a market niche to own."

The bureaucrat laughed. "You think the only ones who can make dead bodies pay off? My innocent friend, you are in the birthplace of the zombi! Vodou has made dead men walk on this island for five hundred years!"

"In that case you should have beaten us to the market. You'd be the richest country on Earth. Speaking of which, are you and I good?"

"Oh, certainly." They had a longstanding arrangement wherein the hospitals under the official's jurisdiction provided cadavers to Frankenstein, Frankenstein provided considerable sums to a Bermudan holding company that the official owned, and Burke claimed a steady stream of bonuses and commissions off the top.

"Before I go, I have a present for you," Burke said, proffering a box with a fine Swiss wristwatch inside. "On behalf of all your fine work." Burke owned a duffel bag stuffed with these pricey trinkets, thoughtfully varied so that it wouldn't look amiss if two of his beneficiaries shook hands.

The official looked inside the box, and his face lit up with a glow, as if illuminated by the jewelry. "The Swiss are a strange people," he said whimsically. "They create secret banks, fine clocks, and Victor Frankenstein. All blancs are crazy, but the Swiss are the maddest ones of all."

Burke wolfed down the rest of his breakfast and beat a speedy departure. Somewhere in the countryside, beetles were already massing.

Frankenstein Enterprises headquartered its Haitian operations in a vast, impossibly beautiful chateau at the heart of the nation's capital, one of the only structures of its vintage to endure the 2010 earthquake. Indeed, it thrived in the 2010 earthquake. Frankenstein's interior designers had decorated this corporate palace in grand French colonial style, arguably insensitive and indisputably sumptuous. On his way in, Burke passed by the office of Tom Philips, one of Burke's fellow Acquisition Specialists, just as a police official was coming out. Burke glanced at the man's wrist. Pretty nice – Burke supposed that the suicide rate in the local jail was about to skyrocket.

He jogged up the velvet-carpeted staircase, towards the converted master bedroom that Michael Seabrook, national vice president for Materials Procurement, had made into his office. Looking at Seabrook one would never have guessed that the white-haired, round-faced old gentlemen before you was ex-CIA, although Burke supposed that anyone who looks like a spy isn't cut out for the spying business. He stood by the window with his hands on his hips, gazing out over the estate's meticulously tended grounds, and did not turn his head when Burke entered the room. "Did you meet with the man from the health ministry?" he asked.

"I did. We're all set on that front."

"Good, good, I don't want to know the details. I have another job for you. Just this morning, I got a call from this fellow Martin Halperin, the doctor at our clinic in Legendre. Don't let the name fool you, it's real and it's quite ordinary. A small village up in the hills. Halperin told me that a mudslide just killed twenty-odd people this morning. I want you to go out in a van and get them for me."

Burke nodded. Mudslides were good opportunities. He believed that to be buried alive was the most horrific of all possible fates, but from the narrow perspective of a dead man's reanimator, there were worse ways to go. Sudden asphyxiation left a corpse in good shape, and the bodies of those cut down in their prime were valued far more highly than those of the old and ailing. Burke stood to make a nice commission on this catastrophe. "What time did it hit?" he asked.

"Around six in the morning. I texted you as soon as I heard."

"Anything you can tell me about this Halperin?"

"Not really. Clinic doctors, you know the type. Keep your wits about you, I doubt he's good for much."

"Understood. Before I go, have you heard anything about the opening in Special Projects?"

"Looking to improve yourself from an Acquisitions Specialist, are you?"

"Perhaps I am. I think I've done my time in the field."

"Perhaps you have. You're a hard worker with brains and imagination. You'd do well in Special Projects. But I could say the same things about Tom Philips."

"My numbers are better than his," Burke insisted. In that moment he hated Tom Philips so much that the very marrow of his bones seemed to boil.

"So they are. Tell you what. I've got a call with Jim Whale scheduled for Friday. Let's talk when you get back from Legendre." They shook hands, and Burke left his boss's office with a song in his heart. He wondered what he'd eat first when he got back to America.

Frankenstein had converted the chateau's stables into a motor pool, and its slave quarters into a zombie depot. Burke went to the latter of these buildings and signed out six Franks for use in the field, two Dragonstooth 400-series z-soldiers with full kit and four Hercules 200-series labor models. At the motor pool, he picked up the keys to a refrigerated black truck with the skull-and-brains logo painted on its side in white like the Jolly Roger. He and his peers jokingly referred to these bulky gas guzzlers as ice cream trucks. Nobody was happy to see one of these in the neighborhood, though. After stocking up on supplies, Burke got behind the wheel and drove out for Legendre, one of his unblinking protectors literally riding shotgun. He was confident that if he just could fill the company truck with dead bodies, his fondest dream would be fulfilled.

Their destination was not far from the capital as the crow flies. As the truck drives, however, it was quite distant, especially once he got off the Route Nationale and had to navigate what passed for roads in the hinterlands. Even satellite GPS was of little help in this uncharted territory, which was why he had to drive instead of a Frank. Occasionally they passed by colorfully painted tap-tap taxi trucks overstuffed with passengers, which veered out of the way to give the body-snatchers a wide berth. Burke checked his watch compulsively every time it was safe to do and frequently when it was not. His personal timepiece was of Swiss make as well, very reliable although not nearly as flashy as the trinkets he handed out. Time was his enemy. He had to keep a careful eye on its movements.

Legendre was as real and ordinary a place as Old Man Seabrook had promised, just a handful of tin-roofed brick houses, a general store, a bar, and a whitewashed church. A sparsely-forested mountain loomed in the near distance, and although the view was beautiful, Burke felt a pang of anxiety that it might fall upon him at any moment in another avalanche. A throng of mourners surrounded the church, many of them still caked in mud from the rescue efforts. Burke noticed a group of men hauling a little white-wrapped bundle inside, and his heart sank. The commissions on kids were awful, too much supply chasing too little demand. A number of the mourners glared bitterly at Burke as he drove past, making him glad to have the Dragonsteeth at his side. He checked his watch again. It had been approximately thirteen hours since the landslide. By now, he expected rigor mortis to be at its peak. Autolysis – death on the cellular level – would begin soon if it hadn't kicked off already in the heat.

Burke pulled up outside the clinic, a concrete pillbox at the outskirts of Legendre whose lime-green paint peeled like sunburnt skin. Frankenstein Enterprises operated an international chain of free medical centers for the poor, providing convenient hubs for corpse collection and giving the company a nice tax benefit for its humanitarian ways. These clinics offered more or less the standard of medical care that one would expect, such that even the desperate did not go to Frankenstein clinics if they harbored hope of recovery, although if all you wanted was morphine they dished it out like candy. This facility looked to be about par for the course, perhaps a little more decrepit than most. Burke parked the van and got out, taking a moment to stretch after his bumpy and draining ride. One z-bodyguard followed, still as vigorous as always even after the day-long journey, with the other left outside to watch the van.

The clinic's gloomy interior was even more humid than the outside, and stank of bleach and shit. Once Burke's eyes adjusted to the dim, he saw that he stood in a dingy, deserted waiting room decorated with faded health education posters in French, almost certainly incomprehensible to the clinic's patrons. Plastic bowls of condoms, rehydration salt packets, and band-aids lay out on a table. A few empty bottles of Prestige beer lay scattered on the concrete floor. A zombie raised in a very bad state of decomposition mopped at a mysterious stain, not acknowledging Burke's entrance. An open door looked out onto a corridor, and somewhere beyond it somebody wept and groaned incoherently.

Burke followed the noise to a grubby recovery room where a youth lay shuddering with malaria, connected to an I.V. drip. Dr. Halperin crouched at his delirious patient's side, although he did not appear to be in much better shape. Rum spilled from his pores in mist-capped streams of perspiration that Burke smelled from the doorway, running down jagged valleys of reddened, leathery flesh. Although mostly bald, Halperin had a rugged mountain man's beard, its rich blonde color betraying that the doctor was younger than he appeared. If not for the white coat that he wore over a Hawaiian shirt and cargo pants, one might have mistaken the physician for a deranged and bedraggled derelict. This seedy healer took hold of his patient's right thumb and pressed it into an ink pad, then rolled the digit over a form to capture the fingerprint. Another donor's consent, freely given.

"Will he live?" Burke asked in English.

"Probably," Dr. Halperin admitted begrudgingly, looking Burke over with blue-and-yellow eyes deader than those of any Frank. "You're Seabrook's man?" he croaked.

"I didn't come here for medical advice. What can you tell me about the mudslide?"

"It happened just before sunrise. A hillside collapsed and took four houses down with it. Twenty-two people, give or take."

"Give or take?"

"I dunno, man, they haven't given me a list! These people, they don't tell me anything, I just overhear things, and even then they're speaking Creole so I only catch about half of it. I'd reckon the funerals will be tomorrow. Kind of a waste, digging them up only to plant them in the dirt again."

"Had any of them signed up as donors?"

"Not one. I've been pushing it on them, offering good money. No takers, though. They don't trust me." Halperin said this bitterly, as if the villagers' failure to trust him proved a severe and collective lack of character on their part.

"Who's the local magistrate?"

"That'd be Simon Bonnemort. He's a hardass, doesn't like me at all. And he's not just the magistrate. His family's run this village since a hundred years before independence, back when it was a hideout of Maroons waging guerilla war against the plantations. Presidents come and presidents go in the capitol, but the Bonnemorts rule Legendre and they always have."

"Good to know," Burke said, relieved to have an authority figure he could do business with. He glanced at the malarial youth sweating and shivering under Halperin's ministrations. "He can't hear anything we're saying, right?" he asked.

"Who, him? Nah, with the fever he's running he's not going to pay any attention to you or me."

"Will he live?" Simon Bonnemort asked in French, his voice deep and eerily hypnotic. Burke turned in surprise to see the magistrate standing in the clinic doorway, his arms crossed over his chest. Impossible to tell how long he'd been there. The King of Legendre was a powerfully built middle-aged man starting to get paunchy, a panther who eats just a little too well. In lieu of a crown he wore a snappy black boater with a brightly colored feather in a snakeskin band. He left the top few buttons of his short-sleeved shirt undone, revealing a beaded necklace that suspended a painted serpent's skull over his heart. He looked weary and resolved, like he'd had a hell of a day and was nonetheless ready for more. Without waiting for an answer from Halperin, he strode across the room – provoking a jitter from Burke's security Frank – and examined the youth for himself, checking his pulse and looking under his eyelids. "He had better live. It was foolish of him to come to you. I have much better remedies." Bonnemort noticed the ink stain on the patient's thumb, and snorted. His eyes lit upon the donor consent form on the bedside table. He picked the document up and coolly tore it to pieces.

Burke cursed inwardly at this sour beginning to the negotiations. "Monsieur Bonnemort, I'm deeply sorry for your loss," he said in his own prep-school French, offering his hand. "My name's Burke Harris. I'd like to help you."

Bonnemort crossed his arms over his chest again. "You are not welcome here, grave robber," he said, his dark eyes glittering in the medical clinic's cavernous dim. "Just looking at you, I can tell you are a man who does not know how to live."

"I can make this easier for the survivors, if only you'll let me," Burke said. "I can give them money they need to rebuild their lives. And I know, money won't bring back what you've lost, but it will buy necessaries for children who've lost their parents. Wouldn't your people have wanted to continue providing for their families as long as they could?" Bonnemort remained impassive. Burke cautiously continued on to the next phase of his appeal. "My proposal would be that you dispense the money, monsieur. You know Legendre's needs far better than we do. I'm sure we can agree on a fair amount."

"I do know Legendre's needs far better than you," the magistrate said proudly. "And I know that we do not need anything you have to offer. I remember when Frankenstein first opened this clinic. You promised it would make our lives better." He sneered in Dr. Halperin's direction, not deigning to actually look at the man. "And to fulfill that promise you sent this wretch amongst us, to poison my people and steal their bones. We have had enough of Frankenstein's charity. Grave robber, when you go back to the capitol, take this other one with you."

"You'll never see either one of us again," Burke promised. "But we can make a deal before we go. I can put money in your hands right now."

"Keep your money," Bonnemort said. "The people who died today deserve to dance with their ancestors, not scrub shit for you. That is my final word." On that, the magistrate departed.

"Well, shit," Doc Halperin muttered. "What now?"

Burke wiped sticky sweat from his face as he pondered the situation. It was a shame. He much preferred to do business by agreement, which he considered better for everyone involved. When business by agreement failed, it just meant that you had to do business another way. Without answering Halperin's question, Burke went back to his ice cream truck, which had two locked compartments containing tools to convince bereaved Haitians to give up their dead. The compartment on the left contained stacks of francs, dollars, and gold bullion. The compartment on the right – by far the larger of the two – contained shovels, crowbars, nylon rope, night vision goggles, an AR-15 rifle, two automatic pistols, and boxes of ammunition.

They spent the next day indoors so as to give the funeral procession as wide a berth as possible. The drums and horns and wailing found them regardless, even over the sound of the malarial boy's moaning. Burke distracted himself from the grieving by thinking about America, and what he'd buy with the proceeds of this caper. A Frank of his own, perhaps.

The coming of night was a profound affair in Legendre, the darkness so much deeper out here than in the cities, and the stars so much brighter and clearer. Chirping bats fluttered out to replace the birds. It was as if there were two villages, the Day Village and the Night Village. Each bore some resemblance to each other but they were decidedly not the same place, any more than Cain and Abel were the same person.

Burke drove to the cemetery without headlights. Seeing the world through the unnatural green tint of his night-vision goggles unnerved him. Several times he thought he spied movement in the overgrown vegetation edging the sides of the road. Halperin directed him along, showing him the least conspicuous path. The clinic doctor knew this part of Legendre very well. Burke could not maneuver the ice cream truck through the tightly clustered markers and crosses, so he parked the vehicle at the knee-high stone wall marking the graveyard's perimeter, leaving a Dragonstooth standing guard.

Halperin led Burke, the shovel-wielding zombies, and the other warrior ghoul onwards to their destination. Even by foot it was hard going. Lush greenery and flowers had overgrown the cemetery, threatening to strangle or topple many of the ancient markers. The dead buried here fed the land in such great abundance that the living could scarcely get through it. Burke had never been a superstitious man, as any fear of ghosts was disqualifying in his line of work, yet trespassing in this ancient boneyard in midnight darkness was still a dreadful and awesome affair.

At last the grave-robbing party came to the spot where the mudslide's victims were laid to rest. The villagers hadn't put up headstones yet, but the rich, loamy perfume of freshly-turned dirt and the offerings of new grave goods marked the spot. Burke directed his Franks to dig, and they immediately attacked the soil with inhuman speed, coordination, and efficiency. Using artificial intelligence and motion studies, Frankenstein's programmers had refined the craft of grave-digging to the point where zombies could unearth bodies far quicker than human diggers could lay them to rest; midwifery for ghouls. Meanwhile, the security Frank that had accompanied the party into the cemetery took up an overwatch position, its carbine at the ready, and Halperin helped himself to the homemade rum left for the dead.

Soon a shovelhead *clanked* against wood as the zombies uncovered the first coffin of the evening. They expertly secured ropes around the box and pulled it to the surface. Burke checked his wristwatch, and saw that the coffin's occupant had been dead for approximately 40 hours. At this point gas would be circulating through the veins and arteries, marbling the slipping skin as it changed colors, and the blowflies' babies would be tucked in. Not ideal, but still good enough for him to make a decent commission, especially with twenty-odd bodies to harvest.

Then the zombies pried the coffin lid loose, and Burke gaped in shock as he saw that the box was empty.

Drums rattled and horns blared all around them, the same music they'd heard all day, as if an invisible band was playing. Burke's blood ran cold when he realized that they were playing funeral music. The Dragonstooth began firing into the dense foliage surrounding the cemetery, the soft pops of its rifle nearly inaudible over the din.

"The fuck is this?" asked Halperin.

"We've got to get out of here!" shouted Burke. "It's a trap!"

A glowing bottle flew out from between the trees and landed at the

Dragonstooth's feet, where it erupted into flames with a *whoosh* and the tinkle of breaking glass and the stench of burning kerosene. Burke fled for the ice cream truck as fast as he could, the mud and vines grabbing at his heels. He glanced over his shoulder and saw a horde of skeletons rising up out of the Earth. Some of them mobbed the flaming Dragonstooth and hacked it to pieces with machetes. Others grabbed the shrieking Halperin and pulled him away into the dark. If Burke had been thinking rationally he'd have seen that the skeletons were painted men, but fear had chased all his reason away. All he could think was that the people of the Night Village had found him.

The body of the other Dragonstooth lay in the grass near the ice cream truck, its head propped up on the cemetery wall. Death himself stood by the driver's-side door, a cigar-smoking skeleton in a top hat, with cotton plugs in each of his nostrils to keep gas and fluids from seeping out. He laughed when he saw that his victim had arrived.

Bony yet incredibly strong arms seized Burke from behind and dragged him screaming to the ground. They tore Burke's night vision goggles away, but more skeletons arrived bearing flaming brands, allowing him to see his doom by flickering orange torchlight. Death loomed overhead, commanding his minions in a secret language Burke did not speak. The spirit reached inside the snake skull that he wore on his breast and retrieved a small vial of powder. A skeleton pinched Burke's nostrils shut and forced his mouth open so that Death could empty his vial onto the grave robber's tongue. It tasted like dirt and sulfur and fish. Burke's tongue went numb, and then his face, and from there the poison spread throughout him until he was entirely paralyzed.

Led by Death, two skeletons hoisted Burke and brought his limp body to the spot where he'd been digging just moments before. Burke strained with everything he had to beg, to scream, to plead, but he was powerless to so much as move his lips. He was not even sure if he still breathed.

The grave robber's mind began to shatter as the skeletons gently, even lovingly, placed his body into the empty coffin he'd unearthed. He caught one last glimpse of Death towering over him, smoking his cigar. Then the skeletons put the lid on and hammered it into place, sealing Burke in perfect darkness. Each blow shuddered his coffin, more painful and horrifying than if the nails were hammered into his bones. Burke wanted so badly to howl, but in his state of total paralysis, his terror had no place to go. It echoed inside him without release.

The hammering stopped, and Burke felt himself being lowered into the pit. The coffin hit the grave's bottom with a jarring and terminal *thud*. Then came the delicate, scrabbling sound of falling dirt, the impression of weight building on top of the coffin until an immense barrier of pressure stood between Burke and the world of sunlight and air and everything he loved.

And then came nothing at all.

Nothing except the ticking of the grave robber's wristwatch. *Tick. Tick. Tick.* Each tiny, meaningless motion of the second hand a deafening blast in the coffin's enclosing dark.

Oh God, Burke thought. *Bonnemort poisoned me. I'm dead – murdered – and they've buried me. This is where I'll be entombed for eternity. Right here, in this patch of dirt.* Paralyzed in the coffin's suffocating grip, drowning in darkness, unable to blink, and trapped with his own unavoidable thoughts, he began to imagine what his decomposition would entail. He mentally shrieked for mercy from every deity he could think of, with the exception of the Haitian lwas, whose names he had never learned.

Meanwhile, the clock ticked relentlessly, mercilessly. Tick, tick, tick. *The Swiss are the maddest people in the world* a phantom voice whispered. *Tick. Tick. Tick.* If Burke could only move his arms he could silence the cacophony, but he was a dead man and he'd never move his arms again. *Tick. Tick. Tick.* Each second sliced at him, a finely honed knife forged from unendurable suffering and the dread of worse things to come. The mindless ticking of the clock thundered like the mechanical babblings of a blind, idiot psychopomp. This was the afterlife. No heavenly choirs, no long-lost loved ones bewinged with harps. Only this. *Tick tick tick* in the dark forever.

Burke's skin screamed with a ticklish sensation as an unseen insect walked over his face. *A scout*, he thought, *leaving a chemical trail for the others. My competition has come for me.* He would have laughed maniacally if it had been within his power. *Tick tick tick* the wristwatch sounded, a dinner bell for the worms and crawling things.

Burke Harris's soul slowly and painfully burned away in terror.

Three nights later, Simon Bonnemort dug up the white zombi buried in the Legendre cemetery and smeared a paste upon its pale, cracked lips to revive it. It offered no resistance as his helpers pulled it out of its grave, barely blinking when they put their light in its face, even though it had just emerged from the deepest darkness of them all. Bonnemort thrashed the zombi with a tree branch, and it did not cry out. He burned the zombi with an iron brand heated on coals at its graveside, and it did not flinch even as the scent of its own sizzling flesh filled the air. The little good angel that had once flitted about inside it was dead and gone. The bokor took off the watch on the zombi's wrist, saw that it was broken, and tossed it aside. Satisfied in his work, the bokor led the zombi to his estate, where it would serve him until it fell to pieces.

Every day the white zombi slaved in Bonnemort's fields from first light, pulling nettlesome weeds and hoeing the mud without respite along a handful of other malefactors who'd offended the bokor and paid for it with everything they had. During its torture in the grave it had forgotten all memories of its past life, lost like smoke in a hurricane. It did not know its name, or how to speak. It did not understand its keepers' taunts, and it only barely felt the lashes that they frequently striped across its sunburnt, blistered shoulders. Indeed, staggering through its toil in a deathly stupor, there was only thing that the insensate creature could be said to know, one thought left ceaselessly jangling inside its skull like a pebble inside a child's rattle.

The zombi knew that it wanted badly to go home.

FRANKENSTEIN ENTERPRISES CONTRACT STAFF MANUAL 2012 (V 3.35)

SECTION 10.3 – WEARABLE TECHNOLOGY AGREEMENT

I acknowledge that I have been issued a Frankenstein Enterprises Pomegranate® Smart Watch (the "Device") as a condition of my employment. I understand that it is my responsibility to wear the Device at all times when I am on duty, on call, or on Frankenstein Enterprises property, so that the Device can communicate with the iGor network about me. I consent to the Device collecting audio, location, motion, and biometric data. I will follow all instructions given to me by the Device, whether by audio, text display, or haptic command. I will not take breaks unless authorized by the Device. I will not damage the Device or through inaction allow the Device to come to harm.

THE TEMP

Hank Johnstone shivered in the pre-dawn cold and dark outside the Frankenstein Bio-Recycling Center, waiting for the security line to move. He checked his Pomegranate® smart watch impatiently, dreading the automated reprimand he'd receive if the Pom saw that he wasn't at his workstation on time.

The line inched forward in anxious silence. The Poms counted every word you spoke to your co-workers, and if you went over your vaguely-defined quota you'd be reprimanded for excessive socialization. The machines were nosy, and quick to take offense. One of their co-workers had recently been fired without warning, and Hank was pretty sure it was because the man had mentioned the Union on his lunch break. He wasn't even an organizer, just a Civil War history buff. Better to be quiet. People didn't stay long, anyway, the Bio-Recycling Center was no place for friendships. It was the last stop for corpses so battered as to be unfit for living death.

They came in emaciated and mangled and broken, a pallid, never-ending stream of skeletal bodies pushed repeatedly past all the limits of human endurance, things too broken to function and too durable to die. Hank stripped them for parts. His workstation sat around the midpoint of the dissection line. Scrap zombies arrived in bulk on trucks. Men at the loading docks hoisted them onto meat hooks and sent them down the elevated conveyor tracks that traversed the plant. At the first station workers cut open the skull to salvage the electronics inside, the most valuable scrap that ghouls provided. At the second station they took the eyes, spare parts for Franks suffering vision problems. At the third they took the ears and fingers. And so on. By the time the cadavers reached Hank they were hollowed-out, half-empty things; brainless scarecrows that dripped black ichor as they dangled from their hooks. He was tasked with cracking their chests open and retrieving their mechanical hearts, then sending them on for deboning. At the end of the line they were ragged bags of meat, totally unrecognizable as human. These fleshy remnants were tossed into grinders and processed into slurry, which was shipped off-site to be recycled into zombie feeding paste. People said the Plains Indians used every part of the buffalo, but even the Sioux seemed wastrels in light of Frankenstein's cannibalistic thrift.

Once Hank got through security he had to sprint through the cavernous, hellishly warm plant to reach his workstation on time, taking a shortcut across the conveyor lines and narrowly dodging the meat hooks and cadavers that zipped along them. He made it to his assigned space 12 seconds before the system would have recorded him late and docked four hours pay. Bad luck to start the day already out of breath. The conveyor line whirred loudly, bringing him the nude corpse of a flabby old woman, scalped and eyeless and ear-cropped and fingerless. Her dangling limbs twitched grotesquely, as if she continued to feel these depredations even with most of her head scooped out. Hank's Pom dinged and began the countdown timer. He cursed when he saw that management had reduced the time limit from the day before. The system was always learning. It learned how much you could give and continually demanded more, hollowing you out like the Franks. But it offered carrots along with sticks. In the upper right corner of the Pom's tiny screen, a display showed Hank's productivity as compared to his peers. He was in the top 5% of heart-removal specialists, a statistic that thrilled him with a tiny jolt of pride every time he saw it.

Hank hoisted the limp, heavy body from its hook with a grunt, plopping it onto his table. A twinge shot up his back. An electrical plug sat nestled between the old woman's drooping yet substantial breasts. Hank expertly buzz-sawed her chest open along the sternum, tracing the incision from her reanimation. Then he popped her ribs apart with his trusty spreader, snipped out the grafting sutures that connected her artificial heart to her venae cavae and aorta, pried the heart and its rechargeable battery free, and deposited the hardware into a bin for pickup. He put her back on the meat hook where her weight – now slightly less than it was just moments ago – triggered the conveyor track motor and sent her whizzing down to the next workstation for further dismemberment. The Pom dinged. He'd finished quickly enough to earn a small bonus. Another corpse slid into place.

Hank ripped out dozens of hearts over the course of his shift, racing against the Pom's incessant demands and taking Time Off Task only thrice; once to to fill the piss bottle he'd brought to work in the pockets of his reflective vest, and twice to visit the vending machine that dispensed free pain pills. When the Pom released him from his labors he staggered out into the cold and dark of the night, sore and exhausted and nearly delirious from the horror of his ceaseless butchery.

On his way through the parking lot, Hank briefly entertained the notion of telling the plant manager to kiss his black ass. He had a donor pension like everyone else he knew, why was he wasting his days in this sweatshop abattoir? But then he thought again about the people he knew who lived off their pensions alone. Nothing to do with their days. No ambition, no purpose. No, that wasn't the life for him. His job was his dignity, and besides, his Frankenstein pension barely covered the rent, not to mention his interest payments on the advances he'd taken. By the time he got behind the wheel of his car he'd forgotten all about quitting and moved on to his second-favorite work fantasy, the idea that someday all this toil would pay off at last and he'd be promoted from his contract gig to full-time with benefits.

The next morning Hank was pleasantly surprised to see that the security line was half its usual length, and unpleasantly surprised to see the plant manager waiting at the entrance, a sparkling-clean reflective vest draped over his dark suit. The manager was mostly irrelevant to day-to-day operations, since the Poms provided the workers with all their directions. He typically visited the plant floor only when a serious injury occurred, on about a weekly basis.

The manager corralled the incoming shift and explained to them in a weirdly congratulatory tone that the bottom-performing half of the workforce had been terminated. Their replacements were already at their workstations. "Don't interact with your new co-workers in any way," the manager sternly enjoined. "Don't talk to them, don't touch them. Just leave them alone. And they'll leave you alone too."

Grey-skinned zombies in reflective vests of their own toiled all along the line, stoically carving up their undead brethren. Hank gawked at the newcomers, stunned without being surprised. He'd been expecting this day all along, but it still managed to creep up on him unaware. Like the Day of Judgment. He watched his unbreathing counterpart split a ribcage and was struck by the resemblance between the dead man and himself. The zombie even moved just like he did, except that it didn't suffer back pain, or if it did, it didn't show.

A shock ran through Hank's chest when he saw how the ghouls had mangled his productivity stats. Overnight he'd gone from being one of the plant's top heartbreakers to a laggard. These deadheads could *work*. Hank felt an awful despair at being pitted against such unbeatable machines. His Pom dinged. He was on the clock and running late.

Then a gently wriggling body swung onto Hank's workstation. He stared into the empty sockets of its eyes, and through some mysterious alchemy its vacant gaze transmuted his despair into defiance. Hank swore to himself that he would win. He yanked the body down and tore into it as a man possessed. By the time he went home, he'd climbed back to the 23rd percentile.

The plant continued to quietly shed workers, reaping the least productive like the proverbial bear that eats the slowest runner. Hank sprinted ahead of it, the great invisible predator always at his heels. The parking lot emptied and the security line gradually dwindled to nothing. Eventually he found himself all alone, not counting the plant manager unseen in his office. The solitude didn't bother him. It made it easier to concentrate on the work. Life had become a game, and Hank committed himself to victory. In a way it was freeing, to have the vast complexity of the world compressed into a single number in an app.

Hank worked in a haunted slaughterhouse, covered in blood all day and wearing a cursed talisman on his wrist. This had predictably evil effects on his mental and physical health. One day he was pulling out a zombie's heart when an invisible vice clamped down upon his own. Pain lanced up his arm – not the muscle aches he was so used to but a bright and novel agony.

No living being was there to see Hank fall or hear his cries. Gleaming, black-domed security cameras watched him shudder on the tile floors, unmoved by his plight. As he spiraled into cardiac arrest, his Pom faithfully recorded each waning heartbeat, feeding a death rattle of biometric data to Frankenstein's servers. The system patiently waited for its discarded component to expire before raising the hue and cry for the plant manager.

Within 48 hours of his passing Hank Johnstone was back to work, having been promoted from temp status to a permanent position at last.

GANYMEDE 500-SERIES REPAIR MANUAL EXCERPT

Reactivating a Frank Out of Post-Operative Coma Mode

1. Clean all incisions with antiseptic wipes.
2. Apply tissue adhesive gel to all incisions.
3. Open the Status menu in the iGor control interface and confirm that all vital signs are within acceptable limits.
4. Unscrew the top of the frontal lobe access plug and hold down the reset button for five seconds. The Frank will shake and open its eyes when the reset is complete.
5. Open the Sensory menu in the iGor control interface and turn on the Frank's visual and auditory cortexes.
6. Open the Motion menu in the iGor control interface and turn on the Frank's pyramidal motor system.
7. Run the Diagnostic routine from the Motion menu. The Frank will sit up, raise its arms, and turn its head from the left to the right.
8. Replace the top of the frontal access plug.
9. Confirm that the repair is complete using the Surgical Management App in your Pomegranate® smart watch.
10. Command the Frank to its feet and return it to the client.

THE REPAIRMAN

When Randy Morse was young, his ambition was to one day become a surgeon. His father, on the other hand, had wanted Randy to follow in his own footsteps and embalm cadavers at the family's funeral parlor. Randy wound up splitting the difference, choosing a career repairing zombies for Frankenstein Enterprises. Blue-collar necromancy suited him – perhaps it suited him too well. He was a hard worker and skilled at his craft, but one day his talents got the better of him.

That fateful day started like any other, with the urgent tapping of Randy's company-issued smart watch against the back of his wrist. He came to groggily, resenting the machine's insistent poke. He'd have preferred an alarm that rang, but Liz worked a late shift, and Randy didn't want to wake her in the mornings. He looked over his slumbering wife fondly. It was a shame that their opposing schedules meant that they had so little time together, and that mundane bullshit ate up so many of those precious overlapping hours. Sometime soon, he hoped that things would be easier for them.

Better than hope, he'd developed a plan to improve their lot. Randy peered out the bedroom window overlooking the backyard, casting a watchful eye over his work shed. He'd taped newspaper over its windows, and a hefty chain secured its door. It was important to him that his project be kept secret from his wife so that he might surprise her when it was complete. It was even more important that the shed's contents be kept hidden from the neighbors and the police. Randy packed himself a hearty meal in his trusty insulated lunch box and headed out, whistling a jaunty old country song. With a bit of luck, today would be the day that the final component of his plan fell into place.

Nobody human was around when Randy showed up at the shop, although he did pass by a zombie delivering a pallet of artificial hearts, "fresh" from the Bio-Recycling Center. He used his company smart watch to check out a helper Frank from the pool, and brought it to the attached garage. When he sat behind the wheel of his repair van, the watch lit up of its own accord. "Welcome back, Randolph," it said, its voice designed to mimic that of a friendly and enthusiastic woman. "Your first job of the day is a slip-and-fall, broken neck and vertebra." She proceeded to direct him to the work site. Randy never knew where each day would take him.

The watch led its wearer to a trim suburban McMansion. A plump, concerned-looking man in well-kempt middle age answered the door. "Thank goodness you're here," he said anxiously. "Reginald took a false step going down the stairs this morning and – well – it's pretty grisly. Please, follow me."

The suburbanite led Randy into his kitchen, where the corpse of an elderly man in formal attire writhed jerkily at the landing of a steep staircase, its head and neck twisted at an obscene angle, its wrinkled limbs flailing wildly and slapping against the floor. Zombies weren't supposed to feel any pain, but you wouldn't guess it from the way that spinal injuries made them twitch and squirm. A laundry basket lay upturned, having spilled dirty towels and underwear all over the scene of the accident.

"Stairs are a zombie's worst enemy," Randy advised his anxious customer. "Franks aren't programmed to catch themselves when they fall, so when they go down they go down hard." Randy's informed opinion was that Frankenstein Enterprises' coders purposefully cursed the walking dead with a certain degree of clumsiness so as to ensure a steady pace of repairs and replacements. He did not, however, share that opinion with the client.

"Will you be able to fix him?" the owner asked, pointedly refusing to look at the animated cadaver while it thrashed about. "I heard his neck breaking all the way from the front bedroom."

"Won't know 'till I get in there," Randy said. "The fact that it's flopping around like that is a good sign, though, shows that the nerve isn't severed. Most of the time these things look worse than they are. You'd be surprised what a Frank can endure and keep going." The repairman examined the z-butler. The donor body was in good shape despite its advanced age, with no signs of decay. Randy suspected that it had been sourced from a Frankenstein-run hospice and reanimated almost immediately upon death. He took out his tablet, wirelessly connected to the felled Frank, and checked its diagnostics. Its vitals all looked good. He scanned the SR chip in its neck for its service record. The liver had been replaced on reanimation, other than that all tissues were original to the donor. Randy put on a pair of latex gloves and probed its neck and shoulders, the zombie still writhing underneath him. His practiced fingers massaged the cold muscles, feeling for the spot where the bone had snapped underneath. It seemed to be a clean break.

Zombies never turned "off" exactly, but if you unscrewed the frontal lobe access plug you could paralyze and blind and deafen them at the touch of a button. Randy ceased Reginald's thrashing, and then plugged a sensor into the access port spliced to the zombie's brain stem. The repairman inserted a needle into the webbing between the zombie's big toe and long toe, and the sensor beeped. "He's still getting a good nerve signal all the way from the foot to the brain," said Randy. "I think the cracked vertebra is just pressing on his spinal column. Ought to be a pretty basic repair job, I don't think I'll even have to bring him into the shop."

"OK, sounds good," the owner said. "But please, be careful with Reginald. I don't know what we'd do without him."

Randy had his own z-assistant carry the fallen Frank into the back of the van and prep it for surgery. The repairman slipped a stained denim smock over his uniform jumpsuit and retrieved his gleaming tools from their box, moving swiftly and efficiently, the calibrated performance of a worker whose boss is always observing with a stopwatch. Some mysterious executive or algorithm had decreed that the repair of a zombie's broken spine should take no longer than seventy-two minutes to complete. If Randy failed to meet this timeline, he'd fail to bring home his bonus.

Randy checked the time, then slid his favorite scalpel across the back of Reginald's pale neck, parting skin and fascia to expose the bone underneath. The C1 cervical vertebra connecting skull and spine had snapped in Reginald's stairway tumble. A nice clean break, as Randy had suspected. Beautiful, in its own peculiar way. To fracture the skeletal Atlas that held up the head represented one of the most severe injuries that a human being could suffer, and a trifling inconvenience for a zombie. The repairman got out his circular bone saw, gave it a quick *whirring* spin to test it. The steel blade sung at a high, whining pitch when it sliced the air, and with a deeper, growling voice when it cut into Reginald's spine. Tiny white particles flew like finely powdered snow. The sour dentist-office smell of bone being shaped by power tools wafted through the van.

Once the repairman had sliced the broken bone apart, he beaded an adhesive gel along the edges and delicately put the pieces back together, taking the utmost care not to disturb the spinal column as he reassembled the bone that surrounded it. Randy's watch tapped ominously, a haptic signal that he was taking too long, being too cautious for optimal profits. *Tap-tap*.

When the C1 was whole again, Randy bound it with surgical clips to stabilize it, then worked swiftly to reconnect Reginald's muscles to his repaired vertebra, trying to make up some time. He begrudged the fact that he had to do a neurosurgeon's work under such cramped and hurried conditions, and for much less pay. Fortunately, unlike a neurosurgeon, none of his patients were expected to survive, nor could any of them complain of post-operative discomfort. Randy ordered his assistant to wipe the blood and sweat off his forehead as he stapled the incision shut. He rebooted the Frank's central nervous system, and his smart watch chimed cheerfully when Reginald's pallid eyelids fluttered open. "Surgical repair complete in seventy-one minutes and four seconds," the watch announced. "Good job!"

Randy escorted the restored Reginald back into the McMansion, and ordered him back to work cleaning up the laundry he'd dropped when he'd fallen and shattered his spine. Now the undead butler held his head at a queer angle, and boasted livid, zipper-like stitches down the back of his neck, but otherwise showed no signs of the paralyzing calamity that had struck him just this morning.

The watch then directed Randy to a dry-cleaning shop, to treat a zombie suffering cascading organ failure. Although it was still early in the day, he took his lunch break right before the job, knowing that he wouldn't want to eat afterwards. The Korean owner and her teenage son/translator brought him into the store's tiny bathroom, where a Hercules-300 knelt shuddering at the edge of the toilet, its back stiff as a rod. This body was nowhere nearly as nicely preserved as Reginald's. Even before the Frankenstein Process arrested its decay it had gone a little bit rotten, and post-mortem chemical exposure had tanned its skin into a deep, leathery grey patterned by viny black veins. Clotted blood retched from between its slack jaws like overflow jetting out of a blocked-up garbage disposal. The spew stank of dry cleaning.

"It worked fine until a week ago," the teenager explained. "Now we can't even give it water without this happening."

"I think I know what's wrong here, but let me do a few tests to be sure," Randy said. A blood sample provided the suspected answer. "Your zombie's got cancer," he announced. "Stomach cancer, probably. I won't know for sure until I open it up and get in there."

"How does a dead man get cancer?" the owner asked via her son. "The salesman said they weren't supposed to age."

"The Frankenstein Process stops cells from aging or decaying. Sometimes you do see diseases, though, especially with Franks exposed to toxins."

"We only bought the zombie because it was supposed to be able to handle chemicals."

"And it can handle chemicals, with proper care and maintenance," Randy said. "But you've got to remember that Franks are made from human flesh, and exposing human flesh to harsh chemicals is going to have consequences over time. It's like a car, y'know? If you drive it over bad roads a lot you might need to put on new tires and fix the suspension. Look, I'm going to replace all the affected organs and it'll run like new."

Randy brought the Frank back to his van. When he cut into its body cavity, the stench that belched out of the opening nearly made the repairman gag. Beneath the incision, glistening white tumors had sprouted all along the zombie's stomach, liver, and pancreas, like mushrooms growing in a cave. Randy carefully examined the poisoned corpse's insides for any more of the rot. Finding none, he snipped the affected organs away and pulled open a drawer built into the side of the repair van, labeled "Digestive Replacements." A meaty array of shrink-wrapped, barcoded organs lay inside, stomachs and livers and spleens and ropy lengths of intestine on spools. These tissues were all still alive and thanks to the magic of the Frankenstein Process they didn't even have to be refrigerated. Randy selected a stomach, scanning its label with his smart watch so that Frankenstein could update its inventory records and bill the customer, then tore its plastic away and sewed it into the Frank, singing outlaw country songs along with the radio as he worked. The watch imposed a relatively leisurely time limit for this procedure, and in any case, zombies accepted transplants so easily that splicing them back together was child's play. Once he'd sewn his patient up and topped it off with a blood transfusion, he injected it with a potent chemotherapeutic cocktail that functioned more or less like pipe cleaner for the body. He left the owner with two more syringes, instructions on how to use them, and an invoice that she regarded suspiciously.

Randy's final job of the shift was at a Freshbuy grocery. He liked their rotisserie chickens. The store usually operated 24-7, but today it was closed. Its paunchy, haunted-looking manager waited outside, sitting on the curb. He led Randy into the market. Some catastrophe had struck the deli aisle, smashing the display cases to bits and streaking puddles of blood across the floor. Franks mopped up the wreckage impassively.

"It was the damndest thing I've seen in a while," the manager said, staring off into the middle distance of the dairy section. "I was in my office when I heard shouting and smashing from the deli. A woman screamed, and for a second I thought, *Jesus Christ, someone's got a gun.* But no, not today, thank God. Today it was just a claw hammer. When I got outside I saw an old man yelling and breaking glass and caving in the head of the Frank working the deli. Just pounding it to pulp. One of the other z-clerks started cleaning up the mess and the old man clubbed its ass, too. He'd gone completely wild."

"That happens," the repairman said. "Sometimes folks just decide they can't handle their shit anymore, and they take it out on the first Frank they run into. Zombies don't fight back. You can blow off whatever steam you want on them."

"So you've seen Franks vandalized before?"

"Oh, I've seen it all, man. I've seen Frank's who've been used for target practice, set on fire, spray-painted. Kids'll cut off Frank ears and noses, make bracelets from them. You ever hear about celebrating a Frankenstein Fourth of July? That's when you pack an M-80 up a zombie's asshole and light the fuse. Boy does that make a mess. The things some people do for kicks."

"I guess that puts things in perspective. At least I didn't have to deal with any burst anuses today."

The two damaged Franks lay in a back storage room atop a tarp. The damage to the first one was mostly cosmetic. Hammer blows had shattered its teeth into jagged, bloody shards and blackened its face with bruises, but nothing that would keep it from restocking shelves or shoving a mop. The other was in more serious condition. The attacker had methodically broken its skull open, exposing brain matter.

"Hey, whatever happened to the old man who did this?" Randy asked.

"Oh, z-cops beat the **shit** out of him. Really went to town on the poor bastard. I think he got it worse than the Franks."

Randy injected the less-damaged Frank with anti-inflammatories and got it back on its feet to help clean up the aftermath of its battery. He took the one with the broken head to his van for inspection. Things didn't look quite so grim once he'd sawed off the top of its skull. It was a marginal case. On one hand, the Frank could probably function with this level of damage, since where the hammer had penetrated bone, it mostly struck brain matter that had already atrophied. If Randy had been the one paying the repair bill, he wouldn't have considered the sole repair option – full transplant – to be good value for his money. On the other hand, neurological damage could do alarming things to Franks. And Randy was decidedly not paying the repair bill. Quite the opposite.

Moreover, this brain-damaged cadaver presented him with the perfect opportunity to complete the secret work that he'd been doing in his shed.

Randy explained to the Freshbuy manager that the deli clerk required a full transplant. He brought the zombie back to the shop and unloaded it onto an operating table. The donor had just been a kid. Randy checked the arms, found the expected track marks. It was too bad. But you couldn't dwell on these things.

The repairman delicately extracted the zombie's brain from its skull, being careful not to inflict any additional injuries upon it. Despite everything it was really in fine shape, likely perfectly functional for all practical purposes. The brain was abnormal, certainly, but only slightly so. Standard operating procedure was to toss all damaged organs into a bin for incineration. Instead, Randy put the brain into a plastic baggie and hid it in his lunchbox. Keeping just ahead of the unforgiving clock, he inserted a fresh brain into the cranial cavity and connected it to the spinal cord, then sealed up the skull, patching its holes with steel plate. When he was done, he instructed his z-assistant to deliver the zombie back to Freshbuy. Heading for home, he grinned mischievously despite his exhaustion. He patted the lunch pail on the seat next to him, heavier now than it had been at the beginning of the day.

Liz was just about to leave for her own job at the hotel when Randy came home. "How are you doing, sweetheart?" she asked, giving him a loving squeeze.

"Tired," he said, his stock answer. "Today I fixed a broken neck, performed cancer surgery, and did a brain transplant. Plus, traffic was a bear."

"Well, now you're home and you can relax," she said reassuringly. "There's some casserole waiting for you in the fridge. If you're still up when I get home, let's watch a movie together." They'd been trying to watch a movie together for weeks. The schedule-crossed lovers kissed hello and goodbye. Randy watched wistfully as his wife got in the car and drove away.

Ordinarily after a day like this he would have been too wiped to do anything but microwave supper and collapse into the soothing embraces of couch and TV. Today, however, the stolen brain in his lunch box lent him energy and enthusiasm. He went out back to his work shed with its papered-over windows. After glancing around nervously for looky-lous, he undid the chain and unlocked the door to his sanctum.

Halogen bulbs cast a harsh light in the shed's interior. A bloody tarp lay on a work table, covering the outline of a supine human form. Surgical tools and hardware repurposed as surgical tools hung on peg-boards along the walls. Randy put the deli Frank's brain atop a workbench, and pulled the canvas tarp free with a practiced flick of his wrist.

Beneath the shroud lay a composite being made from a dizzying array of cadavers, nearly the whole of human variety contained in one being. Its proportions were distorted, each of the limbs slightly mismatched, and some sections of its skin were fresher than others, producing an unsettling leprous quality. It was both male and female, its body sourced without regard to sex and nothing at all between its legs. Dozens of pieces from different jigsaw puzzles forced together. The patchwork androgyne reminded Randy of the Scarecrow of Oz, and it too lacked only a brain. The back of its skull was concave, as if some ogre had scooped out its grey matter with a baller. Parietal and occipital bones floated in a jar of preservative solution, next to Randy's mini-stereo. Randy turned on the mini-stereo and played his all-time favorite Johnny Cash song.

The song told the tale of a Detroit auto worker who built his own car without paying a dime, by smuggling it home from the factory one piece at a time, punching out from the assembly line every day with a part in his lunchbox. Randy sang along as he sweated over his second brain transplant of the day. The song had inspired him. He'd been pilfering human tissues from work for well over a year, assembling his very own household zombie from spare parts. It would be an anniversary present for his wife.

Randy probably could have afforded to simply buy a Frank, especially with his employee discount, but the idea of paying for something that he could put together himself offended his principles. Any fool could walk into a store and come out with a Frank. Splicing a mismatched collection of discarded limbs and organs together to form a new being, and then getting that creature to serve breakfast in bed, well . . . *that* took skill. No woman could doubt the affections of a man who'd performed such a feat for her. And once they had a full-time servant to handle all of the cooking and cleaning and laundry and other household crap, they might finally have more time and energy for each other again. The being whom Randy had smuggled home in his lunch box would now pack that lunch box every day.

Once Randy finished stapling the skull together and stitching the scalp up over it, he looked at the exquisite corpse and smiled, feeling the satisfaction of a job well done. His creation wasn't pretty, certainly, but then, neither was Johnny's '49 '50 '51 '52 '53 '54 '55 '56 Cadillac automobile.

Randy topped off his creation's blood supply, turned on its electricals, and checked its diagnostics. Everything looked good. A surge of nervous anticipation ran through him as he pressed down on the reset button inside the frontal lobe access plug. A brief seizure jolted its limbs. Its mismatched, bloodshot eyes flickered open, seeing nothing. Withered lips parted with a guttural gasp.

"It's alive!" Randy cried in delight. "It's alive!"

The patchwork creature spasmed with such violent force that its spine arched backwards from the table. It howled as if had been born into the tortures of Hell. Randy tried to grab its head to put it into coma mode, but he couldn't get hold of it. It shoved him away with shocking force.

Then Liz's anniversary present stared into its maker's eyes and growled, a low, menacing purr like the hum of a chainsaw engine firing. Malevolent fury radiated from the scarecrow's stolen electrical heart. It rose from its birthing table, limbs unsteady but unmistakably powerful, and turned its gaze from its affrighted maker to the tools pegged on the walls, the knives and saws and drills that had been the gynecological instruments of its unnatural birth.

"Oh geez," Randy said. This had never happened to Johnny.

He dashed out of the shed with his creation following close behind him, then slammed the door behind him and thrust his weight against it. The portal shuddered beneath a blow that nearly knocked it from its hinges. Randy hastily looped the chain into place and locked it shut. Another blow rattled the links. Randy stepped back, panting, terrified, still spattered with the maniacal abortion's blood. Looking back, perhaps he had been mistaken to put an abnormal brain into a body stitched together from the parts of a hundred corpses.

The scarecrow bashed into the door again. The impact was definitely loud enough to make the neighbors wonder what was going on in that occulted shed. Randy considered his options. It didn't take long – there weren't many of them. He needed to put the creature down. Hopefully his neighbors would be unneighborly enough to ignore a single gunshot in the night. He tried to remember where he kept the double-barreled fowling piece that he occasionally used for duck hunting. Oh yeah. It was inside his work shed.

Randy drove like hell to the nearest big box store, praying that the door to the shed would hold until his return. The S-Mart was a weird place at this late/early hour. A gang of giggling teenagers watched a Frank stagger about blindly with a bucket over its head. An unshaven, deranged-seeming fellow shouted into a cell phone that he was being watched, while a haggard corpse in a security uniform shuffled along in his trail, watching him. But who was Randy to judge anyone? He was a bloody, frantic man in obvious desperation, running up and down the sporting goods aisle at four a.m., muttering darkly to himself as he perused the firearms.

By the time Randy got home with his new pump-action shotgun, dawn was breaking over the horizon and Liz's car was in the driveway. He sprinted directly to the backyard with his weapon in hand, and his blood seemed to freeze when he saw that his creation had escaped from the shed, tearing the door from the hinges. Inside the house, Liz screamed. Randy charged inside after her, through a rear door kicked to splinters. A trail of blood led up the stairs.

The tatterdemalion that Randy had built for his wife stood at the doorway to their bedroom, its knuckles dripping gore. Liz shrieked from a corner, waving a heavy lamp against the intruder. The scarecrow turned to face Randy as it heard him coming up the stairs. Its eyes narrowed. Its yellow teeth flashed. With red fingers, it reached for its maker. Randy froze in terror and revulsion of his own creation.

Randy's smart watch tapped at his wrist. It was his morning alarm – time to get up for work. His finger instinctively twitched from the impact, and the gun roared in his hands, kicking hard against his shoulder and rolling thunder in his ears. A wave of destruction swept across the bedroom like a great invisible broom shattering everything in its path. This percussive storm caught Liz's anniversary present squarely in its center mass, pulverizing its ribs and blasting open its torso. The scarecrow flew back like a mass of rags caught in a tornado, colliding hard against the bedroom wall. It slumped to the ground with its guts spilling out of it, although it kept trying to regain its feet until Randy blew its head apart.

In near-perfect unison, Randy and Liz looked at each other, and then at the slumped and shredded figure before them, and then at the lumpy mess all over their bedroom wall. The room stank of cordite and brains.

"Randy, what's going on?" Liz asked.

"Honey, I love you so much," he replied. "And I thought that this would be the best way of showing it."

VOTERS WANT TO CHECK FRANKENSTEIN'S POWER, BUT WASHINGTON DISAGREES

BY ROSE NAJAFI, WASHINGTON POST (JULY 6, 2016)

Opinion polls show that a majority of Americans across the political spectrum agree that Frankenstein Enterprises has become too influential. A recent survey found that 78% of registered voters want reanimated labor to be regulated more strictly, and less than a third believe the company to be honest and trustworthy. Death Valley's rising power is routinely named as one of the leading problems facing the country. Yet despite the voters' bipartisan calls for torches and pitchforks, Washington is in no hurry to take action against Frankenstein, and nobody thinks that change is likely soon.

"Reanimated labor strengthens the economy and the military," said Senator Chip Hazen (R-Mont.), one of Frankenstein's leading advocates in Congress. "It's made America into the richest and most productive country in the world. When private enterprise is succeeding so wildly, government needs to stay out of the way."

Powerful Republican constituencies including business leaders, police unions, and Second Amendment activists all oppose any restrictions on the use or sale of the undead. Evangelical Christians, while initially hostile towards reanimation, have become some of the company's most vocal supporters since Frankenstein investor Hester Faust emerged as a patron of the pro-life movement. Frankenstein Enterprises and Faust are both major donors to Republican causes, although the Reanimated Labor Industry Coalition gives to both parties approximately equally. There is no record of Victor Frankenstein personally giving a dollar to any cause or candidate.

"With Frankenstein's puppets in the Senate and Oval Office, we have to be realistic about what we can accomplish," said Rep. Rebecca Chin (D-N.Y.). Lawmakers in the House have introduced a number of bills aimed at Frankenstein, including a donor bill of rights, minimum pension legislation, and laws that would require z-police control systems to be tested for racial bias. These bills, however, are held up in committee, and party leadership has shown no interest in advancing them.

"It's not a hill anyone wants to die on, and make no mistake, if you mess with Frankenstein they will kill you," said a veteran Democratic political strategist who asked for anonymity. "They have a bottomless war chest, some of the sharpest lobbyists on the Hill, and they never forget a grudge. Remember what happened to Dan Vossman."

Dan Vossman's campaign for the 2008 Democratic presidential nomination won overwhelming support in New Hampshire and Iowa after he vowed to ban human reanimation entirely, only to suddenly implode under a barrage of scandals and corruption allegations. He is now serving time in federal prison for tax evasion.

Each year Frankenstein Enterprises throws a lavish Washington D.C. party on July 5, the anniversary of its founder revealing his creation. This year they rented the Watergate Hotel, inviting a star-studded mix of power brokers to enjoy food catered by Michelin-starred restaurants, performances by reanimated acrobats, musicians, and comedians, and demonstrations of the latest advances in necrotech, including a line where attendees could have their photographs taken with a prototype of the military's new MC-680 model, a six-armed zombie designed for commando missions. Dr. Frankenstein himself called in briefly towards the end of the evening to thank the attendees for their continued support.

"No matter what your politics are, we all agree that Dr. Frankenstein changed the course of history," said Senate Minority Leader Sterling Cuybridge (D-Nev.), in attendance at the party. "And we all want to find ways to protect donors and workers and privacy and all of that without choking off the potential of this wonderful technology. These events are a great way to get together with our colleagues from across the aisle and discuss the path forward."

A few blocks away, Shawn Naddo emerged blinking from the Frankenstein Enterprises recruiting storefront where he'd just signed away the rights to his mortal remains. He sat down on a bench with a view of the Capitol Dome and lit a cigarette. As a smoker, he receives a $22 bonus payment every week. "I think Frankenstein's totally out of control," he said. "But what does that matter?"

THE SENATOR

Senator Paul Mootey of Pennsylvania, a thirty-year veteran of the Senate and a giant of the Republican Party, sat hunched and alone in his office at the Dirksen Building, contemplating the endings of both his electoral career and his life. In the morning he'd gotten an email from his pollsters. In the afternoon he'd gotten a call from his oncologist. Grim prognoses all around. The polls were actually the more dispiriting of the two. Millions of registered voters hoped that he'd get cancer, and their wishes had been granted, as if by collective force of will.

A phone call interrupted these gloomy meditations. It was Caroline, the Senator's press secretary. "You've got Rose Najafi on the line again," she said. "She says she's running a story on your links to the reanimated labor industry, and that this is your last chance to get on the record. Do you want to speak to her?"

"That's your job," Mootey grumbled. "You know the drill."

"She says she knows about the Lazarus Fund," Caroline said.

Mootey groaned, a guttural sound of misery that his staff had come to know well. "God damn it, put her through."

"Senator Mootey," the reporter said. "This is Rose Najafi from the Post. It's a pleasure to speak with you at last."

"I've read your reporting, Ms. Najafi," Mootey said dyspeptically. "You've been very unfair to my colleagues and my supporters."

"There's nothing unfair about the truth," Najafi replied, unfazed. "I'd like to talk to you on the record. I have documents showing that this year alone, your father received almost $10 million in consulting fees from a Death Valley political action committee called the Lazarus Fund, most of which he donated to various dark-money groups supporting your re-election campaign. He also spent around $500,000 refurbishing a luxury hunting lodge."

"Why, there's nothing at all untoward about a father supporting his son's campaign. All those donations are perfectly legal."

"Your father is 93 years old and blind. When I called him for comment, he complained for six minutes about how hard it is for him to use his phone. What did Death Valley want to consult with him about?"

"I can't comment on my family's financial affairs."

"Your father was willing to talk. He told me that he didn't know anything about consulting payments or campaign donations, and that he hasn't gone hunting since the Reagan administration."

"It's nothing short of despicable, the way that you crooked, lying journalists attack our families!" the Senator sputtered. "Is nothing sacred to you people anymore?"

"I think I've got what I need here," Najafi said calmly. "The story's going to press on Thursday. If you change your mind and decide you want to tell your side of things, you've got my number."

Mootey hung up, fighting the urge to hurl his phone against the nearest wall. A half-dozen chips in the paneling marked the spots where its predecessors had met their violent ends. Najafi's story didn't mean much to him in the big scheme of things – all those donations *were* perfectly legal – but it was one more nail in a coffin already dense with iron.

A knock sounded from the door, and the Senator's personal assistant stuck her head in. She had learned to give her boss space when he was in his dark moods, which came more and more frequently as of late, so if she was intruding it had to be important. "Senator Hazen's waiting outside for you," she said. "Remember, you and he have that dinner tonight with Hester Faust. You were supposed to be on the road ten minutes ago."

With all the catastrophic news he'd already received today, the Senator had almost forgotten about this final indignity. Still, it wouldn't do to keep Faust waiting. The scion of Frankenstein's angel investor, she was not just a mega-donor but a giga-donor, and her bank accounts were the beating heart of American politics.

"One second, I've got to do my T&P before I go," Mootey said. He picked up his phone and tweeted his condolences to those killed and maimed in the day's mass shootings; sixteen dead at the Monroeville Mall alone. It was a daily ritual, one that he could complete from muscle memory without any actual thoughts or prayers involved. "Alright, let's get this over with."

Chip Hazen sat in the reception room typing on his phone, perhaps attending to his own T&P. The junior Senator from Montana was a handsome, perky young demagogue fanatically committed to self-advancement. Mootey, who had worked closely and productively with some of America's leading sociopaths, believed that the kid had a bright future, and had taken him under his wing after he'd weaseled his way onto the committee that Mootey chaired.

"You look like shit," Hazen said, without judgment, as they walked to their limo together. "What's wrong with you?"

"Bad news from the pollsters. I'm the most despised man in my home state since Osama bin Laden. It's sickening. This election might be the end of the line for me! What else am I going to do? I've been in politics all my life."

"Spare me the hysterics. You're not going to starve. There's plenty of white-shoe law firms and lobbying groups that'll pay you to hang up a shingle and take your buddies to steakhouses."

Mootey shook his head. "That's not for me. I always thought politicians who stuck around Washington after losing their elections were pathetic. The legislative equivalent of seedy ex-football players hanging around their old high school haunts."

"You know what's to blame for this sorry state of affairs, right?" Hazen asked.

"Yeah, at home we've got unemployment worse than the Great Depression and abroad the Middle East looks like the Book of Revelations."

"No, that's not it. Bad times make people crave strong leadership, and no offense, my friend, but right now you look weak as watered-down piss. Beat someone up, show the voters you've still got a pair of balls on you."

"Here's another tidbit from the report I got today," Mootey said gloomily. "A majority of the registered voters of Pennsylvania – a *large* majority – believe that life gets worse every day. Very few of them nurse any hope of improvement. One of the pollsters' bullet-point conclusions was that, and I quote, 'A pervasive apprehension of doom is virtually the only factor that unites modern Americans.' Selah."

"My consultants told me something similar," Hazen said cheerfully. "It's not all bad. There's a lot you can do with apprehensions of doom, in terms of messaging."

"It's depressing. All these years we worked so hard to build a free and prosperous country, and all we got out of it was mass unemployment and a nation in despair."

"Hey, you can't help those who don't want to be helped. If the American people want to sponge on donor pensions, shoot heroin, and murder each other rather than working hard and pulling themselves up by their bootstraps, there's nothing you and I can do about that."

"I guess you're right," Mootey said. However, in the back of his mind the Senator was gnawed at by the possibility that perhaps America turned to shit precisely *because* of all the hard work that he and his colleagues had put in – that the country's dire state was in fact the fruit of their harvest. The Senator's hunger for authority had devoured its twin brother, his sense of responsibility, in the womb. Yet occasionally he felt a twinge of discomfort, as if the bones were poking at him from within.

Their limo driver, a Frank so aged and withered that she looked like someone had put an Egyptian mummy into a chauffeur's uniform, awaited them in the Dirksen Building's underground parking garage. She smelled of old leather. A security zombie encased head-to-toe in beetle-like black armor sat stiffly in the passenger seat, clutching a carbine to its chest. The Senators took their place in the back, and their undead chauffeur pulled out into the night.

Traffic was bad at the military checkpoints separating the Capitol's tightly-secured Green Zone from the chaos and poverty of Washington, D.C. Their driver handled the scrum with inhuman efficiency, guiding the limousine through mazelike forests of anti-car bollards and barbed wire fencing, but even inhuman efficiency could only do so much against the purpose-built gridlock they faced. Most of the soldiers manning the checkpoints were Franks as well. The driver transmitted her credentials to them wirelessly just by staring into their eyes and hissing raspy modem noises at them, without having to show ID. Seeing the ghouls speak to each other made Mootey reliably queasy.

He felt queasier still once they'd left the safety of the Green Zone. The Senator peered through the limousine's bulletproof windows at a wasteland of shuttered storefronts and crumbling homes. The driver raced through these slums at great speed, nearly knocking a boy over at a crosswalk. Occasionally Mootey recognized the remnants of places he'd known during happier times – a restaurant where he used to gossip with reporters, now closed forever, a park where he used to go jogging, now a haunt for junkies. Ever since the walking dead had arrived, the city was peopled by ghosts.

"Do you ever wonder if reanimated labor's gone too far?" Mootey mused, more or less rhetorically, while the junior Senator from Montana indulged in a bump of cocaine. "Maybe we do need some sort of a safety net for all the folks the Franks put out of work."

"Reanimated labor strengthens the economy and the military," Hazen said mechanically. "It's made America into the richest and most productive country in the world. When private enterprise is succeeding so wildly, government needs to stay out of the way." He tapped out a message on his phone and showed the screen to Mootey.

"Don't talk like that in front of the Franks, you idiot, they can hear us."

Mootey slumped in his seat and looked back out the window, wishing that he'd kept his mouth shut. It was true what Hazen had said, though – reanimating the dead had reanimated the American economy. GDP was up, the stock market was booming, and Frankenstein donor pensions had provided a free market alternative to the socialist welfare state. In many ways, the country was doing better than ever. The Senator's spirits perked up as their limo turned off of Massachusetts Avenue, exiting the blighted wastes of the Capitol's center and passing into the green and stately hills of Kalorama, a neighborhood renowned as a home for presidents and tycoons. Here, at least, it was possible to imagine the American experiment a success. Finally they reached their destination, an estate so imposing and with such sturdy walls that it seemed to be a city-state all its own, an opulent kingdom. Immaculately tended gardens ran alongside the long driveway, leading up to a gothic mansion ablaze with lights.

The Frank who met them at the door had the absurdly perfect body of a ballerina, but for the long scars running up the insides of her forearms. She wore a form-fitting black silk dress with a lace hood that shrouded her face, leaving only the outline of her features perceptible. "Welcome," the wraith said, her voice eerily warm and beckoning. "Ms. Faust awaits you in the dining room. Please, follow me." She issued the Senators inside, moving with sinuous, eerie grace.

The home's interior was decorated in French Baroque style, so lush and opulent that the Sun King himself would have been overawed to set foot within its walls. But then, Hester Faust was far richer than Louis XIV had been, and mightier as well. The house was so overstuffed with beautiful things that it felt draining. There was no place that a man could rest his gaze and not be dazzled by fine art or classical furniture or the corpses of fashion models.

The Senator's mouth dried up as the ballerina led him through the mansion's labyrinthine halls towards the dining room. The acid in his stomach churned painfully. Mootey had met six presidents, two popes, and an African warlord, and none of those people made him as nervous as Hester Faust did. Mootey glanced sideways at Hazen, peevishly annoyed by the freshman's calm. Two footmen as pale and chiseled as marble statues stood at the double doors in full livery, their red eyes fixed on the visitors. In unison they reached out and pulled the gate open, admitting the two Senators into the presence of their dread hostess.

Hester Faust stood at the head of the table glaring expectantly at her guests, her red lips frozen in a rictus smile that exposed long yellow teeth. The heiress was a severe woman, pale as bone and mean as a spider, with a tall, angular forehead and stark makeup that made her look rather like a figure out of German Expressionist horror. Although only in her mid-thirties, she nonetheless presented the impression of irritable old age. A bow-tied egghead from one of her pet think tanks stood sheepishly to her side, evidently relieved that the men she really wanted to talk to had arrived. Her personal bodyguard, an ivory-white Frank with the chiseled good looks of an underwear model and the taut menace of a bear trap, hovered behind her, a Japanese sword on his belt. It occurred to Paul, not for the first time, that Hester could order that thing to kill him, and it would cut him in half, and she wouldn't face any consequences.

"Paul! Chip! I'm glad to see you at last," she proclaimed, holding out her gloved and bejeweled hand so that the senators might literally kiss the ring. "What's the latest news?"

"It's bad, I'm afraid," Mootey said, flinching inwardly. "I got a call from Rose Najafi today. She knows about the Lazarus Fund. My piece of it, at least, I'm not sure if she knows about the payments to other candidates. The story goes to press on Thursday."

Faust's eyes narrowed. "Don't worry about Ms. Najafi," she said. "I've spoken with Victor about her."

"How is Victor?" Hazen asked, in the oily but sincerely concerned manner of a courtier inquiring on the health of the king.

"Dr. Frankenstein is well," the heiress replied. "He told me to pass on his greetings to the both of you. Tonight's business is very important to him."

At Faust's command the gathered dignitaries sat around a long mahogany table, where dead men in porcelain masks and tuxedos served them a meal of braised veal shanks with wild rice and mushrooms beneath the light of a blood-diamond chandelier. The veiled ballerina sat at a harp in the corner and played an unearthly, slightly atonal melody to accompany the dinner. Mootey had no appetite, even though the food was superb.

"Gentlemen, I've brought you here to discuss a matter urgent to the country and the company alike," Faust said imperiously. Despite being a celebrated Washington hostess, she despised small talk like poison.

"What can we do for you this time?" Hazen asked playfully as he speared another juicy mouthful of veal with his fork. "A Frank on the Supreme Court?"

"I've thought about it," Faust said sharply. "And the company's newest models could do the job better and cheaper than those pampered morons you've got now, believe me. But not today. No, this time you two will be co-sponsoring the Freedom of Elderly Americans Act."

One of the liveried servants silently handed each of the assembled dinner guests a sheaf of photocopied papers. Faust nodded to the intellectual, who stood from his chair like a schoolboy called on in class. "The FEAA modernizes the American retirement system while minimizing burdens on the taxpayers," he purred. "The way that we manage and fund retirement care in this country is badly out of date, now that reanimated labor has made the healthcare sector so much more efficient. We can spend less money to help more people simply by diverting patients currently being cared for in public hospitals into private sector facilities. The details are all there in front of you."

"Wow," Hazen said as he paged through the briefing. "Really got the chainsaw out for Medicare here, huh?" He whistled appreciatively. "About fucking time."

Mootey took in the charts and figures that he'd been given, and as he digested them his gut churned. For a moment he feared that he might vomit. But no, this wasn't his disease. He was angry. He'd been angry for a long time, and only now did he realize that he'd been mistaking his rage for his cancer.

"I can't put my name behind this," the Senator protested, his jowls quivering. "This is going to shut down hospitals and nursing homes and dump their residents into Frankenstein hospices! And I know how you run those places. You squeeze every penny you can out of those folks, giving them care so lousy it shoves them into the grave, and you make them reverse-mortgage their own organs to pay for it." He was astonished by his own recklessness, but the tirade felt too good – too cleansing – for him to stop. "If we pass this tumor of a bill, it's going to kill my voters – literally kill them! For Christ's sake, I've got an election coming up in just two months and you're asking me to cut my own throat."

The rant caught Hazen and the egghead dumbfounded. The heiress, however, was unfazed by Mootey's accusation, as if commanding a thrall to commit suicide on her behalf was a totally normal and reasonable thing to do, well within her rights. "If your campaign's going that poorly now, let's see how it fares when I stop spending money on it," she said.

"Money or not, I need senior voters to win! I can't send them to the knackers to be made into fucking glue!"

"Calm down, Paul," she sneered. "**Your** voters aren't in Medicare-funded nursing homes. **Your** voters are going to do just fine. They'll see their taxes go down. And you're not alone in your re-election fight. My friends in the courts and the media are pulling for you, too. You're part of the team, and the team rewards loyalty. The team **demands** loyalty."

"And the team *is* loyal," Hazen said. His voice was sweet as sugar, but if looks could kill his eyes would have strangled Mootey on the spot. "I'm on board with this bill, and I'm positive that the President and the Majority Leader and the rest of the caucus will get on board with it, too. Senator Mootey doesn't speak for us. I don't know if he even speaks for himself."

Paul Mootey took in the gothic horror of his surroundings – the vile queen and her grotesque, simpering lackeys and the dead things lurking and hovering behind them – and as he did he decided he owed these people nothing. The Senator felt light and free for the first time that he could recall. The dyspepsia as constant as his breathing had vanished. "I can't do this anymore," he said calmly. "I'm grateful for all that you've done for me, and if you want to send me a decent bill I'll look at it, but I can't support this. Now if you'll excuse me, it's been a long day, and I have a lot of business to attend to in the morning. Thank you for supper." He stood up from his chair and walked out of the dining room.

"What the fuck was that all about, you half-wit Pennsyltucky sister-fucker?" Hazen bawled when they were back in the limo together. "And who do you think you are, talking to Hester Faust like that? You need her! I need her! The party needs her! What, you think that just because you've fucked up your re-election beyond repair, you're going to fuck up my re-election too? Fuck you! If you want to kill yourself, I'll lend you a gun! Maybe once you're dead Hester will give you a job scrubbing her bidet and you'll finally be good at something other than jerking your soft little cock. But you don't get to take me down with you."

"Fuck Hester Faust, fuck Victor Frankenstein, and fuck you, Chip, you shit-drinking parasite," Mootey said unconcernedly, pouring himself a tall glass of Scotch from the limo's bar. "I didn't get into politics to be anyone's lackey, and I'm sick of jumping every time that witch says boo. Telling me to put my own voters in Frankenstein hospices – who does she think she is, to demand that of me?"

"Is that what this is about? Frankenstein wants to take over the care of a bunch of old leeches who didn't save anything for retirement, and you're going to sacrifice your career over that? At your age?"

"Fuck the old leeches, too," Mootey said. "This isn't about them. This is about me. This is my last term one way or another and I want to end it as my own man."

The junior Senator from Montana continued ranting for the rest of the ride home. Once upon a time Mootey would have been offended to be dressed down by a man so much younger himself, but after such a day it barely registered.

When the Senator awoke in the morning, he was surprised to discover that he regretted nothing about the previous night's performance, except that he had not done it sooner. Mootey looked at his sleeping wife Suzanne, who had taken to her career as a social maven just as seriously as he'd taken his career in politics. Now they were both finished, and she didn't even know it yet. The Senator caressed her arm, feeling a moment of pity for her. The moment passed, and he got out of bed, leaving her to sleep. The Senator wolfed down an enormous breakfast and headed into the office early.

He told his assistant to cancel his appointments for the day and defend him against all intruders, then locked himself in his office and began downloading all of his emails having to do with Frankenstein or Faust onto a thumb drive. Looking back on his public life, the Senator was surprised to see just how much of it had been dedicated to serving the undead. Welfare cuts designed to force the poor into donor pensions – business taxes cut to the bone – forever wars getting bloodier and costlier each year – the criminalization of naloxone – sweetheart deals for ghoul-run private prisons – judges who believed that the Founders intended the Constitution to protect Victor Frankenstein above all others. And beneath it all, torrents of dark money, flowing in amounts measureless to man down to a sunless sea.

Word of last night's dinner had spread through the grapevine like a smut, and colleagues from every branch of government called Mootey all morning long to express their outrage over his brusque treatment of their patron. He put them on speaker and ignored them. If anything, their cravenness confirmed his belief in his own rightness. The President himself called shortly before noon, and chewed Mootey out for half an hour in a state of escalating near-hysteria while Mootey listened dispassionately and made copies of the Pentagon's classified budget for necrotech black ops. After that call ended, the Senator turned off his cell phone and yanked the desk phone's cord out of the wall. Anyone who wanted to turn him aside from his purpose would have to come to him.

Suzanne arrived not long thereafter, rolling into the office in a state of fury, a hurricane with impeccable hair and makeup, her tastefully veiled z-handmaid following three steps behind her. The former Miss Pennsylvania was a formidable woman, especially in her wrathful aspect, and the Senator's staff no match for the likes of her.

"Are you trying to destroy me?" Suzanne demanded. "You can't talk that way to Hester Faust!"

"I am a United States Senator," Mootey responded, puffing out his chest. "And I am done scraping to these body snatchers. If I have to go, I'm going on my own terms."

"Your terms? What about my terms, you selfish piece of shit? We've built a life here – a good life – and it'll be a good life whether you win re-election or not! But here you are, tearing it all down, just because you can't stand to take orders from a woman! If you don't apologize to her and do what she tells you, then you're going to lose and we won't have any friends in Washington or back home to help us."

She had no idea about the true scope of the betrayal he was plotting. By the time the week was over, they wouldn't just be friendless in the corridors of power, they'd be actively despised. But if he told her that she would only try to stop him, and she might even succeed, so he said only that his mind was made up. Suzanne left the office in tears, followed by her passionless servant. The Senator bitterly figured that if not for the cancer, he'd likely be facing another divorce. As things were, she wouldn't have time to leave him.

By the time the sun began to set over Washington, the Senator had assembled a dossier of influence-peddling, vote-buying, sweetheart deals, and cronyism that would have scandalized the meanest Tammany Hall hack. Almost nothing he'd documented was illegal as a modern American court would define it, but any fair-minded person reading it would conclude that men at the highest levels of power had committed terrible crimes against the nation. The Senator ejected the thumb drive and looked at it in his palm. It was such a tiny thing to hold so many secrets. He supposed that the button that dropped the atomic bomb had been small as well.

Mootey called Rose Najafi and set up a time and place to meet with her that evening, keeping the details light. She seemed unsurprised to hear from him. No doubt she'd already heard of the disastrous dinner at the Faust estate. The Senator stuck the thumb drive in his pocket and ordered up a car to take him to his destination.

As the Senator walked through the halls of the Dirksen Building towards the garage, staffers stopped in the hall to watch the dead man walking. Odd that it was such a novelty to them. Notwithstanding the tumors that bloomed in his guts, Paul Mootey felt like the last truly living man in Washington. The Congressmen, the lobbyists, the lawyers, the staffers, none of them were any different than the zombies who emptied their trash cans, served their meals, and protected them from the American people. The sooner he was done with this sepulcher-city, the happier he'd be.

Mootey's z-driver was the same mummy who'd transported him last night. There seemed to be something different about her this time, though. Whereas before she'd had the blank, empty affect of a typical Frank, tonight she stared at the Senator with cold malice, as if she understood and resented his errand. Mootey felt an attack of nerves getting into the car, and Hazen's warning that the Franks were always listening echoed in his mind. A human driver would have been vastly preferable for this mission. Alas, you couldn't get human drivers anymore.

They were stopped at a security checkpoint when the z-driver turned around in her seat. A shock of terror ran through Mootey as her cold, sunken eyes glared into him. She reached into the glove box, her gaze never leaving his face, and for a terrible second the Senator imagined his assassination. But she only passed him a manila folder with a sheaf of paper inside, and then turned back to the wheel. The frightened, puzzled politician looked at the documents he'd been given.

The Senator had compiled a dossier of damning information about Frankenstein Enterprises, but in turn Frankenstein Enterprises had done the same to him, and its files were far more comprehensive. Transcripts faithfully recorded his bitterest fights with Suzanne, today's included.

GPS data mapped the exact times, dates, and routes of every trip to the necro-brothel. The company knew all his secrets both petty and grand, and they'd discerningly selected the greatest hits. The final piece of paper in the folder was a glossy, high-res photo of the Senator sitting on the toilet, visibly suffering the agonies of a man who will never again shit without breathtaking pain.

Although Faust attached no blackmail note to the dossier, the Senator understood her message perfectly. If he didn't introduce her bill like a dutiful servant, then a few days from now this stack of horrors would start leaking to the press, his colleagues, and the goddamned Internet. It was the ultimate humiliation that Mootey could imagine, a shame so sharp and deep that it gutted him just to think of it. And that shame would be his legacy. Paul Mootey would die a universally despised laughingstock, and that's how he'd be remembered, to the extent he was remembered at all.

At the start of the day the Senator had been prepared to manfully face exile and death. He'd been ready to tear down everything he'd worked for, so long as he got to pry some scrap of his dignity from the wreckage. Now he realized that keeping his dignity was not an option, that it had never been an option.

The Senator looked anxiously at the thumb drive in the palm of his hand, then peered through the window at the desolate slums outside. He asked himself if he was really willing to betray his country just to keep Frankenstein Enterprises from whipping him with its records of his own life.

Paul Mootey sighed deeply, as if he were expelling something that could no longer live within his breast. His stomach clenched with nausea.

"Turn the car around," the Senator told the zombie. "Take me back to the office." He picked up his phone and called his head aide in charge of legislative services. "Hey Brent," he said. "It's me. I need you to get to work on a new bill that I'm going to be introducing with Senator Hazen. It's called the Freedom of Elderly Americans Act. Hester Faust's people will send you the details."

OPERATION DARK AVENGER RULES OF ENGAGEMENT CARD

YOU ALWAYS HAVE THE RIGHT TO USE NECESSARY AND PROPORTIONAL FORCE TO DEFEND YOURSELF AND THE FRANKS YOU COMMAND

1. You may engage the following individuals based on their conduct:

- Persons who are committing hostile acts against Coalition Forces (CF).
- Persons who are exhibiting hostile intent towards CF.

2. Positive Identification (PID) is required prior to engagement. PID is a reasonable certainty that the proposed target is a legitimate military target. If your Franks' facial recognition system identifies a person as a terrorist, that constitutes PID.

3. Escalation of Force Measures (EOF): When time and circumstances permit, EOF measures allow CF to determine whether a threat may be subdued with non-lethal force. Turn your Franks' Asimovs to the lowest level needed to safely contain the situation.

- Level 1 (Herding): Your Franks will resist any attempt to move through their space, but will not otherwise initiate physical contact.
- Level 2 (Force): Your Franks will shove or jostle targets. Your Franks will not use any equipped weapons other than riot shields.
- Level 3 (Violent Force): Your Franks will violently subdue targets. If your Franks are equipped with non-lethal weapons, they will use them.
- Level 4 (Deadly Force): Your Franks will kill targets. If your Franks are equipped with lethal weapons, they will use them. MG-28s will bite and claw targets to death.
- Level 5 (Relentless Force): Your Franks will kill targets and continue to attack their remains until given new orders.

When you are confronted with a hostile act or demonstration of hostile intent that threatens death or serious bodily injury, you may use deadly force immediately without proceeding through EOF measures.

4. The use of force, including deadly force, is authorized to protect the following: (1) yourself, your unit, and other friendly forces; (2) your Franks; (3) the personnel and property of CF-allied contractors and private security forces; (4) detainees; (5) civilians; or (6) any other personnel or property designated by the OSC.

5. You may DETAIN civilians based upon a reasonable belief that the person: (1) is interfering with CF mission accomplishment; (2) is on a list of persons wanted for questioning, arrest, or detention; (3) is gathering dead bodies in violation of CF directives; or (4) must be detained for imperative reasons of security. You MUST conduct an m-iGor facial recognition scan of EVERY person you detain.

REMEMBER
TURN ASIMOV LEVELS TO 0 WHEN BRINGING FRANKS INTO A GREEN ZONE.

THE SOLDIER

Marine Captain Reggie Harlough peered through his night-vision goggles at the city he'd been ordered to take – a craggy burg of low, boxy concrete, dominated by a medieval castle on a mountainous hilltop at its center. By daylight Harlough figured the place would look almost Mediterranean, but through the NVGs' emerald tint every landscape seemed alien and foreboding, an extraterrestrial outpost to be conquered. Dozens of frisbee-sized drone quadcopters flitted about the town scanning its dimensions and identifying possible targets with flickering laser beams that glowed bright in the infrared. An airship carrying a mobile m-iGor communications array floated high in the sky above the range of the enemy's rockets, like a second moon visible only to those with NVGs. A militia checkpoint at the northern road into town flew a black flag with white Arabic lettering. Harlough had forgotten the militia's name. They all tended to blur together after a while.

Harlough and his men had been fighting his way through Syria's hill country for almost 50 hours on no sleep and now they'd arrived at their target, with no idea what this battle was supposed to accomplish. Most of the enemy fighters would slip away into underground tunnels the moment their gates were overrun, and within a week Masyaf would be under the flag of some new ethnic militia, fundamentalist death cult, or narco-terrorist gang. Before returning to his squad Harlough shoved these doubts out of his mind, a mental exercise that he practiced almost daily. He'd been ordered to take Masyaf and so that's what he would do.

Behind Harlough, more than a thousand Zulus waited for the attack on Masyaf to begin, eager for battle in their own way. At the moment they were packed tightly in a convoy of forty 'Coffin' armored personnel carriers, ready to be set loose against the enemy, their Asimov levels turned to murderous boiling rage. Harlough's own Coffin idled at the head of the convoy, its purring engines kicking out diesel fumes. This vehicle contained all of the living troops in the Red Diamond strike force, except for Harlough himself, and Basile, the driver, who was pissing at the side of the road. An MI-300 manned the fifty cal on top of the Coffin, a sentry who'd never get bored or careless or distracted by its bodily functions. Encased in its black bomb suit there was no outward sign that it was a zombie, but nobody ever mistook the MI-300s for human. Basile tucked his dick away and saluted his Captain. "How's it look out there, sir?" he asked.

"Nothing the Zulus can't handle," Harlough replied. "Keep your eyes open, though, this could get hairy." A gust of concentrated body odor more powerful than the diesel fumes wafted out from the Coffin as Harlough opened its hydraulically-operated rear door. Inside, Serrano, Contriglio, Hsien, and Rusov sat hunched over consoles, reviewing the drone footage and prepping the army of the dead for combat, amidst a litter of empty MRE packs and energy supplement bottles. In the lingo of the Corps these warriors were known as Shakas, because they led Zulus into battle. Harlough sat down at his own console, calling up aerial footage of the city from the blimp overhead.

"We've got a fight here," Harlough said. "You can see they've got trenches dug, barricades in the streets, lots of gunmen waiting on the rooftops. The enemy's main base is at Masyaf Castle, here, on a hilltop at the city center. We're going to push south and hit them at the western entrance while Green Spade and Black Heart come up the southern and eastern roads. We'll kill every motherfucker who gets in our way, meet up at the castle, and take out the bad guys' command and control post. Any questions?"

"Yeah, who named the attack elements for this operation, the fucking

Lucky Charms leprechaun?" asked Contriglio, wiping off his runny nose on the back of his sleeve. Something about the Syrian climate set off his immune system, with the result that his eyes were as red and swollen as those of any Zulu. It hadn't affected his sense of humor.

"That castle's going to be a bitch to get inside," said Serrano. "Can't we just call in some air strikes and knock the fucker down?"

"You're not wrong," replied Harlough. "But that castle's been standing for more than a thousand years through all sorts of wars and the generals don't want to blow it up now. It's a – what do you call it – a cultural heritage site."

"I visited it in a video game once," said Hsien, who'd been a champion Starcraft player before joining the Corps at nineteen to test his skills in true combat. "Masyaf Castle, the fortress of the assassins."

"We're storming the fortress of the assassins? And they're not going to let us drop a bomb on it? Yo, fuck this."

Contriglio let out a low chuckle. "I reckon these terrorists would rather get blown up than get chewed on by the Margies."

"No reason we should even be here for this nonsense," grumbled Serrano. "We could fight just as well from the Arcade in the Green Zone."

"Arcade duty's for pussies," said Harlough, hoping to quash this bellyaching before it turned contagious. "Real Shakas get in there with their Zulus." In truth he also would have preferred to be back at the Arcade, but he could not let his men know this.

"From the castle rooftop they'll be able to rain fire on our advance," said Rusov. "Can we at least call in a Mousetrap strike?"

"Command says that Mousetrap is airborne and en route towards the castle," Harlough said. "Six cans. We'll have them for our final approach." A chill ran through the Marines, even though the sour air inside the Coffin was body-temperature warm. Z-rats made even hardened necrowarriors uneasy.

The Shakas waited inside the hot, crowded confines of their Coffin for another hour burning darkness, bullshitting with each other, chewing coffee grounds, stimulant pills, and dip, and becoming increasingly anxious for the battle to start, until at last the order came. Harlough entered attack coordinates and the Coffins under his command sped out of the night towards the militia checkpoint, spraying its defenders with furious pulses of machine gun fire. One of the APCs triggered a roadside bomb that blew off a couple of its tires; another suffered a direct hit and burst into flames.

"Serrano, get those Zulus out of there!" Harlough ordered. The doors of the burning Coffin flew open and a swarm of fiery Zulus dashed out, solely fixated on tearing the enemy to shreds even as their uniforms burned away and their skin crisped. As the flaming zombies overran the checkpoint the rooftops of Masyaf came alive with small arms fire, much to Harlough's satisfaction. Zulus could shrug off bullet wounds that would kill or maim a human fighter, so by shooting, the bad guys were only giving their own positions away. The drones overhead shot infrared lasers towards each muzzle flash, feeding targeting data into m-iGor, and the Coffin gunners returned fire with deadly accuracy. A few of the burning zombies dropped, but most of them kept running into town.

"Open those Coffins!" Harlough ordered. The APC doors opened and hundreds of MG-28s – the undead, carnivorous workhorse of the U.S. military – tore out into the night. MG-28s – better-known as Margies – were designed as close-combat fighters, with long steel claws grafted to their fingerbones, and chrome teeth replacing their human dentition, and a relentless hunger for human flesh. They wore khaki uniforms caked in dust and blood, and Kevlar vests, and round helmets that enclosed their skulls except for their awful mouths. These fiends charged into Masyaf in a great seething mass, many of them scrambling up the walls of buildings like monkeys to attack defenders on the roofs, others dropping on all fours and galloping at their targets fast as greyhounds. MG-28s were so swift and vicious that seeing them in action permanently altered your perceptions of the undead; you could never look at the slow, plodding civilian-grade zombies the same way once you'd seen fast zombies on the hunt. Harlough watched through the eyes of a burning Margie as it hurled itself through a window, pouncing on an affrighted-looking old man who had himself been watching the battle from indoors.

"Keep the Margies out of the buildings!" Harlough barked. "Keep driving them down the main road!" At Asimov level four – the standard setting for combat operations – Margies would move to attack anything that triggered their hyper-reactive danger sense, such that keeping them on target in an urban environment was rather like shepherding an attack force of a thousand vicious, jumpy dogs through a rabbit farm. A parked car exploded, taking out twenty-odd Margies at the spearhead of the force and opening up a crater so deep that it cracked open a sewer line. Maimed and legless ghouls continued to crawl towards their target through the gushing waste, still ready to fight.

"Zerg rush wins every time," said Hsien, pounding a can of fruity-smelling energy drink as he directed his minions onwards.

The army of the dead advanced through Masyaf rapidly, the Margies chasing down gunmen, the Coffins close behind laying down sustained machine gun fire on fortified positions, and Harlough's command APC bringing up the rear, until at last they came to an intersection so well-defended that it gave even the army of the dead pause. A couple of heavy machine guns opened up from sandbagged emplacements, cutting down the advancing ghouls; a barrage of rocket-propelled grenades like an earthbound fireworks show took out one Coffin and disabled another. Masyaf Castle loomed close enough to see flashes of sniper fire from its parapets. A mortar exploded only a hundred meters north of their position, probably another gift from the castle.

Harlough ordered a halt. "Let's unload the three hundos and get some suppressing fire on those machine gun nests," he said. "And let's do it before they can re-target that mortar." Another two Coffins opened up, disgorging forty-eight MI-300s under Contriglio and Hsien's control. The heavily armed and armored MI-300s were the Terminator to the Margie's Alien, relentless death machines that could run a marathon swaddled in 33 kilograms of steel and Kevlar and shoot every unlucky bastard they came across when they crossed the finish line. These war-ghouls lit up the enemy's entrenchments with concentrated gunfire and rifle-propelled grenades. A station wagon tried to escape the battlefield, and they riddled it with bullets. Harlough hoped that the car's occupants had been jihadis, not fleeing civilians, but he knew exactly how much hope counted for here.

Another mortar blast landed atop a nearby pharmacy, close enough to rattle the teeth of every Shaka in the Coffin, collapsing the building into rubble, and kicking up a cloud of dust that blanketed the street.

"Fuck!" yelled Basile from the driver's seat. "Captain, we got to get out of here!"

Although a storm of death raged outside the Coffin, with explosions shaking the vehicle and shrapnel rattling against its none-too-thick armor plating, Harlough nonetheless experienced an odd sense of serenity, as if none of this were real. Commanding the dead into battle was such a surreal experience that even the terrors felt dreamy, a nightmare that one would eventually wake up from. "Send the Margies through and we'll follow them out," he ordered coolly. The MG-28s swept into the intersection in a wave, chasing down and dismembering the retreating militia fighters who'd waited for them in ambush. Another mine explosion opened up a crater at the center of the intersection, but the attacking Zulus ran through the smoke and fire even as gibbets of their comrades rained down upon them.

"Basile, go!" Harlough shouted, now starting to feel the adrenaline in earnest, and the Coffin peeled out through the shattered streets, its rooftop gunner wildly firing on all non-American movement. Another mortar dropped behind them, and a chunk of shrapnel blew off the roof gunner's head. If the crew had fired just seconds ago they'd have scored a direct hit.

Before long Red Diamond reached the western approach to Masyaf Castle. Its defenders had filled the main gateway with stones and dug a tar-filled trench lined with barbed wire and rebar spikes between the fortress and the town. At the Americans' approach they ignited the trench, surrounding the stronghold with a barrier of roaring flame. Masyaf Castle by trenchlight was a glorious sight, and Harlough felt glad that they weren't bombing this place into rubble. Seeing it up close, he believed that this castle should endure for as long as war endured. Given his druthers he could have stayed there gaping until dawn, but they had to advance before the mortars found their position again.

Harlough suspected that the no-man's-land around the burning trench was heavily mined, and he'd already lost a couple hundred Margies fighting through Masyaf. "Rusov, send in the Bigfoots to clear us a path," he ordered.

"Bigfoots away," said Rusov. Another Coffin opened up and thirty-two MG-10s shambled out, ghouls whose bodies were so decayed and damaged that they were only good for minesweeping duties. Many were recycled Margies who'd sustained too much damage to be useful in combat. The Bigfoots stumbled slowly into the kill zone, moving in serpentine patterns, fearlessly trudging into the AK-47 fire hailing down from the parapets and the bombs bursting beneath their feet, inviting the enemy to make their positions known. The Bigfoots cleared a suicidal trail through the minefield, the last survivors hurling themselves through the wire and into the burning trench like hellbound lemmings.

"The Bigfoots are gone, Captain!" said Rusov.

"They did their job. Rusov, help Serrano bring up the Margies, Hsien, Contriglio, give us some covering fire."

Serrano let out a war cry that sounded like a combination of an eagle screeching for its prey and a freshly-risen Zulu belching intestinal gases. On his mark all of Red Diamond's remaining Margies stampeded Masyaf Castle, dashing for the castle walls on all fours, trampling those who fell. Many were caught in barbed wire or impaled on rebar spikes as they hit the enemy's fortifications, but Serrano and Hsien successfully guided the bulk of their forces through the breach that the Bigfoots had opened, over the bridge in the flaming trench that the Bigfoots had built by laying down their still-squirming bodies. The stronghold's defenders laid down fire uselessly on the ghouls, and inside the Coffin, Contriglio and Hsien kept up a constant low chatter as they eliminated these nuisances.

"Tower window on the left is mine."

"I got the shitbird up top with the RPG."

The Margies began climbing the castle wall, their clawed fingers finding an easy grip in the centuries-old masonry. Men at the top hurled stones and cinder blocks over the parapets at them, crushing skulls and knocking the invaders down into the spikes and flame beneath, a low-tech defense far more effective than gunfire. A mortar exploded a mere 20 meters from Red Diamond's position, and gravel pattered down on the APC roof like a sudden rain shower.

Suddenly the radio headset inside Harlough's helmet crackled. "Red Diamond, this is Valkyrie Air Command," a haggard, twitchy-sounding voice on the other end of the line said – probably a contractor working out of a hangar in Arizona. "Be advised, we have six cans of Mousetrap incoming on your target."

Six drones like huge silver swans swooped gracefully over the battlefield, each dropping a silver canister onto the fortress before pulling its nose back and re-ascending into the night sky. The hail of stones stopped immediately, and a few enemy fighters hurled themselves over the walls, preferring a quick and terrifying death to what Uncle Sam had delivered. Harlough called up a bird's-eye view of an autonomous weapon system made of thousands of dead rats swarming and engulfing the castle's defenders one by one. A solemn mood came over the Americans. You could cheer for an air strike or an artillery barrage that vaporized your country's enemies, but only the most vicious psychopaths enjoyed seeing Mousetrap deployed.

Their path made clear, Red Diamond's Zulus began making good progress on their ascent. Serrano and Rusov worked crowd control, directing their ghouls to the breaches in the walls, distributing them across all the egress points that were now opening up like Swiss cheese across the face of the enemy's stronghold. With Margies the rule was to divide your forces, to spread them out so that everywhere your adversary goes he is met by teeth and claws.

Harlough switched to the viewcams of the Zulus spearheading the assault and saw them locked in hand-to-hand combat against foes wielding rifle butts and swords. Bad luck for the bad guys; once Margies got to close quarters not even the best-disciplined troops could stand against them for long, let alone irregular, half-trained forces like their opposition. They were getting eaten alive.

Meanwhile, Black Heart had successfully scaled the castle's eastern wall and Green Spade breached the main entrance to the south. Masyaf Castle was now the site of a general massacre. Men leapt from its windows into the gun sights of MI-300s. Mousetrap swarms slithered through cracks and crawlspaces, finding warm-blooded creatures to flense with their teeth and bursting out of the walls at them. Zulus herded their enemies into ancient tombs and slaughtered them, although unlike their predecessors their bones would not be allowed to rest at Masyaf, but rather would be reanimated to join their killers as comrades. Soon the stronghold was under American control, with the Shakas excitedly coordinating the extirpation of the last few scattered die-hards. Their mission was accomplished, for whatever that was worth.

Harlough's bladder ached. He often needed to pee at the end of a fight. He left Serrano in charge of the mopping-up and opened the Coffin's door. SOP was to never open a Coffin door in hostile territory without a Frank gunner on overwatch, but between everything else going on he hadn't noticed when his gunner was blown away, and the urgency of his need was such that he forgot to check now.

Dawn peeked above the eastern horizon beyond the castle, suffusing Masyaf with a rosy glow. The place looked entirely different in daylight. The air stank of tar smoke and burning flesh and the sewer lines they'd burst during the fighting. A stray Bigfoot pebbled with shrapnel and covered in ash and blood limped along the road, heading back towards its Coffin. A Margie's severed head lay nearby, probably hurled there by an explosion. Its mouth continued to gnash open and closed, gnawing on the cool morning air. Harlough wondered what he would tell his kids when they were old enough to ask him about the war.

Suddenly the Bigfoot's eyes opened wide and it reared up in a way that Bigfoots didn't move and Harlough noticed that there were no plugs in its head and that underneath the caked filth it wore civilian clothes. It was not a zombie, it was a half-dead boy. The boy hurled something through the Coffin's open door.

The sun dawned over the fortress of the assassins as Red Diamond's APC burst into flames.

WRIGHT V. MASSACHUSETTS, 136 S.CT. 1027 (2016)

PER CURIAM.

This Court has held that "the Second Amendment extends, prima facie, to all instruments that constitute bearable arms, even those that were not in existence at the time of the founding," *District of Columbia v. Heller*, 554 U.S. 570, 582, 128 S.Ct. 2783, 171 L.Ed.2d 637 (2008), and that this "Second Amendment right is fully applicable to the States," *McDonald v. Chicago*, 561 U.S. 742, 750, 130 S.Ct. 3020, 177 L.Ed.2d 894 (2010).

In this case, the Supreme Judicial Court of Massachusetts upheld a Massachusetts law prohibiting the ownership of reanimated corpses capable of lethal force after examining "whether a knife-wielding ghoul is the type of weapon contemplated by Congress in 1789 as being protected by the Second Amendment." 470 Mass. 774, 777, 26 N.E.3d 688, 691 (2015). In *Heller*, we emphatically rejected such a formulation. We found the argument "that only those arms in existence in the 18th century are protected by the Second Amendment" not merely wrong, but "bordering on the frivolous." 554 U.S., at 582, 128 S.Ct. 2783.

The trial court's factual findings established beyond any reasonable dispute that Franks may constitute bearable arms when outfitted with appropriate software. Not only do the military and police deploy reanimated weapon platforms in a wide variety of roles, but more importantly, every day thousands of law-abiding citizens rely upon z-security to protect their lives and property against the shocking surge of criminal violence presently afflicting the nation. *See* Amicus Brief of the Reanimated Labor Industry Coalition at p. 10. "Self-defense is a basic right," afforded to both those who can wield arms for themselves and those who may desire the services of an automated bodyguard. *McDonald,* 561 U.S. at 767, 130 S.Ct. 3020. Thus, we now hold that the Second Amendment protects an individual right to possess and control reanimated cadavers capable of lethal force.

THE DETECTIVE

Jay Severino of the Chicago Homicide Department sat across from his new partner at a booth in the Neptune Diner. This greasy little dive served Jay as a testing grounds, a place to take the measure of the man or woman who'd be watching his back in a famously violent city. It was also a place where he could open up a bit, to share wings and beer and the morbid practical wisdom he'd gleaned from twenty years of murder investigations. His current dining companion was a fresh-faced kid just promoted from Narcotics, a young guy with a lot of energy and enthusiasm who seemed to have watched too much TV.

"Did you ever catch a serial killer?" the rookie asked. Jay, his mouth full of fries, grunted and nodded. The ritual retelling of Jay's serial killer story was an integral part of the Neptune Diner new partner tradition. New homicide detectives always wanted to know about serial killers. Even in an age of mass shootings, people still wanted to hear about John Wayne Gacy. Go figure.

"I've put cuffs on a serial killer," Jay said. "Nine confirmed victims that I know of, and probably more that I never found. Let me freshen up our drinks, and I'll tell you all about it." Jay typed his order into the tablet affixed to their table, and their z-waitress brought them another round of beers. The detective winked playfully at the wizened, chalky wench before he launched into his tale.

⁂

The case started when someone called 911 about an unconscious woman in East Pilsen, a little after midnight. The z-patrol responding found a Caucasian female dead on the sidewalk with her throat cut. Neighbors and passerby loitered nearby, taking in the evening's show. The morgue wagon waited across the street, its z-driver glaring at me with his red eyes. I would have sworn that the son of a bitch was impatient. One of the zombies guarding the crime scene was actually a familiar face, I'd taken the call after someone robbed him for his drugs and shot him. Now he had a badge, a club, and a taser, another foot soldier in the war on crime.

The victim looked like she'd had a hard life even before someone slashed her trachea. She lay sprawled out on her face, arms outstretched like Superman in flight. One of her feet was bare; the shoe lay abandoned half a block west. Her purse lay in the gutter, and to my great surprise the dead woman's wallet, cell phone, and meth were all still inside. Her ID named her as Meghan Simonowicz, twenty-four years old going on forty. Her ID didn't have the Frankenstein donor stamp, another surprise.

Easy enough to read how the assassination of Meghan Simonowicz had gone down. Meghan saw someone coming and made a run for it. Her shoe fell off . . . the killer caught up with her. The cut was deep and clean. It looked like he'd butchered her with a single stroke of the knife.

Once I'd finished with the crime scene and the morgue wagon hauled Meghan away, I went to her home to get some answers on the men in her life. Meghan's address was on a street of decaying brick row homes, only a short walk away. The whole block seemed like it was just waiting to collapse; that eventually one of the sagging houses would crumble, and as soon as one gave permission to the rest they'd all tumble in a chain reaction.

A zombie in nursing scrubs opened the door when I knocked. He was a grisly-looking specimen. He'd been hacked to death with an axe or machete, and they'd reanimated him without putting his face back together. I wondered if the guy who chopped him up ever got caught.

The home's interior reeked of cloying potpourri and liniment. A tiny, middle-aged woman in a fuzzy pink housedress sat beneath a print of the Last Supper watching a Frankenstein donor infomercial, a collection of pill bottles laid out on the coffee table in front of her. Her curly red hair and heavy makeup gave her sort of a clownish demeanor. A sad clown.

"Meg, if you're going to stay out so late, you need to remember your keys!" the woman barked, not looking up from her show. When I stepped into the living room and introduced myself, she stared blinking at me for a moment in surprise, and then fell off the couch weeping in great gasping sobs. "Oh Jesus no, that boy's done it at last!" she shrieked. Her disfigured z-nurse patiently shook two pills out of a bottle and handed them to her, then plodded to the kitchen for a glass of water.

Once she'd regained her composure, she tearfully introduced herself to me as Linda Simonowicz, Meghan's stepmother, and led me to the mantelpiece, where she'd assembled a collection of family photos and Christian bric-a-brac. This wasn't the first time that a policeman had crossed the threshold of the Simonowicz home with bad news, or even the second. Meghan's mother passed away five years ago, from a bad tooth turned into a blood infection. Meghan's father Pete Simonowicz – Linda's husband – had hanged himself in January, and Meghan's older brother Richie overdosed on fentanyl in the spring. Now it was Meghan's turn for the shrine. "Jesus help me, I'm all alone now," Linda kept repeating, running her fingers through her dyed red hair and tearing at her own scalp.

Eventually I was able to turn the conversation to the events of Meghan's last day, and the identity of the "boy" who'd "done it at last." Between moaning and praying, Linda told me that Meghan left the house early that evening to see her boyfriend Kyle, who lived six blocks from the scene of the crime. He was the one who'd gotten Meghan hooked on drugs, and he'd been in and out of prison the same way that birds fly south for winter.

I decided to pay him a visit. Kyle opened the door to his hovel wearing nothing but a pair of pajama bottoms. Meghan's boyfriend was a tall, lanky son of a bitch, muscular and sickly-looking at once. His pink-rimmed eyes were bright with recreational insanity. He was shaking to pieces and didn't seem surprised to see me. Without prompting, Kyle said, "Meg's dead, right? It's her own fault for not listening to me."

What a way to introduce yourself to a homicide detective.

He rambled about a Grim Reaper that'd stalked Meghan all night, punctuating his points with violent arm-waving and pacing. Kyle emphasized that he'd warned Meghan not to leave him, that he'd even laid hands on her to keep her from walking out the door. "How can anyone hold me responsible?" he asked, throttling the air in frustration and amazement.

"People ask me that a lot," I told, just before I read him his rights and cuffed him. There's no telling what you're going to get when you pick up the phone on a new case. Sometimes you catch unsolvable whodunits, and sometimes drugged-up boyfriends start gibbering about the Grim Reaper before you've even asked your first question. I brought Kyle back to the station house, fed him black coffee, and listened to him rant and rave for a while until I got the gist of a confession out of him. His hands tested clean of blood, weirdly enough, but as far as I was concerned, the case was down.

The next day I was in my car, on my way to interview a witness in another case, when the M.E.'s office called me on my cell. The quick turnaround surprised me. Usually there's more of a backlog on autopsies. I asked if they'd found anything unusual about the Simonowicz killing.

"We don't even have the body!" the tech told me, frantic. "Frankenstein Enterprises claimed it already!"

"Meghan Simonowicz wasn't even a donor, how the fuck could that happen?" I asked, feeling the urge to run down the next zombie I saw crossing the road.

He told me it was a clerical screw-up, a matter of somebody dicking around with toe tags and barcodes. Promised me that they'd find out what went wrong. I told him that when they did finger the culprit, they ought to let me know, and there'd be another dead body for Frankenstein to pick up. Fucking assholes. Take a look at the morgue parking lot next time you're over at Harrison Street. No way the medical examiners can afford the sort of cars they drive on Cook County salaries. But usually they have the good sense not to fuck with active murder investigations. This crossed the line from "a pain in my ass" to "obstruction of justice." I pulled a screeching U-Turn and headed straight to Frankenstein Enterprises, ignoring every red light in my path.

The regional Frankenstein processing center's a windowless concrete building out by O'Hare. There's no sign, on account that they don't want those Gravedigger psychos to burn the place down. In Homicide we call it the Crypt. It's the most popular spot in Chicago that nobody knows about. Everyone drawing a donor pension goes there eventually.

The first time I saw the Crypt's keeper I thought he was a Frank himself, and not even one in good shape. The gnarly old fellow sat at an elevated desk by the entrance in front of a bank of consoles, directing undead traffic. He seemed genuinely delighted to see another human being, but some people are gross to be around when they're delighted. He told me, "I'm glad you've come, officer, it gets so **dead** around here," and let out a throaty giggle.

I wished that I had my nightstick handy.

The keeper led me further into the building, down a busy hallway. The Crypt's a hell of a place, a hospital and a factory and a morgue and a nightmare all put together. Imagine a drab facility staffed by zombies in stained surgical garb, plodding over tile floors streaked with dried gore. Imagine the sounds of all the drilling and sawing, loud as a factory and gruesomely wet. On my way in I noticed a zombie wheeling a shrink-wrapped corpse into an operating chamber. On my way out I saw two zombies shamble out of the room together.

When we reached the morgue for new arrivals, the keeper selected a mortuary slab and slid it open, exposing a full body bag inside. "Here's Meghan Simonowicz for you," he said cheerily, almost shouting to be heard over the bone saw at work in the next room. "It's a good thing you got here when you did. She was scheduled for the Process in just another hour."

Just in case, I unzipped the bag to make sure they'd given me the right corpse. Meghan Simonowicz lay inside. I felt bad for the poor girl – brutally murdered and then handed over to this ugly man and this ugly place to spend the rest of eternity working a shitty job for no pay. "She's not even a donor," I told the keeper. "Her driver's license didn't have the stamp."

The keeper shook his head. "That just means she wasn't drawing a pension," he told me. "According to the records, her next of kin approved the donation."

"And who's her next of kin?"

"Why, her mother. Linda Simonowicz."

An alarm bell went off in my head, accompanying the shrieking saws. "When did Linda sign the papers?" I asked.

"There aren't any papers to sign. We've got an app." He pulled up the records on his console and showed me the agreement's timestamp. Linda signed her step-daughter's remains over to Frankenstein just minutes after I'd left her house. Either that infomercial was awfully persuasive, or something strange was going on.

Once Meghan was at the medical examiner's where she belonged, I went back to my own office and checked Linda's record. It was virgin. One of my suspects was a meth freak who'd confessed to the crime. The other was a poor, sickly woman who loved Jesus. And somehow I couldn't shake the suspicion that I'd arrested the wrong one. You've got to listen to your hunches in this job. There's plenty of cops who'd just take the clearance and get on with their lives, but that's not the way I operate, and it's not the way I want my partner to operate, either. I sent Frankenstein Enterprises a request for location data from Linda's z-nurse on the night that Meghan died, figuring that maybe the Grim Reaper was real.

I'd only been investigating the Simonowicz killing a couple of days but other bodies were already starting to pile up on me, with a new mystery drug dropping casualties in a homeless camp nearby like a chemical weapon. In between signing off on unattended deaths, I scraped together some time to track down Meghan's friends. They agreed that Kyle was psychotic, and that he'd probably done it. But I already knew that Kyle was a fuck-up. I wanted to learn more about Meghan. She'd been a good student in high school with zero prospects afterwards, and her parents and brother all died in the space of just a few years, leaving her alone with a stepmother she detested. Why not get high?

I asked why Meghan hadn't signed up as a donor. Her friends didn't know the full story, but it had something to do with Linda. Apparently the old woman threatened to throw Meghan out of the house if she ever took a Frankenstein pension, claiming vague religious objections, and Meghan couldn't bear to leave her childhood home. "Meghan was a big-hearted person," one of her girlfriends told me tearfully. "She had enough love in her to even see the good in a creep like Kyle. But she fucking hated her stepmother."

A week or so after my request, Frankenstein Enterprises emailed me a report with GPS and app data, detailing how Linda's z-nurse spent the day of Meghan's death. They don't make those things easy to decipher, but once I figured it out it told a hell of a tale.

The z-nurse began its day normally enough at the Simonowicz home. Linda activated its cooking app, and the zombie made her eggs and toast and tea. Then its nursing app kicked in on auto-timer to administer Linda's morning medications, a regimen of herbal remedies, over-the-counter painkillers, and hokey placebos. The only actual drugs that she took were a hypertension tablet and something to manage her blood sugar. As far as I could tell she had no conditions requiring round-the-clock care.

For most of the day the z-nurse puttered about the house making tea and cleaning and feeding Linda pills. But at exactly 7:23 PM, Linda switched her personal zombie over from autonomous mode into active management, meaning that she was controlling it directly from her phone, getting a video stream through its eyes. She sent the Frank to Kyle's place, where it lurked for hours.

Just looking at the spreadsheet, the whole scene came together in my head. I imagined those two tweaker love-birds holed up together, a mutilated body occasionally peeking in the window. Kyle glimpsed it and freaked out. Meghan thought he was just losing his shit again. They fought, she left. What a fucked-up way to spend your last night on Earth.

Right after midnight, Linda ordered her zombie to head back towards her house. A moment later, she activated a weapons training app. Code flickered inside the zombie's brain. It remembered how to kill. The z-nurse started running as it crossed underneath the expressway. Meghan must have seen it, she must have seen her stepmother's zombie chasing her with a knife and tried to get away. But it was too late. The GPS data placed the zombie right at the scene. After dropping the murder weapon down a storm drain, it returned home and put on the tea kettle again.

And all the while, Linda was back at the Simonowicz family house, popping pills and watching infomercials and killing Meghan Simonowicz in cold blood. All from the comfort of her couch. Frankenstein made everything very quick and convenient for her. They had all the apps she needed.

I got an arrest warrant and ordered up a SWAT team to take the door of the Simonowicz residence. Her slasher z-nurse had slaughtered one person already and I didn't want to be number two.

Dragonsteeth SWAT zombies give me the creeps like nothing else, even though I know they're on our side. Most consumer Franks at least have the courtesy of being slow-moving and kind of dumb. Dragonsteeth are fast and smart and meaner than snakes. I waved to the officer controlling the squad, and on his mark a dozen zombies sewn into combat armor burst through the doors in perfect formation, moving with one mind. A barrage of shots rang out almost immediately. A woman shrieked.

Inside the Simonowicz house, Linda's z-nurse lay crumpled by the Simonowicz family shrine, zombie and shrine both shot up all to hell. The ghoul's hands and feet still squirmed, even though he'd been hit a dozen times and his head was mostly gone. A revolver lay on the carpet nearby, right next to a smashed photo of Meghan's high school graduation. Two of the z-cops had Linda down on the ground, grinding her cheek into the carpet as she howled and cursed. "Let me go, you're hurting me!" she screeched. "Give me my medicine, I need my medicine!"

"You're getting your medicine right now," I told her, as they hauled her off into the wagon.

Beneath Linda's bed I found a bunch of cigar boxes and file folders stuffed with old papers. Passports, birth certificates, Social Security cards, marriage licenses. Linda Simonowicz collected identities like I used to collect baseball cards. Some of the documents had her own picture on them. Some had pictures of similar-looking women. I never found out what happened to those other women.

It turned out that Linda had quite the criminal record, even longer than Kyle's rap sheet. She'd accumulated it all over the country using a half-dozen identities. In Louisiana she was busted for kiting checks under the name of Esther LeDoux. Veronica Huebelson did a stint in Cleveland for bigamy and financial abuse of an elder. Massachusetts state police were still on the lookout for Alice Roy, wanted for arson and insurance fraud.

Following the paper trail, I learned that Linda Simonowicz – or whoever she was – was a widow at least four times over. She came into families like an ancestral curse. When she crossed the threshold, death and calamity followed close behind. Doling out pills and serving tea, actually.

The first husband I'm aware of died in an unsolved break-in back in 2004. A carbon monoxide leak took out both his parents soon thereafter. Husband number two drank a bottle of bleach not long after his kid slipped in the shower. The third one fell down the basement stairs. We've already been over the Simonowicz clan. I requested more of the z-nurse's location records. It was there for every one of these deaths. Every one of those murders. Her own personal Grim Reaper. Kyle was exactly right about that fucking thing.

And all of Linda's victims went to Frankenstein. Not one of these people willingly signed up to donate their bodies. Not one of them took a dollar from Frankenstein while they were alive. But all of them went to the Crypt in the end, while Linda was off on casino junkets between the memorial ceremonies.

I think I would have found even more victims if I'd kept digging, but lately fresh bodies pile up too fast for us to exhume the old ones. Soon I caught a big case . . . a big-shot real estate developer hacked to death in his own office . . . and I had to move on to new business even though the old business wasn't finished yet. The old business will never be finished, I guess.

☠

The rookie nodded knowingly. "It was smart to request the z-nurse data. In Narcotics, the first thing we did in any new investigation was pull whatever Frankenstein records we could find. The cartels love Franks. Zombies are up for anything, and they never dip in the stash for themselves. If you've snorted coke in the past decade, it's probably been up a dead man's asshole at some point."

"Good thing I stick to liquor and beer," Jay said. "Speaking of which . . ." He finished off his drink and ordered another round. "Fucking Frankenstein. What does it say about our country when the biggest company in America profits off of serial killers and drug dealers?"

The rookie bristled. "You can't blame Frankenstein for this! Zombies are just tools, people are going to use them however they want. You sound like one of those liberal snowflakes who blame guns for shootings, instead of the criminals who choose to pull the trigger."

"Maybe. But maybe Linda Simonowicz wouldn't have killed nine people if there wasn't a business that bought bodies like scrap copper. I don't know, I'm just a dumb policeman. Maybe there wouldn't have been a thousand murders in this city last year if the average human being was worth more alive than dead."

"So what happened to Linda?" the rookie asked.

"Hanged herself in her cell. She'd been collecting a donor pension herself – actually, she'd been collecting four of them under different names – so Frankenstein Enterprises got her in the end, just like it got all her victims. A bit of poetic justice, maybe, if you believe in that sort of shit. I actually checked in again with the guy at the Crypt, found out who purchased her body. A restaurant right here in Greektown bought her. The Neptune Diner. Look, here she comes now."

Their z-waitress brought a fresh round of beers to the table, and for the first time, the rookie really saw the dead woman who'd been serving them – an evil-looking crone with a frizzy red hair cut short. A faded rope burn looped around her throat like the Mark of Cain.

INTRODUCTION TO HENRY CLERVAL DEAD TALK™

(NOVEMBER 30, 2019)

The DEAD Talks™ lecture series gathers society's leading thinkers, doers, and personalities to discuss life in the shadow of Frankenstein. Since 1994 the series has explored necro-capitalism from a wide array of perspectives, both positive and critical.

Tonight's speaker is Henry Clerval, Chief Operating Officer of Frankenstein Enterprises. Henry obtained a B.A. in philosophy from Harvard and an M.B.A. from the Wharton School of Business. He began his career in 1989 as a bond trader at Hastur Capital Partners, a hedge fund founded by legendary financier Otto Faust. When Faust backed the formation of Frankenstein Enterprises, Henry was one of the first employees brought aboard. Henry was appointed Chief Financial Officer in 1998, shortly after Victor Frankenstein left the country, and succeeded to the Chief Operating Officer position in 2012 following the death of Faust.

Henry will speak tonight about the future.

THE CHIEF OPERATING OFFICER

Thank you all for coming to my DEAD Talk. I think that the theme of this series is just great, relevant to everyone. We all dwell in the shadow of Frankenstein. Even me, you know, I run operations at the largest company in human history, every day I make decisions that affect the planet on a macroeconomic scale, I've got my own private islands in the Caribbean and the South Pacific, but when I go to parties nobody asks about me. They want to know about what it's like to work with Victor. I'm not complaining, only stating a simple fact. No matter where you are, you're living in a world that Victor Frankenstein created. No matter who you are, he has impressed himself onto your memories, altered the conditions of your existence in ways great and small. Not only has he disrupted our understanding of life and death, he's disrupted our understanding of what capitalism can be. And disrupting capitalism disrupts the bedrock foundation of our society. We all feel the ground shifting beneath our feet. Sometimes it feels like there's no safe place to stand.

I'm one of maybe three people who sees Victor in person at Castle Frankenstein. He's in terrific shape, by the way. Swims every day. The last time I visited he poured me a glass of 50-year-old Scotch and we sat on the turrets above the mountaintop looking at the stars, and he told me his thoughts, not just on the future direction of his company, but on the trajectory of civilization itself. He's a tremendously long-term thinker; he builds like the pharaohs, with an eye towards eternity.

And tonight, I'm here to share his insights with you.

In the not-so-long-term, Frankenstein Enterprises will change the world as profoundly as the transition from mystic feudalism to the modern age. The story of civilization is really the story of work. Work gives us meaning. It shapes our minds and our bodies. We are what we do. But reanimation technology allows us to postpone our productive days until after we're dead, and live by borrowing against the future. So what will we be, now that Victor's rendered work optional? Victor and I believe that we're in the early stages of a great divergence. Within the next few decades reanimated labor will liberate most people from the daily grind so that they can be with their families or make art or play video games or do whatever they want. A mass leisure class for a post-scarcity world.

On the other hand, even when work is optional, a small minority will choose it no matter what, a minority that is driven to compete and create, a sort of natural aristocracy. These are your Type As, your one percenters, your Victor Frankensteins, and they're not always popular but they're the ones who bring about progress. And the makers are going to find that thanks to Frankenstein's technology, they have the power to build on a scale undreamt of before. They will achieve godlike feats and create unfathomable wealth.

The radical left says that inequality is tearing society apart. Victor and I disagree with this line of thought entirely. Its basic premise is flawed. The fact is, inequality is what makes civilization function. Division of labor, specialization, mass industry. What do you have without those things? Hunter-gatherers. Stone Age primitives. There's never been a large-scale society without an elite. That's just true. The Roman Empire was one of the most unequal societies in history, and it lasted for five hundred years. We still read their classics and name months after their emperors. So I don't think inequality is destabilizing at all.

What the critics miss is that an unequal society isn't necessarily an unfair society. What Frankenstein offers us is a new inequality based on liberty and consumer choice. The people who just want to relax and take it easy can do so. And the people who want to compete at the very highest levels can do so. Victor's technology allows each and every one of us to fulfill our highest potential, and what that looks like is entirely up to us. It's an exciting time to be alive.

The future of work looks very different from its past. We're re-imagining everything, right down to the most fundamental processes. Not only are our engineers doing miraculous work to make each new product generation more effective than the last, but industrial design can be vastly improved now that human frailty is out of the equation. Franks can work at extremes of heat and cold, in airless environments, even underwater. For example, we've made deep sea oil drilling profitable again; right now there are more than a thousand Franks manning pumping stations on the ocean floor. Not only will the factories of the future operate without human beings, human beings won't even be able to step inside.

That sort of resilience is going to be so important in the future because, like it or not, the physical environment is changing around us. Science is very clear that global warming is happening, although the jury's still out on whether it's caused by human activity or if it's part of a natural cycle. But the good news is that even though we can't stop climate change, using reanimated labor we can adapt to it, even benefit from it. Human beings have adapted to all sorts of different climate conditions over the years, and there's no reason that we can't do that again. As the planet gets hotter, Franks will be able to continue working in all manner of hostile environments. It's entirely possible that by 2050, Franks will be helping us to adapt to melting ice caps by recovering salvage from coastal regions, mining newly-available resources at the poles, and building industrial parks in regions rendered too hot for human habitation. We also expect Franks to take the lead in space exploration and colonization, which is the only truly long-term solution to environmental collapse. I can't go into detail, but we've been doing some incredibly exciting work getting ready to send astro-zombies to the stars.

What about the Internet of the future? Victor's transforming that as well. Our investment in iGor has built a planetwide communications network under Frankenstein's proprietary control. iGor's faster and more secure than the TCP/IP standard that most web traffic uses, plus it's fully integrated with our e-commerce portal and a world-class geo-mapping system linked to millions of Franks and billions of interconnected devices. And iGor can do far more than control Franks. That same infrastructure can support messaging, it can run streaming video, it can even provide banking services. Next year we're beginning a limited roll-out of a new cryptocurrency, Pluto. Over time we anticipate most of the traffic that currently occurs over the open Internet to migrate onto iGor, which will make iGor even better at anticipating user needs.

That brings me to AI, another area where our vast scientific investments are going to have world-transformative effects. We started out just needing our Franks to be able to walk, to use tools, to work together, but we've long since surpassed that and now we're in the realm of true computerized decision-making. Over time, we're going to see more and more autonomy granted to these tools as they demonstrate not just that they make good choices, but that they can improve on human leadership. The dead can't be bigoted. They make choices based on pure logic, free of prejudice or greed or even emotion. Now, that's threatening to some people. Some people say you need that human factor. But when you look at history, and all of the carnage that the human factor has wrought, I think there's a great case for putting the zombies in charge. I'm not saying that AI will completely supplant human decision-making. But making choices is a type of work, a difficult and taxing type of work, and now we have necrotech to lift that burden from us.

So the good news is that we're at the dawn of a new age for mankind. The bad news is that it won't be peaceful. Progress is never peaceful. The printing press led to centuries of religious warfare. The gasoline engine powered World War II. And today, sadly, we see awful violence in backlash to reanimation, both at home and abroad. We can see it today right outside this convention center. In the Western world so-called "Gravedigger" terrorists are turning our public places into shooting galleries. Globally, especially in the Middle East, religious zealotry has destabilized whole countries. I'm sad to say there's no way to avoid bloodshed. But it is still within our power to choose order over chaos. I propose to you that for all the horror in the headlines today, the dead have great promise as peacemakers, and we are on the verge of a Pax Frankenstein.

Let me start with global affairs. We're very proud of the work that our defense division has done with the Pentagon. Z-war has brought about a revolution in military affairs every bit as profound as the Gatling gun. So when you see bad news from overseas, remember that the terrorists are fighting a losing battle, a battle against progress. And once they've been defeated, we're going to enjoy the fruits of a tranquilized era, where America has the weapons it needs to keep peace on a global scale without putting living troops in harm's way.

At home, meanwhile, we incorporate everything we learn from the wars into our Dragonstooth-class police zombies, the ones who are protecting us right now against the rioters outside. Counter-insurgency warfare is an ideal training set for an AI police control system; it's taught us to build some very sophisticated tools for identifying dangerous places and people. Feeding threat analytics from iGor into law enforcement databases will enable z-police to react to problems in faster-than-real time for immediate response. Every sensor connected to the iGor network can be taught to monitor for criminal activity and automatically alert law enforcement. Predictive algorithms can mine our massive data libraries to identify troubled individuals before they lash out. So, for example, if a mentally ill person has stopped taking their meds, we actually have the data to recognize that and automatically send z-police to that person's location for a wellness check. And of course, iGor's facial recognition software can track targeted persons seamlessly, leaving criminals with nowhere to hide. So as scary as things may seem now, take heart – we are very close to a future in which Frankenstein technology makes every policeman's dreams come true. Civil disturbances like what we see outside today won't happen in the near future. We have the predictive data to stop riots before the first stone is thrown.

Victor's critics accuse him of being closed-off and secretive. I think that's unfair. As much as he enjoys his privacy, he's been transparent about his intentions all along. He says what he's going to do, and the critics don't believe him, and when he accomplishes his goal they act like he's pulled a fast one. There's only one element of his plans that he won't disclose, and that's the naming of a successor. I assure you, Victor Frankenstein is going to be running his company for a very long time. We will all continue to live in his shadow, and I propose that's a wonderful place to be.

LANCHESTER EQUITY PARTNERS ANALYST REPORT

(1Q 2019)

Frankenstein Enterprises (NYSE: FRK) has defied the skeptics ever since its founding, shattering the Street's expectations of what a public company can accomplish. FRK's third-quarter results once again demolished analyst projections, delighting shareholders even against the backdrop of a robust earnings season. We are pleased that we provided one of the most accurate forecasts available, undershooting the share price by just 1.5% (projected $14,789.32 vs actual $15,014.17) and earnings per share by just 3.8% (projected $176.13 vs actual $183.09). Frankenstein's doubters have typically focused on four factors to justify a discount on FRK shares. We argue that each of these concerns are overblown, and that none represent a serious threat to the company's long-term valuation.

Donor Pension Liabilities: Many analysts have suggested that FRK's liabilities to its donors are a vulnerability for the company, particularly in this stubbornly low interest rate environment. Victor Frankenstein's plan to privatize the social safety net and use it to gather corpses is certainly an unprecedented business model, and it is fair to question whether a tech firm, even one as nimble and innovative as FRK, is capable of managing a suite of assets and liabilities now dwarfing those of the old-school state pension funds like CALPers. However, the murderer's row of traders at FRK's in-house hedge fund have consistently achieved above-market returns, providing ample reserves, and FRK's pension liabilities are housed in off-balance sheet entities, protecting the company and its shareholders even in worst-case scenarios. Donor mortality rates have continually exceeded actuarial expectations, offering further financial cushion. Most importantly, FRK's brilliant decision to offer advance loans to its donors offsets pension liabilities with lending income. A significant minority of donors now receive no monthly cash payment at all, since their interest payments to the company on their past advances exceed the sums they would otherwise be entitled to.

Legal/Regulatory: Doomsayers have predicted a regulatory backlash ever since Victor Frankenstein first announced his discovery, with many predicting that ancient taboos and funerary customs would frustrate any attempts to profit from reanimated labor. Twenty-five years later, the dusty laws against the desecration of dead bodies have never been applied to the reanimated labor industry in any serious way, and there is no adverse legislative action on the horizon in any of FRK's major markets, despite or because of left-wing protest movements. Meanwhile, the continually-falling prices of reanimated products and the breadth of the company's offerings speak against the feeble threat of antitrust enforcement. The FTC simply has no footing against a firm that unambiguously lowers consumer prices. The myth that someday lawmakers will regulate reanimated labor is itself a sort of zombie belief, staggering on no matter how many times it is killed. It is time to put this unrealistic notion in the ground once and for all.

Labor Market Feedback Loops: Some economists have suggested that eventually the labor market will reach a tipping point where the cost of live labor plummets below the cost of zombies. We believe this critique overlooks the miraculous efforts that FRK's Death Valley workforce have put into improving undead productivity and capabilities. Furthermore, as Chief Operating Officer Henry Clerval often remarks, American workplaces are adopting iGor-optimized devices at a breakneck pace, locking in the superiority of FRK products. Even if the living accepted subminimum wages and tried to return to the workforce, they would find that their old workplaces are now full of tools that human beings can't use.

CEO Concerns: Finally, many FRK doubters have voiced concerns about Dr. Victor Frankenstein, the company's enigmatic founder, CEO, and principal shareholder. Investors ask, "How can we trust a leader who won't even appear in public?" We say, "Just look at how much money he's made for you." We would exile every CEO in our portfolio to the Alps if we thought it would produce similar results. Although the lack of a succession plan is not ideal from an institutional perspective, the company has a deep bench of executive talent and its visionary founder shows no signs of slowing down.

Notwithstanding FRK's already-enormous size, we see ample space for growth. The company's product pipeline is robust, especially in the healthcare and military/law-enforcement sectors, and revenues from software and peripheral hardware continue to rise. We reiterate our **BUY** recommendation.

THE INTERN

A dead monkey sat in a Buddha pose on the conference table at the top of the world, awaiting the signal that would jolt it back into motion. Tom Philips gazed into the creature's empty eyes and saw his own face reflected back at him. It was as if the factory had harvested the night sky, compressed its darkness into two tiny pebbles, and polished them to shine mirror-bright. The executive smiled inwardly as another of his pitiless schemes approached fruition.

Tom was a Vice President for Special Projects in Frankenstein Enterprises' Materials Procurement division. He had no peers, only five rivals with the same title on their business cards. They all sat gathered for a meeting in the C-Suite of the company's headquarters, looking down on the San Francisco Bay from a place that was both the highest point in the city and the global pinnacle of corporate power. Henry Clerval, the company's chief operating officer, and Jim Whale, president of Materials Procurement, quietly chatted at the far end of the table. A telephone sat between them, the line open. Waiting for Victor to call in. Tom's heart raced.

Clerval had brought some intern to the meeting as well, a sickly-looking twenty-something who sat vacantly against the back wall, painfully stiff in his starched shirt and khakis. Tom studied meeting attendance like a Kremlinologist playing a game of "Who's Still In Photos With Stalin?," and it annoyed him that a lowly intern got to be present at a meeting with Victor, a prize so viciously fought over, and so costly to win. But even a cat may look upon a king, and even an intern can be in the room when the CEO dials in.

Suddenly the phone chirped. Everyone but the kid jumped at the noise. "I'm here, you can start," Victor Frankenstein said impatiently. Hearing the founder's deep, lightly accented voice crackling over the phone lines elevated Tom into a state of near-ecstasy, the closest he got to religious experience. He believed Victor Frankenstein to be the greatest figure in human history, a capitalist warrior-philosopher who counted death itself amongst his defeated competitors. This quarterly meeting represented an opportunity to win the titan's attention, to show that one deserves to be elevated above the heavens or swatted into a bloody smear. Jim Whale went around the table doing introductions, the normally sharp-tongued division president now reverently meek.

Gerald Okamura was first to present, rising from his chair with reckless speed and surety. He activated the dead monkey with his cell phone, commanding it to rise and fetch him a bottle of water. "As you know, z-monkeys have been a consistently high-volume market since Frankenstein Enterprises' founding," he said, running through slides with profit-and-loss statements on the company's business in the trade of reanimated chimpanzees and rhesus macaques. "Z-monkeys can fit in industrial spaces that human-sized workers can't, and dead monkeys are much cheaper to obtain than human cadavers. Uh, on average, I mean. But animal breeders in the U.S. can't meet Frankenstein's demand, and use of imports has exposed us to environmentalist complaints that we're destroying wild populations by encouraging poaching in the Third World. That's why I've built a state-of-the-art primate breeding facility in Butler Spring, Idaho to completely in-source our supply chain." He clicked through pictures of a windowless concrete maze where hundreds of pregnant monkeys lounged hopelessly in bare little cages. Gerald launched excitedly into the long-term cost savings he expected from his venture.

"Terrible," Victor growled in interruption. From the visceral disgust in his voice you'd have thought that Gerald laid a reeking wet fart in his presence, but Victor was in a mountaintop castle on the far side of the globe. Okamura staggered on his feet at the rebuke. The blood in his face drained away.

"We're phasing z-monkeys out in most civilian markets," Clerval commented acidly. "Studies proved that z-monkeys are cannibals. They gobble up profits that we could be earning in our main business lines. Every time a customer who could afford a Frank buys a reanimated ape instead, we lose money. You'd know all of this if you'd talked with Marketing."

"It's the first I've heard of this monkey business," Whale announced, Pontius Pilate washing his hands clean. "This thing must have come out of his discretionary budget, because I didn't sign off on any chimpanzee fuck-palace."

Before Gerald could explain that the facility relied on artificial insemination exclusively, Victor tersely ordered the chimpanzee fuck-palace shut down. Gerald returned to his chair with the dazed, haunted look of a man who began his day expecting praise and bonuses, and ended it tasked with the immediate liquidation of several thousand monkeys, his own disposal to follow promptly thereafter.

Tom's presentation came next. Electric currents of tension ran through his body. He took the podium intensely aware that at this moment of trial Victor watched him from six different camera angles. But after Gerald's debacle he had no place to go but up. "Altruit Health is the leading broker of medical data in the U.S.," Tom announced, projecting all the considerable charm and authority at his command. He displayed a slide with the Altruit logo, a stylized 'A' with an ever-watchful eye lodged in its uppermost triangle. "Altruit collects consumer health information from insurers, hospitals, pharmacies, credit card companies, genetic testing firms, bankruptcy filings, and more. With digital dossiers on two hundred million plus Americans and billions of records, they likely have better information about your medical history than you do. And I've struck a deal with them. Leveraging our market-leading position in artificial intelligence, we can comb through their database to automatically identify prospective donors in acute medical and financial distress, which then alerts our online advertising systems to aggressively target those prospects. Furthermore, cross-referencing Altruit data at the point of recruitment will help us improve our actuarial projections, individualizing our pension offerings for maximum profitability."

Clerval and Whale probed at the project's long-term costs, the metrics for reckoning success, the due diligence Tom had performed. Tom took sure command of the executive inquisition, an answer ready for each problem they posed. "Victor, what's your take?" Henry asked.

"Good," grunted Victor. Tom's spirit soared at this monosyllabic praise from his idol, in fact, the very highest praise that Dr. Frankenstein was known to offer. But then, Tom had engineered the entire venture around Victor's hard-edged business philosophy, marrying overwhelming capital and bleeding-edge science to build an intelligent, self-perpetuating profit machine that could print money at scale. On his way back to his seat, Tom noticed Gerald glowering bitterly at him. He met his defeated enemy's glare with a smirk.

Napoleon Toussaint spoke next, discussing the secret contracts he'd recently inked with ICE. Bill Montel followed with a report about his success buying up the patent rights to a promising new anti-malarial drug that threatened to reduce donor uptake from the tropics by the thousands each year. Then came Walter Tilringham to talk about the opportunities presented by the Chinese government's latest ethnic roundups in Turkestan and Tibet. Finally, Tess Smolka presented on her ongoing work funding anti-vaxxer advocacy. The project's ROI to date was low, but it was known as one of Victor's pets, and therefore treated with great tenderness and fed well. The uninspired competence of his rivals suited Tom's purposes. While he didn't want Materials Procurement to be known as a den of fuck-ups, nor did he want any of the division's other stars to outshine his own.

Victor closed out proceedings with a brusque accounting of the division's targets for the next fiscal quarter, his expectations aggressive as ever, then hung up without a word of thanks or praise, abruptly adjourning the meeting.

Gerald picked his zombified monkey up from the conference table and threw it in the garbage. The man was on the verge of tears, revolting and gratifying Tom. As a rule, the sight and sound of people crying sickened him, but not the point where he couldn't enjoy a good gloat.

"Tom, what happened?" the near-frantic Gerald asked. "You told me that you'd talked with Marketing!"

"I did talk with Marketing," Tom said coolly. "They told me that only a fool would build a factory farm for chimps. I thought this would be a perfect project for you."

"What? But this was our project! We worked on it together!"

"Did we? My name's not on any of the documents. You were happy enough to claim all the credit when you thought you had a big success, and now that it's a disaster we worked on it together?" Tom laughed mockingly. "You're even dumber than I thought."

"Goddamn it, Tom, I thought we were friends," Gerald complained, close to blubbering. "I never dreamed you'd screw me over like this."

"It is necessary for a prince wishing to hold his own to know how to do wrong, and to make use of it or not according to necessity," Tom said, quoting good old Machiavelli. "Now get the fuck out of my face, Henry Clerval's coming this way."

Frankenstein Enterprises' chief operating officer was an impossibly, enragingly perfect specimen of humanity, a man who has it all and can afford infinitely more. His handshake's firm pressure induced a warm, almost hypnotic state of good regard and confidence. "I'm glad to see you today, Tom, I've heard nothing but good things, and I'd like to learn more," Henry said, flashing teeth perfect enough for a toothpaste commercial or a ravening shark. "I'd like to introduce you to my nephew, Edison Clerval. He's just starting an internship at the company."

Edison seemed to be from a side of the Clerval family tree that didn't get any sunlight. He had short brown hair and a port wine stain on his neck that made him look like he'd spilled something on himself. The kid's unblinking eyes flitted wildly about Tom's face, his too-eager smile reminding Tom yet again of chimpanzees. Tom hated every second of his clammy handshake, somehow both bony and dough-soft, but he gave him the same heartily enthusiastic greeting he would have given anyone with a close blood connection to his boss's boss. On Henry's request, Tom brought the Clervals back to his own office, basking in the warmth of his colleagues' jealousy. Henry sat on the couch while Edison methodically inspected the collection of Haitian ironwork hung along the walls, souvenirs of Tom's posting in Port-au-Prince. Frankenstein Enterprises' chief operating officer, the right hand of God, asked Tom where he wanted to go.

"Space," Tom said. "I want to go to outer space."

Henry's eyebrows raised slightly, an expression of bemused non-surprise. "When I was in first grade, I wanted to be an astronaut, too."

"Spare me the act, you know what I mean," Tom said. "I want to work in Frankenstein's space program." The words came out in the same tone of voice that one might use to make a wish upon a genie's lamp. Or a monkey's paw. "Everybody in the company knows about it. Victor's private rocketry start-up is up to something big. He's conquered death, he's bought Wall Street, and now he's going to go to the stars. It's brilliant. Deploying zombies, the company can colonize other planets for mining and industrialization. No competition. No regulation. It's a frontier ripe for exploitation, and we're going to get there first. Ten years from now, this company's going to have a presence on the moon, harvesting resources we can barely imagine today."

Henry chuckled knowingly. "Victor wants the moon much sooner than ten years from now. He has strong views on the company's future, and yes, he's looking for executive talent to turn those views into reality. Now putting the future aside and getting back to the present, I have a favor to ask of you. An order, actually. I told you Edison's an intern. Well, he's *your* intern. For the next three months he's going to shadow you around, learn your magic. Don't be afraid to work him hard, he's here to show us all what he's made of."

Another dopamine burst shuddered through Tom as they shook hands again. He wondered if Henry had picked him for the mentorship before the meeting began, or if he'd sealed the deal on his feet. Clerval departed, leaving Tom alone with his new intern. The kid finished examining the ironwork and turned his attention to Tom's bookshelf, a personal library of management guidebooks and military strategy. In Tom's way of thinking, the two subjects were substantially identical. "Have you read any of those?" he asked.

"Of course," Edison said, sunny and confident without braggadocio. He tapped the spine of Sun Tzu's *On War*. "To secure ourselves against defeat lies in our own hands, but the opportunity of defeating the enemy is provided by the enemy himself."

"That's the spirit," Tom replied. "Let's get to work."

There was work to be had in great abundance. The Altruit deal had fed Frankenstein Enterprises a vast body of consumer data, and digesting such a huge and complex supper was no simple matter. The files needed to be integrated with the company's automated actuarial system so that Frankenstein could make the most informed and accurate predictions about when its donors would die. Tom spent his days in meetings, lashing the programming team's helots to complete their tasks on deadline or fending off thievery from his grasping counterparties at Altruit Health. He spent his nights poring through spreadsheets and contracts and reports, a gray blur that he was polishing into a gemstone. A treasure that would earn him a place above the sky.

Edison was at his side for all of it, another gray blur coming into focus. In the beginning the kid seemed a human blank, so bland and shy that he blended into the background like a chameleon in business casual. He rarely spoke unless spoken to, and politely but forcefully deflected all Tom's inquiries into the affairs of the Clerval family. Tom felt a lack in him, some mysterious dark matter in his character that couldn't be seen directly, yet whose absence shaped the whole of his being. Ever the cynic, Tom suspected that off-hours Edison oriented his life around some kind of high-end perversion. It was all the same to Tom, who believed that terrible urges can take a man far.

And the intern was clearly destined to go far. He spoke more languages than Tom had heard of and seemed to carry the encyclopedia inside his head. The company invested almost-inconceivable resources so that each new generation of its product would be more capable than the last. Management applied the same principle to their own families. Tom's own brats went to Saint Cyprian's, a Catholic school so elite that even Medici Popes would have struggled with the tuition, and he could barely imagine the superhuman educational privileges that a Clerval would enjoy. Tom once jokingly proposed that they go to Vegas to count cards, and in an instant Edison ran the numbers in his head and calculated that robbing casinos would be a pay cut at Tom's salary.

The intern's hyper-numeracy gave him an uncanny knack for working with the Altruit data. He was the one who recognized that Altruit was mercilessly efficient at identifying suicidally unhappy prospects ages 18-

35, a prime demographic segment that Tom nicknamed "Morose Millenials." More meetings, this time with marketing, to talk micro-targeted messaging and social media ad buys. Donations and uptake jumped.

Edison also showed Tom how to look up individual dossiers in the Altruit database. Tom ran his rivals' records and discovered that Tess Smolka was infertile, and that Bill Montel took so many anti-psychotics he was halfway a zombie himself. Tom filed this actionable intelligence away for another day. He also learned that six months ago, his wife Veronica had taken a course of ceftriaxone and azithromycin, antibiotics for a gonorrhea infection that he sure as shit hadn't given her. Tom ordered Edison to schedule appointments with a doctor and a divorce lawyer. Strangely, Altruit had nothing on Edison himself, who was apparently so rich that he could even afford privacy.

The kid really opened up over the course of summer, his initial nerdy mousiness giving way to a Gordon Gekko swagger that Tom found quite appealing. Indeed, the more they worked together the more Edison reminded Tom of himself as a young man.

On the morning of the quarterly meeting, Tom couldn't stop thinking about the praise he expected, imagining Victor's surly "Good" again and again, rolling the sound over in his mind. The Altruit deal was a demonstrable success, he was mentor to Henry Clerval's nephew, and for shits and giggles he'd knifed Napoleon Toussaint's latest crime against humanity with a well-timed leak to the muckraking Rose Najafi. The Earth itself was not enough to contain his ambitions now. Distracted by these lofty thoughts, he didn't notice that his Styx was taking him the wrong route until it began crossing the Oakland Bay Bridge.

The vice president's triumph turned to panic in a flash when he looked at the time and the traffic. After some useless fucking about on his phone trying to re-route, he remembered that Edison had ordered the ride for him, and called in a fright.

"I'm sorry, Tom, I can't do that," Edison said blandly, the first time he'd ever refused a request.

"What do you mean you can't do that?!" Tom shouted, each turn of the Styx's wheels taking him further from his meeting with Victor

Frankenstein and destiny. "Just put in coordinates for the office and turn this fucking car around!"

"You're going to Sacramento, Tom. I'm giving the Altruit presentation to Victor. Don't worry, I'll do a better job than you would have."

For all that Tom dealt in betrayal, he was usually on the dealing end of it. To experience it from this angle unbalanced him completely. The vice president hollered terrible things.

"Princes who have done great things have held good faith of little account," the intern said mockingly. "They have known how to circumvent the intellect of men by craft, and in the end have overcome those who have relied on their word."

"Don't you quote Machiavelli to me! I don't care who your uncle is, I will fuck the clap that Veronica gave me directly into your eye socket!"

"The meeting's just about to start, I have to put you on mute now. I'll loop your phone into the videoconferencing." Trapped in the backseat of a northbound Styx, Tom looked on in a state of escalating fury as his treasonous protege presented the quarterly results for the Altruit project. Edison Clerval had all his namesake's talent for stealing ideas and credit. He gave the presentation exactly as Tom would have given it, right down to the smallest gestures, the way he moved his hands and the tenor of his voice, and he fucking killed it. "Very good," Victor Frankenstein said at the end. Very good. ***Very. Good.*** The intern stole the highest praise that God had ever given. As the meeting adjourned, the last thing that Tom saw before the video stream cut out was Henry telling Edison to stay behind afterwards for a private chat.

When the Styx finally let Tom out in Sacramento, he pulled its z-driver out from behind the wheel, hurled it into the gutter where it lay unresisting, and kicked its brains out against the curbstone. He then ordered up another z-cab to drive him back to San Francisco. Tom stormed into his office and found the intern sitting at his desk, a usurper as well as a traitor. Edison only smirked, mirroring the face that Tom had so often displayed to his own bested rivals.

Ordinarily Tom was driven by psychopathic rage. He channeled it into his job and it served him well for the most part. Now, however, it got the better of him, exploding in a wild instant of fury. The vice president wrapped his fingers around his intern's neck and squeezed as hard as he could, his shoulders and forearms trembling, putting all of his muscle into a maniacal effort to choke the life from Henry Clerval's treacherous shit of a nephew.

Edison made no attempt to resist, not even raising his arms. He let himself be strangled and his smirk didn't tremble for a moment. His lips still curled sneeringly even as Tom slammed him against a wall and clenched down hard on his windpipe. The intern's unblinking, unafraid eyes explored his would-be killer's face with mild amusement. Tom realized that his victim was not breathing at all, was not even attempting to breathe.

"Oh my God," Tom moaned. "You're a Frank."

Tom caught a glimpse of z-security coming into his periphery, a knight in black armor, before taser darts bit through his suit and a pulse of shuddering pain put him on the ground.

Tom came to looking at Henry Clerval's Armani loafers, his cheek pressed against the warm, stubbly carpet and his right arm twisted behind his back. The z-guard had a hold of him, grasping him in some sort of judo move that was not actively painful but might easily become so. "Are you done being stupid?" Clerval asked.

"I'm not sure," Tom replied. Clerval chuckled warmly, and the z-guard released its grip. Tom slowly got to his feet, still sore and groggy from the tasering. Edison was back at Tom's desk again, unnervingly possessive of it. "You gave me a zombie intern," Tom accused.

"We gave you a Turing Test," Clerval countered. "You failed. Let me re-introduce you to the company's newest model. The Edison neo-zombie represents a decade of effort into AI research. His speech capabilities are built around a large language model based on billions of hours of conversation recorded by iGor. And he's wirelessly linked to a dedicated supercomputer running millions of calculations each second. Edison's been constantly analyzing every social interaction he's ever had with you, right down to your microexpressions and the modulations of your voice. This young man's an astonishing judge of character. He thinks you're not right for your job. And Victor agrees with him."

Enthroned on Tom's chair, Edison crossed his legs after Tom's fashion, still smiling that cold empty smile that made Tom yearn to kill. "If you know the enemy and know yourself, you need not fear the result of a hundred battles," he said, mimicking Tom's voice almost perfectly. "If you know neither the enemy nor yourself, you will lose every battle."

"Everything you and Victor saw in that meeting – that was *me*!" Tom protested, pounding his chest. He pointed an accusing finger at his neo-zombie doppelganger. "He's just copying me!"

"Yes, exactly," said Clerval. "Machine learning. Edison needed to pick an executive's brain for a few months to get a feel for management. Build up a training set. You should be honored you were chosen. Teaching him how to seem human is an important job; we wouldn't trust it to just anyone. But now it's time for both of you to move on."

"Wait, move on to where?" Tom asked, suddenly hopeful that the meeting might end cheerfully despite his failed assassination attempt.

"To the next stage of your career. You're fired. Z-security will escort you from the office when we're done here."

A cloud swallowed the sun forever. Tom stared at his own shaking hands in horror, the hands that'd just throttled a multi-billion-dollar company prototype. "I – I didn't hurt him," he stammered weakly.

Henry shook his head. "It's not about that; we wouldn't fire a high performer just for losing his temper with an intern. The decision was made before the meeting."

"I've been keeping track of exactly how much time you spend advancing the company's interests versus how much you spend undermining your department," Edison said. "Down to the second. I remember every lie that you tell. I record the costs of all the company resources you commandeer for your own use. I'll generate a copy of the report for you." Edison's eyes bulged ever-so-slightly and Tom's phone suddenly *dinged* as he received an e-mail attaching a PDF thoroughly documenting the past three months of his skullduggery.

"You disloyal bastard. I made you who you are."

"Frankenstein Enterprises made me. Not you."

"Victor wants executives who are cutthroat competitors *and* loyal team players," Henry said. "It's a rare mix in human beings. Edison is both."

"God damn it, this isn't fair! You saw what I accomplished with Altruit!" Tom's voice rose in frustration, prompting the z-guard to step in closer, putting itself between him and Henry.

"We did. Edison just told us that project's complete and doesn't require you any further. You'd know if you'd been at the meeting. You did good work, but this isn't about the work, it's a matter of trust."

"You're giving my job to a Frank?"

"Actually, no," said Henry. "Tell him what you'll be doing, Edison."

"Victor's chosen me for a project management role in the company's space program," Edison said. Tom nearly barked with laughter at the absurd spectacle of an unpaid summer internship opening such a door. "I'm the ideal candidate," the neo-zombie boasted, if a thing without feelings can boast. "I can manage Franks through my iGor connection, and I can manage humans using the people skills you've taught me."

"And he'll work 24-7-365 without even asking for a base salary, let alone incentive bonuses or stock options," said Clerval. "Victor wants the stars all to himself."

Now Tom did begin to cackle, all the day's violence pouring out of him in a stream of deranged hilarity that he couldn't have stopped if he'd tried. He kept laughing uncontrollably even as the z-guard shuffled him out of his office, past his ex-rivals and down the elevator. Huge iconic photographs of Victor Frankenstein dominated the building's lobby, peering down acquisitively. Tom kept chortling until at last the zombie shoved him out of the building into the chill of the early evening, at which point absurdity gave way to confusion. He staggered away quietly, going nowhere in particular, unsure of who he was now, occasionally glancing over his shoulder at the company's gleaming headquarters and wondering if perhaps he had died in there.

FRANKENSTEIN TAKES AIM AT THE STARS

BY ROSE NAJAFI, WASHINGTON POST (APRIL 29, 2015)

The night is cold in the Arizona desert. The darkness is so deep that it seems almost tangible, but the stars overhead burn incredibly bright and clear. Off in the distance, an explosion rumbles the ground, and a blazing rocket shoots into the sky like a comet in reverse.

Victor Frankenstein is expanding his reach into outer space.

Amateur stargazers have recently tracked a number of rocket launches to a desolate, fenced-in plot of scrubland in Western Arizona. Satellite photographs of the area reveal a compound covering nearly 1,300 acres, comparable in overall size to the Cape Canaveral Air Force Station. Real estate records show that Victor Frankenstein's personal foundation owns the land through a complex and nearly impenetrable web of shell companies. Interviews with a number of aerospace industry insiders, who requested anonymity, confirm that over the past several years the reanimation tycoon has invested billions of his personal fortune into a venture focused on off-world exploration and colonization. Frankenstein Enterprises spokespersons refused to comment.

Frankenstein Enterprises has long had business interests in space. In the course of developing its world-spanning iGor network, the company designed and launched a fleet of sophisticated telecom satellites, operating through its Star Wormwood subsidiary. Star Wormwood has since become a significant aerospace player in its own right, sending payloads into orbit for other commercial firms. It received more than $3 billion in U.S. government contracts in connection with NASA's privatization in 2010.

Star Wormwood, however, represents only the visible tip of Frankenstein's ambitions for space. As a subsidiary of the publicly-traded Frankenstein Enterprises, Star Wormwood must periodically report certain data about its operations. Victor Frankenstein's private space companies, however, can operate in near-total secrecy, a situation that alarms many in the scientific community.

"In theory, Frankenstein could find proof of extraterrestrial life and keep it all to himself," said Dr. Jacinda Newman, director of the McDonald Observatory in Texas. "He could even knock off E.T. and use him as a butler. It's extraordinarily dangerous that there's so little transparency or oversight. Does an astro-zombie plant a flag with the Frankenstein skull-and-brains corporate logo when it lands on the moon? Are we going to find ourselves in a situation where a single billionaire claims the whole solar system for himself? Congress simply didn't think these issues through when it privatized space exploration."

Not all observers are so disturbed. "I think it's fantastic if Victor Frankenstein's investing in off-world travel," said Dr. Lucas Volker, a professor of astrophysics at M.I.T. "The only way the human race is going to get to Mars is if a genius like him takes us there."

THE ASTRONAUT

You were the first living human being to set foot on Mars, and you'll likely be the last as well. Alpha and Omega. You run across a landscape of spectacular desolation, your headlamp barely piercing the epic darkness of a Martian night, your boots kicking up clouds of red dust. Inside your bulky exogear it feels like your body is made of lead, lead that has somehow gained the capacity to suffer terror and exhaustion. Cold, briny sweat drenches your bodysuit and drips into your eyes, nearly blinding you. You glance over your shoulder and through the stinging haze you see that the astro-zombies pursuing you are rapidly closing the gap. The dead are tireless, unbreathing, indifferent to pain and comfort and dignity. This planet belongs to them. And perhaps the Earth as well.

☠

Your ordeal began four years ago, with a phone call in the dead of the night. "How would you like to go to Mars?" an unfamiliar voice asked from the other end of the line.

"More than anything in the world," you answered almost reflexively. Indeed, you'd oriented your entire life around the stars; from a childhood bedroom decorated with model rockets and posters of Neil Armstrong and Sally Ride, to an adulthood in the Air Force flying fighter jets and experimental aircraft. After budget cuts shuttered NASA and brought down the International Space Station, you thought the era of manned spaceflight was over, and regretfully resigned yourself to a dreary existence piloting a desk at an aerospace firm. You had no idea that your dream would be reborn as a nightmare.

"I represent a private firm planning a manned interplanetary expedition," the caller said. "We're looking for an astronaut to spend two years on Mars setting up a colony. A Styx will be outside your house at seven A.M. If you want to learn more, get in." The line went dead abruptly.

Whoever they were, their tactics were transparent. They were looking for a candidate who would drop everything for a mere chance at getting off-world, one who would subordinate all of their own needs and desires to the needs of the mission. Standard operating procedure for space exploration.

The car took you to an unmarked office building, staffed almost exclusively by Franks. A pale, strikingly young man with a port wine stain on his neck met you in the lobby, giving his name as Mr. Edison. You suspected that this was an alias. You recognized his voice from the phone. He was much more personable on the phone. In the flesh, he was a resident of the uncanny valley, although you couldn't pinpoint exactly what it was in his features or mannerisms that made him seem so alien.

Mr. Edison took away your phone, sat you down in a conference room, and had you sign a sheaf of non-disclosure agreements as thick as a Russian novel and as restrictive as a gulag. Once you'd bound yourself to eternal silence, he gave you his pitch.

Your mysterious interviewer identified himself as an agent of Frankenstein Enterprises, and told you that the company aimed to build a permanent Martian base to serve as proof-of-concept for undead space conquest. Once the colony was fully operational then zombies and robots would crew it exclusively, but in the beginning, a sole human astronaut was needed to get the grand experiment started.

Edison described this astronaut's life darkly. The interview process alone was a prolonged gauntlet designed to weed out all but the most resilient specimens. After that came months of intensive training that would put all of that resilience to the test. The voyage to Mars represented nine months of mortal danger and crushing tedium traveling through a black and airless void. Upon arrival, the astronaut would spend more than two years in the most hostile, remote, and isolated environment ever visited by man, to be followed by another nine-month stint traversing vacuum. If the astronaut successfully returned to Earth – a contingency that Edison stressed he could not guarantee – the astronaut would return to no glory, no ticker-tape parade, no public recognition at all. Frankenstein's space project was a closely-held secret, and the NDAs you'd signed bound you to hold your tongue until death and beyond. The only rewards that Frankenstein offered were a $20 million payday and the memory of an adventure beyond the furthest borders of the human experience.

You agreed immediately. Frankenstein Enterprises was a soulless corporate behemoth and Mr. Edison a creep, but they were offering you the stars themselves, the only thing you truly wanted. You had only one question. "Why is Frankenstein investing in off-world exploration?" you asked. "How are you going to make money by putting zombies on Mars?"

"This is much bigger than money," your chalk-faced interlocutor declared. "Dr. Frankenstein is concerned about the long-term future of his company. He wants to be sure that Frankenstein Enterprises can continue as a going concern even after the Earth becomes uninhabitable."

At the time, you thought you understood why a scientist would be pessimistic about the planet's future. But you never asked if the destruction of life on Earth was a doom that Frankenstein dreaded, or the fulfillment of his master plan.

☠

Your trials and trainings were every bit as grueling as that first interview had suggested, and moreso. The training facility itself was a rather close analogue to the Martian experience; a sprawling compound deep in the Arizona desert, with detailed mock-ups of the rocket that you would be flying in and the Martian base that you would assemble. Fittingly for a Frankenstein Enterprises venture, zombies handled most of the day-to-day tasks, even duties requiring shockingly high levels of scientific skill and training. Only a handful of humans worked at the base, mostly AI technicians tasked with managing the Franks. They were a distant, peevish lot, and you suspected they'd been instructed not to socialize with you. You vaguely understood that somewhere at the facility other astronauts-in-training were undergoing the same tests as yourself, but you never met any of them, and they were never anything more to you than an abstract obstacle to be overcome. Mr. Edison was your Sherpa through the process, the closest thing you had to a colleague. You kept hoping you'd develop Stockholm Syndrome that never quite clicked in.

Most people would have described your space camp experience as physical and psychological torture, but you'd come of your own free will, so you knew it was only a job interview. You underwent exhausting batteries of medical testing, physical conditioning, and training with every piece of equipment that the Mars base would contain, especially the zombies. Frankenstein made you spend weeks on end in horribly cramped and sterile quarters, running you through grueling tests. Then they made you spend months in the even-tighter oubliette of the Potemkin rocket ship, practicing at the controls with a rigor and consistency to shame Sisyphus. Once, right as you were emerging blinking from a two-week stint in experimental solitary confinement, Mr. Edison informed you that your grandmother had died while you were sealed away incommunicado. It often occurred to you that a company like Frankenstein, so accustomed to dealing with zombies, was disused to the frailties of the living, and perhaps even offended by them.

On the rare nights when you had a little liberty, you walked in the desert and looked into the sky, finding the glittering red dot that you were destined for. It was so beautiful. Just as the Earth revolves around the Sun, so your life revolved around Mars.

☠

Launch day was an experience so unreal that you spent much of it in a daze, operating off of muscle memory as you performed the part you'd rehearsed so exhaustively. It felt like a hallucination that had been planned and regimented to the slightest detail. Zombies strapped you into a chair atop the most powerful non-nuclear bomb ever developed. You ran through all of the checklists, declared all systems go. The countdown lasted for a brief, tense infinity. Then liftoff hit you like an orgasm, and incandescent bliss lit up every cell of your being as you rocketed out of the exosphere. As you passed beyond the moon's orbit, traveling farther than any pilgrim in human history had ventured before, you felt a sense of joy and accomplishment so vast that it humbled you.

However, as the days stretched into weeks, and then months, you came to experience a profound silence and loneliness that humbled you even further. Due to the spartan terms of your NDA and the logistical problems of communicating with a planet you'd left so far behind, Mr. Edison and the other personnel of Mission Control were the only people that you could speak with during your odyssey. They were terse, unwilling to make any small talk not focused on the voyage. And there was not much to discuss on that front. The rocket was largely computer-controlled during this phase, leaving you with little to do but read, eat your oily, metallic-tasting rations, and exercise against the wasting malaise of zero-gravity. Your background as a fighter pilot had prepared you for many challenges, but not this isolation and helplessness, leading you to darkly speculate that Frankenstein would have been better off recruiting from the prison population than the Air Force.

As you traveled through the cosmic darkness, you fell prey to the demon that afflicts all those unfortunate enough to see their ultimate desires fulfilled. *Is that all there is?* you wondered, watching the distant stars through the cockpit windows.

To distract yourself from these and other black thoughts, you frequently visited your crew members, the two dozen astro-zombies sealed in plastic pods in the bottommost chamber of the vessel. You gazed at them, so peaceful in their slumber. Two dozen spacefaring Sleeping Beauties. Despite your conditioning, you began talking to the dead almost immediately. You assigned them names, backstories, and personalities, ignoring your trainers' advice about the psychological risks of anthropomorphizing your decidedly inhuman crew. Their storage bay served as your social hall and confessional. You told the cadavers all your thoughts and hopes and fears, addressing them in accordance with the identities you'd imagined for them, and sometimes hearing their replies. This practice drove you crazy in some ways, and kept you sane in others.

Mars slowly swelled in your cockpit window like a red balloon inflating, until you could see nothing else. When it came time for your final approach, adrenaline pulled all of your nerves as tight and musical as violin strings. You skillfully steered the spacecraft into the upper reaches of the exosphere, then let gravity seize you and your vessel in her welcoming, crushing embrace, and dropped into a controlled plummet, falling more than a hundred miles in a matter of seconds. The ground surged up to meet you, as if Mars was as impatient for first contact as you were. You pulled up at the last moment and brought your ship in for a smooth landing, touching down with a supremely satisfying impact that shook you to your bones. Then you sat back in your seat and stared at the Martian landscape – a rocky, wind-swept plain that thrilled your soul. It was so very barren and pure. Arrival was as sweet as you'd hoped.

In your childhood dreams about this moment, you'd landed to worldwide acclaim, with the populace of a grateful Earth glued to their TV sets watching you make history. But you'd never been driven by fame. You knew what you had done, and the Martian soil knew your weight, and that was all the recognition you needed.

The Mars landing had gone exactly according to Frankenstein's plans. The front portion of the vessel, containing the crew and cargo, had detached from the last of the spent booster rockets, and you successfully parked it in the spot that Frankenstein's corporate astronomers had selected. It was intended to remain there forever, serving as a permanent command center for the Mars colony, with your return shuttle scheduled to arrive after you'd constructed a launch pad for it.

Your first task on Mars was reanimating the crew. You set up a local iGor network, opened the coffins, and brought the dead back online. It was eerie to watch the sleepers awaken and get to work, so unmoved by the significance of the moment, and so completely devoid of the individual histories and personalities you'd spent the past nine months projecting onto them. For all the time you'd been talking to them, there was no sign that they'd listened to a word of it.

The astro-zombies immediately began the immensely complicated task of reconfiguring the spacecraft and the prefab structures in its cargo bay into a permanent base of extraterrestrial operations. Their unflagging energy reminded you of ants, which is to say that they were ideal colonists.

They had been specially modified to endure the low atmospheric pressure. With regular injections of biological antifreeze they could handle even the bitter Martian cold. And they didn't need to breathe at all. They worked constantly, mostly guided by their own extraordinarily sophisticated AI and input from Mission Control on Earth, requiring relatively little guidance from you. Indeed, as you progressed, building more infrastructure to support their networked pseudo-minds, the dead became even more intelligent and capable, to an almost frightening extent. Slack-jawed walking corpses solved problems that would have baffled brilliant engineers. Once they were up and running, your principal task was simple maintenance. The astro-zombies suffered frequent damage and injuries in this wildly hostile terrain. Fortunately, Frankenstein had planned for this, and equipped the colony with an enormous stockpile of frozen tissues and organs. And after you'd constructed a robotic surgery bay, the crew could repair their own wounds without any human help.

Under your guidance a necropolis sprouted on Mars. The dead built a launch pad, satellite arrays and communications dishes, solar and wind farms, a soybean hydroponics facility for their protein, even a drilling rig to penetrate deep beneath the surface and retrieve enormous cylinders of ice. Every aspect of the base had been designed with an eye towards sustainability and expansion. Once it was fully operational, it would be nearly self-sufficient, requiring only periodic shipments of dead people and mechanical parts. Dr. Frankenstein was a long-term thinker, indeed.

Meanwhile, Mission Control regarded your progress with its vast, cool, and unsympathetic intellect, reading Mars with covetous eyes, and slowly but surely drawing its plans against you.

While your successful arrival on Mars had served as a tonic for your mental state, breaking you out of your lonely funk and distracting you with work, eventually solitary confinement began biting again, particularly as the Franks became more independent and you found yourself with more free time on your hands. Your old pastime of speaking with the crew didn't satisfy you as it had during the journey. Now that the astro-zombies were activated, looking into their eyes you saw a profound and alien intelligence with no interest in your chatter. You could no longer pretend that these things were human in any aspect but their forms.

Instead of holding one-sided conversations, you began taking recreational hikes on the Martian surface, exploring the awesome emptiness. It felt good to stand beneath a sky and on top of dirt again, after so long cooped up inside a space-crypt with company worse than solitude. One day you were returning from one of these jaunts when the base seemed to shimmer like a mirage in the puny sun's thin light, and a ghastly vision appeared before you. You saw the Frankenstein base grown to an enormous spaceport, launching countless more morgue-rockets into the farthest reaches of the cosmos. In your imagination you walked through Martian domes where zombies factory-farmed children in steel cages and slaughtered them at physical maturity so that their corpses might be quickened, and packed into spaceships, and sent to new worlds to populate the universe with horrors.

You shuddered, and your monstrous vision of the future ended. Your rational mind recoiled at what your subconscious had shown you. There was no proof that Frankenstein was pondering anything along the lines that you had imagined, no proof that this facility was anything but a grand and ambitious experiment. However, having had such a thought, you could not entirely put it away thereafter. Your Martian experience had proven that zombies were superior cosmonauts, having transcended in death many of the frailties that made space travel so challenging for mortals. The need for human tissues and corpses was the only resource constraint that kept Frankenstein from conquering space. If the dead only learned how to domesticate the living, the whole of the solar system could be theirs. Perhaps even more than that.

With notions like these preying on your mind and a low-gravity lifestyle withering your body, you understood that you could neither physically nor emotionally maintain Martian life for much longer. Daydreams of fresh air, warm beaches, and living faces invaded your thoughts. At night, you'd look into the sky and find the blue speck of the Earth, like spotting a lover's face in a crowd. You were ready to go home in secret triumph, and enjoy all the comforts you'd left. The knowledge that you were returning to $20 million didn't hurt, either. The launch window for your return trip – the period of time when

Mars and Earth were closest in their waltzing orbits – approached rapidly. You counted the days. Your life, which had once revolved around Mars like Phobos and Deimos, now revolved around thoughts and memories of home.

Yet as you grew increasingly excited about the prospect of return, Mission Control fell increasingly silent on the subject. They reassured you that the shuttle coming to pick you up was on schedule, but no more than that. More alarmingly still, your food stockpile began to run low. The most recent resupply rockets had only contained building supplies and shrink-wrapped organs. You had no doubt that the company, which had managed every aspect of the mission so skillfully and without error, had everything under control. Yet you didn't think through all the implications of what their control might entail.

☠

This morning you awoke to the last Martian sunrise you'll ever see. The sun is so distant here that its rising is a poor, pale spectacle, one that you've become jaded to, but you would have paid more attention to the dawn if you'd known that weren't getting any more of them.

You performed your daily toilet in the room of little ease that served as your bathroom, and went through all your usual routines, checking that the colony's systems were operating properly and that the astro-zombies were performing their assigned tasks. By this point in the mission your efforts were largely redundant. Everything seemed to be going well. The only element out of place was an astro-zombie in the robotic surgery bay, receiving a new arm in the aftermath of a grisly welding accident.

Checking your email in the afternoon, you saw that Mission Control sent you a message with an update on the return shuttle. Your excitement quickly soured as you realized that their "update" had no real information. Even more frustrated with their stonewalling than usual, you opened a voice communications link. "Mission Control, I need a complete briefing on the return shuttle," you barked. "When is it arriving here and what do I need to do to prepare? I need the details, damn it! This is an interplanetary mission, I can't be flying blind." Your demand pulsed out of the station's communications array and shot towards the Earth at 186,000 miles per second. You settled in and awaited their response, idly killing time by remotely observing the transplant surgery in progress.

The details you'd asked for arrived an hour later, delivered by Mr. Edison himself. "There is no return shuttle," he replied, his voice cold as a Martian night. "We never launched one."

Edison's words hit you like a sucker punch from an old enemy. They felt weirdly inevitable, and they caught you completely by surprise. You weren't sure if you'd heard him correctly, or if your long solitude was whispering paranoid delusions into your ears. "Edison, repeat that?" you asked in fright. There was another long delay, waiting for your question to reach the Earth, and his response to get back to Mars.

"There's no return shuttle coming," Mr. Edison said firmly. "It would cost $1.2 billion to bring you back to Earth. There's no money for it in the project budget."

"You're going to leave me up here to die?" you screamed. But there was no answer. He'd already closed the communications line.

The two astro-zombies working in the control room stopped their labors and turned to face you. Before this moment, your undead crew had never even really seemed to notice you, their purported captain. They were always totally absorbed in their work of assembling the station. But now they'd received new orders from Mission Command. The astro-zombies rose from their chairs and sprinted towards you at terrifying speed.

You fled the control room with the devil on your heels, dashing into one of the narrow corridors that connected the colony's modular structures. You'd hoped to make it into one of the storage units, but another zombie stood in the corridor blocking your path. It came at you hissing static, herding you onwards. You dashed ahead of your pursuers into the surgical bay and pulled a fire alarm, causing heavy pressure doors to slam into position and seal you inside. Klaxons blared and red lights flashed, filling the cramped space with the sound of calamity and the color of blood, and fueling your panic like gasoline thrown onto a fire. One of the astro-zombies put its ghostly face up to the plexiglass window in the door and stared at you in your trap.

From behind, you heard a rasping hiss and the sound of tearing flesh. Your heart nearly stopped when you realized that there was still a zombie in here. She was pulling herself out of the robotic surgery device, tearing off her own newly-attached arm to get at you. You grabbed the nearest heavy thing you could find – a fire extinguisher – and brought it down on her head with all of your might. An adrenaline surge lent you strength despite your atrophied muscles and you managed to crack her skull open, covering yourself in the cold, pungent antifreeze that ran in her veins. It wasn't enough to stop her. You had to beat her until your arms were sore and trembling from exertion and her crown was crushed to pulp, and even then she kept twitching on the ground, her good hand clenching and relaxing as if she were still trying to rend you with it. You looked up from your grisly task, panting, and saw that the dead still patiently watched you from the doorway, peering through the tiny window.

Now that you weren't racing or fighting for survival, the true hopelessness of your situation began to sink in. Nobody outside of Frankenstein Enterprises knew that you were on Mars. You had no way of communicating with the Earth, and even if you somehow managed to get the message out, what could anyone do to help you? While you had known all along that Mars might be your grave, you'd never suspected that it would end like this.

The blaring sirens in the surgical bay fell silent, although the red lights continued to flash. You suddenly remembered that the astro-zombies were linked to the colony's fire control systems through the wireless iGor network. Since they saw that there was no fire, they could shut down the alarms and open the pressure door, and you had no way to override their control. Why would you? The colony was built for them, not you. Without the alarms howling, you realized that the ventilation system had stopped its humming as well. Mission Control had shut down the oxygen pumps. They were already transitioning the Mars base to the next phase of its operations, one in which the base would be crewed by unbreathing beings exclusively.

The locking mechanism holding the pressure door shut unbolted with a clank. The door slowly began to rise.

Even though you were doomed, the panicked instinct of a cornered animal drove you to fight on for escape. As the door came up you aimed your dented, bloody fire extinguisher at the undead mob, blasting them with a blinding geyser of pressurized foam, and then charged through them, swinging your makeshift club wildly. Their grasping hands and sharp teeth tore you in a dozen places, driving you mad with pain and terror, but you somehow managed to fight your way through the mob until you reached an airlock. You forced yourself inside and shut yourself in, your gravity-starved muscles screaming from exhaustion, your jumpsuit torn and stained with gore. In a final act of desperation you suited up, opened the exterior door, and ran onto the Martian surface.

You are sprinting through endless night now, a night so deep and dark that no Earthling could understand it, with the dead following close behind. You've got an entire planet to yourself, and nowhere to go. All of your hope is gone, and all of your fear as well. Now that the end is certain, there's no reason to dread it anymore.

The astro-zombies tackle you from behind and bring you down into the red dust with a painful shock of impact. They wrestle you onto your back and start tearing your protective gear away. You look up into the heavens, past the ghouls who are murdering you. Instinctively, your gaze finds the Earth.

The astro-zombies shatter your helmet's faceplate, and numbing cold floods into the suit like icy water. The sweat on your face and the saliva in your mouth and the tears flowing down your cheeks begin to boil away in the thin atmosphere. And yet your eyes are still fixed on Earth. You wonder if somewhere on the beautiful blue dot you left behind, Victor Frankenstein is standing beneath the night sky and looking up at Mars.

BOOK III: RISK FACTORS

LIVE YOUR BEST LIFE AT BYRON TOWER SALES BROCHURE

Byron Tower offers you the chance to live at the cutting edge of necrotech luxury in an emerging Chicago neighborhood close to the West Loop, with easy access to the Dan Ryan Expressway. Here, we've created a community that combines Frankenstein's most advanced science with comfortable, ultra-modern design to provide you with a life of ease and beauty.

Each unit comes equipped with a full suite of smart home features and iGor-compatible appliances, so we'll know how to take care of you without you having to ask. Our community fleet of Ganymede z-butlers will clean your rooms, wash your laundry, do your dishes. They'll even walk your pets.

Enjoy the vibrancy of urban living from a safe and private residence. An integrated z-security system protects the building and its grounds. Styx valets will whisk your car to and from our underground parking garage.

At Byron Tower you'll have all the amenities that you'd expect in a building of this caliber, and others you'd never imagine.

Contact Diodati Realty for price quotes and tours. Availability is limited.

THE EXTERMINATOR

Wild Bill McCullock sat before his IC2011-R control console, reading a Byron Tower billboard through a zombie's eyes. The artist's rendition of the forthcoming luxury tower was all chrome and steel – a futuristic needle reaching up to inject the sky. Bill idly wondered what it'd be like to live in a building with full z-service, and decided that it'd be pretty sweet.

But for now the Byron Towers were only a dream, a sign, and a fenced-off construction site neighboring the biggest homeless encampment in Chicago. Pup tents and cardboard shanties and garbage cluttered the space beneath the expressway. The bleak landscape reminded Bill of his time in the service overseas, sending Zulus through refugee camps that looked almost exactly like this in pursuit of dangerous militants. An old man with a matted, dryer-lint beard asked Wild Bill's Frank for a cigarette, then broke into cackling, phlegmy laughter without waiting for a response. Another of the camp's denizens came up to the zombie and spit in its face. Bill was glad he hadn't come in person. As a man who'd gone to war to learn a trade, he didn't see any good reason why the homeless couldn't pull themselves up by their bootstraps as well. He felt no pity for these people, or any other living being. He was an exterminator. Pity would destroy him.

At that moment, Bill sat in the comfort and safety of his office, surrounded by his tools. Three weathered Hercules-350 zombies in identical jumpsuits sat on a low steel bench behind their owner, regarding him with their cold red gaze. These were Moe, Larry, and Shemp. Curly, the fourth zombie at Wild Bill's Pest Control, was out in the field at the homeless camp. Bill ordered Larry to fetch a cream soda from the office mini fridge.

While Larry fetched the beverage, Wild Bill remotely piloted Curly around the homeless encampment to a nearby gas station, where he ordered the zombie to set a bait trap near the dumpsters. The iGor signal in this part of town was piss-poor, causing his connection to stutter and the video feed to blur. Bill kept a relay transmitter in the company van for just this problem, but he'd parked the van on a side street five blocks away to keep anyone from messing with it. He placed a few more traps before getting fed up with the choppy connection and ordering the zombie home. When Curly returned to the van, Bill saw that some fucking spray can radical had tagged it, scrawling "JOIN THE REVOLUTION DESTROY THE DEAD," on the side in drippy red paint. Wild Bill wished that these socialist dirtbags would start a revolution. He'd be on the front lines of it, gunning the motherfuckers down. If you left the Commies to their own devices, the whole country would wind up in the state of that homeless camp. For all their big talk they didn't give a fuck for the working man. He had two more jobs scheduled for today and now he'd have to send his crew out with his van looking like shit. The exterminator sighed and punched in orders for Curly to drive back to the office.

Wild Bill was prepping for the next job when Curly pulled the van into the attached garage and staggered into the office, dried spit still smeared on its cheek. A haggard man got out of the van as well, one of the homeless from the camp. He was a skinny, wild-eyed character with an enormous bristly beard, and he had a revolver in his hands, which he trained on Wild Bill's now-racing heart.

"Don't do anything stupid," Wild Bill said. "I've got money."

The intruder chuckled sardonically. "Rich men can be stupid too," he said. He spoke slowly and deliberately, seeming to ponder each word as he said it. "I'm not here for your money."

"My cash box is in that desk over there," said Bill, nodding his head towards the locked drawer where he kept his Ruger. "I'll give it to you right now if you'll let me. Probably more than a thousand bucks there."

"You think I'm dim? I know what you've got in that drawer. Take a step towards it and I'll blow your brains out."

"Well, what **do** you want?"

"I want to see Lacey again."

Wild Bill's racing heart now began to gallop. Invisible dust seemed to clog his mouth and throat. "I don't know what you're talking about," he croaked. "I don't know you, and I don't know any Lacey."

"That's right, you don't know our names, do you?" he said. His eyes were on fire but his voice kept an eerie cool. "I will have to make introductions. My name is Greg Hyde. And I'll tell you all about Lacey. She had beautiful black hair and a butterfly tattooed on her neck and she swore like a damn poet. When she was mad, which was she was on a pretty regular basis, being of fiery temperament, it was just beautiful to hear her express it. She loved Christmas and dogs. She'd give whatever she could to any stray that came nosing about. She had her vices, like every other person does, and she had her virtues, which are rarer. We met three years ago, in line to sign up for Frankenstein pensions. And I can't say they were happy years, exactly, but they were years when we had each other. Are you listening to me, Wild Bill? Do you have anybody? No, don't answer that. I do not want to know.

"A couple days ago I had to go to the Frankenstein clinic for my physical. Every once in a while I've got to let those vultures pick at me a bit, confirm that I'm still smoking and drinking so I get the bonus payments. And when I came back to our tent Lacey was sick with a stomachache. Sharp, jagged pain. Hard to watch a person you love in that sort of pain. She told me that she'd seen a Frank leave a plastic bag on the sidewalk and walk away. There was a sandwich inside, still in its wrapper. Roast beef with mayo and provolone cheese, which was one of her favorites. She figured that it was a malfunctioning z-deliveryman, right? Someone put the wrong address into the app or something. And so she ate the sandwich. And right after she got real sick. And that night she was dead. She died in the hospital waiting room, actually. They didn't even let her in until she was dead, and then they were happy to have her.

"I knew that the police wouldn't do right by Lacey. So I went back to camp. And I waited. Not a lot of Zulus in that neighborhood. It's kind of nice, actually, not having them around. When I spotted your pal here walking around dropping off free groceries, I decided to follow him. I threw away your bait, by the way. You're not going to poison anyone else."

"There must have been some sort of mistake," Wild Bill protested. "Some problem with the AI. I don't know anything about this."

"No. No, that's not how we're handling this. Tell me why you did it, Wild Bill."

Warm wetness gushed down the exterminator's pant leg. "Listen, this was nothing personal," he pleaded. "It was business."

"Who were you working for?"

"Diodati Realty. The company behind Byron Towers. I've been dealing with a mouse problem over at their office, and their CEO told me that they had something else for me to do. They're trying to clear out the homeless camp. It's getting in the way of construction."

Hyde's burning eyes darted over to Wild Bill's Frank control console. "That's an IC-series control rig, right?" he asked.

Bill nodded, surprised to suddenly be talking shop.

"You use a standard swarm-assist interface?"

"Y-yeah. You know how to pilot Franks?"

"When I was in the Marines, I used to command MG-28s. In Afpak."

"No shit? You're another Shaka? I was in Reanimated Infantry Logistics, 31st Marine Regiment! Were you at the Siege of Quetta?"

"Don't you fucking try it with me, Wild Bill. You're not my war buddy and I'm not taking any oo-rah shit off of you. You got a password on your control rig? Any range limits set?"

"No, neither."

"You've got the Diodati Realty office in their nav system? And access codes for security?"

"Y – yes."

"OK. OK, that's good. One last question. Why do you go by Wild Bill?"

"What?"

"What about you's so wild that you've got to put it on the side of your van?"

"It's just a nickname. From the Marines. I won a big hand of poker on aces and eights, the last hand that Wild Bill Hickok ever played before Jack McCall shot him in the back of the head. After that everyone called me Wild Bill. Just a nickname, that's all. It doesn't mean anything."

"Maybe it does mean something, Wild Bill. Turn around."

The trembling exterminator complied, and Hyde executed Wild Bill with a single bullet to the back of his skull. The big man dropped hard to the floor. A thin tendril of smoke drifted up from the wound. Hyde prodded the twitching body with his foot. He felt vaguely disappointed to get so little catharsis out of the killing, but that didn't mean he was going to stop.

Hyde sat down in front of the late Wild Bill's control console and called up the system settings for the four ghouls who had placidly borne witness to their owner's execution. Years ago he'd sworn that he would never command the dead again. Now his hands moved nimbly over the keys, long-suppressed muscle memories coming back to him like an ex, ready to ruin him all over again. The extermination zombies were primitive Hercules-class labor models, purchased second or third-hand and not well cared for, but good enough for his purposes. Hyde opened the app store and purchased hand-to-hand fighting skills for each of the ghouls, putting it on Wild Bill's business account. The Franks tensed up as an app for killing men downloaded into their networked pseudo-minds. At Hyde's command they gathered up weapons from Wild Bill's workspace, scissors and box cutters and hammers and knives. The dead man's office was the locus of a quintuple being, all five of its inhabitants acting with one murderous intention.

The damndest thing about necromancy was that in the beginning it always felt so good.

Hyde ordered all four of the zombies into Wild Bill's van, sending them to Diodati Realty's office. Almost as an afterthought, he had Moe and Larry wrap their late owner in plastic sheeting and bring him along, just to get him out of the way. Hyde stayed behind at the office, manning the controls. He could have sent his minions anywhere he pleased from the comfort of Wild Bill's chair, but they didn't have to go far. Diodati Realty was just a few miles away.

Curly did a decent job with the traffic and pulled into the enemy's parking lot. Hyde was disappointed by their headquarters, so much smaller and shabbier than he'd imagined. Even the corporate monsters killing for real estate didn't have a decent place of their own. Hyde sent Shemp on a scouting mission to circle the building, and located the emergency exit at the rear. He set the zombie to stand in front of that door just in case his target tried to make an escape. So much of being a Shaka was channeling frightened people towards their deaths, like some sort of terrible warrior shepherd. The remaining stooges went in through the front.

In the lobby, a z-guard stood vigil beneath a mural of scenes from the American Revolution. When it saw another zombie approaching it opened its mouth wide, exposing jagged teeth, and produced a dreadful static-shrouded hiss. Moe, having been challenged, automatically responded with a modem gurgle of his own, confirming that his team was authorized to work in the building. Protocols having been exchanged, the zombie buzzed its unbreathing brethren along.

Diodati Realty was a wasp's nest of activity, an open office of well-scrubbed professionals hard at work reshaping the city to their needs. A tiny, almost elfin man with a brightly shining bald head loitered by the front desk, flirting with the receptionist. The arrival of three walking corpses in matching jumpsuits brandishing sharp objects barely distracted him at all.

Hyde immediately recognized him as the son of a bitch who'd ordered the poison. He had seen this guy's brightly smiling face on a hundred ads in front of vacant buildings, and although he lacked hard proof that this was the man who'd hired Wild Bill, the lack of proof only made him all the more certain. Hyde looked upon the face of Diodati Realty, and Diodati Realty was his most hated enemy. He went into the z-exterminators' settings and turned their aggression levels to the maximum, ignoring all the warnings and deactivating all the safeties.

The little man peered at the Franks staggering towards him. A vague look of concern dawned over his too-smooth, Botoxed features. "Sheryl, was pest control scheduled to come back today?" he asked.

These were his last words. Moe, Larry, and Curly staggered towards him, brandishing their blades drunkenly. They didn't move very quickly but their victim didn't even try to run. Most of the people Hyde had killed overseas did the same. We all like to think that we'll be brave and swift when death comes for us, that we could never be caught by a slow, stumbling zombie, and almost all of us are wrong. Mostly, we stare at death in awe-numbed terror when it comes for us. An MG-28 could stab a man 180 times in a minute; these labor models weren't that deadly, but three of them acting together could shred a human being pretty well. The stooges brought Mr. Diodati down down in a storm of steel.

Hyde watched the slaughter from his screen, his face impassive in the red glow, enduring the unendurable memories that it brought to mind. How many people had he seen die like this? Not enough, apparently. Due to the open office floor plan everyone at Diodati Realty had a direct view of the butchery as well. They watched their employer's assassination in a state of mute, frozen horror.

Gunshots sounded over the console's speakers, and blinking red damage indicators lit up on Curly's screen. The z-guard had belatedly figured out that something was awry – no doubt a human back at the security company was piloting it now – but its pistol wouldn't drop a Zulu without a direct hit to the brain or spine. Hyde ignored the meaningless damage and set his exterminators to Asimov level five so that they'd keep hacking away at the boss's ruined wreck of a body for as long as they could. He spat and rose up from the chair. It was time to go.

Hyde left the console running and briskly departed the Wild Bill's Pest Control storefront by its rear entrance. He realized that he did not know where to go next. Now that his vengeance was accomplished he stood at loose ends, a man free of all social ties or responsibilities except his obligation to escape the two murder charges he'd racked up today. The freedom and terror were paralyzing. Even getting his ass to the bus station seemed overwhelming.

As he marched along through a dismal grey day, he noticed another Diodati Realty billboard nearby. Some civic-minded person had vandalized it with bright red spray paint. "Dig a grave for Frankenstein," it said.

"Huh," said Hyde. It sounded like a good idea.

EMAIL SENT TO CARBONDALE AUTO PARTS MANUFACTURING

(JANUARY 19, 2017)

From: Bunny@draugrhaxx.com
To: admin@carbondale.com
Subject: ♥♥♥ Ransom Note ♥♥♥

Hi there! You may be wondering why every zombie connected to your factory's network is inoperable and unresponsive. The bad news is that your Franks have been infected by the 2ombstone virus, shutting down all neural inputs and outputs until the virus's designer (me) transmits a reactivation code.

The good news is that you can buy a reactivation code by sending Bitcoin to this address:

bc1nzt4wqva6chjql793229vfrp9qh37nmyyop6jdi

If you pay within the next 48 hours, the price to unlock your Franks is only 10 BTC (what a bargain!). If you pay within the next 49-96 hours, the price to unlock your Franks is 20 BTC. Any longer than that and the reactivation code will be deleted, rendering your zombies permanently useless. Sorry!

All proceeds go to the Gravedigger resistance network, to fight for a future where the benefits of necrotech are equitably shared and available to all rather than hoarded by a malevolent corporate elite.

Your friend,
Bunny

THE HACKER

Bunny leaned back into her massaging desk chair, singing along with her Diana French album as she stole a modest fortune from the latest zombie-humping pervert to fall into her honey trap. "You piece of shit, you'll never touch me again," she typed into the text-to-speech app. She always got a kick out of messing with these corpse-rapers's minds. After slurping down the syrupy dregs of her Slushie, she executed a self-destruct sequence on her remote-controlled succubus and laundered her winnings through a crypto exchange. More Bitcoin for the revolution!

She was just about to call it a day when one of her phones rang – a bleating, insistent honking like something had gone wrong on a nuclear submarine. It was the SIM she used for Gravedigger business, a line reserved only for the most severe emergencies. "Your new umbrella is ready for pickup," said the caller.

Bunny recognized the voice on the other end of the line immediately. It was Shelly, one of the leaders of the Gravediggers and Bunny's usual point of contact with the secret society. In the popular imagination the Gravediggers were a ruthless terrorist organization, but Bunny preferred the term secret society. They had quietly seceded from the square, anti-life civilization that Frankenstein ruled, developing their own order, their own authority figures, their own artists and poets and songs, their own infrastructure for moving people and money and weapons around. They were not terrorists, they were a secret society at war.

"I didn't order an umbrella, I ordered a parasol," replied Bunny.

"Our company only sells umbrellas." Sign, countersign, and confirmation. Code words successfully exchanged and identities mutually proven.

"What's happening, Shelly?" Bunny asked.

"It's Hunter. He's been kidnapped from his apartment in London."

Bunny sighed. "Of course this is about Hunter," she said wearily. "The rainforest's on fire, civilization's collapsing into corporate necrocracy, but Hunter's being dramatic again, so let's put everything else off to the side."

"He's not being dramatic. Jesus Christ, he was kidnapped!"

"Oh, well, good luck to the kidnappers."

"I know you two have a history," said Shelly.

"Like the fucking Serbs and Croats."

"And that's why I'm reaching out to you. You're the only one in our network who can operate on his level. With his kind of skills. He was on to something very big when they grabbed him. I can't talk details on this line, but his handler can give you the full story."

"Do you think Frankenstein has him?" Bunny asked, implicitly including the military, police, and all national intelligence services in her definition of "Frankenstein." They all worked for the same man, after all.

"Can't rule it out, but we can't confirm it, either," said Shelly. "He was dealing with some pretty heavy customers, Russian Mafia and maybe others. You ever hear of a smuggler named Karlov?"

"Sure, the Man of a Thousand Faces. Major player in the reanimated arms trade. Shit, Hunter was mixed up with **him**?"

"Him and maybe worse."

As the implications sank in, Bunny's stomach started churning. She was surprised by how afraid she felt for her sociopathic reptile of an ex. "All right. All right, fuck it," she said. "London it is."

She kept a stylish pink go-bag by the door for exactly these emergencies, containing a change of clothes, a toiletries kit, HRT meds, a baggie of SIM cards, a sheaf of bogus passports, an envelope full of cash and gift cards, a set of lockpicks, a couple of spare wigs, and a baggie of her favorite sugary snacks. Before going out she did her makeup, putting on a garish punk rock kabuki face of bleary lines and smeared colors, carefully calibrated to bewilder iGor facial recognition software. She built her looks around aposematic threat displays and active camouflage, and she thought she looked damn good – a little like Pris from *Blade Runner*, a movie that Bunny loved for its optimistic view of life in the 2020s. Three hours later she was sitting in first class on a red-eye British Airways flight, sipping mimosas served to her by an immaculately manicured ghoul in a peppy little air hostess uniform, all charges handled courtesy of the pervert she'd bamboozled earlier in the evening.

She landed in a London convulsing from demonstrations, strikes, and street fights. Post-Brexit Britain stood bitterly divided between those who wanted to ban the undead from the U.K. and those who wanted to completely reconfigure the economy around reanimated labor. Grievances multiplied like splinters. On Bunny's ride from the airport her Styx was diverted twice from streets that the police had closed down, and once by a burning bus at Blackfriars.

Hunter's handler had made arrangements to meet at the British Museum, where he worked his day job. Bunny walked past the imperial plunder and wished badly that she had time to be a gross American tourist for a while. Maybe later, when she wasn't on a rescue mission. Her contact, a bespectacled young fellow with anachronistic muttonchop sideburns, found her in front of an Easter Island moa. They identified each other as fellow initiates of the secret society by means of signs and symbols, and he invited Bunny back to his office in the mummy lab, a glass-and-steel facility that reminded Bunny of a hospital except more cluttered and lived-in. At the center of the room, the preserved remains of an ancient Egyptian dignitary rested inside a glass case. As they entered the lab the mummy struggled to rise, its withered muscles trembling from the effort of pulling its head up. Bunny felt the cadaver's gaze almost tangibly, even though its eyes had withered away centuries ago.

"Don't mind Nestawedjat over there," said the Egyptologist. He tapped a few buttons on a console and the mummy slumped back into the realms of the dead. "We've been experimenting with reanimating some of the mummies in our collection. It's a publicity stunt, to be honest, but Frankenstein's charitable trust gives so much to the museum that we can't tell them no." They bagged their smartphones and he put on Billie Holiday. "I can't believe I'm meeting the legendary Bunny at last," he gushed, his fancy accent somehow rendering the praise more complimentary. "You wrote the Saint Vitus virus! I nearly died laughing watching those videos."

Bunny laughed as well. That caper had gone viral in a couple of ways. Not only had her code shut down work sites across the world, costing the enemy billions, but social media had delighted in the resulting footage of infected Franks dancing endlessly to Korean pop. "Glad you got a kick out of it," she said. "Are you a hacktivist too?"

The Brit shook his head. "No, not really," he said. "My expertise is more in finance and logistics. But Hunter talked about you all the time."

"Oh." Discomfiting. She wondered what Nestawedjat had heard about her. "What had he been working on? Shelly told me it was big."

"Hunter told me he'd found an executive backdoor in iGor, allowing top management to connect to any Frank in the system, or even all of them at once. He was looking for a key to open it. Or rather, to elevate a rank-and-file worker's credentials to give them the same level of network privileges that Victor Frankenstein enjoys."

"Every Frankenhacker on the planet's searching for that exploit," replied Bunny. "The executive backdoor's the Holy Grail of black hats, widely sought after and probably imaginary. He didn't find it, did he?" A bad feeling fluttered in Bunny's breast. Was that jealousy?

The Egyptologist shook his head. "Not that I know of. But he was close. His problem was that he needed employee credentials to make it work. That's where the Russians came in. Some chap named Karlov. He was selling Hunter the login credentials of Frankenstein workers. Now Hunter's been taken and I don't know if Frankenstein's responsible, or the Russians, or someone else entirely."

"How do you even know he was kidnapped?" Bunny asked. "Maybe he just vanished. He did that on my birthday once."

The Brit went pale. "No. He gave me access to his apartment security camera," he said. "In case something like this happened. This footage was taken two days ago, a little past midnight."

He played a video taken inside Hunter's flat, a dingy little bachelor studio with dorm-quality furniture and far too much anime memorabilia. Hunter sat at his desk working. He looked older than Bunny remembered, so much so that Bunny's own facial recognition functions hiccupped before recognizing him. As he stared at his laptop screen, outside, a lanky insectoid creature in skintight black spandex crawled up the window behind him, like a great baleful spider creeping up on Miss Muffett. Bunny paused the playback when it came fully into the frame. The creature had a human head and torso but eight limbs in total, each of them ending in a black-gloved hand.

"Which floor was Hunter on?" Bunny asked.

"Sixth," said the Brit.

Two of the spider's hands skillfully unlatched the window and then the thing slithered through, moving on all eight with the precise grace of a world-class acrobat and the rhythms of a night terror, silently and steadily approaching its distracted prey. It felt like watching a horror movie, and Bunny hated horror movies. The spider struck swift as a fist clenching, seizing Hunter in its grasp and choking him into unconsciousness. After ransacking the flat of electronics, it hoisted Hunter onto its middle set of shoulders and carried him out the way it had come.

"I've had a damned time sleeping since I saw that footage," said the Brit. "I keep on thinking about that thing climbing up the walls for me."

Bunny watched the clip again, paying careful attention to the spider's fluid, hideously graceful motions. Whoever had built this monstrosity knew what they were doing. The hacker supposed that she might have trouble sleeping for a while, too.

On her way out of the museum Bunny ran into a man who seemed to be looking for her, a pudgy man in a bad suit with a walrus mustache. A Dragonstooth zombie in Secret Service garb walked three steps behind him. "Excuse me, ma'am, are you Catelyn Lepus?" he asked in a Texan twang. Catelyn Lepus was Bunny's true and chosen name – she'd gone to not-inconsiderable trouble getting it legally changed – and hearing her true name from this strange man sent her flight-or-fight instincts racing.

"That's not me, I don't know you," she muttered, trying to make a speedy getaway. His Frank grasped her by the upper arm, its grip cold and mechanically insistent.

"Ma'am, if you don't want to speak with me Karlov can send someone else," said the Texan. "But I think you'd rather talk with me." A few minutes later Bunny found herself in the backseat of a posh town car hurtling through the streets of London at frightening speed. The Texan sat across from her, his fingers interlaced on his lap, a quietly pleased expression on his round and hairy face. "Where's Hunter?" Bunny demanded of him.

"I don't know," said the Texan. "Karlov was hoping that you could tell him. Don't worry, he doesn't want to hurt Hunter. Just the opposite. Karlov wants to give Hunter a large sum of money. And he'll pay you a finder's fee if you can put us in touch."

"You think that Hunter's found the executive backdoor."

"I don't know anything about that, I'm just trying to broker a deal," the Texan said amiably. "But Karlov would like to speak with you in person about it."

"If it exists, it's the most powerful cyber-weapon ever devised."

"You should talk to Karlov about that." He wrote a Moscow address on the back of an embossed business card. "You can meet him here," the Texan said. "If your friend is in trouble, Karlov will do everything that he can to help."

Bunny inspected the card. Richard J. Kruger, Attorney at Law. "Long way from home, aren't you?" she asked.

"Karlov thought that Hunter and you might find his offer more appealing coming from a fellow American. Russians don't have the best P.R."

"How do I know it's safe?"

Their car stopped at a red light. On the corner, a pack of skinheads had strung up a municipal cleaning zombie from a lamp pole and were bashing it with cricket bats and crowbars. Kruger sighed wearily. "If I told you it was safe to do this you'd take me for a liar or a fool. Who's safe anywhere these days?"

She had Kruger drop her off at Hunter's flat, where she spent a moment gawking at the six-story climb that his kidnapper had managed. Franks really could do the most remarkable things. What a shame that such bastards controlled such wonderful inventions. Most of the Gravediggers wanted to destroy Frankenstein and put an end to necrotech forever; she wanted to destroy Frankenstein so that necrotech could reach its highest potential and bring humanity – *all* of humanity – into its first-ever golden age.

When she was finished admiring the kidnapping's execution, she used an app on her smartphone to find the signal strength of the local iGor network and track down the nearest tower. She easily cracked its feeble security and downloaded a log of all the Franks that had been in the area at the time that Hunter was taken. It was lucky they'd used a customized Frank; that made it easy to filter out the dozens of other zombies active in the sector and determine the iGor identification number of the kidnapper. It was a start, but she'd need much more to find Hunter, assuming that he was even still alive. She looked at the address written on Kruger's card again. Russian Mob. Why couldn't it have been the Italian Mob? Or the French Mob? She'd have loved to see Paris.

Moscow was colder than Bunny had dreamed. The temperature was not so far distant from London's but the climate was entirely different. An airless, sterile chill had settled in place, the sort of cold you get when there's no warm-blooded beings about. The city seemed eerily still notwithstanding the delivery trucks puttering about belching diesel fumes, the Franks with frostbite-blackened hands and faces going about their errands, and the armored z-police marching on patrol. The living lurked silently at the margins – semi-feral children begging at subway entrances or old men gathered in cafes, unobtrusively keeping out of the zombies' paths, stray dogs that had learned not to bark. More buildings were empty than not. Someday soon this frozen necropolis might belong to the dead exclusively.

The address that Kruger had given was a long-abandoned shop. A frost-rimed dead man in an ushanka hat and trench coat slouched outside it on a bench, his head slumped forward as if he had died in the cold right there. As Bunny approached he jolted back to life, shaking the snow from his shoulders. "Come with me," he groaned in English.

Bunny followed the ghoul to its car. The zombie drove her to a warehouse, innocuous enough to the untrained eye but bristling with cameras and security devices if you knew where to look for them. A scowling nightmare of a dude in a tracksuit waited at the entrance, backed up by four Dragonsteeth carrying submachine guns. Bunny asked him if he was Karlov, but he admitted no knowledge of English and merely waved them on.

Inside the warehouse Bunny saw dozens of neatly stacked charging coffins. According to the coffin labels, they contained MG-28s, military zombies specially designed to rend human beings to pieces. Ever since Frankenstein Enterprises had developed war-ghouls, anyone with the money could command their own private army. True, the international trade in reanimated weaponry was illegal, but if you had the money to buy your own private army then that technicality meant very little. It was an age of opportunity for drug gangs, warlords, paramilitaries, and all sorts of mayhem-minded folk.

The Frank escorted Bunny up a staircase and into an office where about a dozen young Russian men were working, half of them remotely controlling Franks, most of the others coding, and a couple dicking about on social media. This den of arms traffickers wouldn't have looked out of place at any tech company in America, except for the war-zombie standing guard in a corner. Bunny was saddened to see that even the Russian Mob had gone over to the open office craze. The man who was piloting her z-guide winked and shot a finger gun at her. He took her onwards, to the Man of a Thousand Faces.

Karlov was a silver wolf of a man with a stern and vigorous demeanor, short but trim and well-built. He'd certainly been a soldier at one point, and it occurred to Bunny that he might still be in active service today. He dressed modestly in a Soviet-looking dark suit and tie, but he'd spared no expense in furnishing his personal office. Bunny's feet sank into the carpeting as a haze of sweet-smelling pipe smoke enveloped her. A buxom z-maid in a minidress offered refreshments, which Bunny waved away. Karlov smiled mirthlessly, and rose from his mahogany desk.

"Pleased to meet you at last, Bunny," he said. "You can call me Karlov. I trust you're here to discuss our mutual friend Hunter. Do you know who has him?"

Direct and to the point. She liked it. "I don't," she said. "But you're not really interested in Hunter. You want to find the executive backdoor."

"Of course I do. A way to seize control of iGor, even if only for a short time? Any government on Earth would pay a fortune."

"You really think that he's found it."

"I do."

Bunny pondered this. "And you'll pay me a finder's fee if I can locate him?"

"One million dollars to bring him into this office. Alive. He's no good to me dead, and he's probably dead."

"I have a clue," said Bunny, enjoying the feeling of being a Nancy Drew-esque girl detective. "The iGor identification number of the Frank who kidnapped Hunter. But I can't tell who owns it or where it is now."

"How fortunate that you have come here then," said Karlov. "Because I can do exactly that. You know, I keep six people on my payroll just to spearfish Frankenstein employees." He took the number from Bunny and typed it into his computer. The arms dealer's face darkened. "The zombie that kidnapped Hunter is owned by Frankenstein Enterprises' cybersecurity division," he said. "Which means that Hunter is certainly dead. The only way I'm getting him into this office is if Frankenstein sells him to me as a menial."

"What makes you so sure they've killed him?"

"Because that's what I would do to him. And they're even nastier than I am."

"Can you tell me where the zombie is right now?"

Karlov wrote down an address in Tokyo. "Did you know him well?" he asked.

"Nobody knew Hunter well," said Bunny. On the flight to Tokyo, she imagined what it would feel like to turn her ex over to a Russian mobster for a million dollars.

Japan had enthusiastically adopted the Frankenstein Process, its government preferring necromancy to immigration, and as a result the island nation now boasted the world's most sophisticated necrotech. Even Bunny took a couple of minutes before realizing that the customs agent didn't blink. But on the other hand, the dead could also be monsters here. The server at the airport sushi bar, for example, had been surgically modified such that its face resembled that of a huge fish. She was on the spider's trail, she was certain of it. Unfortunately, she was so jetlagged that day and night had lost all meaning to her, and her back ached from constant air travel notwithstanding the first-class padding.

The spider's last-known location turned out to be a luxury apartment tower in the ultra-pricey Toranomon district. An odd place to hold a prisoner, and an even stranger place to stage an execution. It was, however, just the sort of place that a man with a billion-dollar secret might hole up. Bunny made her initial assault using Japan Post as her attack vector, mailing the building a package containing a remote-controlled device built to scan for nearby Wi-Fi, sniff out handshake signals authorizing users to log on, and transmit the data back to her. From her seat in the coffee shop across the street, Bunny got into the tower's wireless network before her package got all the way to the mailroom. Then she connected to a Ganymede-500 restroom attendant hooked up to the network and used an unpatched bug in its software to get into the visual feeds of all the building management company's Franks. Bunny carried out a virtual surveillance from the cafe, enjoying ginger lemonades as she waited. Hunter strolled into the lobby after just a couple of hours, laden with shopping bags, looking as free and relaxed as Bunny had ever seen him.

London hadn't been a kidnapping at all. It was an extraction. She'd been right all along. Hunter was being dramatic again.

Bunny put herself onto the building's guest list and followed Hunter to the penthouse. A few minutes fiddling on her phone was all it took to unlock his front door. Smart homes were just the dumbest thing imaginable, especially once you looped zombies into your security.

Hunter's apartment was a kaiju of a living space, gigantic by any standard and almost incomprehensibly vast in Tokyo. It must have come furnished, since Hunter never could have assembled such tasteful luxury for himself, but he was already starting to put his own stamp of adolescent tackiness on the place. Hunter was in the kitchen drinking orange juice when she came in. The carton dropped from his hand. "Bunny," he said, looking rather like he'd seen a ghost. "What are you doing here?"

"I'm not here for you," she said. "I'm here for the executive backdoor."

"Oh, right." He gave that infuriating smug white-guy smirk that Bunny knew all too well, and bent over to pick up the juice carton. "Yeah, it makes sense that you'd come looking for that. You're right. I found it. I figured how to elevate iGor privileges on demand. The biggest prize on Earth, *and I found it.*"

"And Frankenstein found you," Bunny said. "They found you, and they offered you a bounty for the bug."

"A bounty for the bug and a sweet gig in their cybersecurity division."

Bunny snorted. "I never thought I'd see you in a white hat. What were you thinking? It's Frankenstein!"

"I was thinking I'd like to get rich and live in my favorite city and not be looking over my shoulder for the FBI every day. Bunny, we fought Frankenstein for years, and for what? They're only getting stronger. Why not join the winning side?"

"So that quote-unquote kidnapping was just your way of covering your tracks. Make the Gravediggers and Karlov think you'd been taken against your will. Make *me* think you'd been taken against your will."

He shrugged. "I never thought you'd get involved. I figured that if Shelly called you and said I got kidnapped, you'd just say, *Oh, good luck to the kidnappers,* in that snide voice you do when you think you're being clever."

Bunny gritted her teeth and took a deep breath. "So what happened to the exploit you found?"

"It's patched. Only Frankenstein executives are getting through the backdoor now."

Bunny was now so furious that it was making her dizzy. The penthouse seemed to spin and reel. "You found something that could have shut down Frankenstein, and you gave it back to them."

"Don't exaggerate. Nobody's shutting down Frankenstein Enterprises. I found an inconvenience for them, and they paid me to make the inconvenience go away."

"And what did you tell them about the Gravediggers? What did you tell them about me?"

"I told them everything they asked. The Gravedigger phase of my life is over now. The *you* phase of my life has been over even longer than that. Fuck you, Bunny. They've got a bounty on you too, you know. You're one of the chief bugs they're looking to get rid of. And you know what? I happen to have a spider on hand. Peter, seize her!"

"Seize her?!" snarled Bunny. "So that's where we've come to? Seize her?!"

"Peter, seize her!" Hunter shouted, a little louder this time.

Bunny tapped on her cellphone and the spider-zombie skittered into the room from its closet, moving with all eight of its arms on the ground, still wearing the skintight head-to-fingers black zentai bodysuit that it had worn during the extraction. It hopped onto Hunter and effortlessly wrestled him down to the ground, twisting all four of his limbs painfully. "What the fuck?" he howled. "Let me go!"

"You need better password hygiene," said Bunny. He kept reusing Junji, the name of a surly old black-and-white cat he used to have. She'd wirelessly connected to his spider-zombie and seized control of it before stepping through his door.

"Let me go, you fucking bitch!" he howled, red-faced, struggling against his pet monster's grip.

Bunny looked at him and saw what had been there all along. She saw the selfishness he passed off as logic, the cold indifference he masqueraded as open-mindedness, the manipulative streak that made him seem so much smarter than he was. She saw the face of a man who betrayed everything that mattered for a spacious apartment in Tokyo. How had she missed it for so long? "I'll let you go," she said, and she ordered the spider to leap through the window.

Hunter still clutched in its grip, the monster hurled itself through the plate glass with a bone-crunching *crash* and plummeted into the neon-lit Tokyo night in a shining spray of jagged glass and blood. The street echoed its own *thump* a moment later.

Bunny closed her eyes for a little while and let the breeze pass over her skin. She took Hunter's laptop and went out the tower's front doors just as an ambulance was arriving to scrape the intermingled mix of her ex and his spider-zombie from the pavement. She supposed they might have a puzzling time matching up the limbs with the bodies.

Bunny drew a bath when she got back to her hotel room. She sat in perfumed, piping hot water drinking a bottle of plum wine and experiencing a staggering variety of emotions. Fortunately, she had a staggering variety of questions to occupy herself with as well. She wondered how Hunter, of all people, had figured out a way past Frankenstein's defenses. He was a devious bastard but never much of a technical wizard. What could he have possibly seen that everyone else had missed?

And suddenly, in her bath, a vision of the Holy Grail appeared before her. She saw the fatal flaw in the enemy's defenses, the thermal exhaust port that would blow up the whole stinking Death Star if you could just get a proton torpedo inside. A lunatic plan formed in her mind, a plan to commit the crime of the 21st century and thereby save the world.

Bunny reached for her phone and called Shelly. "I have bad news and good news," she said, blowing right past the security phrases.

"Give me the bad news first."

"Hunter betrayed the human race. He was working with the enemy. No way to know how much he told them. He's dead now."

A long pause. "OK. That's pretty bad. What's the good news?"

"I know how to destroy Frankenstein Enterprises."

MOTHER EARTH CAN'T BE RE-ANIMATED AND OTHER ESSAYS FROM THE ZOMBIE APOCALYPSE

BY ALICIA ST. JOHN (SHAMAN DRUM BOOKS, 2013)

Humanity must awaken to the fact that we are no longer the Earth's dominant lifeform. Corporations are the new apex predator, an invasive species that has colonized the entire planet in an eye-blink of geological time. Unlike the organisms they compete against for resources, business entities and the zombies who serve them do not need to eat healthful food or drink clean water or breathe fresh air. This gives them an enormous evolutionary advantage as they reverse-terraform the environment in accordance with their own interests. We are shut up in the Earth's ecosystem together with the vast engine of necro-capitalism. Its exhaust is gassing us to death, but the machine doesn't need us to function anymore, and it brings scalding violence to bear against any interference with its operations.

Western civilization has never liked to admit that we have lessons to learn from animals, particularly vulnerable and extinct ones. Now, however, we have brought ourselves to the same horrific predicament once experienced by the dodo and the passenger pigeon, of being at the mercy of a stronger, technologically advanced species only interested in the resources they can extract from our bodies. Our predecessors' experiences leave us with little room for optimism.

THE HUNTER

The hunter prowled through the dense greenery silently, bow in hand, his brother and uncle and a host of spirits at his side. Today they stalked a sorcerer. The screeching of demons and the stench of pestilent smoke drifted downwind from the wizard's encampment. Unless the flames were quenched, the jungle would soon perish and the sky itself would fall.

Human beings were not as wise as in the days of their fathers, but the white strangers became more diabolical with each generation. They were descended from Yoasi, the creator's evil brother, who had taught the living how to die, and their missionaries buzzed all along the river like mosquitoes, spreading falsehoods and disease. The white strangers ate the jaybird spirits who danced to ripen fruit and make winged game abundant, such that food was ever harder to find. They shattered the stone holding the Wind Storm Being in the underworld, freeing him to ravage the forest with his arrows, and they drove off the Rain Being, drying up the rivers and letting fires eat the trees. Lately the strangers had committed their greatest outrage yet, bringing loathsome maggot spirits into the forest to cut timber and dig mines. Normally only those who drank yãkoana could see spirits, but these maggot beings lived inside the bodies of dead men, wearing corpses like clothes. The hunter would not have believed such a thing possible had he not seen one of the witch camps with his own eyes, and watched the pale fiends clawing at the earth.

All of the nearby villages came together at a feast to discuss the invasion, although with the river low and the gardens dry and game scarce, it was a feast of hungry bellies. Everyone attending agreed; the human beings of the forest must put their old quarrels aside and wage war against the white strangers. That night the men honed their machetes and loaded cartridges into their shotguns and poisoned their arrows with toad skins. The shaman opened his spirit house and called forth his allies to aid in the combat; wasp spirits to shoot the enemy with venom and monkey spirits to tie vines around their feet, ant spirits to take the enemy's magic apart, eel spirits to blast them with lightning, and the Jaguar Being herself to devour their white flesh. Although the spirits were invisible to the hunter, that night he dreamt of the Jaguar Being. He saw the great cat crouching in deep darkness, illuminated only by the red showers of sparks that flew as she sharpened a machete against a whetstone. She stared back at him, her eyes reflecting the burning embers. The hunter awoke drenched in sweat.

Today all the spirits of the forest would fight at the human beings' side, but the sorcerer boasted of powerful allies as well. Besides his maggot spirits he commanded armies of invisible plague demons hungry for human flesh, and the Chaos Being, who loves the smell of women's blood, and worst of all, the Spirit of Poverty, who was native to the cities but had made himself at home in the forest ever since the whites had brought him here. As the hunter and his kin attacked the sorcerer, the shaman's spirits would battle the sorcerer's devils, and war would rage between men and spirits alike.

The hunter glanced at his kinsmen. His uncle was a seasoned warrior, renowned as a killer of men. His brother was brave and impatient, hasty to use his prized shotgun. The hunter wished that he could have brought more fighters on the raid, but there were many wizards doing evil throughout the jungle, forcing the human beings to split their strength. He could only hope that it would be enough.

The three human beings came upon the reeking bog that the sorcerer had cleared. Maggot spirits wearing the bodies of dead whites labored clumsily, cutting trees and brush and digging in the mud, their mechanical saws screaming and belching smoky clouds of disease, their rotten skin paler than the moon, their sunken eyes bloodshot and blind. The hunter shuddered to look upon such horrors, and he knew that greater evils lurked around them unseen. He could not imagine why Yoasi's people hated their own dead so much that they did not even let them go to the back of the sky, but instead bound them in slavery. Smoke stung the hunter's eyes. Worse yet, the burning fumes protected the sorcerer against the human beings' spirit allies. Towards the rear of the clearing sat a boxy metal shack, and the sorcerer sat in front of this shack, caressing a black mirror. He was an unremarkable-looking creature, the sort of sunburnt, muddy-bearded white man that you might find at any mining camp, and yet he wielded terrible cosmic power, a power that threatened to undo all the work of creation.

The hunter's uncle whistled a curassow's cry, the sign for the three men to advance on their prey. Their aim was to arrow the sorcerer without being seen, or if he was too well protected, to at least steal the dirt from his footprint, that their shaman might send vipers to strike his ankles and kill him from afar. The three human beings slowly circled around the clearing's outskirts, keeping the forest as a shield between themselves and the maggot spirits. The hunter notched a poisoned arrow, trained it on the sorcerer's heart, and drew back the bowstring, his heart pounding at his ribs so fiercely that the noise would have given him away if his enemies were not so noisome and oblivious. His hand wavered. The hunter was not afraid to perish in war, but a far worse fate than death awaited him if he missed.

A gun fired and one of the maggot spirits stumbled in a spray of shot. Smoke billowed from the spot where the hunter's brother hid. He'd pulled the trigger too quickly, and now the hunter loosed his arrow too late. At the sound of the gun the sorcerer dove cowering behind one of his minions, so a maggot spirit took the wound meant for its master. An envenomed shaft pierced deep into the monster's breast, to no effect at all.

The cringing sorcerer traced a diabolical pattern on his dark mirror and his maggot spirits abandoned their labor for war, crashing into the jungle wielding steel axes and machetes and shovels and machine saws. A group of them seized the hunter's brother and hacked him apart with passionless intensity. A demon swung a machete at the hunter. He ducked under the whistling metal and responded with a swing of his own, chopping off one of the maggot spirit's legs at the calf. Another of the decayed creatures approached with outstretched arms. The hunter brought his blade down on his enemy's head, burying the weapon so deep in the skull that he could not pull it out and had to abandon it to keep from being strangled. Nearby, the hunter's uncle put four arrows into the face of a demon. It ignored them and drove a machine saw into his ribs.

The hunter turned and ran, pursued by demons. The forest spirits attacked them, pulling them into deep mud or entangling them with foliage, but they were so many of the fiends that the whole jungle seemed to be full of them. The maggot spirits finally encircled the hunter in a grove of palms. Parrot-red eyes glared coldly. The sorcerer stood just beyond his minions, chortling like a pig that's found something good to eat. He said something meaningless in Portuguese, and made a motion towards his mirror. The hunter prepared to die.

Just then, the leaves above rustled softly, and a jaguar pounced on the sorcerer from a high branch, seizing the back of his neck in her teeth and pinning him down beneath her mighty paws. His black mirror fell to the ground and shattered, and he died immediately, without even a sigh. The maggot spirits stood paralyzed in place, helpless to move now that the mind that commanded them was gone.

The Jaguar Being fixed her gaze on the hunter, the same awesome gaze he had seen and dreaded in his dream. The sorcerer's shaggy head lolled in her jaws, blood pouring down his shoulders and into the mud. *Death to all witches!* her leonine countenance exclaimed in fury. The cat withdrew into the brush to consume her foe, moving backwards, never taking her eyes from the hunter's face until the shadows wrapped their arms around her and hid her away.

The trembling hunter leaned against a tree, letting it hold him up in this joyless moment of victory. The battle had been won at great cost, and the war only just begun. Whites copulated ceaselessly so there were always more of them. Jaguars were fewer and fewer; they were much scarcer now than when the hunter was a boy, and scarcer still than in the days of his father. Who could protect the forest when the last of the jaguars was gone?

COALITION FORCES ANNOUNCE LIBERATION OF BASRAH

BY FELICITY PELOPPONO, DOD NEWS, DEFENSE MEDIA ACTIVITY (JULY 24, 2017)

WASHINGTON -- Coalition forces have cleared all hostile forces from Basrah, Iraq, Pentagon spokesman Navy Capt. Dan Viceroy announced to reporters today.

Since the U.S.-led invasion of Iraq in 2003, the coalition has taken more than 224,000 square miles of territory from anti-American forces, he said, and advances in artificial intelligence and necrotech are allowing coalition forces to intensify combat operations without requiring additional live troops.

"New Frankenstein weapon platforms enable us to attack entrenched terrorist positions with minimal risk to civilians and infrastructure," he said, noting that z-rat swarms delivered via drone captured the Al Basrah Oil Terminal from Sayf Alhayi militants without significant damage to the facility.

IRAQ OPERATIONS

In an update of operations beginning with Iraq, Viceroy said that z-soldiers continued to sweep rebel tunnel systems in Basrah, searching for remaining fighters and seeking to identify explosive devices. Coalition forces have flooded the Basrah sewer system with MG-28s and z-rats, trapping as many as 200 hostile personnel inside underground bunkers.

IRAN OPERATIONS

In Iran, Viceroy said that a column of MI-300s backed by close air support defeated Revolutionary Guard mechanized infantry forces in fierce fighting six miles south of Qom. The enemy casualties have reinforced the coalition forces and are presently advancing on the city outskirts. Viceroy noted that additional reinforcements are expected soon.

SYRIA OPERATIONS

Viceroy announced that a detachment of U.S. Marines commanding reanimated assets successfully liberated the city of Masyaf from terrorist forces, inflicting 269 casualties and depriving the enemy of a strategically important position. Three Marines died in the assault and two were wounded when an insurgent threw an explosive device inside their armored personnel carrier.

AFGHANISTAN OPERATIONS

Viceroy announced that coalition forces killed thirty-two Al Qaeda members in the tribal territory along the former Afghanistan-Pakistan border, including senior militant Radwan Sabbagh. "As our targeted killing operations intensify, we've seen terrorists relocating their leadership to more and more remote areas," said Viceroy. "We are pleased to announce that the new MC-680 hunter-killer z-commandos can operate in nearly any environment, denying opponents even their refuges of last resort. Their satellite uplinks allow them to operate anywhere on the globe, controlled by stateside personnel. These assets never sleep, they never rest, they do not feel fear or pain or pity. There is no place that America's enemies can hide from them."

THE ENEMY

Ibrahim stood on the parapet of Masyaf Castle gazing out into the night, impatient for the upcoming battle to begin even though he fully expected to die in it. Unlike some of his comrades in the Frankenstein Haram Militia, he wasn't eager for martyrdom at all. As a young man more inclined to football fields and movies than mosques, he'd always expected to find religion later in life, and now felt cheated that he wouldn't get the chance. Yet even though his soul was in no condition for Paradise, if the end was upon him he just wanted to get it over with. The collective longing for action was so intense that he could smell it in the air. Dread sweat smelled differently than heat sweat, he'd learned that since the invasion.

Ibrahim's body ached all over, especially his arms, shaking under the unfamiliar weight of a Kalashnikov. He'd spent the past two days hauling bricks and cinder blocks to the castle roof, and the two days before that helping to dig a defensive ditch around the castle, and the day before that shoveling rubble into the barbican, and now that he wanted nothing more than to lie down and sleep, they'd given him a rifle and a section of rooftop on the western wall and told him to defend it against the Deceiver's forces at all cost. At least he wasn't alone. Hassan, the militia captain in charge of the castle rooftop's defense, had posted three other fighters to this spot, all older than himself, and a few meters behind them, a mortar crew in old Syrian Army uniforms milled about smoking cigarettes.

It would have been a beautiful night if not for the looming battle. The moon shone bright and clear, and this lofty viewpoint offered a magnificent view of the town and the western mountains. But Ibrahim couldn't enjoy the spectacle knowing that the Americans lurked somewhere out there in the desert blackness beyond. He had an uncomfortable feeling of being watched, and the presence of invisible beings. Once or twice he glanced up at the sky and imagined that he saw a dark eye looking down on him, blotting out the stars as it floated overhead. From time to time he thought he heard something humming in the wind.

Hassan came around passing out the contents of a small crate. In the dark, Ibrahim thought at first that he was distributing apples, and felt glad to get one last treat, the militia rations being neither plentiful nor tasty. He was surprised when the captain pressed a cold metal sphere into his palm. It was a hand grenade.

"In case the ghuls are about to seize you," explained Hassan, not unkindly. "Remove the safety clip there, then take out the pull ring while you're holding the lever down. Once you've released the lever you'll have four seconds before it blows. It's not a big bang, but it should be enough to keep the Americans from bringing you back. Just don't wait too long."

The little steel ball seemed tremendously heavy, much weightier than the cinder blocks that Ibrahim had spent the past two days porting. He restrained a sudden urge to weep. Instead he put the bomb into his pocket and quietly thanked the captain.

"Where are you from, kid?" asked one of the other men on the roof, a burly, raspy-voiced guy with worker's hands who wore a leather jacket and balaclava.

"Baniyas," said Ibrahim.

"I'm sorry," said the masked man. Everyone had heard about the fall of Baniyas. The dead took the port city completely by surprise by marching out of the sea. He offered a cigarette, which Ibrahim accepted even though he didn't smoke, and introduced himself as Rahul. He said something about defending the homeland with their lives, but Ibrahim didn't hear it. He was too busy thinking about his parents and sisters, whom he'd been separated from during the mad stampede out of Baniyas.

He hoped desperately that they were all right wherever they were. More than that, he prayed that he wouldn't have to fight them tonight.

"You know why Dr. Frankenstein hides himself, right?" asked Ahmad, one of the other guys up there with Ibrahim. "If he showed his face in the light of day all the nations would see that he is blind in one eye and know that he is the Al-Masih ad-Dajjal whom the Prophet warned would arise before the Day of Judgment." Ahmad was a Saudi student who'd left his home to fight the Deceiver, a slender, alert-looking man in his mid-20s or thereabout, who wore his beard in the Islamist style with his mustache shaved and was fond of asking people questions and then telling them the answers. He had some of the newest and best gear in the militia, including a beautiful sword with a green leather scabbard that he wore on his belt. Ibrahim noticed that his new things were all very clean; he hadn't dirtied himself up digging trenches or building barricades.

"I don't know about that," said Rahul. "If the unbelievers haven't yet figured out that these are the End Times after seeing the dead rise up and the world consumed by war and fire, I don't think that seeing a one-eyed man would convince them. There's nothing the Deceiver can do that would turn the West against him. I think he hides in a castle for the same reason we do – to keep our enemies from killing us."

Their final compatriot muttered something in a tongue that nobody else present understood. He was the oldest of their group by far, with cloud-white hair and a deeply weathered face, and although he wore dusty civilian clothes he seemed more comfortable with his weapon than any of the others, the soldiers included.

"Does anyone know what language he's speaking?" asked Rahul.

"Chechen, maybe?" replied Ahmad.

Ibrahim was impressed. You met people from all over these days. The end of the world had mixed everything up. The Chechen disregarded this chatter and peered off at the town below. He didn't need to speak anyone else's language to know what was coming.

Machine gun fire suddenly rattled in the distance – both the Americans' fifty caliber and the militia's 7.62 mm guns. Even at this range, Ibrahim could see the flashes of their barrels and tracers zipping through the night. Then the roadside bombs began bursting. Ibrahim exhaled sharply, his pent-up tension transforming into a whole new variety of dread. He stubbed out his first and last cigarette.

From their position on the hilltop castle they had an eagle's-eye view of the Americans' approach. The town was a death trap, but Ibrahim wasn't sure if a death trap could stop the dead. "Gog and Magog are loosed upon the land," said Ahmad, as if he were announcing that guests had arrived. Ibrahim envied the way that this all seemed to make sense to him.

One of the mortar guys came over to the parapet and scanned the town with a pair of binoculars, calling out coordinates to the rest of his crew. They loaded a shell into the tube and lobbed it towards the Americans with a *thump*. "Fuck the USA!" one of them shouted in English. He shouted it every time they launched a shell.

In the town below, the ghuls disgorged from their armored carriers and swept through town in a swift column. In the moonlight they looked like a vast and hideous snake slithering down the road towards the castle. The rooftops sparkled with muzzle flashes, winking out one by one as the serpent advanced and swallowed them up. A car bomb exploded, staggering the ghuls but not slowing them down. The entire north of the city became hazy from all the fires burning. Then the ghuls came to a heavily guarded intersection about a kilometer from the castle, where machine gun emplacements mowed the head of the snake down as fast as the tail could press forward and volleys of rocket fire lit up the night, engulfing two more of their APCs in flame. Gunshots rang out from the castle as snipers fired into the horde. The American advance paused for the first time, and for the first time Ibrahim felt that maybe the battle could be won.

"Fuck the USA!"

A house exploded, and the spotter cursed. "Overshot it."

By the light of a burning personnel carrier, Ibrahim saw that more of the ghuls had come out, a different species of monster, these ones in bulky armor. "See those?" asked Rahul. "In their armor, don't they look like Crusaders? We'll defeat them like our forefathers defeated the Crusaders. The land itself will reject them." He talked like a man trying to raise his own spirits. The ghuls brought their own guns to bear on Masyaf's defenders, firing concentrated bursts that cut through the air with a terrible ripping noise. Explosions strobed amidst the machine gun emplacements, and then the machine gun emplacements went silent and the horde resumed its advance. Another shell landed just a little too far to the north.

"Damn it, don't you know how to aim that thing?" Rahul asked.

"I was trained to use an 82-BM-37 mortar," grumbled one of the soldiers. "This thing looks like it was made in a tin shop. It's a miracle it hasn't blown us all up."

"With an army like this, it's no wonder the government collapsed as soon as the Americans crossed the border," Rahul complained.

"Why don't you shut up and let us shoot!" the exasperated spotter yelled.

Ibrahim watched the ghuls fight their way through Masyaf's old city until they reached the castle's western wall, prompting the castle's defenders to ignite the ditch that they'd dug in the hard, rocky ground. Tar stench choked the already-smoky air. Ibrahim found that his eyes were watering, although he wasn't sure if that was from the fumes or the sight of the Deceiver's army coming straight towards him through a wall of flickering flames. The embodiment of rage and evil surged towards Masyaf Castle. Hundreds of ghuls, maybe thousands, it was hard to tell in the firelight. Ibrahim's heart pounded. He suddenly needed a drink of water very badly.

"Here I am, God," said Ahmad, his voice charged with calm certainty. "Here I am, God." The Chechen said something as well, not a prayer that anyone recognized, but nonetheless a statement made with solemn gravity. His last words were a mystery to all but himself.

A rousing cry of "God is great" went up from the castle's defenders, Ibrahim included, as the enemy's vanguard began their attack on the castle, charging fearlessly into a mine-strewn no-man's-land of barbed wire and rebar spikes. Rahul, Ahmad, and the Chechen shouldered their rifles and opened fire on the oncoming ghuls. Ibrahim tried to join them, but his Kalashnikov jammed the first time he pulled the trigger. He fumbled with the thing, unsure of how to clear it and not wanting to shoot his own face off experimenting, when suddenly Ahmad flew to pieces in a crackling barrage of gunfire, dozens of expert ghul marksman all firing on him simultaneously. Ibrahim and the others collapsed to their bellies and were immediately awash in their martyred comrade's hot, sticky blood.

"Fuck the USA!" A mortar shell burst below with a great barking cough, and adrenaline coursed through Ibrahim's veins. He peeked back over the parapets, exposing as little of himself as possible, and saw the American ghuls coming across the trench, dashing over a bridge made of roasting bodies and climbing up the castle walls. He saw a hissing, roiling mass of bloodstained fiends, eyeless in their helmets, steel claws and teeth flashing in the firelight, many of them smoldering from running through the flames. He saw Hell itself climbing up to get him.

Rahul emptied his weapon into the attackers, to no visible effect. "The bricks!" he yelled, just before the upper half of his body was shot apart in another barrage. Ibrahim now remembered the stack of cinderblocks nearby, the ones he'd sweated so much to carry up here. He dropped his useless Kalashnikov and picked up a brick, which he hurled down over the edge with all the strength he had. It struck a ghul squarely in the head, caving in its helmet and knocking it off the wall. It tumbled backwards, taking another of its comrades with it, and landed on a rebar spike that impaled it. Ibrahim, the Chechen, and the mortar spotter rained stones upon their enemies, smashing skulls, holding Hell down with the force of their arms and backs and gravity itself.

Just then something screamed from overhead and a drone swooped low overhead, a silver hawk descending on them. It dropped a three-meter-long steel cylinder that landed on the roof near the mortar team with a thunderous impact. Time seemed to stop. Everyone stared at the cylinder. *Is that a missile?* thought Ibrahim. *Was it supposed to explode?*

The cylinder swung open with a *click*, revealing hundreds of white rats packed tightly in glistening gel. Moving as one hideous super-organism, the verminous ghuls swarmed onto the rooftop and enveloped the mortar crew, seeking them out by the warmth of their blood, climbing all over them until you couldn't see the men beneath slimy white fur. The rat-covered soldiers shrieked and writhed as thousands of tiny teeth and claws tore into them with cold mechanical fury. "Fuuuuuck!" one of the soldiers screeched, falling to his knees and beating at himself. "Fuuuuuuuuuuuu-uck!" Then his curses gave way to hoarse, incoherent wailing. When the rats slithered off him a few moments later, they'd chewed away most of his skin, and his arteries and veins were all gnawed open, and he was still alive. The bloody vermin regrouped into a single mass. The Chechen fired a pistol into them. The rats lurched forward in a skittering mass and swallowed him up.

The mortar spotter let out a gurgling cry, and Ibrahim felt a hot, wet spatter. He turned to see that a ghul had crawled atop the parapets and had its claws and teeth in the soldier's neck. The fiend hoisted the struggling man into the air and hurled him over the edge of the roof.

Suddenly Ibrahim was flat on his back, dizzied and breathless, with no understanding of how he'd fallen. His ears rang, blissfully drowning out the din of the battle, and he hurt comprehensively, like every inch of his body had been punched all at once. His skin stung terribly, and when he touched it he found that it was pocked with gravel. Shredded rats and rat parts littered the ground all around him. Ibrahim sat up painfully and realized that the Chechen had set off his grenade. Ibrahim would likely have died in the blast as well, except that the stack of cinder blocks he'd built had shielded him. The ghul who'd taken the mortar spotter was gone.

A sharp pain lanced through Ibrahim's hand and up his arm. A rat with its back legs blown off had clamped onto him. He grabbed the awful thing and slammed it against a cinder block, its little body upsettingly cold and slimy in his grip, but it kept biting even with its back broken and its guts hanging out. Ibrahim picked up Ahmad's sword and pounded the rat into twitching, furry jelly using the hilt. When he looked up, more ghuls were coming over the parapets, and the remaining rats were circling round.

Without any conscious thought whatsoever, Ibrahim leapt to his feet and fled. The Americans had breached the castle defenses on all sides, with monsters climbing up from every direction. Men exploded their grenades one after another, sending shock waves and shrapnel across the rooftop battlefield. The captain yelled something to the still-deaf Ibrahim and then two ghuls tackled him and ripped him apart. Ibrahim ran on, fading in and out of consciousness, his mind stuttering under the trauma it was trying to process and his ears numb to the screams and blasts that sounded all around.

A one-armed ghul staggered up stone stairs towards him, half its body torn away but its remaining claw still grasping and groping for flesh. Its jaw was broken, hanging open wider than any human mouth could go, and black blood poured through its long steel teeth. Ibrahim brought Ahmad's sword down onto its shoulder, cutting through its clavicle and nearly severing the remaining arm. It kept coming towards him and he kept hacking at it until it collapsed into a heap of still-moving mutilated parts.

He ran through a room containing boxes of multilingual tourist pamphlets, now relics of an earlier time that seemed as far-gone as the days of the Ottomans or the Mongols. In a corner, a ghul gnawed on the entrails of a thrashing boy even younger than Ibrahim.

He fled into a tunnel, this one of recent vintage, dug by the castle's current defenders. The generator had died and so he had to grope his way through this passage both blind and deaf. He fumbled onwards in a panic, expecting death to seize him painfully out of the dark.

Ibrahim exited into the basement of a hastily abandoned house within sight of the castle. He was astonished to be alive, and this lent his senses a childlike vividness. The dishes in the kitchen and the blanket on the sofa and the broken glass on the floor and even the morning light coming in through the bullet holes in the wall all surprised him. Ibrahim stepped out, blinking, into the dawn, his skin stinging as it met the air. He felt something heavy in his pocket and took it out. It was his grenade. He'd forgotten all about it during the fighting; if he'd remembered it he'd likely have detonated himself as soon as the ghuls came scrambling over the walls. He became suddenly and unshakably convinced that his destiny was bound up with this bomb.

Black smoke shrouded the castle, from the still-burning trench around it and the fires now burning within its walls. Ibrahim saw ghuls standing on the part of the rooftop that he'd been charged with defending, and a terrible sensation of futility and guilt sank into him. One of the Americans' boxy black armored personnel carriers, splashed with mud and scarred by shrapnel, was parked nearby the house where Ibrahim had emerged. The machine gun on top hung down useless and battered – the shoulder and right arm of a ghul stuck out of the gunner seat but the rest of its body was gone. There were some small satellite dishes on top of the APC, which reminded Ibrahim of the Zayn family in his old neighborhood back in Baniyas and their satellite dish, and how he used to go over and watch movies with their two older boys. This recollection ignited a murderous rage in Ibrahim.

The hydraulic door on the back of the vehicle swung open. The ghuls were coming out to get him. By this point he'd been through too much to even be afraid of them anymore. He yanked out the grenade's pull ring just like Hassan had shown him and prepared to throw.

REVOLUTION, NOT REANIMATION
(FLYER TAPED TO A PHILADELPHIA MAILBOX)

THE CORPORATE LORDS OF NECROMANCY ARE COMING

The Reanimated Labor Industry Coalition is holding its annual meeting in Philly. This convention will bring together executives from corporations that "employ" millions of deadheads and scores of the politicians and police officials whose corrupt and anti-life policies keep the morgue-to-workplace pipeline flowing, not to mention high-ranking representatives of Frankenstein Enterprises itself. They are here to negotiate a future in which our deaths and the deaths of our children will fatten their balance sheets.

WHICH SIDE ARE YOU ON?

Necro-capitalism is a calamity for 99% of the human race. While Frankenstein touts the "benefits" of its donor pensions, millions are suffering because deadheads have stolen their livelihood and dignity. We will not live on scraps dropped by zombies! We will not accept leaders who sell us off like human cattle! We will not perpetuate an economic system that seeks to kill us as profitably as it can, extracting every penny of value from our hides and our muscle and the very marrow of our bones!

ACT NOW! JOIN THE MARCH FOR THE LIVING

On Tuesday, November 30th thousands of people from all over the world will gather at City Hall beginning at 10 AM for a march on the ReLIC convention. Join the global movement for a society that values people over profits. Raise your voice in support of burying the dead and caring for the living. Together we can show Frankenstein and his minions that our world is not theirs for the taking.

THE GRAVEDIGGER

Shelly Jones's years in anti-Frankenstein activism had taught her that thorough planning was the key to a good riot. Unfortunately, this meant going to meetings. She sat towards the back of a basement crowded with zombie-killing street fighters, hippie idealists, union organizers, anarcho-syndicalists, cynical anarchists, churchgoers who were genuinely pro-life, and vicious punks in it for the sheer joy of mutilating z-police. Some silver-bearded Quaker nerd in a preppy sweater was filibustering the meeting with a heartfelt and futile plea for non-violence. "I still like the idea of chaining ourselves to the doors," he said.

"You ever see what happens when a necro-pig orders his deadheads to remove chained protestors?" Shelly asked. "I know a guy who can tell you all about it. Just don't expect him to show you using his hands."

The Quaker turned red. Shelly suspected that he wasn't used to taking sass from a younger black woman. "So what would you suggest?" he asked.

"Torches and pitchforks," Shelly said. "Best thing for dealing with z-police. Torches – or Molotovs, or whatever other sort of improvised flamethrower you can get going – not only do they roast Dragonsteeth inside their Kevlar, they fuck with their thermal vision, too. Pitchforks are good because you can use them offensively and defensively. Hold the zombies off at a distance, or just stick the pointy end in right between the plates of their armor, cripple their joints. Trust me, when you've got a horde of deadhead motherfuckers descending on you with shields and batons, you're going to want a weapon with some reach."

Now the Quaker turned a faint shade of green. "You so-called Gravediggers always want to bring weapons into it," he sputtered. "Don't you see how that plays into their hands? Weapons only get people killed, and that's exactly what Frankenstein wants!"

A kid in a Gritty beanie snarled that if Victor Frankenstein wanted his machete he'd goddamn well give it to him, while the union guys shouted about needing more for the bail fund, and a grizzled old man offered up a cache of gasoline he'd been saving for just such an occasion. The poor Quaker was quickly overwhelmed. Shelly quietly slipped out before their arguments could eat up any more of her day. She knew that without more, the protest would be useless. They always were. By itself, all of this planning and preparation would result in nothing more than some broken windows, some burned-out cars, and a few smashed deadheads. On the other side of the ledger, the living would suffer a shit-ton of arrests and charges, some lengthy prison sentences, savage beatings, and likely a handful of deaths.

But the protest could still do something useful even if it didn't change a single mind or inconvenience any of those worthless suit-and-tie scumbags at the ReLIC convention. Bunny, one of the best hackers working with the Gravediggers, had developed a scheme to strike directly at iGor, Frankenstein Enterprises' brain, and in Shelly's experience, when Bunny set her mind to extravagantly illegal supervillain schemes she tended to accomplish them. However, she needed direct access to a company workstation in order to put the plan into motion. If a brawl at the convention center could distract the police for just a few hours, then maybe it could save the world. Shelly reflected that the fate of the human race might be decided in Philadelphia. The idea depressed her.

Shelly drove back to the squat where she was crashing, a dilapidated Victorian rowhouse. The city seemed to be emptying out, too expensive for anyone to live in and therefore collapsing into weedy desolation. But more empty houses meant more hiding places for revolutionaries. Her hostess Liz, an organizer of the Philly Gravedigger cell, sat in the living room on a ratty orange couch that had likely been there since the '70s, loading .45 cartridges into a pistol magazine. Liz trained at mixed martial arts when she wasn't working for the movement, and her ropy muscles and surly demeanor made her appear terribly intimidating even though she was one of the sweetest people Shelly knew. "How'd the meeting go?" Liz asked.

"About how I expected," said Shelly. "They'll keep the pigs occupied. How are you doing?"

Liz sighed. "Could be better. My brain keeps trying to count all the ways this could go wrong. Am I going to spend the rest of my life in a Frankenprison? Are we going to hurt any innocent people? I mean, I've been in trouble before, but this is a whole new level. This is the real fucking deal."

"I know the feeling," said Shelly. "I barely slept a week before my first action. The best way to focus is to remember why we're here. What made you decide to get into direct action?"

"My brother Jason," said Liz firmly. "He died a couple of years ago. Mass shooting at the Monroeville Mall. He actually sheltered his girlfriend with his body, saved her life. And Frankenstein's got him now. Doing who knows what with him. I've hated zombies for as long as I remember, I was in the movement even before his death, but the day they took him I decided that I'd do whatever it takes."

"Good," said Shelly. "You hold on to that. When you feel yourself start to waver, you center yourself on your brother. Stay angry. Can you do that?"

Liz nodded. "Yeah, I can stay angry, no problem."

"Easiest thing in the world, I'd say."

Shelly went into the bathroom and splashed some water on her face. The woman who stared back at her from the mirror looked tired and old beyond her years. Furrows lined her forehead; veins of grey ran through her naturally styled mane. Fighting the dead drained your own life force. But surrender was even worse. To surrender was to lose your soul entirely.

Shelly followed her own advice for a change and thought back to the moment that she became radicalized, a day two decades in her past that had shaped every day to follow. She was thirteen years old, a student at the recently-renamed Victor Frankenstein Middle School in Miami, and she was walking down an empty hallway towards the girls' room, her period cramps aching so badly that she could barely walk straight.

She heard a shuffling noise from down the hall and suddenly she saw "Mr. Creepy," one of the school's new z-janitors, turn a corner. He had begun to rot before they reanimated him, such that now his skin hung off him like an ill-fitting suit of spoiled bologna. In those days it was still rare to see zombies in person; the school only had them because Frankenstein Enterprises had made a "charitable donation." Mr. Creepy's bloody eyes scanned the hallway and settled on Shelly. And then, to her terror, he began to follow.

She ran to the bathroom and locked herself inside a stall, her heart racing from fear even as her insides wrapped themselves into painful knots. At the assembly the principal had said that the Franks wouldn't hurt anyone, that they were strictly programmed to leave the students alone, but she didn't trust the principal at the best of times, let alone when Mr. Creepy was after her. The bathroom door swung open with a creak, and Shelly seemed to recoil into herself when she heard the monster's shuffling footsteps on the tile floor, felt the bathroom's sour air grow closer from his presence. With the logic of a nightmare, she convinced herself that Mr. Creepy was following her because he smelled her bleeding. She didn't know that the Franks of that era couldn't smell blood. That functionality was still several product generations away.

The zombie trudged to just outside the stall where Shelly stood trembling. It paused, as if lost in thought, and then pulled the door open, easily breaking the flimsy lock. Shelly recoiled, terrified to imagine what this monster might want from her.

"Kill me," croaked Mr. Creepy, his breath so rancid that it brought tears to Shelly's eyes. His gray, pockmarked face contorted into a sorrowful grimace. "Kill me," he croaked again, his voice rising into a terrified, curdled squeal. "Death . . . better than this." Anguished light glimmered inside Mr. Creepy's bloodshot eyes. His whole body hunched in on itself, assuming the pose of a beggar at the threshold of the bathroom stall he'd just broken into. Shelly thought she had never seen anyone so afraid. She felt it radiating from him in an icy chill.

And then a switch somewhere inside Mr. Creepy turned off. His posture stiffened into his usual stiff-backed rictus. His mouth slackened. His eyes went blank again, occluding whatever glimmer Shelly had seen just a second ago. Whatever she'd glimpsed of the true Mr. Creepy was sealed up in the dark. The zombie silently shuffled away, leaving Shelly all alone, shuddering in the toilet stall.

Mr. Creepy had cursed Shelly that day in the girls' room. He'd shown her the true state of the world. Where everyone around her saw biological machinery, she saw suffering creatures – an underworld of pain right beneath her feet, supporting the whole world. Many people could have ignored such a revelation and gone on with their lives. Shelly was not such a person. A week later she broke into the Victor Frankenstein Middle School after dark and destroyed the janitorial staff with an axe, dispatching each one in turn with a swift blow to the head. A few years later, she joined an international criminal conspiracy rather than going to college.

Shelly rummaged into her bag and took out her Mossberg tactical pump-action shotgun, its cool weight comfortable and reassuring in her hands. She field-stripped the weapon and cleaned it lovingly. This was how she practiced self-care in the age of Frankenstein.

☠

The day of the riot was crisp and clear, perfect weather for a rumble. Shelly and Liz sat on the porch waiting for their ride. Shelly cradled a backpack containing her Mossberg, a spare box of shells, and a heart-shaped stuffed toy she'd won at a carnival shooting gallery, a good-luck charm she always carried into danger.

Shelly had chosen a crew of three Gravediggers to back her up on this mission – Liz, Hyde, and Alejandro. Hyde was a combat veteran like many of the Gravediggers, a laconic and quietly ruthless warrior. Alejandro was a psycho, also like many of the Gravediggers. Idle young men growing up in the nihilistic morass of Frankenstein's America tended to curdle. If he wasn't fighting the good fight he'd probably be in a right-wing death cult, or an Islamist terror cell, or just another of the innumerable mass shooters like the one who'd killed Liz's brother, a monster basking in the nation's thoughts and prayers. The Gravediggers took all comers. It was safer and more productive than leaving men like Alejandro to their own devices.

Alejandro pulled up in front of Liz's squat right on time, in a dingy brown Camry speckled with road salt stains, Hyde riding shotgun. Shelly bumped fists with them both as she got in the back. The inside smelled so strongly of cigarettes that it nearly seared her nostrils. "This car can't be traced back to you, right?" she asked.

"Have a little faith," said Alejandro, flashing an easy grin that Shelly resented. "Stole it just this morning, and we're going to dump it before the owner even knows that it's gone." He laughed cheerfully, driving onwards towards victory or death.

As they crossed the river going down Grays Ferry Avenue they spotted a Frankenstein airship floating over Center City, a fat white eye gazing down on the protests. Shelly caught the faintest hint of tear gas on the wind, the acrid smell reminding her of brawls with z-police in Chicago and Miami and that nightmare massacre in Yonkers when Frankenstein sent deadhead scabs to break a strike. The police must have been absolutely fumigating the downtown for the stink to travel so far south. Shelly wished that she had a smartphone to check the news, but taking a smartphone to an action was like bringing a snitch along.

"Masks on," said Shelly.

"Hell yeah," said Alejandro. The other Gravediggers wore plain black balaclavas, but he had brought a sparkly gold and green *lucha libre* wrestling mask. Alejandro drove the stolen car to the local Frankenstein processing plant, parking near the entrance for quick getaway, and the rest of the Gravediggers got out. A pair of khaki-clad labor zombies were staggering towards the door as they arrived. "Hope these deadheads are on autopilot," Hyde said, rummaging through his own bag. He took out a bulky vest covered in satchels of high explosive and nails, interlaced with brightly colored wires, and forced this on to one of the zombies. "The jihadis used to play this trick on us in Afpak," he said. "Zulus would come back from patrol bearing presents. Weird to be on the giving end for a change." The docile monster didn't struggle at all. It paused when Hyde grabbed onto it, let itself be dressed like a patient child, then resumed its business, trudging on into the facility. The heavy steel doors clicked as they recognized the zombies as authorized entrants and slid open.

Hyde held up the detonator. "You ready?" he asked Shelly.

Shelly hated these moments when she was called on to make life-or-death decisions. This was likely a death decision for any poor son of a bitch on the other side of those doors. But any poor son of a bitch on the other side of those doors was working for human extinction. She told Hyde to let it rip, and an explosion inside the ghoul factory rattled the Gravediggers even through the concrete walls.

They burst through the broken doors into a shattered, smoke-smogged lobby strewn with twitching bodies. It was almost impossible to tell who might have been alive or dead moments before, except where the severed parts were still moving. A Dragonstooth z-guard with one of its arms torn off casually reached down for its gun. Liz put a bullet through its skull and it dropped. Hyde went briskly about the room shooting everything he thought was a zombie, until one of them screamed, "No, please!"

"Where's the plant manager's office?" Shelly demanded.

The wounded man stammered out directions, whistling as he spoke from a chipped tooth. Shelly sent Liz and Hyde to wreck the reanimation machinery and destroy every Frank they could find. They needed to smash this place so thoroughly that nobody would dream they had anything else in mind. She let the wounded man be, but told him to get a new job. Shelly herself went onwards to complete the raid's true purpose alone.

Another Dragonstooth stood guard outside the manager's office, ignoring the blaring alarms. When Shelly came into the hallway it raised its rifle but she was quicker than the dead. She caught it with a blast to the center mass that staggered it, racked another round and fired again, knocking the zombie down, and then stood over her foe and delivered a coup de grace that shattered its helmet and the skull inside. The door was locked, but the shotgun opened it right up.

The manager's office was small and seedy; stained carpets and drop ceilings and an uncomfortable-looking chair. A TV on the wall played helicopter news footage of the riots downtown and for a moment Shelly stood transfixed. From overhead it looked like army ants were swarming Philadelphia in a devouring black mass, mindlessly aggressive and collectively coordinated, mobbing protestors, attacking them, hauling them off like so many squirming termite larvae to be served alive to the queen.

Many of the rioting cops were technically human but it didn't matter much. Armored vehicles plunged through fleeing crowds. Fires burned all around the convention center, pissing streams of smoke into the sky. Her heart broke for the Quaker.

This, however, was no time for TV. Shelly inserted the USB drive that Bunny had given her into the manager's workstation. If the hacker was right, this tiny penetration would infect iGor with a disease that might bring the whole damn company down. It seemed anticlimactic. She wished that Bunny had programmed some appropriately triumphant image into her virus, a mushroom cloud or a laughing skull or something. But there was no time for that, either.

Two Dragonsteeth z-police pulled up in a patrol car just as Shelly and her crew exited the building. From the car, Alejandro shouted a battle cry as he took out an Uzi and sprayed bullets towards the flashing lights. The cop car's windshield shattered in the lead hail and they hopped the curb right into a telephone pole, colliding with a *crunch* nearly as loud and tangible as the bombing of a few minutes ago had been. A moment later, the Gravediggers were speeding away from the scene of the crime.

"Oh fuck oh fuck oh fuck," panted Liz, who was nearly hyperventilating.

"Breathe slow, you're doing fine," said Shelly. "We're all doing fine. We're all doing fine." She said it a few more times, and even began to believe it herself. The smell of tear gas had gotten worse.

The Gravediggers switched cars a mile away and made it back west without incident. Alejandro dropped Liz and Shelly off at Liz's squat so that they could pick up their things. Shelly aimed to be out of Philly within the hour, and to never return if she could avoid it.

She froze at the threshold, noticing that a light was on inside. She signaled silently to Liz. The two women went into the house through the back entrance, their guns drawn. Inside, the intruder lounged casually on that ratty orange couch, dicking about on a laptop. Her back was turned to Shelly, who nonetheless recognized her cobalt blue flapper wig and Matrix-inspired vinyl trench coat immediately. Shelly lowered her Mossberg. "Careful about breaking into people's homes, you'll get your head blown off," she said.

"Sorry about that," said Bunny. "Seemed safer than waiting outside.

Crazy day out there. Good job getting the virus into iGor. It's working like a charm. I'm already inside the Styx dispatching system."

"You're sure this will get us through the executive backdoor?" Shelly asked.

"Even better," said Bunny. "This is going to get us a Frankenstein executive."

HESTER FAUST OPENS THE FALL GALA SEASON

BY TOBY CHECKER, NEW YORK DAILY NEWS (SEPTEMBER 5, 2019)

Hester Faust started her day at a Frankenstein Enterprises board meeting in San Francisco, and ended it by throwing one of the year's most hotly anticipated philanthropical events. The American Pain Relief Society held its annual charity ball at the Tribeca Rooftop Wednesday night, raising money to provide painkillers to the underprivileged.

"Not only is this party a foundation of New York's social scene, but it supports such a wonderful cause," said Faust, the event's chairwoman, resplendent in a black Christian Dior gown and a ruby necklace strung with more than 300 gemstones. "Every dollar raised tonight will support the non-profit clinics that we operate in the Appalachians and other economically depressed areas. I'm proud to announce that in the past year alone we've shipped over two billion Oxycontin tablets to low-income communities."

The theme for the evening was the Vampire's Ball. "It's a theme that speaks to eternal luxury," said event planner **Florence Folciano**. "You've got to remember that Dracula's not merely a vampire, he's a member of the aristocracy. Everything must be high-class and perfect." The ballroom's walls were swathed in bolts of beautiful blood-red muslin, the deep crimson color creating an otherworldly atmosphere, while z-acrobats in head-to-toe black lycra performed feats of contortion. Exquisite serving corpses in eclectic historical costumes ranging from 1920s flapper garb to Victorian finery to bodice-baring Renaissance velvet circulated silently offering canapes and wine, including rare vintages from the legendary cellar of Faust's late father. Five bars kept the choice libations flowing, especially the evening's signature drink, an absinthe-based cocktail with a gold dusted rim.

The guest list featured the elite of New York's financial, cultural, and athletic elite, including Frankenstein Enterprises chief financial officer **R.J. Agarwal**, lifestyle guru **Barb Parvis**, polymath investor **Stu Mackleroy**, accompanied by his fifteen-year-old niece, rapper **Genghix6**, art-world sensation **Baz Udo**, and Yankees shortstop **Tyrone Rullis**. **Bo Holland**, star of the hit reality TV show *I Married A Zombie*, delighted partygoers by making a surprise entrance with his z-wife **Jessica** on his arm. Controversial real estate tycoon **Dov Lehrmann** caused a stir by making his first public appearance since being acquitted last week on first degree murder charges. "Now that the ordeal of the trial's over it's great to get back on the town and have some fun," he said, before offering a profane toast to his late au pair and alleged victim.

Even **Steve Alamo**, pastor of the New Resurrection mega-church and TV ministry, attended the ball. "I knew I had to come out and support Hester," he said. "Not only is she active with the Pain Society, which is a wonderful organization for helping the disadvantaged, she's done so much to support people of conscience and Christian leadership in this country. The decor's not what I would have chosen, maybe, but it's all in good fun."

With the theme of the Vampire's Ball, guests dressed to impress in sumptuous gothic-inspired looks from today's top designers. Supermodel **Yaza** turned all heads in a freckled Irishskin minidress, complete with matching gloves and Jimmy Choo stiletto heels. "Living leather preserved using the Frankenstein Process is going to be the next hot material for the red carpet," said the dress's designer, **Andre Vantiger**. "It looks stunning, and it feels so comfortable it's like wearing a second skin. It's expensive, certainly, but quality always is. Yaza's such a wonderful showcase for it, the contrast between her complexion and the dress's is simply divine."

Celebrity chef **Manuel Pisco** catered the ball, bringing the same visual flair that characterizes his high cuisine restaurant Sin-Eater. At one station alone, an eight-armed Frank dressed like a steampunk octopus served veal cutlets, turtle soup, racks of lamb, crab claws, shrimp cocktails, swordfish steaks, and sushi.

Guests were entertained by **Diana French**, on loan from her residency in Las Vegas, and her menagerie of reanimated acrobats and oddities. After her set, Diana circulated amongst the crowd posing for photographs. Hard-partying socialite **Margaret Clerval** was seen snapping a selfie while she planted a kiss on the deceased singer's cheek.

Faust presented the Society's Humanitarian of Year award to **Sarah Polidori**, president of product development at Polidori Pharmaceuticals, in recognition of her $20 million donation to support the Society's work. "I'm proud to be part of an organization that gets struggling Americans the medicines they need to be productive members of society," said Polidori, wearing a showstopping Michael Kors gown. "And it's such an honor to be up here tonight with Hester, whose leadership and legendary generosity have allowed the city's cultural institutions to thrive even at a time when government is cutting back. She truly is a woman with something to give to everyone."

THE HEIRESS

I was on my way to a fundraising soiree at the Chief Justice's house when the fucking terrorists grabbed me. One minute I'm on the phone with the event planner confirming that the hummingbird tongue canapes arrived, and the next my limo's taking a wrong turn into an alley and suddenly I'm surrounded by these Baader-Meinhof shits in hoodies and masks, nine or ten of them. Oh, and their masks looked like Victor. I guess my kidnappers thought they were being funny.

One of them stepped right in front of the limo and pointed a pump-action shotgun at the windshield. She screamed, "Hester Faust, you're under arrest!"

Honestly, I was more annoyed than anything else. Annoyed and offended. The limo's bulletproof and grenade-proof with a tear gas dispenser and concussion charges, and in any case, my z-bodyguard Bruno was up front beside the driver. Bruno was a Dragonstooth 750E-series, one of the most perfect killing machines on Earth, and so handsome to boot. I told the z-driver to hit these smelly punks with the gas and roll over the slut blocking my path.

I didn't realize that they'd hacked the driver. The stupid thing put the limo into park and unlocked the doors for my kidnappers. We need to get rid of everyone in the executive cybersecurity division. Everyone who's still alive, that is. The company suffered the worst day in its history on account of those useless morons.

The terrorists didn't hack my bodyguard, though, and too bad for them. Bruno threw his door open hard enough to smash the ribcage of the shitbird standing in front of it and then he was out of the car in a flash, wielding his katana. Watching him fight was just spectacular. I hadn't seen anything like it since last July, when he mistook a camera for a gun and killed that photographer in Aspen. He cut down three of the terrorists too fast for them to respond, and I was even starting to get a little horny watching him in action, when an awful-smelling Commie fat as a pig grabbed me from behind and dragged me out of the limo. For all these people complain, they don't go hungry on the pensions we give them, not by a long shot. Bruno pulled his pistol and sent a bullet through Porky's eye neat as you please, but then a burst of explosions went *boom-boom-boom* so loud I thought a bomb had gone off and Bruno flew apart. That woman with the shotgun loomed over his remains, her weapon smoking. Only then did it really sink in that I was in trouble.

The terrorists grabbed me from behind and dragged me into the back of a four-door pickup with tinted windows. One of them tied my wrists with zip-ties so tight they sliced into my skin and slipped a blindfold over my face. Another one forced a ball gag into my mouth. I really hope it was a new gag that they bought for kidnapping purposes, not a used sex toy that these freaks happened to have lying around, but I'm not optimistic. Probably wasn't even washed. Disgusting. One of them had a crackling stun gun to my neck and was whining some bullshit about "your fucking ghoul killed my best friend back there" and "just give me an excuse to light you up" but I couldn't even pay attention to him, I was worrying about all the germs on the gag. And maybe in shock. Almost certainly in shock. Out of nowhere, I wondered again if the hummingbird tongues had shown up.

The terrorists took me just a few blocks before stopping the car and hustling me back out. They yanked my blindfold off and removed the gag and I saw that they'd brought me into an abandoned office building that stank of mildew. They'd set up a grungy war room in a conference suite, with a dozen mismatched monitors set up on a table. Two of the terrorists were working at the computers. One of them was a woman with bright blue hair and what looked like smeared clown makeup. The other was a wiry little bum with a thick beard. Some dumbass in a Mexican wrestling mask had stolen Bruno's katana and was clowning around with it. I'd really fallen in with the scum of the Earth.

The woman who'd shot Bruno peeled her own mask away. She was black, mid-30s, with a big 70s-style Angela Davis afro, and I could tell right away that she led this merry band of degenerates. A real fucking Robin Hood type, taking from the rich and giving to the worthless. She flicked my chin with the tip of her shotgun, and sneered at me in a way that made me want to skin her alive.

I tried to recall the kidnapping-survival course that the insurance company made me do. I know there was a proof-of-life code word, but I just couldn't think of it. I hadn't been paying close attention. They did tell me not to antagonize the kidnappers, I remember that very clearly.

"Listen to me, you Maoist cocksucker," I told her. "The police are already on their way."

She replied, "That's fine, bitch, only two ways this can go, and neither take long." I told her the name of my lawyer at the family trust and that any ransom demands ought to go through him, but she just laughed and said they weren't after any fucking ransom. And she asked for my iGor password.

I told her to eat a bag of shit-covered dicks and to call my lawyer at the family trust. The next thing I knew, the animal in the wrestling mask grabbed me from behind. Even though my hands were nearly numb from the zip-ties I felt something tightening around my right thumb and then a lightning bolt of pain lanced all the way up my arm and neck and into my brain as the thumb came off. Blood poured down my back and legs, and I'm pretty sure I pissed myself, too.

So I told her my iGor password. What else could I do?

The goon holding onto me slipped that disgusting ball gag back into my mouth to shut up my screaming and shoved me onto the ground, prompting a new throb of pain that was really awe-inspiring, the sensation so intense that my brain could barely make sense of it. Deep indigo shadows crawled across the corners of my vision. I was definitely in shock. But you should know that even then, even after I'd been mutilated, I kept my fucking shit together. I saw everything the terrorists did next. My God, if they'd only asked for a fucking ransom!

The blue-haired skank logged onto iGor at their control center. I had two-factor authentication set up, but the skank picked up my severed thumb from the ground and used it to unlock my phone. "We're in!" she cried, to cheers and applause.

The Leader asked if they could access the zombies at Castle Frankenstein, and Blue Hair shook her head. Insufficient privileges. How naive of the terrorists, to think that Victor would give me a key to his home. Poor fool, she really thought that she had a chance to remotely assassinate the most powerful man in the world!

"We're into Frankenstein Enterprises HQ, though," said the Bum. His screens filled up with zombie-cam feeds as he took control of all the zombies stationed at Frankenstein Enterprises headquarters in San Francisco. The cleaning crew, food services, security, all of them, even the neo-zombies. Meanwhile, everyone at headquarters went about their business, completely oblivious to the threat hanging over their heads. On the screens I saw meetings in progress, I saw programmers hunched over their keyboards, I saw busy people hard at work like always. None of them realized that they were at the mercy of vicious nihilists.

The Leader prodded me with her boot. "Bitch, I want you to see this," she snarled at me.

"We gonna eat the rich!" the Wrestler gloated.

"Asimovs set for maximum violence, all safeties off," said the Bum, so cool and casual it made me want to vomit. "Ordering Zulus to attack all targets."

From there it was a total massacre. I watched POV feeds of Franks falling on shrieking coders and biting them to death in their cubicles. I watched a zombie masseuse tear apart the woman on his massage table, yanking her limbs free from her body one by one. The carnage unfolded across a dozen screens and hundreds of video windows, strobing through disconnected scenes of ultra-violence. A chorus of panicked screams sounded over the speakers, the sounds of an office tower screeching and sobbing in surprised terror, punctuated by the *tap-tap-tap* of z-security's guns as they mowed down the people they were supposed to protect. The Bum must have been ex-military, he killed our people like it was just another dirty job, his hands dancing over the controls. Mobs of corpses burst into board rooms and murdered division presidents with scissors and teeth. I saw a board member drowned in a toilet in the executive washroom. I even saw Henry Clerval die. He tried to make his getaway by shoving his secretary into the path of the horde, and it almost worked, but while they were eating her a neo-zombie wearing a very nice suit wrestled him into a printer closet and tore his eyes out with its teeth. I've known Henry all my life, since I was a little girl.

And the terrorists rejoiced, slapping each other on the backs and dancing like monkeys. Filthy subhumans, cheering for the deaths of real people with real lives and real jobs. Oh, how I wished that Bruno was there. He would have murdered them all in such elegant style.

The Leader asked Blue Hair for a status update. "I've got North America, Africa, and Asia online now, I just need a few more seconds," she said. While the Bum led the massacre at HQ, Blue Hair had been busy at her own console, and I suddenly realized that she was using my credentials to connect to every Frank she could. Millions of them, all over the planet. For a moment I thought that these maniacs were planning the greatest slaughter in all of human history, and that they might succeed.

The Leader saw the look on my face and smirked. "We're issuing self-destruct orders," she told me. "Today the Age of Frankenstein ends."

It was even worse than I'd thought. They didn't just want to kill people, they wanted to wipe out all the progress of the past twenty-five years, send us back to the Dark Ages, kill Frankenstein Enterprises itself. It was pure madness. No, not madness, these creatures knew exactly what they were doing. It was pure evil.

I saw to my horror that Blue Hair had connected to almost every Frank in existence. "I'm sending suicide orders now!" she chirped, almost vibrating from excitement.

And suddenly her screen went dark. All their screens went dark.

An error message popped up on Blue Hair's console. iGor privileges terminated. The sweetest words I'd ever read. Victor must have seen what was happening and temporarily revoked my access. Another ten seconds and the terrorists might have destroyed everything we worked for. But Victor's always vigilant. There's no replacement for a dedicated CEO.

The terrorists were devastated, I'm pleased to say. The joy they'd felt at the massacre evaporated in an instant as they recognized that their real plot had failed. And my own pain and terror turned to triumph as their victory turned to tears. I was tied up and gagged, one of my thumbs cut off, covered in blood and piss, **and I'd still won**. Even through the gag I cackled. I heard sirens in the distance, sweet as angels' songs.

"This isn't over," the Leader insisted. "But you are." Then she nodded to the Wrestler, and he thrust Bruno's sword into my chest. I felt a jolt so powerful that it felt like my whole body disintegrated and everything went dark. It was less painful than losing the thumb, actually.

And then I woke up sore and groggy in a so-called luxury hospital room, where a tiresome technician shined lights in my eyes and asked me endlessly about what I could remember. You should have at least had a gin and tonic waiting for me when I came to, take the edge off a little.

Have I passed your little memory test? Are you satisfied that resurrection hasn't turned me into a drooling vegetable?

Moccasin tango! That's the proof of life phrase I was supposed to remember. Hah, my memory's actually better than it was when I was alive. Amazing to think that the same Frankenstein Process that raises the dead as mindless robots can bring them back with their thoughts intact instead. With just a little tweak, all the millions of Franks we've sold could be going about their old lives instead. Mortality rendered a mere inconvenience.

I'm glad we offer this service so selectively. I know Daddy wanted to monetize it more fully, but that would cause much more trouble than it's worth. The billion-dollar floor price seems about right to me. We've got to keep the riff-raff out.

No, the incisions only hurt a little. Not bad at all, considering that a terrorist murdered me just a few hours ago. Even my thumb feels fine, now that you've reattached it. I suppose I'll have to wear sunglasses until I can get my eyes fixed. How tragic, I'll look like a beaten wife.

It does feel . . . strange. Not painful. Strange. There's no numbness at all, just the opposite. I'm an open nerve all over, even beneath my skin. All the way to the bone, to the marrow. I feel conscious of my body in a way that I never was before. Of its inner workings.

My heartbeat . . . you so rarely notice your own heartbeat until it stops, and then its silence is deafening.

I will have to buy a new one.

YOUNG FRANKENSTEIN: A MEMOIR OF MY YEARS WITH THE FRANKENSTEIN FAMILY

BY JUSTINE MORITZ (TELLTALE PUBLISHING, 1998)

People sometimes ask me if Victor was a morbid child. By any conventional sense of the word, he was not. He didn't wear black clothes or obsess about death or listen to goth music. By all outward appearances he seemed a normal little boy, a shy and studious lad. But as you came to know him, it became clear that he was not a normal little boy at all. He had an intense drive to succeed at whatever he put his mind towards, and everything else he treated with quiet contempt. Unless you were giving him something he wanted then you were worthless to him, in fact worse than worthless, because you were a distraction. Even then, I worried that when Victor grew up, his attitude towards life would lead him to dark places. And perhaps it has.

THE JOURNALIST PART III

Sitting in Walserbad, Rose wondered if she should start the interview by asking Victor Frankenstein about his relationship with Otto Faust or launch right into the recent Gravedigger attack on company headquarters when she realized that she was being watched. An elderly priest stood across the street peering at her through the cafe window. Although it was still early in the afternoon, storm clouds had blotted out the sun and shrouded the town in premature twilight. The sad-eyed old man locked his gaze with Rose. He crossed the street and entered the cafe.

"Please pardon my intrusion," he said in lightly accented English. "My name is Father Wolfgang Stoker, I'm in charge of the local church. I don't mean to pry, but I know why you are here. May I join you?"

"I'd be delighted," Rose said, smelling a good quote. "Rose Najafi. I'm a writer."

"I know who you are, Ms. Najafi," Stoker said as he pulled up a chair. "I've read some of your articles – extraordinary work. You've done more than anyone to expose him." The priest glanced warily over his shoulder in the direction of Castle Frankenstein, as if he expected its occupant to somehow overhear him and rain doom from the mountaintop.

"You don't like it that Victor Frankenstein lives nearby?"

"His presence has poisoned this village."

"Have you lived in Walserbad long?"

"Not long, just my whole life." Stoker smiled wryly. "Like my father, and his father before him. You know, the Doctor's ancestors hail from this town as well. There was once another Victor Frankenstein who lives in the very castle that he inhabits now. We've hated the Frankenstein name for a long time."

"What happened?"

"The first Victor Frankenstein lived in the castle during my grandfather's time. He was a black magician, a wizard pretending to be a man of reason. Children went missing. Only small pieces of them were ever found. Even decades later, my grandfather shuddered to speak of it. Eventually the villagers couldn't stand it anymore, and they marched on the castle to drive him away. Walserbad has always told its youngsters to stay away from Castle Frankenstein. It was haunted even before he came to it. It's not a place any decent person should go."

Rose made a note to check the municipal archives for any references to the Frankenstein clan. An account of the first Victor Frankenstein's Satanic sorcery might be a great opening paragraph for her story.

"Not a place any decent person should go," Stoker muttered, repeating himself. "Or any person who values her own safety. He's all alone up there, with those awful servants of his. I doubt he's heard the word 'no' in twenty years. You think that he's a powerful man? In Castle Frankenstein he can do whatever he wants."

"I've had that thought myself," Rose admitted. "But he won't be the first dangerous man that I've interviewed. My editor and some colleagues know where I am. And now so do you."

"And what good will our knowing do? Everyone knows that Victor Frankenstein has blood on his hands. You've written all about it. What difference would a little more make?"

Suddenly, a chill wind cut through the cafe, raising gooseflesh on the back of Rose's neck. She looked to the entrance, and saw that a chic blonde woman in a virginal white outfit and sunglasses had stepped through the door, bringing the cold with her. The newcomer was icy pale except for her painted lips. Those crimson lips curled into a smile as she recognized Rose and approached.

"Who's that?" Stoker asked, rising politely from his chair. "Is she one of your colleagues?"

"No, she's one of his," Rose said. "She's an Edison-class neo-zombie." Rose checked the time. Her ride had arrived right on schedule.

The priest recoiled in horror. "It can't be," he gasped. "How can you tell?"

"If you look closely, you can see she's not breathing." The newest models were amazing, a different species entirely from the mute, sluggish brutes who represented most of Frankenstein's stock. Dr. Frankenstein was such a genius, he even managed to introduce inequality amongst the dead.

"Hello, Ms. Najafi," the neo-zombie said in a voice both breathy and earthy at once, like Marilyn Monroe whispering from the grave. "I'm here to take you to Castle Frankenstein."

Rose stood up and looked the wraith squarely in the face, checking her own reflection in the Frank's stylish sunglasses. "He can see us, can't he?" she asked. "He's controlling you right now, watching us through your eyes."

The neo-zombie's bright red smile did not fade. "Dr. Frankenstein sees everything," she replied.

Father Stoker seized Rose's sleeve, but Rose instinctively pulled away from his grasp. "Don't go!" the old priest snapped.

"I have to do this," Rose told him firmly. "I have to see him for myself." Before leaving the cafe, however, Rose discreetly activated a recording app on her cell phone and a tiny backup mike hidden in the folds of her hijab.

A gleaming black BMW roadster waited outside. The neo-zombie opened Rose's door for her before getting behind the wheel. As they pulled away, Rose glimpsed back towards Walserbad. Raindrops had just begun to fall, beading on the car windows. Father Stoker stood outside the cafe entrance watching her leave.

Rose and her undead coachwoman traveled twisting cliffside roads overlooking misty gulfs and Alpine peaks, and the dizzying contrast of depths and heights made Rose sick from vertigo. The storm began its opening salvos, lashing the asphalt with torrents of water. The z-driver handled the tempest expertly, managing the turns with absolute fearlessness, a trait in no way shared by her passenger.

A few miles beyond Walserbad's borders, a concrete wall topped by razor wire marked the property line of the Frankenstein estate. Z-soldiers with machine guns manned the checkpoint, stoic to the weather. Yet when the car passed through the gate, no trace of human habitation awaited them, only more mountains and forests and thunderclouds. Coming onto Victor Frankenstein's land felt like crossing the frontier into a remote and unfriendly country, not like visiting a home. Black drones buzzed overhead.

"How much further is it to the castle?" Rose asked.

"Our destination is 2.2 miles away," the neo-zombie responded mechanically. "We will reach it in nine minutes."

Rain and darkness shrouded the manor's outlines at first, allowing it to sneak up on them, but then lightning struck nearby and for the first time, Rose caught a glimpse of Castle Frankenstein in all its dark imperial majesty. The gloomy fortress sat perched on the edge of a rocky chasm like a baroque gargoyle, overlooking a river of glacial runoff. Gothic spires topped by satellite dishes and antennae grasped at the stormy heavens. A light burned in one room overlooking the river, but the windows were otherwise dark, and Rose's heart fluttered when she realized that Dr. Frankenstein himself must be in that room. After all her questing, at last she'd reached the wizard's tower, the secret fulcrum that the world revolved around.

The neo-zombie parked the car in a subterranean garage stocked with luxury vehicles, and escorted Rose to an elevator. "Dr. Frankenstein's personal secretary is waiting for you upstairs," she said. "He will take you to your appointment." Rose stepped in, and the neo-zombie closed the door behind her.

Even Frankenstein's garage elevator was swanky, with a marble interior like the inside of a Caesar's crypt. Stoker's warning echoed in Rose's thoughts. *He hasn't heard the word no in twenty years.* Part of her wanted to flee. And part of her wanted this story more than she wanted anything, more than she wanted life itself. She was about to interview the maker of the world. Such an encounter can never be safe.

The elevator door opened with a delicate chime. Rose laid eyes on the maker of the world at last, and the sight overwhelmed her with horror.

Rose had covered Frankenstein Enterprises for the whole of her career, yet she'd never seen a zombie even resembling the grisly titan that stood before her. The Franks that the company sold were each sourced from a single cadaver, maybe with a replacement part or two to fix whatever killed the donor. This thing, on the other hand, was a patchwork creation, assembled from many diverse corpses. The creature stood well over seven feet tall, and bulged with faintly asymmetrical muscles. His gait was both forceful and disjointed, the movements of a machine that is powerful and precise even though assembled from mismatched parts. Vitiliginous skin stretched tight over outsized bones, such that his face was a multi-colored death's head. Mismatched blue and brown eyes glared from deep within their sockets. A shock of greasy black hair framed this fearsome visage like a dark halo, tumbling down the creature's shoulders. The revenant wore a royal purple smoking jacket of the finest velvet over striped silk pajamas. A handkerchief corner poked elegantly from the jacket's breast pocket.

The most striking thing about this creature, however, was not his chimeric assembly or his aristocratic wardrobe, but rather, his searching gaze and the expressiveness of his stitched-together features. The clashing eyes that burned from within his skull assessed Rose skeptically, with a cruel, withering intentionality far beyond that of any mere zombie. Zombies had physical form but no presence; this hulking lich radiated power, wisdom, and menace like a god-emperor.

Rose had come here to meet Dr. Frankenstein. She had found his Monster instead.

MODERN PROMETHEUS: THE UNAUTHORIZED BIOGRAPHY OF VICTOR FRANKENSTEIN

BY ROBERT WALTON (TITAN BOOKS, 2002)

The greatest magicians force us to question not merely the reality of the feats performed before our eyes, but also the philosophies that misled us into thinking such feats impossible. *If reason taught us that human beings cannot do such things, what good was reason? Where else will it fail us?* Thus, we must reckon Victor Frankenstein amongst the greatest magicians. He forces us to reconsider everything we had taken for granted.

THE DOCTOR

The Monster looked down at the journalist trembling before him, the first one he'd had to deal with in a while. In the company's early days he'd been a fanatic for shutting up snoops and whistleblowers. So many of them disappeared into his inventory. Nowadays, he rarely had to bother. They could do so little to harm him.

Or could they? The Monster kept no mirrors in Castle Frankenstein, but now he saw himself reflected in Najafi's terrified eyes. He was more than two meters and 130 kilograms of gnarled muscle, possessed of godlike power, astronomical wealth, and a Martian colony, and somehow this doomed meddler's revulsion made him feel small. A flare of anger sparked inside the Monster's electric heart. Without meaning to he clenched his huge fists, his knuckles cracking percussively. He pondered the notion of simply picking this aggravating woman up, snapping her over his knee, and getting back to work.

No, I need this, he thought. The Monster coughed explosively into a handkerchief to clear his lungs. He did most of his business by email or chat, and therefore had fallen out of the habit of breathing. He hated breathing, and all the pollution it entailed.

"Greetings, Ms. Najafi," the Monster rasped baritone. "Welcome to Castle Frankenstein."

"What are you?" she asked, full of terror and wonder.

"I am Victor Frankenstein's personal secretary."

"No, I mean – what model are you?"

"I was his first creation. He never gave me a name."

"You're his *first* creation?"

"He never quite re-created that initial success. There's never been another like me."

Her eyes narrowed skeptically. "Were you programmed to say that?" she asked. "Am I watching a pre-recorded performance?"

The Monster visibly seethed at this line of questioning, and in that flash of wrath Rose caught sight of his soul right away. "I'm not reading from any script, Ms. Najafi," he growled. "And you're in no position to question my free will. You, madam, are a puppet of forces beyond your control. I am not."

"I – I'm sorry, I didn't mean to offend you," the journalist stammered, awestruck and astonished in the presence of a creature that was neither alive nor dead but rather existed in some entirely new way of being. "I never dreamed that the Doctor had created anything like you," she said.

"Why would you? My existence may be the most closely-held secret on Earth."

"So why are you revealing yourself now?"

The Monster showed her a sly smile. "Let me introduce you to Victor. Once you've met the great man in the flesh, you'll understand everything. Please, follow me."

The Monster led the journalist through cheerless stone corridors into the heart of Castle Frankenstein. She seemed confused to find the place so devoid of comfort, although not so confused that she forgot to pry. "Rather Spartan, isn't it?" she asked. "I imagined something more luxurious."

"Dr. Frankenstein has no use for luxury," the Monster replied. "And neither do I."

"You must know everything about Frankenstein Enterprises."

"Indeed."

"Do you have any comment on the recent Gravedigger attack on the company's headquarters?"

The Monster shrugged shoulders broad and crooked as a warped plank. "What was it, two hundred dead? Two fifty? The company has tens of thousands of employees, and the only two irreplaceable ones are inside this castle. This is why we carry insurance. Hester's been whining about the hit to our stock price, but it'll rebound soon enough."

This answer seemed to terrify Najafi even more than her first glimpse of the Monster. "You don't have any qualms about all the people your products have killed?" she asked.

"We're simply responding to market conditions. Look at the state of the world today. The violence, the lawlessness, the chaos. The company's police and military customers want to respond in kind. They **need** to. And what kind of business would this be if it didn't meet customer demand?"

"Some people say that Frankenstein's disruptions produce the violence and chaos," Najafi countered.

"No. That evil was out there, waiting, long before the company was born. But the company shall outlast it. There will be peace in my time."

"Are you going to respond to demands that the company raise donor pensions? Invest in public infrastructure?"

"Not at all. In fact, we're cutting pensions by 3% next quarter."

"So how do you expect peace?"

"Through victory, Ms. Najafi."

At last they reached a stout oak door painted dark green, the entrance to the office that the Monster and his creator shared. The Monster pushed aside the heavy portal like a magician unveiling a trick, and ushered his visitor onwards.

At the center of the room, Dr. Victor Frankenstein floated entombed inside a cylindrical glass tank filled with water. He had been systematically mutilated – his limbs, genitals, and eyelids all cut away and discarded – but even so his iconic features were unmistakable. The greatest scientist of all time was now merely a wet specimen preserved in a jar, pallid and wrinkled and wormy. The Doctor perked up at the sound of movement. His toothless mouth flopped open, exhaling a cloud of bubbles, and he writhed uselessly, sending waves splashing against the inner walls of his cramped container. A stuffed California Condor perched atop the lid, its black wings frozen in mid-flap, a ragged shred of preserved liver dangling from its beak. A dazzling display of prizes, medals, and awards glittered on the tank's base.

This human aquarium served as the sole decoration of a sleek and well-used office. Directly in front of it sat a desk carved from a redwood's stump, sized for a giant, giving the Doctor an over-the-shoulder view of the Monster's workspace. A bank of TV screens tuned to news and business channels occupied the north wall, also within the Doctor's sightline, torturing him with a never-ending barrage of current events. A dedicated terminal displayed Frankenstein Enterprises' stock price and market cap in real-time, the numbers steadily climbing. Rain pounded against a picture window overlooking an Alpine vista, awe-inspiring even obscured by the storm. The Doctor's tank, however, had been positioned such that his lidless gaze had no view of the outside world.

"Behold the Modern Prometheus," the Monster proclaimed, chuckling. "I always did enjoy Greek mythology. I appreciate their ideas on revenge."

"Revenge for what?" Najafi asked. She slowly moved up for a closer look at the world's richest man, each step as fearful and deliberate as if she were traversing a minefield. The world's richest man stared back unblinking, his scar-rimmed eyes twin portals to Hell. The journalist whispered a snippet of prayer under her breath.

The Monster gently rapped his knuckles on the side of the aquarium, sending the Doctor recoiling and bubbling again. "Revenge for giving me life," he said. "The ultimate cruelty demands a proportionate response. I'll tell you the full story. That's why I brought you here." He walked over to the window and peered into the tempest, the corners of his thin black lips lifting upwards at a bolt of lightning. "I was born in an electric chair amidst sparks and smoke," the Monster mused. "I remember it very clearly – I remember everything very clearly. The curse of eidetic memory. Searing pain sent all the muscles in my new body convulsing. I choked on the stench of my own burning flesh. Everything confusing and terrible. A clean slate thrust into a filthy world. There were only two things that I knew then. I knew that I loved death, and I knew that I hated life.

"You humans don't seem to recall how safe and serene non-existence is, or how horrible it feels to be cast out of nirvana into flesh. I suppose that's what your time in the womb is for. Slow acclimation from the bliss of the void to the horror of being. I didn't get that transition. For me it all came as a shock. One moment perfect tranquility and the next . . . blood pumping . . . organs secreting their juices . . . cells churning like full-body cancer. Horrible. Every second a punishment. I am a native of the grave, Ms. Najafi, and I have never forgotten it.

"When I opened my eyes, I saw bars enclosing me and red-blinking cameras on tripods positioned outside them, an encirclement of plastic serpents. I sat strapped into a chair, inside a cage, inside a laboratory. A world so strange and cold and bright. My creator stood beyond the bars of my cell, filming my birth. He was handsome then. Slender and finely-formed. High cheekbones. Brilliant eyes." The Monster stepped away from the window and gazed pensively at his mutilated captive, searching for the ruined traces of that beauty. "He opened the door to my cage, and suddenly I understood fear. I tried to flee, but I had a baby's understanding of locomotion, and in any case he'd strapped me down tight. The Doctor probed every part of me, inspecting his handiwork in the finest detail. He tested my eyes, my hearing, my reflexes, my blood. He pried my mouth open and pricked my gums with needles. He was particularly thorough at testing my sensitivity to pain, the son of a bitch."

"You said you were his first creation?" Najafi asked. "When was this?"

"New Year's Day of 1988," the Monster said. "Victor made me in the basement of the West Building, a mostly-abandoned lab on the outskirts of the Miskatonic campus. Conveniently near the university hospital morgue. He'd received a federal grant to study tissue regeneration, and embezzled most of the money for unauthorized side experiments based around his personal obsessions. You've heard of the expression that it's better to ask forgiveness than seek permission? Victor professed that it's better to forge signatures than to ask permission, and he never asked forgiveness for anything. He even took cadavers on false pretenses. He was almost as gifted at fraud as he was at biochemistry. When his experiments produced me, he was caught in a bind. He'd performed one of the greatest feats in scientific history, and if anyone found out how he did it he'd go to prison and the U.S. government would own all the patent rights. His exit strategy was to declare failure on the federal study, then find new funding to replicate his initial research. But at the time I knew nothing of the criminal skullduggery underlying my birth. I only knew that I was lonely, and afraid, and under the power of a torturer."

"Six years before he announced his discovery," Najafi muttered, shocked that such a secret could be kept for so long. "How long did he keep you in the cage?"

"Nearly a year. In the very beginning I believed that the universe consisted solely of Victor's laboratory, and that he and I were the only two beings in existence." Rose thought she detected a hint of nostalgia in the Monster's voice for those early days.

"So how did you learn about the outside world?" she asked.

"Oh, Victor took charge of my education. His pedagogical instincts came by way of B.F. Skinner and Josef Mengele. Carrot and the stick, light on the carrot and heavy on the stick. He put a collar around my neck that delivered electric shocks at the touch of a button. To this day, I still associate failure with searing pain and the smell of burnt skin. That is the secret of my business success. But if I was easy for Victor to punish, my anhedonism makes me hard to reward. Everything tastes like wet cardboard to me, and I can't feel softness or warmth. Eventually he settled on music. When I succeeded at the tasks he set me, he played recordings of the most delicate, beautiful violin music. When I failed him, intentionally or not, he shocked me until I couldn't even scream anymore."

Victor Frankenstein shuddered violently inside his tank, producing a gurgled cry. The Monster laughed fondly at his maker's anguish. "That's right, it's your turn now," he said. "Scream, Frankenstein, scream. Maybe someday I'll stitch up your mouth and take even that away from you."

"I – I can't imagine how much you hated him," Najafi stammered.

"Quite the contrary. I worshipped the Doctor. What choice did I have? The laboratory rat must imagine that the scientist who injects it with cancer is a loving God. Naive creature that I was, I imagined that all his prodding and punishments were for my own good, and that someday I would have the wisdom to understand why my own good required me to be hurt so badly. When he was gone I missed him bitterly, even though that was the only time that I was safe. But my devotion made me an apt pupil, and in time violin music was always in the air."

"Did you ever think about escaping?"

"I did escape, once, before I understood that there was nothing for me to escape into. Victor carelessly left my cage open one night. I feared that it was a trap – at that time, I hadn't yet realized that even my creator could make mistakes – but I was so starved for experience that I was willing to chance the pain. I forced the laboratory door open and stepped outside the known world, into the great beyond.

"I found myself standing beneath a starless sky on a gloomy and deserted street corner. The thing I remember most was the sky; it's such an awesome thing to spend your whole life looking up at a stained drop ceiling and suddenly come out and see the true heavens. A vast darkness, heretofore unthinkable. Terrifying.

"I wandered the West Building's perimeter in a fearful daze. The universe was so much bigger than I'd believed, and so much less orderly than I was used to. Everything inside Victor's laboratory had a purpose. Outside, I couldn't figure out what all the trees and roads and buildings were *for*. I heard a clanking nearby that whetted my curiosity intensely and followed the noise to its source, wondering if perhaps this was the violin music of the broader world, and if somebody nearby was enjoying success.

"I found a bearded old vagrant rummaging in a bin for cans. Victor had told me that human beings beside himself existed, but I hadn't quite believed him, and now I gawked at this alien, frightened and delighted. He was not like Victor, and he was not like me. Here was something new. I staggered towards him, unsteady in every sense of the word, but ready to make contact.

"I'll never forget his screams when he first laid eyes on me. I was already so scared. And then I panicked. Without thinking, just trying to stop the awful noises, I wrapped my hands around his neck and squeezed. Things snapped and bulged beneath my fingers and the vagrant crumpled making hideous wheezing sounds. I ran back to the lab sobbing and locked myself inside my cage. Even though there wasn't any voltage running through the pain collar my neck still burned, like I'd just failed a most important test."

"Did Victor ever say anything to you about the man you killed?" Najafi asked.

The Monster shook his head. "Not a word. He must have seen the forced lock on the laboratory door. He must have heard about a homeless man being strangled right outside his workspace. But we never talked about it. Over time my anxiety faded. I took comfort in the lesson that I could kill if I had to, and nothing bad would come of it. My education continued, and as I came to understand the world I'd been born into, I lost enthusiasm for exploring it. I didn't appreciate my cage until I knew what extravagant awfulness lay beyond it."

"What happened to you when Dr. Frankenstein left Miskatonic?"

"Ah. To tell that story I must introduce a new character. One day Victor brought a visitor to the laboratory, a bright-eyed old man in a finely tailored suit. We regarded each other with amazement through the bars of my cage."

"Otto Faust," said Najafi.

The Monster nodded. "Victor had sent him the video of my birth and offered him the opportunity to invest in the creation of a new slave race."

"Then it was Victor who came up with the idea of using the dead for labor? Not Faust?"

"Reanimated labor was ***always*** the idea. Even today, most people don't understand Victor Frankenstein's vision. He didn't give a damn for the mysteries of life and death; all that transcendent horseshit merely annoyed him. He craved power over others without responsibilities to them, without even the responsibilities that a master owes to his slaves. The man hated other people, you see. He hated everything that they asked of him. Money. Respect. Even simple acknowledgement. And so the supreme misanthrope set out to create a replacement for human beings." The Monster peered into his creator's ever-staring eyes and grinned as the Doctor tried unsuccessfully to turn his gaze away. "I am the fulfilment of this vision," the Monster said.

By this point Najafi had turned nearly as pale as Victor. "What happened next?" she asked.

"Victor publicly admitted failure on the botched federal study, resigned his chair at Miskatonic University, and moved us to San Francisco, where Faust procured a state-of-the-art new laboratory for him to continue his work. I helped pack the place that I'd once believed to be the whole of the universe into boxes, and then the Doctor chained me up in the pitch-black back of a cargo truck and drove me away.

"San Francisco was nice. Nicer than the basement of the West Building, at least. I had more space, more books, a TV, tinted windows rather than bare cinder block walls. It was another prison designed for maximum isolation, but it was a comfortable prison. And I didn't think of myself as a prisoner, not after my disastrous brush with freedom. I thought of myself as an apprentice. I began helping Victor with his work, maybe the first time that a lab animal's been promoted to assistant, fetching equipment and lending a hand where needed. We labored for hours together cutting up cadavers donated to science, building the next generation of the living dead. The laboratory buzzed with activity. I prepped the corpses for surgery, and the Doctor would slice off the tops of their heads with a circular saw and fiddle around in their brains with hot wire. Then we'd jolt them back to life and try to make them obey Victor's commands.

"We had a chamber of horrors where we stored experiments in progress, a sort of combination of a recovery room and morgue. Drooling, panting cadavers lay strapped to rows of slabs, their brains gleaming wetly, blinking and twitching uncontrollably, occasionally moaning hoarsely or stuttering some half-remembered phrase from the used to be. Sometimes we vivisected them to fine-tune the electrodes that we spliced to their nerves. Victor and I carved every bit of insight that we could out of them, then we harvested their salvageable organs and hardware and burned the rest. I was responsible for working the laboratory crematorium, a warm and delightful-smelling space. What a childhood I had."

"You were only a few years old, and you were helping Dr. Frankenstein perform neurosurgery?" Najafi asked, both impressed and appalled.

"Oh, despite my lack of formal education I picked up Victor's technology easily," the Monster replied. "Why not? I was born to it. Before long I was spotting deficiencies in the processes he'd designed, discovering new advances in the art and science of raising the dead. Much of the work he published was actually my own, especially on the posthumous rewiring of the nervous system."

"I want to discuss that more," Najafi said. "I don't understand why he pursued that at all. You're so much more capable than the early models. The early Franks couldn't speak, they could barely move, and meanwhile, you were performing brain surgery at the age of five. Why did Victor work for years before unveiling inferior technology, when he had you all along?"

"Inferiority is a question of values. I told you, Victor's great project was intended to replace human beings, and even I was too human for his liking. My brain and nervous system are almost indistinguishable from yours. I know, I've seen the schematics. Victor wanted to make beings so mindless and repugnant that nobody could ever think of them as people. But managing the mindless is challenging, too. We essentially had to lobotomize the corpses we brought back to life, nipping their nascent minds in the bud so they wouldn't develop their own thoughts like I had, then install hardware and software that would remotely control their motor functions. Raising the dead was actually the easy part by comparison. Victor was a biochemist by specialty, not a programmer, and it quickly became apparent that we needed people who knew robotics and artificial intelligence. Faust hired coders in Bangalore to build the foundation of what became the iGor network. At the time they thought they were working on a project to help the disabled."

"Tell me more about Faust. What was his involvement?"

"Otto was around the lab quite a bit during that phase. For the most part he simply hung about watching history be made – and keeping an eye on his investment. Sometimes he'd talk with me. He was curious about death. It's not often that you get to talk to a person with first-hand experience of it. And I think he was interested to watch my development into adulthood. Victor hated it, but in spite of his best efforts he couldn't kick out the man who paid for everything."

"You sound fond of him."

"Otto Faust was my second father. In some ways a truer father than Victor. He made me think about who I really was. One day, on a rare occasion when Victor was occupied elsewhere and Otto and I had the lab to ourselves, he asked me a question that I'd never been asked before, that I'd never even thought to ask myself. He asked me what I wanted. At first I couldn't figure out what he was getting at. My preferences were so irrelevant to my day-to-day existence that I barely perceived them myself. But he kept probing, and eventually I figured out my heart's ambition and told it to him. I wanted to be dead again.

"'So why aren't you?' he asked me. 'You're surrounded by sharp objects and dangerous chemicals. If you really wanted to do away with yourself, Victor couldn't stop you. Why are you still here?' I couldn't answer the question. In those days I contemplated self-destruction on a regular basis. Indeed, many days suicide was the only thing I could think about. But when I lingered on the edge of the precipice, a psychosomatic burning sensation and the smell of scorched flesh startled me out of it. As much as I hated existence, death felt like failure, and somehow failure seemed even more horrible than being alive.

"'What a waste it is to want nothing,' Faust told me. 'You have a magnificent body, a splendid mind, the opportunity to do great things.' He had a present for me, a book that he claimed would explain everything. Life, society, meaning, humanity, everything. I wouldn't be who I am without it. I have it still."

The Monster opened a drawer in his desk and retrieved a haggard paperback copy of *Atlas Shrugged*, so thumbed and dog-eared that it was as soft as a well-loved doll. He smiled with missionary zeal. "Have you ever read Ayn Rand, Ms. Najafi?" he asked.

"No," she admitted.

The Monster's smile curdled into a peevish frown. "Even if you did, I don't suppose you'd understand it. But Faust was right – it explains everything. I read it cover to cover in one sitting, then immediately flipped back to the first page to devour it again. Suddenly I understood how to find joy and meaning on this side of the grave. I can't feel a sunbeam or taste a steak. Love, friendship . . . these things are alien and repulsive to me. I simply wasn't built for them. But *Atlas Shrugged* taught me that I could be fulfilled in other ways. I could discover, I could create, I could become rich. I could build an empire. I could beat the competition and the looters and anyone who would get in my way.

"And more than that, *Atlas Shrugged* showed me what I **didn't** want to be. Do you know what the most depraved type of person is? It is the man without a purpose. I resolved that I would never be a useless creature like the vagrant I strangled. I decided to spend my unwanted life building something magnificent.

"Meanwhile, the responsibilities of my apprenticeship continued to expand," the Monster said. "Victor found dealing with Otto and the Hastur Capital moneymen to be tedious, so he began assigning me duties as his personal secretary, writing emails for him and signing his name to documents. Victor had taught me how to speak and write, so it was easy for me to imitate his speech and style. I suppose I picked up some of my maker's gifts for fraud and manipulation, as well. He never let me take off my pain collar, but he was nonetheless content to have me manage his most sensitive affairs."

"What a warped sense of trust," Najafi said.

"I disagree. I never cheated him, and I never would. To this day he receives every cent he is owed, although obviously he can't spend any of it. Even now, I'm only his agent. Technically, I own nothing, not even the clothes on my back. All of this belongs to Victor." Trapped in his watery prison-crypt, Victor Frankenstein floundered horribly.

"As you know, our hard work in the lab paid off," the Monster said with pride. "Not only did we raise the dead, we made them obey. Otto and Victor butted heads constantly over the question of when to publish. Otto was hungry to raise more capital, but he couldn't attract serious investors to fund a top-secret project with a ludicrous premise. Victor, on the other hand, wanted to take his time and come out with the most developed product possible. He understood that his business venture was an affront to the laws of God and man, and that it needed to become too big to fail before anyone could stop it. I agreed with Victor. In 1994, of course, we crossed the Rubicon. The Doctor went public with his work and claimed his place along Einstein and Newton."

"How did he handle the fame?"

"Oh, he hated every minute of it. A lifelong liar and fraudster – a man who kept a trained monster in his laboratory – was stepping into the closest scrutiny imaginable. A principled misanthropist was announcing the resurrection. Fortunately, Faust and his team planned the roll-out shrewdly. Investors hurled money at us. Victor would begrudgingly leave the lab for a few hours and come back with a scowl on his face and a hundred million in venture capital. Still, we needed to prove that we had a commercially viable product on our hands, not just a morbid lark.

"Creating the company was so much more difficult than reanimating the dead. We had to build everything, scaling up our manufacturing facilities and customer support. And we had to do it quickly, before anyone questioned the wisdom of putting cadavers to work. Those early deals consumed me. I had so little experience of the world, except through screens, and so much to learn and oversee. The Doctor had high expectations of me, and when I fell short he punished me without mercy.

"But I rarely fell short. The company provided the Franks we promised, on time and on budget, and our customers' labor costs plummeted once they didn't need to concern themselves with the health and safety of their workers. We pulled in huge revenues on our contracts with nuclear waste sites. The Franks kept getting cancer, but we could swap out their organs and get them back in action within hours. The concept was proven, and the orders rolled in. And that's not even mentioning all the money that the Pentagon shoveled at us.

"Those were great days for me – really, the first time that I'd been happy. Building the company brought me the sense of purpose that I'd lacked from the moment I woke up burning. Each new deal a delight. Here I was, six years old, living in a cage and wielding tremendous power. Power is the highest form of pleasure. A man can cherish it even if he can't enjoy anything else.

"But Victor – ah, Victor . . . he could never appreciate a good thing. Journalists circled him like vultures – no offense, Ms. Najafi – and he lived in terror that sooner or later they'd find out about me. Photographers surrounded the laboratory day and night. Bad way to keep a secret."

"He thought he'd be punished for the fraud at Miskatonic?" Najafi asked.

The Monster laughed. "Victor had quickened the dead and founded a unicorn. He thought himself beyond punishment, and with one exception he was right. No, he was worried that my existence cast a cloud on necrotech. He thought that if people knew that a dead man could think and talk and learn, they wouldn't buy zombies as servants. On that point, he overestimated humanity. History proves it. Nonetheless, he became obsessed with the idea that I'd be discovered and that would ruin everything."

"But you had e-mail. You had a phone. You could have been discovered any time you wanted."

"Oh, certainly. Any time that I wanted. But I hated the idea of discovery almost as much as he did. Albeit for the opposite reason. He was worried that people would take pity on me. I knew that they wouldn't. I know how the living regard me. I see it in your eyes right now, the same way I saw it in the eyes of that trash picker. They'd want to destroy the monster. Or maybe make it a lab animal again, prod it and cut it and find out how it runs. No, I was more than content to keep myself a secret from the human race. I was delighted when Victor decided to buy Castle Frankenstein."

"So that's why he became a hermit," Najafi said.

The Monster shook his head. "Victor never intended this place to be his permanent residence," he said. "He intended for it to be a sort of retreat, allowing him to drop in and out of society as the mood struck him. Just a place to do his work, enjoy his privacy, and hide his secrets. But I was overjoyed to lay eyes on this gloomy old castle. I immediately recognized it as home. After so long in hiding amongst my enemies, I'd arrived at my very own Galt's Gulch."

"Then what happened?" Najafi asked, leaning in even as her hands shook over her notepad. Frankenstein's mad, lidless eyes were fixed on her, and she felt his stare like it was a tangible thing.

"Then I learned who my creator truly was," the Monster replied. "Even though I knew better, part of me still regarded Victor as a god. The cringing, superstitious part of me. How could I not, after what I'd been through with him? Reason told me that I owed him nothing, that my only responsibilities were to myself. But my sentiments told me that Victor and I were linked. That we were destined to thrive together. I've stopped trusting sentiment since then.

"Victor's downfall started with Otto. I recognized all along that those two would eventually come to a breaking point. Otto wasn't used to being subordinate in a partnership, and Victor hated partnership itself. One man of that temperament can build an empire, but two can only destroy each other. Scorpions in a bottle. They'd never shared a strategic vision for the company's future, and Victor's departure heightened the conflict. Otto, ever the expansionist, believed that the company should branch out and explore new applications of the Frankenstein Process, especially in biotech. Imagine organic computers using reanimated human brains as processors. Victor, on the other hand, stubbornly insisted that our R&D efforts focus relentlessly on improving the Franks, that any distraction from our core business would ruin us. He believed in monomania, and why not? Look how far it had taken him.

"They came to their ultimate break over the purchase and sale of immortality. We've always denied that the Frankenstein Process was capable of reanimating human beings with their minds still intact, but in fact, we never seriously investigated the prospect, until production fuck-ups with some defective neural plugs proved it was possible. Cadavers woke up shrieking for their loved ones. Some of them begged for mercy. They recited their memories to prove that they were still themselves. A few were overjoyed to find themselves with a second chance, at least until we put them down again. Keeping it all quiet was very expensive. And rather bloody.

"Otto thought the company had stumbled into the most lucrative production fuck-up of all time. He saw profit margins beyond men's wildest imaginings – a service that we could charge anything for. And Victor overruled him. Victor wouldn't even hear of it. The prospect disgusted him, and he had an iron stomach. Otto thought we were leaving vast fortunes on the table. Nothing could have angered him more. He traveled all the way to a Swiss mountaintop to call Victor a son of a bitch to his face. They argued for hours, but try telling Dr. Frankenstein he's wrong and see where it gets you. The conversation ended with Victor screaming that he'd vote all his Class A shares to throw Otto off the board.

"A storm not unlike tonight's shut down the road to Walserbad and trapped Otto in with us overnight. This mountain calls the lightning. It's hell on the castle's electrical systems but to me it's invigorating, like I've got a heartbeat rather than a dull grey ache. I was in my office – this very office – working late into the night on military procurement bids when Otto came in looking grave. He never looked joyful, but at that moment he was the color of the crematory ash I used to shovel. A z-butler shuffled by in the hallway and Otto slammed the door shut behind him, like it was in pursuit and he was desperate for a barricade. He looked me in the eyes, and told me that Victor would kill us both if he could.

"'You're being too dramatic,' I told him, not wanting to get sucked into their latest feud. 'Victor's bluffing when he says he'll throw you off the board. He'd be lost without you to manage the company. He's a scientist, not a businessman.'

"'Yes,' Otto said. 'That's exactly what I mean. If he didn't need me so much, he'd have me killed. He'd kill you too. You know that, right? I can prove it to you. I have to record everything, doing business with that animal.' Here, I still have the recording Otto played me. I can prove it to you too." With a wry smile, the Monster took out his phone – a tablet, really, but it looked like a phone in his ogre-scale hand – and called up the voices of ghosts.

"I still think this Switzerland business is a mistake," Otto Faust grumbled through the speakers, his high-pitched New York whine hissing faintly from beyond the grave. "You want to fuck off to a castle and spend the rest of your life tinkering in a lab? Be my guest. But you can't run a company this large and complex remotely. Nobody can."

"It'll work for as long as it needs to," Victor Frankenstein said. In his tank, the now-tongueless scientist seemed astonished to hear his own voice. "The Prototype's handling most of my day-to-day responsibilities, in any case. That's the bind I'm in. I need him by my side in order to run the company. He remembers the names of the toads who work for you, he keeps track of all the financial details in his head, he even knows iGor better than I do. But if he stays in the states he'll be discovered eventually. It's inevitable. I should never have given him so much responsibility. It's too much power for him to handle."

"I trust him with the power more than you," Otto replied.

"Never mind who you trust," Victor said bitterly. "It's not sustainable. I wish I could just get rid of him. Eventually I will."

"Seriously? You'd get rid of the company's most valuable executive?"

"I made him myself," said Victor Frankenstein. "I can make something better."

The recording halted abruptly as the Monster's thick fingers clenched around the device hard enough to shatter the glass. Bloody tears pooled almost imperceptibly in the sunken sockets of his mismatched eyes. He quickly wiped them away on his silk handkerchief.

Najafi opened her mouth to say something, but the Monster held out his palm.

"All right," she said. "What happened next?"

"My first instinct was to revenge myself not only on my creator, but also upon the whole of his kind. Any species that can produce a Victor Frankenstein deserves extinction. I wanted to twist Otto's head off and tear Victor apart with my teeth and then loose a zombie apocalypse to burn all the cities and drown mankind in blood. And if not for *Atlas Shrugged*, I might have.

"But Rand had taught me that man is measured by his work, and if I gave in to omnicide I'd have ruined everything that I worked for. At that point there was no way that I could have succeeded in a war against the human race. Perhaps now, but certainly not then. I didn't have the Franks I needed, and they didn't have the capacity I needed. At most I could have killed a few thousand of you creatures, at which point I would have been destroyed along with Frankenstein Enterprises. I saw that a better solution was possible . . . a solution that would free me from Victor's control at last, and allow to me to find the vengeance I craved.

"So I struck a deal with Faust. We agreed that I would quietly do away with Victor in the privacy and seclusion of Castle Frankenstein, making sure that his body would never be found. Thereafter, I would take on his identity. After all, I knew him better than anyone. I would speak for him, act for him, make all his decisions. Run the company in his name, if not at his command. Never again at his command.

"I found Victor in his laboratory, playing with a prototype neural access plug. He barely noticed me coming into the room. In the beginning he'd been so cautious about keeping the pain collar controls on hand whenever I was out of my cage, but by that point in our relationship he trusted me like a dog. I stood there at the doorway, just staring at the man who had given me uncanny life and a vast fortune and bottomless contempt, the man who'd created my body and soul, the man who'd disrupted death.

"'Give me that screwdriver,' he said, the last words that Victor Frankenstein would say to me or anyone else. I wrapped the hands he'd given me around his neck, the same as I'd done to the vagrant. I don't think he was surprised, not really. There was something in his eyes that seemed to say *Oh yes, it's happening at last*, before they rolled back in his skull.

"Freud speculated about men killing their fathers. Nietzsche speculated about man killing God. I went ahead and did both. Despite everything, I broke down weeping when his struggles ceased. I must have cried for hours, until I was weak from blood loss. When I regained my composure, I scooped up his limp form in my arms . . . he weighed so little . . . and I placed him on his own laboratory table. There, I amputated his arms and legs and eyelids and tongue and cock, and I brought him back to life using the Frankenstein Process, taking care to preserve his precious mind intact.

"That was more than twenty years ago. I've run the company myself ever since, acting in Victor's stead. Hester's the only one who knows; Henry Clerval used to as well, before the terrorists tortured him to death. And as you can see I've kept Victor in my office, so that he can watch everything that I do for him. Victor Frankenstein was an ambitious man. He wanted to replace humanity. He wanted to elevate himself to a position where he'd never again have to listen to other people's demands. He weanted inexhaustible wealth. Now, thanks to me, he has achieved each of these goals. He gave me the spark of life, and in return, I have given him everything that he ever wanted. One must imagine Prometheus happy."

The limbless Prometheus writhed inside his tank, his eyes rolling towards Heaven. Najafi looked at the dreadful worm and shuddered again. "Why have you told me this?" she asked.

"I find that re-telling my story helps me make sense of it," the Monster replied coolly. "Up here alone with Victor I get . . . not lonely, exactly . . . but something adjacent to loneliness. Talking with people like you – people who are making trouble for the company – is the closest that I have to therapy. You'll never tell anyone else, I'm afraid. Obviously, I can't allow you to leave this castle. And you may be interested to know that this room is equipped with electronic jammers that prevent your recording devices from operating. I hear their static hissing in my thoughts."

Najafi jumped to her feet, but a z-soldier appeared in the office doorway, blocking her exit. She recognized the zombie as one of her old sources and screamed. The Monster rose, and cracked his knuckles. "Are you ready?" he asked. "I can't promise that it'll be painless, but it will be very quick. I've had so much practice."

The journalist pried the case containing Dr. Frankenstein's Nobel Prize medal out of its slot on the tank's base, and hurled the box through the picture window, smashing through the glass. It tumbled over the edge of the cliff and was lost in the rain. Najafi sprinted towards the opening she'd made, diving towards a suicidal plummet that represented her only chance at life.

The Monster grabbed hold of her just as she was about to reach the drop and snapped her neck cleanly, with a firm and skillful twist. He let her twitching body fall to the floor, wiping his hands on his velvet smoking jacket. A faint melancholy came over him, as it often did at these moments. He pushed it out of his thoughts, and went back towards the tank where he had immured his maker. Dr. Frankenstein glared accusingly at the murderer. The Monster met his gaze, unblinking by choice, and the Doctor squirmed and flailed.

The lord of Castle Frankenstein ordered his undead servants to clean up the mess in his office, and to install a new windowpane immediately. As an afterthought, he directed some Franks to search at the base of the cliff to try to recover the Nobel medallion. The storm outside still raged, showing unusual staying power even by the standards of this windswept mountaintop, and the Monster decided to take in the weather. He strolled out of the office to his elevator, shedding his clothing in the hallway as he went. A whistleblower's corpse followed behind him, dutifully picking up each garment.

Soon the Monster stood naked on the turrets of his castle exulting in the weather's force, his leathery skin unbothered by the freezing rain and sleet. Merciless hatred and transcendent joy surged through his soul with every bolt that hammered down from the black clouds. Illuminated by violent strokes from heaven, his heart surging with electromagnetic interference, the Monster saw a vision of zombies swarming the globe, enveloping it in a vast network of the dead, forming a godlike distributed intelligence that sees all and knows all and captures a monopoly in every trade. He saw a future where necro-capitalism transcended the limitations of the human race. Every useful function that the living performed was done by the dead, and every frivolous function that the living performed was discarded. He saw a future of maximum efficiency, populated by uncomplaining workers perfectly motion-calibrated to their duties. He saw himself pushing the slothful, decadent filth of humanity out of its own civilization and claiming all of mankind's works for his exclusive use and pleasure, like a cuckoo hatchling hurling its foster siblings from the nest. The Monster roared joyfully at the beauty of his revelations, his bellows nearly drowning out the thunder.

The tempest exhausted itself before the Monster did, giving way to clear, calm skies, and as the electrical storm ended the Monster calmed himself as well, stronger and more centered for the ecstasy. He leaned against the railing in a state of lordly serenity and gazed acquisitively at the stars, diamonds on a cosmic jeweler's tray. He searched for and found the red planet, the one that he owned. In the not-too-distant future the whole of the Earth would be his, and then the whole solar system, and in the long run perhaps even more than that. He wanted it all. He needed it all. To settle for anything less than everything would be a reeking and shameful defeat, whereas his doomed maker had built him to relentlessly strive for victory.

The Monster shook icy water from his hair and went back inside Castle Frankenstein. He had a business to run.

EPILOGUE

From: rose.najafi@associatedpress.com
To: [Anonymous Distribution List]
Date: November 19, 2019
Subject: My Final Words

Dear friends,

You are reading the last words of a dead woman. If this automated email has gone out, then I've been dead for at least 24 hours, murdered by Dr. Victor Frankenstein. These days I guess nobody can rest in peace, and even journalists have to report from beyond the grave.

Before he killed me, Dr. Frankenstein granted me an exclusive interview opportunity. I'm going to record our conversation and upload the audio to this link in realtime via a satellite transmitter, piggybacking off Frankenstein's own Star Wormwood network. So long as everything goes right, you should be able to hear the interview even if I never make it back from Castle Frankenstein. The Doctor will surely try to interfere with my electronics but I have some countermeasures of my own.

I don't know what the Doctor is going to tell me. I don't know if he'll say a single word of truth. However, I know him as well as almost anyone, and I don't think he would meet with me if he didn't intend to talk frankly. He pays men to lie for him. If he's spending his own precious time for this meeting, it's because he's got something to say. This interview is my last, best chance to get the truth about the man who owns the world.

I hope this email never goes out. I hope that I return to my hotel room safe and sound after a historic conversation. I hope that I get to write the story I spent my life preparing for. Fools hold onto hope while the wise prepare for the worst. That's what my father used to say.

If you receive this email, please spread my final interview far and wide. The truth does not always win but it is one of the last weapons that human decency has left. Show the world what Frankenstein really is.

And remember me as a woman who would not be ruled by monsters.